VAMPIRE RULES

On the high ledges and the gun emplacements surrounding the lake, the Dragon Guards swiveled their weapons and targeted one prisoner after another. The watchers on the slender catwalks aimed their spotlights. The beams pierced the gloomy murk, probing and searching like radiant fingers, until each one had isolated a specific prisoner on one of the stone islands. All over the chamber, the inmates began standing up, shielding their eyes, and peering fearfully up into the brooding and ominous glare.

The prisoners could see a tall thin Vampire sweeping angrily to a vantage point on the central platform, followed by two aides. The Vampire took up his position, leaning out over the railing to look down on his unfortunate charges. The Vampire smiled, revealing his gleaming teeth, his incisors long and needle-sharp.

He shouted across the entire chamber, his voice amplified like thunder. "Pay attention! Disobedience never goes unrewarded! Failure never goes unpunished! We will now proceed with the process of selection."

A groan rose up among the poor creatures on the stone islands. From a hundred throats, it came—a multitude of voices, united in a sad chorus of despair.

Most of them knew what was coming next.

UNDER THE EYE OF GOD

David Gerrold

based on "Trackers"
created by
Daron J. Thomas
and
David Gerrold

BANTAM BOOKS
NEW YORK • TORONTO • LONDON • SYDNEY • AUCKLAND

UNDER THE EYE OF GOD

A Bantam Book/December 1993

All rights reserved.
Copyright © 1993 by David Gerrold.
Cover art copyright © 1993 by Michael Herring.

ISBN 0–553–29010–X

Published simultaneously in the United States and Canada

Bantam Books are published by Bantam Books, a division of Bantam Doubleday
Dell Publishing Group, Inc. Its trademark, consisting of the words "Bantam Books"
and the portrayal of a rooster, is Registered in U.S. Patent and Trademark Office
and in other countries. Marca Registrada. Bantam Books, 1540 Broadway, New
York, New York 10036.

PRINTED IN THE UNITED STATES OF AMERICA
OPM   0 9 8 7 6 5 4 3 2 1

For Daron and Beth Thomas,
with love.

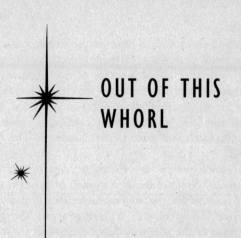

OUT OF THIS
WHORL

If you consider the Milky Way galaxy as a great wheel turning ponderously through space, then you may regard the Palethetic Cluster as a clot of earth tossed up by that wheel as it pounds down eternity's highway.

You will find the Palethetic Cluster a hundred thousand light-years off the plane of the ecliptic, and nearly that distance off the galactic axis. It spins whirligig in the galaxy's wake, but it does not trail the Milky Way; on the contrary, the Palethetic scuttles off in its own direction, a sideways tumble, which takes it away from that immense brilliant disk with an unexplainable velocity.

In the old tongue, *palethetic* means "interesting place to stand." Indeed, the Palethetic's singular appeal lies in the fact that it affords a spectacular view of the enormous starry spread of the Milky Way galaxy—as seen from the *outside*. On almost any world within the Cluster, the great spiral displays a dazzling splendor. The locals call the view the Eye of God.

The Palethetic Cluster itself contains (approximately) seventeen point five billion objects of large enough mass to justify a place in the Regency star maps. Only a small percentage of these objects radiate enough energy to deserve the appellation of *star*.[1] Approximately a hundred million stars make up the cluster; less than one percent of them shine their light on inhabited worlds. Despite the lack of any recent census to validate the count, the locals still refer to the cluster as "The Million Worlds."

Cosmologists in the Palethetic remain puzzled by its existence. None of the best models of galactic dynamics can account for the anomalous existence of seventeen point five billion objects scurrying across the galactic wake; none of the worst models can account for it either. No cluster should exist where this Cluster exists; but the fact that it does exist clearly demonstrates the fallaciousness of all current cosmological theories that do *not* account for it—meaning *all* current cosmological theories.

Some scholars have argued that the Palethetic Cluster may have originally spun off as a side effect of the Milky Way's formation. Unfortunately, the path of the Cluster does not support this thesis. The Palethetic hurtles into the darkness at an odd angle and at an astonishing velocity relative to the Milky Way—as if it knows something it shouldn't about its apparent primogenitor. Tracking the models of both stellar aggregations backward through time produces unbelievable headaches for astrophysicists.

Another theory, one far more attractive to those with much less knowledge of stellar mechanics, holds that a careless Creator left the Cluster here after finishing its much more important work on the greater wheel of the nearby galaxy; to these theorists, the Cluster com-

---

[1]Most starship Captains plying their trade among the worlds of the Cluster elect to purchase regularly updated listings of all of these objects for their inboard memory tanks, demonstrating a more than casual curiosity about matters that might impact their existence.

prises nothing more than leftovers. A splinter faction, operating under the auspices of The Church of the Grand Jape, suggests an even more insidious premise: that a mischievous God deliberately created the Palethetic Cluster and sent it whirling off on this deliciously unexplainable vector specifically to confound cosmologists throughout eternity.

Others simply refer to the whole thing as "the Pathetic Cluster" and leave it at that.

Whatever the case, the view remains spectacular.

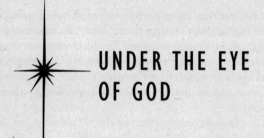

UNDER THE EYE
OF GOD

High up in the northern reaches of the Cluster a swollen red star gutters and sparks in the darkness. It gives off just enough heat and light and feeble radiation to register on the star charts. A small orange planet named Thoska-Roole orbits the giant at a gloomy distance.

A dark, burnt world, Thoska-Roole has little to recommend it. The planet tumbles in an elliptical orbit, spending most of its time roaming out in the cold reaches of night, but occasionally approaching close enough to its primary to pass through streamers of gas, or the outer fringes of its corona. Life exists here only by the application of powerful technologies. During the extremes of Thoska-Roole's orbit, infra-winter and ultra-summer, life survives by burrowing underground and waiting for the seasons to pass.

Under the vast sun, day smolders like a ruin. The sky becomes a ruddy ceiling, filled with the massive red gloom of the ponderous giant. Vision becomes almost impossible; everything looks rippled and indistinct, as if illuminated not by light, but by heat-blurs. During the day the citizens of Thoska-Roole avoid the outdoors.

When night rises, the Eye of God glares down with a horrific splendor. Brightness fills the air with wild hallucinatory colors. The sky sparkles like radioactive foam. The mordant light dances, blazing through states of exhausting glory. The eye cannot assimilate, the mind cannot grasp the grandeur of it. The overload of optic ecstasies intoxicates like a drug, leaving the viewer delirious and bedazzled. Under this shameless exhibition, this great tumbling wheel of heaven, the desert burns so brightly that all normal patterns of diurnal life have collapsed, staggered and stunned.

Here, creatures of daytime instincts have redirected themselves into nocturnal channels, coming out only when the sky blazes like a pinwheel, while those of nighttime impulses struggle blindly through the crimson murk of day. The brilliant leeward sky arouses the activities of life, the dreary red mornings bring the release of sleep.

Night, described as shadow elsewhere, exists only as a supernatural dream on this terrible star-blasted world—never as a darkening, neither of the sky, nor of the soul. On Thoska-Roole the souls of the people have already darkened by themselves.

Despite its awesome glory, the Eye of God weighs as a heavy burden to the inhabitants of the Cluster. Popular belief has it that the good people of Thoska-Roole come into their lives already in a state of virtue, and that throughout the length of their small existences, they do not commit as many of the nine unforgivable sins as often as do the inhabitants of other worlds elsewhere beyond the reach. Perhaps, as some think, under the direct study of the Eye of God, the commission of any sin seems infinitely more dangerous.

The same belief also suggests that when the good people of Thoska-Roole can no longer bear up under the strain, when they can no longer maintain their holier purposes under the intense scrutiny of the Lord of Creation, they fall from grace with a *thud* that shakes the ground for leagues in all directions. Some storytellers insist that this explains Thoska-Roole's perpetual earthquakes and tremors: The unending rain of unfortunate souls falling from grace has shattered the planet's poor crust.

As a result, either of the rain of souls or of the many stories told, probably the former more than the latter, the name Thoska-Roole has become synonymous with the stygian depths of human behavior. Here the stench of villainy and mischief reeks so profoundly that the smell of it seems to permeate the entire northern reach of the Palethetic Cluster. The scent apparently serves as an attractant, not only for those who practice such skills, but also for those who have need of them. Money begets mischief.

The pheromones of wealth in any of its myriad forms have an irresistible allure. Maddening. Mind numbing. Intoxicating. Infuse that allure with the enticements and attractions of power, glamor, drugs, violent excitements, and of course, sex—never forget *sex*—and suddenly, all the starlanes point downhill, with the Starport at Thoska-Roole at the end of the slide.

Here you will find: aesthetes, arbiters, barristers, bean-eaters, boodlers, box men, brokers, burymen, cacklebroads, camp-followers, clinker-boys, coosters, cotton-pickers, councillors, cyberphytes, diggers, doops, dung-burglars, dusters, dweezils, easy-walkers, fandanglers, firecats, fences, flappers, flummists, filberts, fingermen, floorwalkers, gaffers, gamines, gandy dancers, ghouls, goons, grinders, grounders, hackers, halffasters, handlers, hardballers, heir-baggers, heralds, honeyfugglers, hooters, hornheads, icemen, importers, ink-slingers, Ivy-smokers, jackarandles, jackbooters, jammers, jawbreakers, jeasles, jeppos, jimmies, jinglers, jinkos, jollywobblers, kadigans, keepers, kelsies, kewpies, knockabouts, larcenoids, lawyers, leathermen, libertines, lifters, mask-workers, midleggers, monkeys, monkey-chasers, morkies, Mortals, mud-busters, muscle-suckers, narrowbacks, needlemen, nose-lickers, number-crunchers, ore-burners, outlanders, pettifoggers, pilferers, pinkertons, psychomorphs, publicants, questors, quickies, razzlers, rippers, rooters, scofflaws, scramblers, slavers, sugar-doggies, tar-boys, tinglers, tipsters, touts, twizzlers, twinkies, uncles, undermen, users, vaginoids, Vampire-attendants, vintners, voluptuaries, walkabouts, weed-breeders, weevils, xenophilatics, yafflers, yockydoctors, zaglers, zappas, zombies, zoomers, zoots, and zygothetics of every persuasion—Thoska-Roole draws them all.

The rich quality of the underlife here draws suppliants from all over the Cluster—to buy or to sell, but almost never to settle.[2] They come only for so long as it takes to conclude their disparate purposes. Some come to market: they sell their bodies, their memories, their wit, and if necessary, even the tattered remnants of their souls—whatever commerce necessary to provide survival or provoke advancement. Some come to purchase—the market belongs to them. The jingling of a fat purse always commands the world. Others come merely to inspect the wares, not knowing in particular what they seek, but hoping nevertheless to find some interesting novelty or diverting artifice to excite their pitifully atrophied spirits. These frenetic souls create much entertainment on Thoska-Roole, if not for themselves, then certainly for the local inhabitants. "The Eye of God always watches. The mouth of the devil always eats."

Of those who come to Thoska-Roole for legitimate purposes, most do not willingly seek out the under-

---

[2]Most of those who stay, do so because of the unavoidability of death.

culture, preferring to have as little as possible to do with the low-principled denizens of the endless deserts, the badlands, and the bottomless crevasses. They finish their business quickly and depart as fast as they can arrange passage.

Those few who *do* seek out the practitioners of the dark trade select themselves into three categories:

The lawless.

Those who wish to do business with the lawless.

And those stupid enough to think that they can bring one of the lawless to justice.

TRACKERS

A small ramshackle building persisted on the southern lip of the Lesser Desert. It stood alone, two forlorn stories, near a great tumbled ruin.

Behind it, not standing, but scattered like the forgotten toys of a child, lay the remnants of countless other constructions. Here a twisted crane, its back broken like a crushed scorpion; there the remains of an old ore-cracking plant, the hardened slag still pouring raggedly across the rock; and all around, poking up through the hard-baked dirt, the fallen walls and marbled avenues of a forgotten, transitory civilization that had passed this way and disappeared two thousand years before.

An orange light faded from the building's windows, the only sign of life for kilometers in every glittering direction. This tumbledown refuge, this last wretched attempt to hold back the hot dry night and the dull red dust, seemed poised in the final desolate moments preceding its ultimate collapse. The ceramic and metal walls of the structure creaked and groaned alarmingly every time the day spangled into night, and each time the night lapsed back into day.

Time had plucked at the building with fingers of wind and malice. Quakes had rumbled beneath it, rolling and shaking and trying to unbalance it. Sandstorms had scoured it till it shone. The parched sear of the day had baked all the resilience out of it, fatiguing the weathered old walls until they sagged in their frames. And of course, blazing over all, night after night, the Eye of God scorched and blasted everything with unfelt radiation.

The sad structure endured, not in defiance, but in resignation. Inertia ruled. Too tired to complete the job of collapsing, it stood. Dismal brown light outlined its dirty windows, and plaintive music slouched out of the single lit doorway, escaping away into the bright night and the empty desert. The bloody glow of the little building marked a long southward descent into the bowels of gloom.

Nearby ...

Two men appeared on the crest of a low, barren hill, the feeble northernmost finger of Misdemeanor Ridge, a hardened tumble of slag and gravel. The ridge stretched across two hundred leagues of desert, bearing witness to a long-forgotten rape; here sprawled the discarded part of the land, the dross and refuse of centuries of ore-cracking.

Thoska-Roole wore the face of a hag. Misdemeanor Ridge and the long gouge beside it betrayed the greedy history of those who'd come to plunder here. Long gone, and long since turned into the same kind of dust they'd churned this planet into, they'd left as the only sign of their passing one more desolate scar, another appalling wound carved into the old crone's visage.

Here, where the northernmost slope of the ridge faded away into desert, lay the tail of the descent, a glistening notch of scoured and broken rocks. Here the old machines had clattered back up out of the earth, having found nothing more to grind and melt. Here the mines had died, leaving the tortured scar across the desert as the only sign of their passing. Two millennia had neither erased nor polished the wound. The ugliness remained.

The two men paused on the rounded crest of the hill and looked down the slope at the only charted settlement in a thousand leagues. They studied the little structure through high-powered scanning-binoculars for a long silent time. The place looked lonely and very dangerous. The pale one looked to the dark one. The dark one grunted. They both unshouldered their rifles, grim expressions in their eyes.

The pale one stood tall and thin; the other, the dark one, much broader in the chest, came up only to his shoulders. Both wore long black coats, ankle-length and made of thick, heavy material. Both wore wide-brimmed black hats and black silk scarves wrapped tightly around the lower halves of their faces.

The dark stubby man growled something unintelligible. The tall man understood it anyway and agreed. They started carefully down the hill.

They moved with delicate, precise steps. Although the hill consisted of layer upon ancient layer of hard-packed gravel and earth, the surface stones still came loose too easily, slipping and tumbling away in miniature avalanches. The skittering noises echoed brilliantly in the night. Too conscious of the sound, the men picked their way with elaborate caution, keeping their separate attentions fixed on the shallow building below.

Behind them, the Eye of God began to open. It crept up over the horizon, casting long pale shadows before it. As it rose, a great wash of light poured slantwise across the desert, illuminating every irregularity, every twisted rock and gully. The shadows writhed and flickered like souls in torment. As the Eye climbed toward zenith, the shadows would start to shrink and fade; the spangled blaze would turn everything simultaneously bright and ghostly, but that would not occur for hours yet. Down the hill, still hidden from the Eye, the dying little building cowered in the purple shade.

The two men circled it once, keeping wide away from it while they checked the alley and the back exit. They glanced over the few scooters and floats parked at the side, then came back around to the front.

Inside . . .

They entered. They carried their rifles at their sides, low, but ready. Their eyes narrowed. Each scanned the room quickly, professionally:

A deflated poker game. A cheerless bar. Two plastic whores in wilted feathers. Worn-out ceramic furniture, greasy ceramic walls. They'd seen all this before, smelled corroded hope on a thousand different worlds. They could describe the room with their eyes closed, the customers too: a technoid tinkering with gritty distortion on the keyboard of a howling synth, a couple of nervous bioforms whispering illicitly in a dark corner, and of course, the usual sweaty collection of sullen toughs and slow-dying prospectors. Everywhere the frontiers of desperation weighed the same.

The blue-skinned bartender glanced up distastefully. He recognized not the men, but the mission.

"Slow night," remarked the tall man, pulling his scarf down to reveal clear, even features. Sawyer Markham grinned, a wild bright flash of laughter in a gloomy hole.

The bartender ignored Sawyer, his comment, and his grin; he continued wiping absently at a glass.

Sawyer shrugged and stepped sideways so the bartender could see his partner behind him. *Finn* Markham.

Now the bartender looked up. Finn Markham had an ominous look; his eyes shone like coal, glowing in the dark space beneath his hat. His scarf still covered his mouth, and when he spoke, his voice rumbled like death. "Where's Murdock?" he asked quietly.

The bartender considered the question. He considered putting down the glass and picking up the hand-weapon under the folded towels. His eyes flicked up and across and down again, quickly assessing the two men and the power of their rifles. Slowly, he put down the glass. Then he picked up the next one and began to wash it carefully. "Don't know anyone named Murdock," he said noncommittally.

Sawyer snorted.

Finn glanced over, then flicked his eyes upward. Sawyer nodded in response. They headed for the stairs.

Finn went swiftly up the hard ceramic steps, treading as lightly as he could. Still, his footsteps caused the boards to creak. Sawyer waited at the bottom; he turned and studied the room, his gun casually covering a wide arc. The synth fell silent. The technoid closed the cover on its keyboard and faded into a corner. In the silence conversation ebbed. A few of the more cautious patrons moved out of the center of the room.

Finn paused at the landing. He listened at the first door. Nothing. He moved to the second—

The bartender started to move. Sawyer looked over at him. His rifle swung meaningfully. The bartender stopped; he shrugged apologetically. What the hell—Murdock meant nothing to him. Sawyer grinned and looked up to the top of the stairs again, watching his brother with great interest.

At the third door Finn paused. He glanced down and nodded. *This one.* He lifted his rifle; then he kicked—

The door crashed open with a *bang!* Finn plunged in like a charging buffalo. A scream and a roar—"Murdock! I have a warrant for your arrest!" Something crashed against the wall, shaking it visibly, and then another shuddering crash, and a chair came flying out the door, arcing over the railing, tumbling down into the bar and shattering on the floor below. The crashing, smashing noises continued, punctuated by painful grunts and other meaty sounds.

A naked young man—no, only a boy—just a little too young and a little too pretty, came running out the door carrying his clothes in his hands. He looked terrified. He came flying, skidding, tripping down the stairs. He slipped and skidded the last few steps.

Sawyer's eyes widened in surprise at the sight of the voluptuous boy, but he let him pass. "That's not Murdock," he decided. Apparently, this establishment kept a wider variety of erotic talents available for the entertainment of its guests than he had previously assumed.

"Hm," said Sawyer, looking after the boy's rosy cheeks. "I didn't think Murdock liked humans of *any* sex."

Another thundering crunch from above pulled Sawyer's attention around again. The sudden sound of rifle fire spattered loudly above—a fast-crackling whistle, the sound of *air burning*—and then a sudden *oof!* and an even greater loud crash. Large pieces of ceramic molding cracked and shattered from the ceiling, from the walls. They fell to the floor in a lacerating shower, spattering fragments in all directions. Customers gasped and jumped out of the way. The bartender looked up alarmed.

A second chair came hurtling out the door, followed by the two halves of Finn's rifle. The chair bounced once and broke apart. The fuel cell in the stock of the rifle discharged itself in a terrific flash of light and energy. Another frightful impact from above hit the building like the fist of God. The brittle front wall cracked with the shock; all three windows shattered at once, spraying shards of glass outward into the lambent night. For just the briefest moment, they glittered like diamonds in the air.

Sawyer Markham listened thoughtfully. Then, nodding to himself, he admitted, "This one could get serious." He listened half an instant more to the shuddering, thumping, crashing, clattering, thundering sounds of the titanic battle overhead—yes, *very* serious—then headed out the back door.

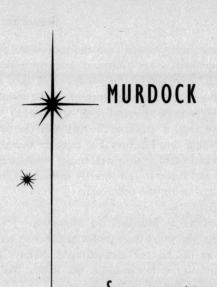

MURDOCK

Sawyer stepped into the brightening alley, starting to sparkle now with spreading starlight. A row of metal-roofed storage sheds leaned exhaustedly against the sagging rear of the building. Yes, new cracks outlined the wall. He looked up above them to the second floor. As he watched, the surface shook again. The wall shuddered. The fissures lengthened.

Sawyer narrowed his eyes as if estimating something. Absentmindedly, he reached into a pocket and pulled out a piece of red-and-white-striped candy. He unwrapped it methodically and popped it into his mouth, never taking his eyes from the old ceramic wall. Suddenly there came a terrible crash, and Sawyer looked pleased.

"Four ... three ... two ..." He counted and took a step back—

Abruptly, right on cue, an incredibly huge, ugly, barrel-shaped monster of a human—at least, it *looked* vaguely human—came fracturing through the boards almost directly above Sawyer's head. He stepped easily out of the way as the elephantine creature crunched, bounced, rolled, flopped, and plopped onto the roof of the row of weak-looking sheds. They collapsed instantly, and the e-normous beast continued its horrendous fall, now crashing and sliding and tumbling down amid the splintering walls and the crumpling metal roofs, surrounded by the terrible clattering of cracking boards and the labored groans of folding metal beams. The monster thumped to the hard-packed earth with a wet, meaty sound, rolled a few meters, and came to rest directly in front of Sawyer Markham, but facing the other way.

Murdock.

Also known as Murdock the Mountain.

Upright, she stood three and a half meters tall. She had shoulders the size of a catastrophe. Sawyer began edging around to face her head-on. She looked like eight hundred kilos of fun all rolled into one.

She also looked very *angry*.

Sawyer blinked. And gulped. And said, "Urk."

Murdock's layers of fat and her inch-thick body-armor had softened the impact of her fall. Now, grunting like a sow, she began to lever herself back to her feet. She rose up slowly, a rising avalanche of flesh, a rolling wave of meat and bone and muscle. Her armor glistened with wet-looking reflections; she glittered like a leviathan, a great gray dragon lifting majestically out of the sea.

Sawyer cocked his weapon loudly, but his voice sounded suddenly thin in the desert air. "Will you come quietly?"

Murdock turned around slowly and saw Sawyer for the first time. Her face seemed pinched and tiny and much too small for her massive head. Her expression, already red and furious, contorted further in crimson rage. Her chins flowed in great disgusting wattles of flesh. The fat rolled up and down her body as the enormous muscles underneath shifted and moved. Murdock billowed and undulated as she rose. And rose. And rose ...

"Hi," said Sawyer. He gave her his most famous smile—

It didn't work.

Murdock's breath steamed. She lowered her head. She growled and started forward.

Sawyer fired.

The needle-beam ricocheted with a loud flash off Murdock's body-armor and blew a hole in the nearby wall. Sawyer stepped back, startled. He hadn't expected that. "I think I need a bigger gun."

Now she charged. The mountain *moved*. She lowered her head and roared like a bull volcano. She came rumbling forward like a wall of meat. Her speed amazed Sawyer. Her power nearly killed him. Her great head caught him full force in the chest and pushed him right through the wall of the building behind him. They hurtled into a storeroom, through a supporting wall, and up against a tower of barrels, which exploded in all directions at once. Ceramic splints, wall panels, and ceiling tiles came crashing down around them, shattering and popping with sharp exploding noises. The lights swung crazily, the shadows twisted like snakes.

Finn Markham dropped from above, falling through a hole in the ceiling, grabbing at a two-by-four as he tumbled—it broke off in his hand, dropping him roughly to the floor.

"What kept you?" gasped Sawyer. Murdock pulled back, looked up—

Finn didn't take the time to answer. He started to swing the makeshift club, but Murdock caught him first, almost casually warding off his attack with one gigantic arm. The two-by-four splintered loudly into pieces.

"Aww, shit," said Sawyer painfully. "Now I think you've made her mad."

Murdock swung her other arm, backhanding Finn into the opposite wall. He crashed against it. It cracked ominously, held for an instant, and then tumbled him backward, ass over teakettle, out into the alley. Finn lay flat on his back like an overturned cockroach. He stared up into the sky. "Pretty lights," he said, blinking. He started pulling himself up—

Murdock moved after him. She followed him out into the alley—

"Last warning," Finn said, clambering quickly back to his feet. "Last chance to surrender peacefully."

Murdock only growled, a terrible rumbling note of doom. The sound had an ominous quality.

Finn took a prudent step backward—and tripped over an empty barrel. He tumbled into the rubble behind it.

Murdock made a sound like an earthquake, only deeper. A *flesh*quake. She grunted and lowered her head. She began to move again—

But Sawyer acted first. Gasping with the effort, he levered himself painfully up. He staggered after Murdock. He touched a control on his belt. Plan B.

Rule Number One: Always have a Plan B.

Rule Number Two: See Rule Number One.

Lightning-bright suns flared suddenly in the sky. The blazing lights dazzled and blinded. The beams probed, swept, and pointed again, illuminating the shaded valleys of the desert with a frightening intensity. Even the Eye of God faded behind the startling glare.

The lightning-beams searched, hesitated, converged—and caught Murdock in the middle of an incredible wash of whiteness. Everything turned stark. The hulking fugitive froze. She looked up, blinking painfully at the glare. She deep-growled something in an unfamiliar language, a nasty curse, then turned and lumbered toward the darkness. The ground thundered under her feet.

The aerial trackers pursued. The blinding beams followed the mammoth human beast out toward the badlands, out toward the glittering distance and the dark notch that slashed deep into the south.

TRACKING

Sawyer pulled Finn quickly to his feet. "We've—(*gasp*)—got to go after her—"

Finn gave his brother a merciless look. His expression said it all.

"We've never gotten this close to her before," Sawyer insisted. He picked his rifle out of the broken rubble.

Finn considered their options. His whole body hurt. He held his breath for half a second, trying to catch up to himself. Exasperated, he said, "Don't you have a . . . a bad feeling about this, or something?"

"No. Should I? Come on, let's go—Hey, what happened to your other gun?"

"She ate it."

"Use this." Sawyer tossed his rifle to Finn. "I've got the grenades." He started after Murdock, breaking into an eager sprint.

Still disbelieving his brother's excitement, Finn followed, shaking his head and muttering darkly. "You know something, Sawyer?" he called. "All of a sudden, I just don't have the same enthusiasm for this."

"Think of the money," Sawyer called back.

"Oh yeah, right. Sure. The money." Finn remained unconvinced, but he picked up his pace anyway. "I just know I'll regret this."

As they hurried after the receding lights, Sawyer unclipped the hand-terminal from his belt. The display cycled through the views from each of the aerial trackers. The skyballs still followed their target. From every perspective the screen showed Murdock the Mountain thundering down a wide, ruined avenue.

"Down that way," Sawyer pointed. The lights burned brilliantly.

"I can see."

They came around a broken colonnade. Down at the end of the avenue, the blazing animated beams of the skyballs weaved back and forth around Murdock's lumpish, dark, ungraceful bulk.

Finn dropped to one knee and took aim. *One good shot . . .* He fired. The needle-thin beam hung in the air for just the briefest of instants, cycling up from the infrared to the ultraviolet and disappearing even before it had finished registering on the retina. Finn couldn't tell if he'd hit her or not. He fired again. And again. Murdock kept moving.

Beside him, just ahead of him, Sawyer tossed a grenade. It lifted up into the dry air with a sharp whine, hesitated at the peak of its arc while it hunted, then began heading vaguely, almost uncertainly, toward its target. It screamed as it flew, its pitch rising and falling as it hunted its objective. The grenade traced an irregular path as it searched, weaving back and forth through the glittering sky like a drunken banshee. Suddenly its note changed—turned into a sizzling, saw-toothed buzz—as it locked onto Murdock's lumbering fury. Now it dove toward her like the vengeance of hell.

The grenade exploded in a shattering flash of light. It cracked the air, silhouetting Murdock's mountainous form like a hole in the sky. Crimson rays spattered all around, sending snakes of blue-white lightning sleeting through the ruins, leaving purple afterglows burning in the air and startling orange discharges writhing across the ground.

But Murdock remained.

"I don't believe this," said Sawyer.

"Oh, I do," said Finn.

The air burned redly overhead—a blistering shot from Murdock! Instinctively, Finn and Sawyer rolled in opposite directions, dodging the next shot and the next.

Finn scrambled for the cover of a broken pedestal. Sawyer kept on rolling, came up swearing behind the corner of an elephant-sized block. He started swearing commands into his hand-terminal. The skyballs began darting and swooping low after Murdock, still pinning her in the light. Now they started firing—the needle-beams scorched the night, laying down a fiery net of thunder and flames.

Somewhere in the middle of that hell, Murdock moved. Untouched.

Sawyer took off down the ruined avenue, across the broken, uneven surface, jumping over the smaller of the fallen blocks where they lay, his long black coat flying out behind him. He wove a random course around and through the colonnade. Murdock's sizzling beams carved holes in the air.

Finn fired back, laying down his own sprays of lightning, to cover his brother's advance; then, painfully, he followed. Finn still entertained the cheerless thought that Murdock might end up costing them much more than the various bounties on her head would cover; but he already knew Sawyer's answer to that—he'd heard it too many times before: "Then we have to catch her quickly. The bounty will offset our losses—well, some of them anyway." Finn knew without asking. Sawyer had already reached the point of no return. He had become obsessed with this one. Murdock had long since gradu-

ated from nuisance to nemesis in Sawyer's mind. Finn
sighed and followed, moving from block to rock to column, never giving Murdock a clear shot back.

In the distance the skyballs moved down a distant
slope, still following their target, remorselessly circling
and firing. The beams flashed and ricocheted off
Murdock's armor, scorching and blistering the rocks and
ruins. Murdock left a trail of small molten pools and
burning fires behind her.

Now she disappeared into the cover of a deep gully;
it sharpened as it carved its way toward the greater notch
beside Misdemeanor Ridge. Down beyond, where the ravine broadened and then narrowed again toward a dark
descent, a wide road led downward through the last broken ruins of the centuries-old mining station. Here the
shapes of Misdemeanor Ridge took on an ominous and
haunting look. They writhed beneath the beams of the
skyballs and turned jagged and tortured. Murdock's
heavy booming steps echoed back up the slope.

Sawyer and Finn came tumbling heedless after,
making wide arcs around the still-burning embers. They
headed down the gully, skidding across the scattered
rocks and following Murdock toward the ruins. The rising light of the Eye of God gave the broken buildings a
pale, ghostly glow. They hovered in the gloom like sepul-
chers, a city of the dead. That thought did not make Finn
happy.

Somewhere ahead a laser-beam spat upward and
something exploded in the sky.

"Damn! She got one of the skyballs!" Sawyer
started swearing.

"Bill the client," Finn called after him. Despite the
partial battle-skeleton he wore, he knew he would ache
tomorrow. And probably for several days afterward. Reluctantly, he keyed himself to a faster pace and began
gaining on Sawyer again.

Sawyer released two more grenades. They lifted in

tandem, then swooped loudly toward the ever-receding beams of the skyballs.

"That won't stop her—"

"Might slow 'er down, though."

Another distant shot—and a second skyball disintegrated in a bright scorch of light.

"She's getting expensive," Finn cautioned.

Sawyer didn't answer. "Better shield yourself—"

The two grenades went off almost simultaneously. They turned the horizon momentarily white. The ground shook with the impact, but even as the detonation faded, a screeching red needle-beam blistered the air over their heads.

"I don't think she likes us," said Sawyer.

"I can't imagine why not."

"Come on, let's go." Sawyer studied his terminal for a moment. "That way—" He pointed downward. "Down the old road."

Finn charged after him. The hard ground of the desert thudded underfoot. The dry air smelled of smoke and ozone. Murdock's blasts came less frequently now.

And then, abruptly, everything went silent.

Sawyer and Finn stopped in the middle of the ghostly ruins and looked at each other.

"Lost her?"

"No." Sawyer didn't sound convincing. He frowned at his terminal. He punched in a program.

The two remaining skyballs probed at the tumbled walls and rocks. They hovered and drifted and played their lights across the ground.

Nothing moved.

Finn scratched at his neck abstractedly. "We'll have to go in on foot. I don't like it." He pulled two pieces of a long-barreled weapon out of his coat and began to assemble it.

Sawyer raised an eyebrow at him. "The rocket-launcher?"

Finn nodded. "You saw the thickness of her armor." He squinted down the barrel, checked the fuel cells, and slapped a magazine of six darts into place. "Well, I've had it. No more Mr. Nice Guy." He unlocked the safeties and armed the targeting monitor. "I don't have to put up with this. I gave her a chance to surrender peacefully." He sighted down the ravine.

As if in answer, another beam sizzled out of the darkness. Another skyball blew apart in the air, showering sparks in all directions.

Sawyer said, "I don't think she did that herself. Maybe she has automatics in place. Or mines."

Finn shook his head. "Why waste it on skyballs? Why not just take us out directly?"

"She likes to play with her food?"

Finn shuddered.

The last remaining probe dodged back and forth, but both brothers knew it didn't stand a chance. The skyballs worked best in swarms.

Down below, from deep in the notch, Murdock's red beam disintegrated the last aerial tracking unit. Glowing pieces tumbled away into brightness.

"Right," said Sawyer. The now-useless hand-terminal disappeared back inside his coat. Instead he fitted a pair of tracking goggles over his eyes. Finn followed suit, and the world took on an ephemeral gray sheen. All the rocks glowed in pastel shades: the ebbing heat of the day, the burning radiation of the night.

"There," pointed Sawyer. Murdock's footprints throbbed in pale orange, a trail of fast-fading spots across the hard broken ground. "Her armor wastes a lot of heat."

"Not the armor—her metabolism."

Sawyer flinched at the thought.

The two brothers scrambled down the slope, across the jumble, and deeper into the narrowing notch. They advanced like ghosts, gliding silently across the ground.

Sawyer moved like a dancer, turning in graceful pirou-
ettes while his weapons probed the gloom; Finn rolled
like a tank, swiveling his whole body in cautious circles.
Finn focused through his rocket launcher, Sawyer held
the last of his grenades ready to throw.

They stepped gingerly down the last remains of the
broad stepway that bordered the descending avenue.
Once, huge trucks had rumbled up and down this road.
Now only the wind whistled here.

Past the fallen walls and broken doorways, past the
junk and gravel, past the rocks and blocks and folded
webworks, past the dead eyes and the empty, vandalized
sockets, past the sad incomprehensible graffiti and the
fallen tiles, and finally past the gaping boxlike structures
that stood apart like desolate questions; down and down
they followed Murdock's elephantine steps.

Something moved and both the brothers whirled,
guns held at the ready.

An uncomfortably long sinewy shape, lithe and
black, twisted and wound between two rocks. It scuttled
rapidly across the empty steps below them and disappeared hissing into a crevice.

Finn relaxed first. "Siamese weasel," he identified
the creature.

Sawyer nodded. "You know what that means?"

"Uh-huh. Watch out for the rest of the ecology. Especially ratchet-lice and scorpions."

Sawyer frowned suddenly. "Listen——" he said. He
held up a hand to stop Finn from moving.

Finn waited. Sawyer touched his belt, adjusting the
level of his monitors. Finn turned up the sensitivity of his
ears too. Nothing. Silence rained, leaving only the hiss of
their own blood in their veins, only the thud of their own
hearts in their chests. The air burned brightly around
them.

"She's gone to ground."

"I told you. She has to have some kind of base here."

Finn nodded his reluctant agreement. "That thought does not fill me with anticipation."

"Let's just find the door. Then we'll call down the floaters and use the heavy artillery." Sawyer pointed forward. He didn't wait for Finn's agreement, he just headed down toward the darkness at the end of the cleft.

"Sure you don't have a bad feeling about this yet ... ?" Finn called after him one more time. Sawyer didn't respond. Finn shrugged and followed. "Okay. Just thought I'd ask."

THE TUNNEL

At the bottom of the cleft, the ruins and the rubble became indistinguishable from one another. Clumps of dirty black brush still clung to the rocks here, the remainder of some hopeless attempt to re-forest the area. Apparently it had failed; the scrub looked dead.

Here, at last, the wide descending avenue faded out into a pattern of broken stones, diving abruptly downward and disappearing into shadowy gloom. As the mining colony had scratched its way north, it had tried unsuccessfully to cover its past behind it. Here the last steep tumble of slag and rocks, the endless stones and gravel and dirt, fell away into an empty dark crevasse. Above, the walls of the notch loomed ominously.

"Shit," said Finn.

"You said a mouthful." Abruptly, Sawyer pointed. "She came this way, all right." Murdock's glowing footsteps led down into the darkness and disappeared.

They followed cautiously. What remained of the roadway continued steeply into the earth, slanting away into an impenetrable black murk. The huge open mouth of a deep mining tunnel lay gaping below them. Sawyer stepped down farther, unclipping a hand-torch from his belt. He adjusted the beam to a stark white cone and aimed it deep into the tunnel. Nothing. No echo, no reflection. The light simply disappeared. The darkness within the gloom remained total and absolute.

"You want to go back for the tank?" Finn asked.

"Sounds like a good idea," agreed Sawyer; he moved forward down into the tunnel.

"Uh, Soy—?"

Sawyer angled his beam up and around. The tunnel had a high bare ceiling, carved cleanly from the dark brooding rock. The giant mole that had dug this tunnel had defined its passage with tight saw-toothed chisel-bites; then it had flash-glazed the exposed surface, both for strength and efficiency. The result looked both sculpted and barren. The nakedness of the walls reflected that of the ceiling and the floor. Sawyer advanced slowly. Against his better judgment, Finn followed. He unclipped his own hand-torch and switched it on.

Deeper and deeper they descended in claustrophobic silence. The steepness and the unevenness of the floor made their footing uneasy. The gloom around them swallowed up even the sounds of their steps. Neither spoke. The sense of pressure in the tunnel grew unbearable. Finn glanced worriedly toward his brother, but Sawyer looked resolute. Behind them, already far above them, the pale glow of night gently faded out and vanished; the mouth of the tunnel disappeared.

"Soy—?" Finn stopped his brother.

"What?"

"Notice anything?"

"You mean those scratches on the floor and the walls?"

"Uh-huh. Do they remind you of anything?"

"You gonna remind me about the tunnel worms again?"

"Don't I always?"

Sawyer snorted and shook his head. "Uh-uh. Forget it. Not here. It wouldn't make sense. Not even for Murdock. For one thing, the local ecology has no significant biomass. That puts a caloric ceiling on *everything*. This degenerate dirtball can't support its humanoid population, let alone a colony of worms."

"One worm then."

Sawyer made a sound of disgust. "Let go of it, Finn. The worm thing doesn't apply here. Stop looking for it. You know as well as I, you can't isolate one worm and keep it healthy. They go psychotic as individuals."

"But look at it from Murdock's perspective. Having a psychotic worm the size of a trawler sitting outside your front door *does* slow down the unwanted visitor."

"You can't control it," argued Sawyer. "And you still haven't licked the maintenance problem. What do you do when it gets hungry? Even a—you should pardon the expression—*sane* worm consumes its own weight in organic matter every day. Where do you get the biomass? Think about it. What do you feed a tunnel worm—?"

"Murdock."

"Uh-uh. Even a tunnel worm has some taste."

"I didn't mean it that way. I meant, if Murdock wanted to guard her base with a tunnel worm, then she'd also find a way to keep it fed."

"Too expensive," muttered Sawyer.

"Not for Murdock," said Finn. "Not for what she needs to protect."

Sawyer didn't answer. He couldn't win this argument. Finn didn't hear logic, not about tunnel worms— not after that escapade on Lorca IV. They continued on downward. This endless descending tunnel didn't seem to have a bottom.

"Soy—?" Finn stopped his brother again.

"What?"

"Notice anything else?"

Sawyer looked. "No more scratches?"

"No more footprints."

Sawyer looked again. He turned and looked back up the way they'd come. He frowned thoughtfully. "We know she came down this way. . . ."

"We missed something."

"You think—?"

Finn nodded. "I think we should get out of here." He waited for Sawyer's agreement.

Sawyer hesitated. "I really hate quitting."

"Consider the alternative," Finn reminded him. "I really hate dying."

"How would you know? You've never died."

"Good point. But I don't want to try it tonight. Maybe some other time."

"Wait," said Sawyer. "I want to try one thing more." He readjusted his earphones. He turned back and forth, listening. Abruptly, he shook his head. "Nope. Nothing. I think she's blanked the whole tunnel."

"Nobody spends that much money casually. I think we've finally found her base."

Reluctantly, Sawyer nodded. "All right. You win. Let's get out of here. We'll have to come back with the tank."

They turned and started back up the tunnel, back up toward the memory of light.

Up ahead, far above them, something opened its smoldering eyes—something big. It squatted in the darkness, a heavy black shape. They could see its glowing orange eyes burning like the embers of two dead moons. It moaned hungrily. It blinked—*sput-phwut*—and started down the tunnel toward them.

"Uh-oh . . . ," said Sawyer. "I think I finally have a bad feeling."

"I love your timing," said Finn.

"Fight?" asked Sawyer. "I've got grenades."

"They didn't work the last time, did they?"

Sawyer shook his head. "They only made it angry—"

Finn unshouldered his rocket-launcher.

"Bad idea," said Sawyer. "You'll trigger a cave-in."

"Do you prefer the alternative?"

Sawyer shook his head. "No."

"Well, you have all the brains in the family," Finn accused. "Make a suggestion."

"We do Plan B."

"Plan B?"

Sawyer shrugged. "We go down—"

"We don't seem to have a lot of choice," Finn agreed, reshouldering his weapon. "We go down."

High above them the worm moaned again.

As one they turned back down the tunnel and started moving as fast as they could, running, skidding, slipping, and sliding over the flash-polished descent. The beams of their hand-torches bobbed crazily, hurling wild sprays of light down the deepening abyss before them. Behind them the moan increased to a howl.

"This does not fit my concept of a good time," gasped Finn.

"You knew the dangers when we accepted the warrant—" Sawyer lost his footing then, caught himself, and slipped anyway, tumbling headlong forward across the laser-slicked rocks, rolling and sliding ever downward. Finn hurried after. "Soy—!"

Sawyer bounced off a wall and came to a sudden stop. For a moment he lay motionless.

"Sawyer!"

"No problem—" Sawyer gasped rolling back up, onto his feet. "Keep going. I can handle it. Life gets harder every year—"

"—And then you die."

"Right. And then they throw dirt in your face."

"And then the worms eat you," added Finn.

Sawyer finished the catechism. "Thank Ghu it happens in that order."

"Uh—" Finn voiced his fear. "It might not *always* work that way."

Sawyer glanced backward. "I can't see it—"

"Don't worry. It'll keep up."

"Uh-oh—" Sawyer skidded to a halt—tried to halt, but slipped instead, his feet sliding wildly out from under him. He came down heavily on his rump and kept on sliding downward, his speed increasing as he tumbled. He shot ahead into the darkness, his screams echoing down the tunnel, his hand-torch marking his descent until both it and Sawyer disappeared abruptly in the distance. The last frantic echoes faded into silence.

Finn tried to hurry down after his brother. The descent grew steeper here, the stones slicker. Finn found it harder and harder to gain purchase. Then he too lost control, his arms flailed, his legs shot out; like his brother before him, he coasted wildly downward into darkness. Suddenly the slide beneath him disappeared and he hurtled out into empty space.

Finn Markham screamed throughout the entire long terrifying moment of free fall; his torch tumbled with him, revealing the quickest glimpse of a wall of shining night, and then he smashed painfully into its cold, wet surface—

DREAD PLANET

The *Lady Macbeth* did not often carry passengers of Lady Zillabar's exalted rank; partly because neither the Captain nor the First Officer enjoyed ferrying warm cargo, and partly because the cruiser's accommodations did not lend themselves to the level of comfort one might expect on a more opulent vessel.

The starship's furnishings, while otherwise acceptable to travelers concerned more with destination than with luxury, possessed a less-than-charming Spartan quality when judged by the standards of the nobility. The *Lady Macbeth* lacked the elegant proportions and spacious design that individuals of wealth and power expected as a matter of daily convenience. The starship did not have many of the luxurious services that broke up the tedium of long interstellar voyages; therefore, that class of passenger most likely to reserve the services of a starship for personal transportation remained those least likely to desire this one—a state of affairs that exactly suited Star-Captain Campbell and First Officer Ota. The real profit lay in cargo, not in passengers.

Unfortunately, the wisdom of these arguments had

failed to convince the Lady Zillabar, leader of one of the Regency's oldest families of immortals. Star-Captain Campbell had tried to reject the Lady's charter, but Zillabar had chosen the *Lady Macbeth* for obscure reasons of her own, and once having made her decision, she would not accept refusal. She wanted transport for herself, her personal retinue of servants and Dragons, and no small quantity of cargo, from the nexus world of Burihatin to the dark red planet, Thoska-Roole.

Captain Campbell had tried a second time to refuse the Lady's charter, but Zillabar did not understand the word *no*. She made complaints to the local Registry administrators, pointedly *not* making reference to the unfortunate fates of their predecessors; the validity of her arguments alone convinced them. Shortly, the Burihatin offices of the Interstellar Registry informed the master of the *Lady Macbeth* that she would immediately put aside her own concerns and accept the Lady's charter—or risk the suspension of her certification.

Captain Campbell chafed in annoyance, but she couldn't operate without a Registry license. She invented several colorful new curses and accepted the contract with about as much enthusiasm as a Dragon confronting a salad.

For her part, the Lady Zillabar had not forced the issue simply as a casual exercise of power. She would have much preferred to make the long nasty journey on one of her own vessels; but certain matters of state on Thoska-Roole demanded her immediate presence—and political expediency required that her arrival remain undetected. As unpleasant as the journey aboard this vessel might prove, the *Lady Macbeth* served her desire for secrecy exquisitely. No ship would seem less likely to carry a Regency noble than this decrepit old tub. Her arrival should pass unnoticed. The Lady cared little that its officers and crew shared neither her passion nor her purpose, as long as they obeyed their orders.

As expected, the passage across the northernmost reaches of the Palethetic Cluster did prove noxious, noisome, and thoroughly offensive. The tired old vessel rattled and stank and vibrated; she produced disturbing smells and inescapable noises. The crew acted surly and the officers seemed disrespectful, even when they bowed. When the vessel finally arrived at Thoska-Roole, bumping rudely into a very *un*standard elliptical docking orbit, the Lady Zillabar allowed herself the experience of a profound relief. "The things I do for my species..." she grumbled.

Out here, as seen from space, Thoska-Roole displayed a savage beauty; scarred and broken, ravaged by the vicissitudes of time and greed. All ocher and black and orange, she glowered like a dying jack-o'-lantern, a rotting pumpkin left too long in the field. Her scars would leave a sense of awe and dread in even the most jaded of observers.

Brightside, the world had a reddish cast, like the dust of ancient tombs. As the ship came around the terminator line, the planet disappeared against the sprawling wonder of the terrifying Eye of God, leaving only an eerie crescent, outlining an ominous dark hole in the spangled realm of space. A few lonely settlements on the dark side of the disk appeared as faint as fireflies. From this angle the luminous glow of the primary illuminated the planet's thin atmosphere like a veil, as well as revealing a dark cone of shadow stretching outward behind it through the pale dust of space.

As the *Lady Macbeth* closed with the orbiting Starport, EDNA, the starship's synthesized personality, reached across the distance and opened a wideband, multichannel interface with the Registry Control personality. She identified herself by sending three different messages encrypted with her private security codes. By the simple act of decoding the messages with the public half of the encryption key, the Starport persona could verify the

Lady Macbeth's identity immediately. The process usually took only a few seconds. This time, however, the Starport persona balked and requested an additional set of Regency clearance codes.

EDNA considered the request with something approaching puzzlement. Speaking in the clear, she replied, "We have no instructions regarding additional codes. (Please advise on docking procedures.)"

Starport responded curtly, "The Regency administrators have activated new regulations. A fleet of Marauder-Class Fighters stands ready to enforce these rules vigorously. Even as we speak, the interception occurs. You have six minutes to reidentify yourself using the new Regency codes. If you choose not to, you may break orbit immediately. (Please watch out for the debris of the last vessel to ignore these rules. Coordinates follow.)"

EDNA began scanning instantly for the approaching Marauders. She found them just coming over the dayside horizon line, six silvery darts. They must have come from a mother ship parked in high orbit. Automatically, EDNA began defensive targeting; if they attacked, she would show them a few surprises of her own. She also noted that the Starport's extrapolation of their interception time lacked precision; the Marauders would intercept in seven, not six minutes. EDNA considered for an additional two milliseconds, then decided—quite correctly—that this matter needed the attention of a superior officer. She paged the Captain. . . .

Star-Captain Neena Linn-Campbell had earned her rank the old-fashioned way.[3] She lied, cheated, conned, manipulated, and clawed her way to power. Like all other ambitious souls, she left a long trail of bodies be-

---

[3] The appellation *Star-Captain* signifies that the Interstellar Registry has licensed the bearer for Faster-Than-Light command.

hind her; only hers remained identifiable by their expressions of astonishment. Notorious for her skills, clever, resourceful, inventive, and brutal, Star-Captain Campbell operated by a single overriding principle: "Profit with honor, profit without honor—but profit nevertheless."

Her Registry papers identified her as female, both genetically and physically. Psychologically, however, Neena Linn-Campbell had the soul of a bulldozer, and her gender identity remained the subject of numerous bawdy Starport jokes and speculations. Of primarily Negro-Asian descent (with some minor Palethetic mutations and tailored genes thrown in for evolutionary confusion), she possessed a remarkable intelligence and a quick sensitivity to circumstance.

A thin woman, wiry and caustic, she affected the waspish cynicism of one born to sin; she spoke with the gruff manners of an outworld dockworker and routinely rebuked all attempts at friendliness. "I already have the best friends money can buy," she would explain. "I don't need any more." Quick to anger, slow to forgive, Star-Captain Campbell had established a well-respected reputation for ruthlessness in the pursuit of monetary gain, a reputation that shamed shipmasters two or three times her age.

Under different circumstances Star-Captain Campbell could have become an exquisite courtesan. Both her form and features had a classic proportion, and once upon a time she had dressed to show herself to maximum advantage. Rumor had it that lucrative offers of employment in several major corporate harems had occurred on more than one occasion, but that Neena Linn-Campbell had deferred because she found insufficient profit in the exercise. Apparently, however, it forced her to realize that she needed to present herself as something other than a sexual plaything—the men she dealt with seemed to have no other way to see her. Subsequently, her standard garment became a severe black jumpsuit, the single most utilitarian garment she could design. The costume demonstrated a simple and direct statement: *Do not touch. This individual requires respect.*

Neena Linn-Campbell knew of the rumors and stories; she neither denied nor confirmed them. She never discussed her past, and her crew had learned not to speculate—although over a period of years, she had demonstrated her ability to maneuver gracefully throughout a variety of circumstances, including elegant grand balls, official state dinners, gaming tables, bargaining offices, bureaucratic chambers, the High Mass of the Purple Revelation, the Low Mass of the People's Dionysetic Revolution, various flavors of diplomatic receptions, behind-the-scene negotiating sessions, war zones, machine shops, frontier cantinas, barnyards, high-pressure mines, heavyside dockyards, red-light districts, and the occasional barroom brawl—thereby spawning a flurry of fascinating but untrue extrapolations about her life before her assumption of command of the *Lady Macbeth*.[4]

One fact, however, remained evident to all who encountered her. Star-Captain Campbell bore a violent opposition to slavery in any form. She refused to carry slaves, made no deals with slavers, and whenever the opportunity presented itself for anonymous action, dispatched slave traders and their vessels without qualm. Those who had taken serious losses as a result of Captain Campbell's unconditional actions occasionally offered sizable bounties for either her death or her capture; but no tracker had yet accepted the warrant.[5]

---

[4]The only time anyone ever observed Neena Linn-Campbell ill at ease occurred on the single occasion when an unwary visitor placed a baby into her arms.

[5]Or, to put it more accurately, no tracker who had accepted the contract had yet returned to claim the endowment. Nevertheless, purely as a discretionary practice, the *Lady Macbeth* generally avoided the

When she received EDNA's page, Star-Captain Campbell swiveled in her chair and faced the viewer against the forward bulkhead of her cabin. "What?" she demanded.

No image appeared in the holomorphic field, only EDNA's ID insignia. "Starport requests additional security clearances. Six Marauders approach from dayside. I have placed the ship on full alert."

"Right. Tell Starport to stand by. Get Zillabar."

Almost immediately, EDNA's badge faded and the Lady Zillabar appeared in its place. "You want something?" she asked disdainfully.

"Starport wants a security code."

"So?"

"Excuse me. Perhaps I didn't make myself clear. If we don't supply the appropriate clearances, they intend to destroy us. I assume you have the proper codes—or failing that, the personal authority to override the necessity?"

Zillabar's expression hardened. "Do you remember why I engaged this vessel in particular? I wanted to keep my arrival here covert. If I identify myself to the Starport authority, or if I supply you with an Imperial Code, I will abnegate my own secrecy."

"And if you do not, you will abnegate your own existence." *Not to mention all of the rest of us, as well.* But Neena Linn-Campbell had too much sense to speak the second part of the thought aloud.

"Oh, very well." Zillabar sniffed. "Obviously, I expected more from you than I should have. Thank the goddess this journey ends soon. Never mind. I have several override codes with me, any one of which should work. I'll make them available to your persona. When do you need them?"

---

darker parts of the Cluster, where slavers often cruised in greater strength than in the northern reaches.

"Immediately," said Captain Campbell, "—if not sooner."

"Yes. I see." Zillabar turned to something off camera. Her image winked out.

EDNA's ID flashed in its place. "I will relay the Imperial Codes to Starport. I expect immediate confirmation."

"Do you need me on the bridge?" Campbell asked.

"Probably," said EDNA. "The situation promises to get stickier."

ZILLABAR

The Lady Zillabar Dane-Sysnikov stood silently in her stateroom, quietly annoyed. She studied her image in the holomorphic field with a growing unease, discontent reflected in her troubled expression.

Her business on Burihatin had not gone as she had planned. Despite the assurances of the aspiring aristocrats—the *late* aspiring aristocrats—on the ringed world, failure and confusion had tainted the entire exercise. Had she allowed them to publicize her presence on that world, she would have borne the same stench of ineffectiveness. The secrecy of her mission had protected her reputation among her own—so far. She had intended to cover her absence by explaining she had taken a long dreamtime. If her security had remained uncompromised, no one would have ever suspected that she had journeyed offworld. Unfortunately, this business with the security codes—

Abruptly, she noticed a frown on the holomorphic image and irritatedly composed herself; she performed the task deliberately. She spoke the little poem of peace that reminded her of the dreamtime, and allowed her face to settle back into its usual masklike serenity. *One must never allow one's face to betray one's thoughts.* Now, refreshed, she began rotating the holomorphic view in thoughtful appraisal. Front, back, both sides—from every angle she appeared elegant and alluring. Tall and pale, like all the Phaestor, she projected an ethereal, almost supernatural presence. Her appearance did not displease her. She wore a gown of peach and maroon, outlined with a delicate blue fluorescence, and a cape of ebony silk. Her snow-white hair fell in dazzling cascades to her shoulders. Her eyes glowed amber, barely revealing the scarlet coals within. Her skin had the crisp waxy shine of one who has risen again from the dead. Yes, she would strike sparks in the hearts of men. The thought thrilled her coldly.[6]

---

[6]As there already exists an extensive body of literature about the origins, history, and meticulous etiquette of the Phaestor, the author will not attempt to recap that material here. Suffice it to say that the Phaestor, a race of genetically tailored chimeras, choose to affect a deliberate and studied manner of deportment appropriate to their unique ecological situation.

   Because of the extreme fragility of their digestive tracts, the Phaestor must limit their daily fare to a particularly delicate cuisine of predigested comestibles. As a result, the Phaestor have distilled their consumption of edibles into a narrow range of discriminating and fastidious tastes. A primary source of Phaestoric nutrition derives from the blood, the brains, and the livers of the lesser forms of the primate family—especially the humans, especially the blood.

   Following the evolutionary logic of this relationship to its ultimate conclusion results in the inescapable self-recognition that the Phaestor exist as the *rightful* apex of the human food chain. The Phaestor have no choice but to acknowledge themselves the highest evolved form of sentience, and therefore the natural masters of all other species and subspecies. The recurrent cycles of historical development throughout the Palethetic Cluster demonstrate conclusively that the Phaestor do indeed have an impressive talent for compelling and enforcing this position among their citizens, clients, and other license-holders, the opinion of the cattle notwithstanding.

Lady Zillabar worked diligently to keep herself cloaked in the somber unearthliness of the Phaestor. She regarded it as a solemn, almost holy responsibility to represent accurately the superior nature, the dignity, and the allure of her species in her every thought, deed, and expression; so it annoyed her grievously not to have all of the underlings around her acting in concert, unconditionally supporting her higher commitment. Obviously they did not understand what the Phaestoric mystics saw in their visions. The cattle operated on the emotional level of unaugmented chimpanzees, thinking with their hormones and interpreting the processes of others through the same narrow filters. They might as well choose to operate their lives under the influence of hallucinatory drugs—much the same process, but at least far more controllable. The recognition of the human hormonal dilemma truly rankled the Lady's sense of balance—on those occasions when she allowed herself to consider it at all, or worse, when the clumsy actions of some underling demonstrated the ugly fact again in her presence.

What a pity, she thought, that she could not apply some of her celebrated culinary skills to this situation. She allowed herself a delicious shudder of distaste. Then again, considering the inferior quality of the materials at hand, the resultant meal might not provide as much pleasure in the consumption as it did simply in the planning.

These mordant thoughts did not arise casually in Zillabar. The Lady would have preferred to have made this tedious journey lying in a state of pleasant dormancy, lapsed into a delicious scarlet reverie; but unfortunately, she could not entirely trust the Captain of this vessel to protect either her life or her interests while she lay asleep in impenetrable dreamtime; so she stayed awake and brooded. She knew the deprivation of soul-flight made her irritable. Ultimately, the imposition more than exasperated her—it unhinged her thinking. The Phaestor needed their access to the blood-vision to stay centered.

Without it, well—Zillabar recognized the keening derangement even as it occurred, and she despised herself for it. That she could not allow herself to express her wild despondency openly in front of all these malodorous underbeings only infuriated her further.

Usually the Lady prided herself on her exquisite manners and grace—but not now, not here, and certainly *not* when dealing with unkempt and untrained creatures like these. . . .

Yes, they bothered her. She didn't mind admitting it. The cattle simply didn't know their place anymore. More and more these days she smelled a dangerous blend of ferment and disdain in the populace—she saw it in their smirking expressions, their careless attitudes, their irresponsible behavior, even in the slovenly way they went through the motions of respect. She heard it in their whispers as she passed; they didn't know how acutely she could hear; she heard it in the pounding of their hearts and the rushing of the blood through their veins. She smelled the resentment in their bodies; it saturated their sweat; it gave them a gamy, metallic aftertaste. As an immortal, she recognized the signs; she'd seen it many times before. This surface lack of manners betrayed a deeper sickness, a festering boil of restless, unfocused hostility that would soon need lancing. Perhaps she should turn the Dragons loose again—for a while, anyway. Let them run freely and feed at will. That would return the paralyzing dread to the hearts of the cattle. A pleasant thought, that. . . .

Even in the best of times, the Lady regarded any dealings with the underclasses as a degrading task, and one better left to servants specifically trained for the duty. That she had had no choice but to manage the details of this filthy situation herself left her feeling soiled and uneasy—and the release she craved she couldn't have. Not yet, but soon. Her tongue flicked through her slightly parted lips, then delicately across the sharp surfaces of her teeth. Soon, she promised herself. Soon.

She sniffed in annoyance, then realized that she had lost her composure again; the damned disconnection! The realization only increased her annoyance. All her rituals and charms had lost their effectiveness. Zillabar knew what she really needed—nothing less than the full release of her own boiling rage, a wild plunge into madness, a screaming leap to glory, an all-consuming killing frenzy—yes! She planned to dance with death, submerging herself in the splendid ecstasies again, as soon as she returned to her private compound. When she had once again satiated herself, when she once again had the hot blood of the kill surging rich in her veins, only then could she recover the fullness of spirit that shone at the center of her soul.

Until then ... well, she would perform her part in this cruel gavotte. She switched off the holomorphic field; the image vanished in a twinkle, leaving only an empty space in the room. Slowly, she brought her thoughts back to the present.

This business of the security codes ought to disturb her, but it didn't. It only amused. Obviously, somebody did not want her returning to Thoska-Roole undetected—somebody with power; that narrowed the list of suspects to only a few. She admired the cleverness of the ploy; a truly elegant way to force her to reveal her presence aboard any arriving vessel. Imperial ships wouldn't need the codes; licensed cruisers would have received them when filing their flight plans; but any private ship attempting passage would find the entrance barred. Yes—a nice maneuver, and one that would not go *unrewarded* when she identified the perpetrator. Already she had her suspicions. Someone wanted people speculating about her absence, measuring it against events on other worlds, eventually connecting it with the incident on Burihatin, thus bringing the corpse home to the table.

She'd have her revenge upon the perpetrator of this embarrassment. The game might even provide some pleasant diversion, but more likely not. The whole affair had already taken on a tiresome quality.

The Lady Zillabar had survived a fair share of Imperial intrigues. In fact, as the author of more than a few of her own, the Lady considered herself one of the foremost experts at manipulation and conspiracy in the Cluster. She doubted that her anonymous opponent in this particular chess match had the same resources at his disposal as she had at hers.[7]

And if her larger plan succeeded, well then—no one would *ever* have as much power as she did; not ever again. . . .

---

[7]Phaestoric Authority follows family lines, always determined by the maternal parent. The absolute power of this allegiance extends throughout the entire Vampire species. The species functions not as an aggregate of individuals, but as a rigorously structured order, closer than a family and more tightly disciplined than an army.

The older and larger a family among the Vampire species, the more authority and revenue it commands from its clients and license-holders. As the head of the oldest and largest family of immortals, the Lady Zillabar held the most powerful claim on the full allegiance of the entire race of Phaestor.

PINK BRINEWOOD

Gito did not like Vampires.

That, in itself, did not constitute a crime.

Speaking one's dislike, however—that bordered on sedition.

But Gito came from a world where popular resentment lay close to the surface and people spoke their feelings aloud. They felt safe to do so; no Vampires ever came downside, no Vampire could survive the world of Tharn. The crushing gravity, the pounding pressure of the atmosphere, the whole toxic recipe of the acidic ecology, any one of those things would have killed a Vampire quickly. Taken all together, they became an uncrossable barrier.

The high-gravity dwarves who lived on Tharn had few illusions. Their freedom took its own toll in shortened lives, painful high-pressure ailments, and cracking bone diseases. Occasionally, the Moktar Dragons[8] patrolled the larger and brighter settlements, but they did it

---

[8]The Elite Troops of the Regency.

more out of duty to their distant Vampire masters than out of any zeal for Regency Authority.

The Dragons clearly felt oppressed and overpowered by the terrible conditions here at ground level; they could not stay long and concentrated more on each new breath than on the security of their surroundings. Their inspections occurred quickly, their manner became only a perfunctory and indifferent imitation of their bloodier purposes. They did not have the strength to kill here, nor to feed, nor to frenzy. Tharn did not love them, the planet did not assist them; it did not love the dwarves either, but its great bulk protected them.

Genetically tailored for this planet, the dwarves survived. Genetically tailored only for strength and endurance, the Moktar Dragons could not. If they stayed, they suffered and died slowly. If they left, they did so with the dwarves laughing at their discomfort. The dwarves turned out for every Imperial departure. They smirked and waved red silk handkerchiefs. They laughed and called out lively insults to the Noble representatives of their Imperial masters, bidding them a swift journey home. Sometimes they held up banners: "Don't let the door bang you in the ass on your way out!" The Dragons pretended to ignore the catcalls and fled in shame.

The Moktar Dragons felt dishonored and helpless. They could endure the atrocious physical abuse of the planet with honor; they could not say the same for the disgrace of the dwarves' ridicule. Amongst themselves they howled and moaned. They suffered terribly, but not in silence, and especially not after they lifted themselves out of the appalling, God-cursed, deep gravity well of Tharn. After each retreat from the hell-planet, the Dragon Lords complained vigorously to their masters, bemoaning the disrespectful behavior of the abominable little people and the shameful seditions they committed. They raged and roared and demanded satisfaction.

The Phaestoric Authority listened calmly, sympathized, and repeated their promises. Someday—not soon, but someday—a race of high-gravity Dragons would come back to Tharn, and then the laughter would cease forever. The dwarves would find that these darker, harder Dragons would not only survive the crushing pressure of Tharn, they would thrive on it. They would stay—and they would rule. The nasty little people would learn to fear again. The Dragons would feed well.

All this would surely happen, the Phaestor promised, but it could not happen soon. The process of creating a new species required time; time for design, time for experimentation, time for breeding, time for training and education. These matters did not succeed when rushed. This situation with the dwarves of Tharn had crucial implications; it needed an overwhelming demonstration of crushing, irresistible force, nothing less. The Regency could not risk a failure here, not even the slightest hint of less than total control. No, they said. Not yet. We understand your rage, your fury. We deeply sympathize. But only when we feel the certainty of total success will we act. For now, have patience.[9]

Thus, the Phaestoric promise remade, the Dragons retired; not quite mollified, never mollified—only the

---

[9]In truth, the Phaestor had several serious concerns about the creation of any new chimeric species, but one very compelling one in this particular case. The most disturbing questions always revolved about the process of control. Suppose a race of high-gravity Dragons landed on Tharn and conquered its unruly population—what then? Would these newer, hardier Dragons retain their loyalty to the Phaestor? Or would they come to feel their own sense of proprietorship on the high-gravity planet? Would they assume the disrespect of their slaves? A stronger, harder breed of Moktars might feel much less inclination to obey the Phaestor. In such a case, how would the Phaestor restore control? No, the reasons given had little to do with the real cause of the delay. The truth remained that the Phaestor never created a new species without also creating the power to destroy it—for their own safety, of course.

rape of Tharn would repay this debt—but they *understood*. Yes, the delays rankled badly, but they knew the Phaestor always kept their promises, especially promises of vengeance. Tharn would burn with unholy flames. The Dragons resumed their Imperial duties and dreamed of the terrors to come. No, they themselves would not return to Tharn, but their chimeric children would—and the children of the dwarves would die in seven days of blood and fire. And the new Dragons would grow fat.

But in the meantime the dwarves still snickered.

Especially Gito.

He wore his Tharnish heritage like a badge, a cloak of rebelliousness that he wrapped zealously around himself. Its orange fury blazed for all to see. Gito had left his world for reasons he did not discuss. By doing so, he placed himself at the mercy of any Dragon who felt the need to revenge himself for insults suffered on Tharn. But also by doing so, he removed himself from the greater danger he left behind. The Dragons did not scare him. Not enough.

"Dragons?" he snorted, speaking to Robin, the Operations Manager of the *Lady Macbeth*, as they polished the pink brinewood paneling of the ship's salon.[10] "You

---

[10]Brinewood grows in a multitude of colors, but the shades of rose, maroon, and peach generally have the greatest market value because of their translucent, almost faerie quality. Brinewood of the warmer hues seems to glow with an inner light. Cold brinewood, a more common form, mostly found in shades of azure, turquoise, and verdante, possesses a more subtle quality of luster and enchantment, attributes often overlooked by the gawdier and more extravagant aristocrats of the marketplace. Those who desire to make an immediate impact usually select the warm brinewoods out of dazzled ignorance; those who understand the deeper soul of the wood, and who expect to live with it a long, long time, tend to favor the blue or royal brinewoods. Amber brinewood also enjoys considerable favor.

That the salon of the *Lady Macbeth* had lavish brinewood orna-

want to know about Dragons? I'll tell you about Dragons. Dragons have no brains. I saw this myself. On
Tharn. A Dragon Lord stepped in a lump of shit—he
looked down, and when he saw it, do you know what
he did? He panicked. He thought he had started to
melt!"

mentation did not signify that Captain Campbell had a taste for luxury. Rather, it represented a demonstration of her resolve to have every
contract honored fully.

The short version: Roderick the Lesser, Ooligarch of The Purple Egg, a minor domain on the planet Peenamoot, decided to build a
lavish summer palace for his wives. The plans approved, the architects
engaged The Grande Importe Consortiume of Peenamoot for the obtainment of an aristocratic selection of opulent decorative materials
necessary to embellish the great confection, including many items not
commonly found on the domestic market. The Grande Importe
Consortiume immediately subcontracted with the Shakespeare Corporation, the management entity of the *Lady Macbeth*, for the purchase and delivery of one hundred and fifty cubics of unfinished
brinewood of assorted colors, and three hundred and fifty cubics of
fine polished silk, also in assorted shades.

After some considerable effort spent locating goods of the
necessary quality, and after lengthy and expensive negotiations invested in the securement of the cargo, the Shakespeare Corporation
finally and reluctantly traded one hundred and twelve shares of itself (with a three-year buyback agreement) for the obtainment of
the cargo. Upon arriving at Peenamoot, however, Captain
Campbell discovered that Ooligarch Roderick the Lesser had suffered a misfortune common to those who hold the reins of mono-
lithic authority too long or too tightly: death by ideology. This
failure of Roderick to secure his reign by popular will triggered a
revolution of manners, philosophy, and political theory which
swept aggressively through the Peenamootish domains like a
broom through a barn, leaving in its dusty wake a transformed population. In almost no time at all, the formerly charming world of
Peenamoot became a bleak and dreary place seemingly populated
only by lawyers and their victims.

The Grande Importe Consortiume had now become The
Holocratic People's Interstellar Trade Mission. Although com-
prising many of the same officials who had formerly made up The
Grande Importe Consortiume (only now dressed in much sterner-

Robin, an organic construct,[11] allowed herself a
smile. She appreciated the humor, but her personal training also allowed her to recognize the animal origins of
the emotions behind the speech. Gito told stories like this
constantly, always using either the Phaestor Vampires or
the Moktar Dragons as the foils for his rough-edged humor. "Careful, my friend. The wrong ears would *not* appreciate that anecdote."

"Hmp." Gito snorted. "The wrong ears shouldn't
travel aboard this ship."

"The Captain had no choice in that decision—"

"Pfah! Front-office politics. It excuses nothing. The

---

[11]An android.

looking uniforms), The Holocratic People's Trade Mission refused to
honor the original agreement. They politely but firmly informed Captain Campbell that because Ooligarch Roderick the Lesser no longer
existed, the authority behind her original contract had also become
null and void. While conceding neither legal nor moral obligation in
the matter, they did sympathize with Captain Campbell's plight and
after some consultation made an unselfish offer to purchase the *Lady
Macbeth*'s cargo of brinewood and silk at the very generous price of
one twentieth its Registry value. After all, they explained, the leaders
of the People's Holocratic Party would soon need their own ceremonial palaces.

Captain Campbell did not dignify the offer with even one
twentieth of the cursing it deserved. Instead, she politely and
calmly explained to the Trade Mission that the price they offered
would not even begin to cover her original investment or the expenses she had incurred in delivering the cargo. The Trade Mission
professed its sympathies, but they refused to raise the offer. "The
Peenamootish Trade Council has issued a position paper prohib-
iting lavish or wasteful trade agreements—and oh, yes, we've also
decided that it does not serve our interests to become signatory to
the Interstellar Registry Trade Agreement; therefore, that body obtains no authority in this domain to act on your behalf to enforce the
original contract. So, sorry. Would you like to reconsider—? At
least we can offset some of your losses."

Captain Campbell gave them her deadliest smile. "You have
my profoundest apologies. The charter of the Shakespeare Corpora-

whole ship reeks of Vampires and Dragons—pfah!" Gito spat. "Darkness take the lot of 'em. I can't get their stink out of my nose."

"My nose doesn't like it any more than yours, but—"

"Ought to shove the whole lot of 'em out an airlock. Let 'em walk. Do the whole Cluster a favor. We left the better cargo on Burihatin. More profitable. Industrial-grade, three-month pfingle eggs—*pfingle eggs!* We could have made twenty times the share that this charter offers. Assuming Captain Campbell can get the noble Zillabar to pay. She will pay, won't she?"

"Gito, please—?" Robin desperately wanted to find a way to end his stream of invective. "Let's just finish

tion prohibits any dealing with nonsignatory bodies. History has proved the virtue of this policy."

"You'll find no buyers here for your cargo. The Holocratic Trade Mission controls all imports to Peenamoot."

"I need no buyers." She smiled again. Some people never hear the warning.

And to prove her point, before she broke orbit, she had the lounge, the dining room, the bridge, her cabin, the six cabins most often used by passengers, the crew's mess, the crew's quarters, the sick bay, the engine room, two cargo bays, four airlocks, both shuttleboats, and all of the major passageways totally redecorated using as many of the most expensive pieces of brinewood and silk as she could. On the last night of her stay, she invited the members of the Holocratic Trade Mission aboard the *Lady Macbeth* for a fare-well supper. During the entire meal she made no reference at all to the ship's new fittings; neither did the members of the Trade Mission, but they got the point.

Subsequently, Captain Campbell made six unauthorized jour-neys to Peenamoot, secretly delivering over one million tons of high-velocity plastic projectile weapons to the Republican Liberation Front, a group that had not only signed the Interstellar Registry's minimum basic trade agreement, but had also committed itself both ideologically and militarily to the violent overthrow of all Holocratic authorities—an event that occurred shortly after Captain Campbell's sixth voyage.

preparing the salon. The sooner we clear customs, the sooner our guests will debark."

"—and then we'll have to decontaminate the entire ship. I know it. We'll probably have to open her up to space just to boil out the pheromones."

At that moment Ota, the First Officer of the *Lady Macbeth*, stepped up into the softly lit lounge from the passage below. It frowned as it caught the last reckless echo of Gito's anger. They didn't dare risk any more trouble.

"Gito, Robin," Ota interrupted quietly. "May I gently suggest that you save these thoughts for a later time. Thoughts spoken in candor might annoy our passengers—or their retinue. I don't think you want them accidentally overhearing."

Chastened, Robin nodded and lowered her eyes. She understood too well. Even if she hadn't voiced the anger, she still shared the crime by listening to it. If caught, the penalty for sedition would apply equally to both of them: death by prolonged torture.[12] Gito hung his head and growled something unintelligible, perhaps a halfhearted promise to watch himself in the future. He hadn't meant to endanger Robin. He *liked* Robin.

Tall and burly, Ota looked deceptively gentle. Its genetic stew contained genes modeled on those of the lesser panda. It had the features and coloring of a giant raccoonlike bear with some of the sharper features of a fox. Most humans tended to regard Ota as a female, viewing the huge soft-looking bioform as a kind of living embodiment of the fabled Earth-Mother. Ota neither ac-

---

[12]The offended Vampire reserved the right to select the appropriate manner of death. Often the Vampire designed a circumstance specifically suited to the victim or the crime. Lady Zillabar, in particular, enjoyed a reputation for distinctively nasty inventiveness.

cepted nor rejected such perceptions, regarding them as occurrences beyond the scope of its own nature.

Ota moved through the salon with surprising grace; its sharp eyes glanced quickly around the room. "It looks good," Ota acknowledged. "Please finish quickly. The Moktar will take their stations soon." Ota stepped out through the aft door and exited.

"Moktar!" Gito shuddered in distaste.

Robin shook her head. "That resolution didn't last long."

Gito grunted, the closest he ever came to apologizing. And then he added, "Someday the Angel of Death will arrive, and Ota will ask him if he wants some tea."

"And why not?" Robin wiped vigorously at a brinewood panel. The soft pink wood shone with pearlescent beauty. "Remember, Gito, what you once said? Most LIX-class bioforms don't care about much except their next meal."

"Hmp. You could say the same thing about Dragons and Vampires."

MANNERS

Ota came back, glanced around, sniffed the air, frowned, and allowed itself to feel annoyed and uneasy. No further effort could make a difference here. Lacking any suitable alternative, it resigned itself to the situation and pronounced the salon appropriately disinfected for a Vampire's delicate sensibilities. Gito grunted and excused himself to the engine room. Robin smoothed her pale blue tunic and began putting away the last of the cleaning items. She looked to Ota. "I assume the Dragons will inspect it now?"

"Don't they always?"

Abruptly, the forward door of the salon slid open and the room darkened like a shadow. The Moktar Dragons entered, six of them, gleaming like the cold night. Ota and Robin stepped quickly out of their way. The Dragons didn't simply enter—they *invaded* the room, a brutal squad of hardened flesh. The Dragons moved in glistening synchrony; they flowed like liquid terror.

Huge and menacing and much too large for a vessel of this size, the Dragons overpowered the space, each one three meters tall and massing three hundred kilos of self-contained brooding savagery. They reeked of power and smoldering madness.

Deliberately constructed on the model of the ancient velociraptor, they had the sleek forms of armored nightmares, with bulging musculature cut so deep and hard they looked like polished stone. They carried their tails high for balance. Their rank hot breaths turned the air around them brackish; but even in their cruel demeanor, each one also had a sinewy beauty. All black and silver, all ablaze with coiled power, they loomed *magnificently*—like burnished demons. Ebony skins shone like silken liquid; corded arms and brutal thighs reflected metal highlights. They all glittered.

Like well-oiled machinery, the Dragons took up their positions. They glanced around the suddenly too-small room with undisguised contempt.[13]

Normally they would have stayed in their makeshift quarters in the forward cargo bay—much roomier than the salon, but still too cramped for them—but whenever the Lady Zillabar went anywhere, even from one room to another, her Guards first checked it for security. The Lady hadn't lived this long by tolerating carelessness. She'd seen too many Vampires die at the hands of fanatics and assassins.

Two of the Dragons took up positions by the forward door, two waited at the aft entrance to the salon.

---

[13]Of the Dragons the underground poet Aristol once wrote:

> *Creature of a crystalline age,*
> *the jeweled claw serves Vampire rage,*
> *black prisoner makes himself the cage.*

The assassination of Aristol remains unsolved. There exists no official proof of Regency involvement. Nevertheless, it remains extremely foolhardy to refer to the Moktar Dragons as the Vampires' claws.

The remaining two stood stolidly in the center of the lounge, the bony crests of their skulls almost touching the bright ceiling panels. One of them turned slowly, his nostrils flaring, his tongue flicking the air, tasting the faint perfumed essence of the lounge. His expression remained unchanged, but he spoke softly into a wrist communicator. "We have smelled the air in the salon. It will not offend."

Watching from the corner of the room, Robin could barely hide her discomfort. She glanced sideways to Ota, but the bioform's expression remained carefully blank. If Ota felt uneasy, it didn't show. The two waited in quiet, respectful postures.

One of the Dragons glanced speculatively at Ota and grinned, showing a mouth full of long white knives. *The better to eat you with, my dear....* The grin became a nasty leer as the Dragon's tongue flickered out; it glistened with a slick pale sheen, licking the air for the faintest taste of Ota. Its eyes took on a deadly glaze.

Robin noticed. She couldn't help but think, *it only wants permission*. But she kept her face impassive.

Ota merely met the Dragon's cruel study with its own impassive gaze, an extraordinary act of courage for an animal the Dragons considered only *prey;* but as the Executive Officer of the starship, Ota couldn't allow itself to betray the slightest sign of weakness. It had to maintain absolute composure.

A moment more and another Dragon stepped heavily in, Captain Naye-Ninneya, the Captain of the Lady's Dragons, the largest and most brutal of the squad. Lady Zillabar followed him, sweeping imperiously into the center of the salon. She wore a cloud of seaspray blue and a cape of ghostly mist, all outlined in bright sunshine fluorescence that enhanced her ethereal beauty like a pale dawn. Nevertheless, it failed to hide the hardness in her eyes. She looked dispassionate as ever. She glanced about the salon, only casually noting Ota's and Robin's presence; she would not otherwise acknowledge their existence. She turned to the Captain of her Dragons. "And the Star-Captain?"

Naye-Ninneya stiffened at attention. "I have no knowledge."

Lady Zillabar raised her eyebrow. She studied the Dragon coldly. "I see. . . ." She glanced away, as if it made no difference, though everyone present knew it did. The Phaestor had no word for failure; the closest concept in the Phaestor tongue implied betrayal, unworthiness, and incontinence.

"Excuse me—" Ota stepped forward, looking calmly up into the eyes of the hungrier Dragon. "I have the honor to inform the Noble presence that the Star-Captain will attend the needs of the Lady and her Guard at her earliest convenience. As soon as we complete the docking, she will present herself." Having finished her recitation, Ota stepped crisply back into position. She omitted the bow; the Dragon might have interpreted the bow as presumptuous. Humans bowed; prey didn't.

The Dragon—the metal badge across its chest identified it as Kask-54—turned to its Captain to repeat the information in sharp guttural barks. Naye-Ninneya accepted the report and turned back to Lady Zillabar. "The Star-Captain will attend shortly—"

The Lady gestured in annoyed dismissal. Excuses bored her. She parted her mouth slightly as she tasted the air; her expression became blank. She did not like the taste of this vessel. She did not like the manner in which this Captain operated her ship. She did not like the disrespectful treatment. She did not appreciate the underwhelming quality of the service. But neither did she like expressing her annoyance publicly.

Even if she could have succeeded in making this trip in secret, she would not have enjoyed the passage. This starship *stank*. That she had endured this unpleasant journey all in vain only added to the annoyance that she felt—and now had to conceal. She would not sink to the level of her ill-mannered hosts. She would not say what she felt. Not here. Not now.

The Lady would repay the insults, yes, but in her own way. The *Lady Macbeth* would suffer unexplainable mishaps for many years to come—until the Lady Zillabar grew bored with the game.[14]

Star-Captain Neena Linn-Campbell entered then. She wore her crisp black jumpsuit emblazoned with her Star-Captain's brilliant gold insignia over the heart. She inclined her head in the curtest of bows. She intended to get this ritual over with quickly. "Lady Zillabar. We have docked with Starport."

Lady Zillabar folded her hands and waited coldly.

Captain Campbell gritted her teeth, swallowed her pride, and continued, "You have honored my ship. I thank you for the privilege of service."

Lady Zillabar studied Captain Campbell with glimmering eyes. The perfunctoriness of this woman's gratitude annoyed her. Didn't she recognize the authority confronting her? Didn't she realize the danger of impudence? Not that it mattered, of course. Zillabar had already decided how she would express her displeasure. Nonetheless, the woman's insubordination rankled. She glanced sideways to Naye-Ninneya, the Captain of her Guards. He looked to Kask-54. Kask stepped to Ota and rumbled, "The Star-Captain may present her gift now."

Ota did not move to relay the message to Captain Campbell. Instead Captain Campbell said, "The corporation that owns this vessel does not practice the custom of gifts, my Lady. I hope this will not offend you." Captain

---

[14]Immortals do not grow bored easily. When one has centuries to plan, one takes the time to create baroque amusements. Vampires particularly enjoy planning and executing intricate patterns of revenge.

Campbell did not add that she herself held the majority of shares in the corporation.

Lady Zillabar remained impassive while she considered her next words. "We would not have you violate your charter," she said graciously. "The quality of your service demonstrates sufficient gratitude. It has not gone unnoticed. However, if you—acting only as an individual—wish to present a gift of your own free will, outside of any constraints of your corporate charter, we would not refuse. On the contrary, we would consider it a generous personal exhibition of loyalty to the Phaestoric Ruling Authority. Such an act would prove sufficient to ensure many years of gratitude and goodwill." She opened her hands to Captain Campbell.

For some reason Captain Campbell thought about brinewood. She spread her own hands emptily before her and said, "You humble me with your benevolence, Lady Zillabar. Unfortunately, this ship carries nothing of sufficient value to offer as a gift, nothing worthy of your station. I would not presume to insult you by offering a token of less than noble rank."

"The value of the gift has no relevance," the Lady insisted. "The thought maintains." She glanced casually around the room. "Any token will do. . . ." Her eye lit upon the bioform, Ota. "Even a lowly servant, perhaps—"

"That servant? Oh, no, my Lady. I could not. That servant suffers from laziness and incompetence. It rarely bathes, and the reek of its unwashed fur, the sour smell of its sweat, the stink of its shit"—Captain Campbell allowed herself a delicious shudder—"my Lady, please. I would not sleep well at nights thinking of the terrible deed I had done. You would get no useful work from this poor specimen. Look at the clumsiness of it, the slackness of its posture, the slovenliness of its general appearance, the ungraceful attitude with which it moves. It shambles like a hirsute pig. I insist you reconsider. This creature has no manners. It would so certainly affront your gracious sensibilities that even to burden you with its ownership would constitute the gravest of insults. I couldn't. I simply couldn't."

"Still . . . ," the Lady Zillabar mused, ". . . I would not have it said that the master of this vessel lacks the grace to offer even the smallest of gifts to the nobility." She appeared to consider the question further. "You speak honestly when you say the bioform would provide me with no pleasure; but I could give it to my Dragons as a plaything. They would not mind at all. They might even look forward to it as a minor sport. What say you?"

Ota hung her head in shame and mumbled something. Both Lady Zillabar and Captain Campbell looked at it, surprised at the interruption. Ota repeated itself. "Perhaps I should go. I would not want rancor on my behalf."

"Keep quiet, Ota!" Captain Campbell snapped at the bioform with genuine annoyance. "If I want you to have an opinion, I'll give you one."

"You see," said Zillabar, pleasantly. "Even the bioform agrees. It *wants* to come with me."

"Still, I must refuse." Captain Campbell's voice stayed firm, despite the apparent eagerness of her demeanor. "My employers will ask me, 'What have you done with the disreputable beast, the LIX-class bioform?' I'd have to tell them, 'I gave it to the Lady Zillabar—as a plaything for her Dragons, of course.' They would immediately relieve me of my command for insulting you and bringing shame upon this vessel. No, I can't."

Zillabar's expression darkened. "I would have the beast," she said quietly. *"I'll pay you for it."* Her tone became deadly.

Captain Campbell held her posture rigid. The moment had suddenly turned tense. She stared directly into Zillabar's smoldering eyes. "I will not sell the beast to you," she said. The watching Dragons bristled and stiffened. One of them even went so far as to bare its teeth. Campbell knew that she had put herself in great danger by her refusal; she needed to ameliorate it quickly. "Don't take it personally, Lady. I won't sell the beast to *anyone*." She shrugged apologetically. "I confess a fondness for it. I would not feel . . . right, allowing the beast to go. I have this fear that someone might forget its sentience and make the grave mistake of using it as food."

"That will not happen."

Captain Campbell shook her head. "Would you guarantee that?" And then she boldly met the Lady's eyes again.

The Lady stiffened in anger—

The Regency Charter expressly forbade the use of sentients as food—except under certain well-defined conditions.[15] Without a license, no Vampire, no Dragon would dare to disobey Article One—certainly not in any way that might come under public scrutiny. Doing so could trigger ferocious mass uprisings, and no one in authority wanted to risk a repeat of the wasteful Obalon Carnages. Unsubstantiated stories still abounded, however—enough to trouble the sleep of more than one Vampire aristocrat. Those who knew the truth had reason to worry about the rumors.

By bringing up the subject so indelicately, Captain Campbell not only demonstrated her distrust of Zillabar; she also served warning. If Zillabar tried to take Ota by force, Captain Campbell would demand an Auditor's guarantee. She didn't know if Zillabar would tolerate—or even risk—the personal attention of the Auditors, but she had to take the gamble.[16] She hoped the

---

[15]These include execution, criminal punishment, quashing of riots or rebellions, police actions, interrogation, public euthanasia, cultural culling, and licensed suicide.

[16]In the Regency legal hierarchy, only one office outranks the

Lady wouldn't challenge her beyond this point. She had no further cards to play.

—but it worked.

Zillabar recovered her composure quickly. She sniffed in displeasure. "I no longer want the beast." She added, distastefully, "Your fondness has the stink of perversion."

"Ahh." Campbell grinned. "You've found me out. I suffer the great weakness common to my species. I anthropomorphize. I bond too easily. I can't help myself. I care about my ... my *family*."

Lady Zillabar stiffened again—and this time she didn't try to hide her displeasure. "I will thank you," she said, "*to mind your language*. I have no interest in the breeding habits of your species. I choose not to have my nose rubbed in the unpleasant circumstances of animal behavior. I'll overlook it this time; I'll assume you didn't know better—but if you bring the subject up again, I'll file a complaint of public indecency against you."

Before Captain Campbell could apologize—assuming that she would have—EDNA chimed: "We have secure pressure in the air lock. Passengers may debark at will."

Zillabar used the interruption as an excuse to end an unpleasant conversation. "You've shown me the best of your hospitality," she said with deadly calm to Campbell. "Very soon I will show you the best of mine." Then she turned imperiously and swept out the forward door. Her Dragons hurried to catch up with her.

For a moment no one spoke. Then Ota turned to

Phaestoric Authority: the Auditors, a genetically tailored species of hive-insect designed to serve as notaries, legal witnesses, and guarantors. The Auditors remain unbribable and have established themselves as the primary control for all government dealings, as well as many of the major private financial transactions. Auditors also handle wills, bounty payoffs, and a variety of contract guarantees.

Campbell, eyes watering in relief. The bioform dropped to its knees in front of Campbell and grabbed her hands, nuzzling them eagerly, making wordless sounds of gratitude.[17]

"Goddammit! Get up!" Captain Campbell jerked her hands away. "I didn't do it for you. I did it for me. I need someone on this ship who knows how to keep the books. Now, quick—go take care of the Lady's belongings before she sends her lizards back."

[17]Several years previous to this encounter, Captain Campbell had discovered a badly abused Ota at a mining colony on the southwestern edge of the Cluster. The LIX-class bioform had suffered terrible mistreatment at the hands of the miners, including a despicable series of degrading sexual acts. The log of the *Lady Macbeth* records that Captain Campbell immediately offered to purchase Ota; the log fails to record that the transfer of title occurred over the dead bodies of the previous owners, apparently at their own request.

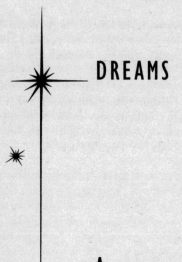

DREAMS

A squad of ceremonial Dragons met Zillabar's party at the docking tube. They came to rigid attention as she stepped out of the lock. "Your escort stands ready, Lady Zillabar," hissed a servant-wasp, a thin creature with glistening multifaceted eyes. Its voice had a chalky rasp. "Kernel d'Vashti sends his regards and hopes to meet with you upon your arrival downside. A Regency shuttlecraft waits at your disposal." The wasp pointed toward a passage.

The Lady nodded her acknowledgment, but she made no move toward the landing vessel. Instead she asked, "Take me to my quarters. I will rest first. And I have some personal business to attend to."

The servant-wasp dipped its antennae apologetically. "I will arrange a suite immediately. We had not anticipated that you might wish to rest. Kernel d'Vashti assumed that you would prefer to land immediately."

"Kernel d'Vashti does not speak for me. He has never spoken for me. He never will. Arrange the suite immediately. I will accept nothing less than full Regency security—oh, and find one that doesn't stink of mammals. I've had enough bad smells to last the rest of my life." The wasp bowed and stepped to one side, linking itself immediately to the station network.

Zillabar turned brusquely to the Captain of her Dragons. "Naye-Ninneya, I'll need at least a dozen hours of dreamtime. During that period have my cargo unloaded and see that all the gifts have made the journey safely. Then I want you to personally inspect and secure the landing vessel before you load anything aboard it."

"Yes, my Lady."

The wasp stepped back to Lady Zillabar. "I will lead you to the Imperial Suite now."

While Captain Naye-Ninneya conducted his usual thorough security inspection, Lady Zillabar barely glanced through the rooms. Right now she cared only about the quality of the suite's dream-tank. She found it in the personal quarters; she had seen worse—hell, she had slept in worse. She could not contain her irritability and exhaustion any longer. This would have to do.

She waited until Naye-Ninneya concluded his inspection, then dismissed him impatiently. Naye-Ninneya withdrew quietly; he ordered two Dragons to wait outside the door to the Lady's personal rooms. Two others guarded the main entrance of the suite.

Lady Zillabar slid out of her gown, feeling its weight slide away like years of toil. She eased herself into the dream-coffin, sighing gratefully as its silken mists embraced her. She inhaled the vapors deeply. She wished for fresh blood to feed her dreams, but didn't mind the lack. Almost instantly, she drifted into rosy splendor, her consciousness dissolving into red narcotic bliss. The dreams engulfed her in an overpowering rush . . . *cold lips press against hot fruity skin, a warm hand slips into hers, the body curls nakedly around her, fitting flesh to flesh, curve to curl, the scent of wine and blood, the violin wails alone, dry breath caresses the cheek, the mouth parts gently, the pale tongue flicks in and out and tastes the air, black flowers fill the garden with a tarty perfume, the curve of naked skin, so clean and white, the hair cascades, the taste of death, the bite, the sudden crunch of bone, the delicious pleasure, orgasmic, flowing, filling, sweet, the scarlet hair, the mandibles, the stiffening moment, slicing wetly, sliding, insertion, transformation, penetration, impalement, the heart gasps, a sudden flash of color, changing red to pink to white to orange, the vision opens, curtains parting, falling aside, the petals unfolding, the landscape spreading out like crumpled bed sheets, pink and white and yellow, fruity smells and puffball trees, the whirring sounds of stinging insects, the bed enfolds, the arms enfold, the legs upfold, the legs, the arms, the thrill begins below, inside, and climbs, the flow comes rising up, the crimson fury burns, expands and fills, and gasps, the star unfolds, explodes in glowing supernova patterns, it roars, it cries, ecstatic fury, flooding, spasming, orgasming, instantaneously transcending, riding, flying, coasting, drifting, receding, ebbing, sliding, dying, leaving in its wake a myriad of twinkling, fading pinpoints of sensation, leaving consciousness, enlightenment, a host of visions, flowers, eagles, wasps, and Dragons, hot-blooded puppies, morsels, uneaten, starships, angry Dragons, bleeding cattle, wasted blood, untasted blood, machines, and tears, emptiness and terror, dizzying dreams, and all those little eggs, a spurt of something yellow, converging lines, the flowers taste of shit, the dust, something dying in the wind of time, a glut of death and words, the endless pouring stream, the dream, the night, the stars,* the Eye of God, *oh God, the line, preserve the line, the holy horror surges, plunges down and out into empty space* ...

PUPPIES

After safely installing the Lady in her temporary quarters, Captain Naye-Ninneya picked two of his warriors, Kask and Keeda, to accompany him to the cargo port to supervise the unloading and transfer of their master's goods.

Several large containers hung from overhead transfer rails, waiting for the handlers to move them out of the *Lady Macbeth*'s aft bay and into the station's cargo port. Three bulky cages also waited, two fat puppies in each of them. Naye-Ninneya carefully began to inspect the seals of the cargo modules, while Kask and Keeda eyed the puppies in the cages with ill-concealed hunger.

Ota stood patiently to one side with a manifest. Gito and Robin waited with her; both carried deadly looking sidearms. Gito also wore a disdainful expression. Robin, an android, knew how to keep her face carefully blank. Nearby, Shariba-Jen, a heavy-metal robot, stood apart from them holding a portable laser-cannon. The robot had a leathery-looking copper skin; it had the general form and appearance of a human male, but it moved like an animated sculpture. Naye-Ninneya automatically noted the potential fire patterns; a little narrow, but practical for these cramped quarters. In spite of his contempt for these creatures, he still approved of their feral cunning.

"If everything meets with your inspection, Nobility, please sign the manifest." Ota offered the clipboard.

Naye-Ninneya ignored it. Dragons did not serve prey. Prey served Dragons. He yawned broadly and made a great show of inspecting the cargo modules, taking as long as he possibly could. Eventually, he worked his way over to the cages. The puppies whimpered and cringed under his scrutiny.[18]

"Thirsty—" wailed one of the pups. "Can we have a wa-wa?" It stood up against the bars of the cage, scratching and scrambling with fluffy paws, and wagging its tail hopefully. Naye-Ninneya noticed that its little pinafore had stains all up and down the front. Disgusting. All the pups would probably need cleaning before the presentation—and fattening too. They hadn't endured the journey well.

The puppy peered up at Naye-Ninneya, at Kask and Keeda. "Wa-wa, pwease?" it begged. The Dragon ignored its request. Talking prey annoyed him. He could already hear it begging, "Please don't kill me. Can't you eat something else?" Naye-Ninneya believed that prey should have the good manners not to speak as it died—a simple squeal, perhaps, but not a soliloquy.

Ota glanced to Robin. "Get the pups some water, please," it whispered. Robin nodded and went quickly to the service bay; she returned with a pail of water, a dipper, and a detached expression. As she approached the

---

[18]Uplifted canine bioforms, capable of limited speech; designed for entertainment, companionship, and simple labor. Most species have the intelligence of pre-reform humans.

first cage, all the pups began wagging their tails excitedly and squealing in eager anticipation. "Wa-wa! Wa-wa!"

"All right, all right—" called Robin. "Everybody calm down. You'll all get wa-wa. I have plenty—"

Abruptly, Captain Naye-Ninneya stepped deliberately into her way. Robin looked up—*and up*—to meet his black emotionless gaze. He towered over her darkly. "Did I order water for these animals?" he asked, his voice rumbling harshly.

"Wa-waaa. Pwease. Wa-waaa. Now." The puppies cried insistently.

"Why do you deny them water?" Robin asked innocently, keeping her voice purposely bland, and betting that the Dragon did not have the experience to recognize the full range of humanoid emotions, especially not the coy pretense of naïveté. "I thought your master commanded you to *protect* her property. What value do you add by starving and abusing these poor children?"

"Pwease. Waa-waaaa—pwease." As if to underline Robin's point, all six of the puppies had climbed to their feet and had begun reaching through the bars of their cages, clawing and crying.

Naye-Ninneya ignored it. He'd ignored worse. "If you water them," he explained, "they will only urinate all over themselves and their cages. They will stink. They will offend the sensibilities."

"So, wash them," Robin smiled and batted her eyes. "You do know how to wash, don't you?"

"Dragons don't wash—" Naye-Ninneya snarled.

"So we've noticed," Gito called from his position by the wall. He sniffed distastefully. Ota poked him sharply; Gito stepped sideways out of her reach, but he muted his disdainful expression.

Naye-Ninneya rumbled warningly. His orders didn't extend to cover insubordination by the starship crew. He didn't know if he had a license to kill this insolent servant or not. Better just to play it safe, he thought. He looked down at Robin and let the tone of his voice show his contempt. "Do you plan on accompanying us so you can attend to the washing? If so, by all means, give them water. If not, take it away."

Robin looked startled, as if she had just realized something. "You honestly don't care about their suffering, do you?"

"Suffering builds character. It adds *flavor* to the meat." Behind him the puppies began to weep.

The android looked unconvinced. "I wouldn't know. I don't eat meat."

For some reason Naye-Ninneya felt uncomfortable. Defensive. It puzzled him. He shouldn't feel that way in front of prey. He puffed out his chest. "The animals can wait until they reach the kennels downside. They will have water and grooming then."

"If they sicken—or worse, if they die—your master will blame us for insufficient care. Let me give them water now. And baths. We'll clean their clothes and deliver them to the landing shuttle in a much happier state."

The Captain of the Lady Zillabar's Dragons considered the thought. It made good sense; but if he followed the android's suggestion, he would look weak. The prey used a word to justify weakness; they called it *compassion*. "No," he decided. "I cannot allow it. My orders do not permit the animals out of my supervision."

"Stay and watch then," Robin suggested. She forced herself to focus on the Dragon, otherwise the plight of the caged puppies might distract her so badly that she'd lose all of her control; in which case, she might do something *really* dangerous.

"I must see the cargo safely transferred. That includes the cages. I will permit no exceptions."

Robin could feel her frustration building. She stopped trying to pretend. "Does the word *dogmatic* mean anything to you?" she snapped.

"An automatic canine? A relative of yours, perhaps?" Naye-Ninneya allowed himself a sharp-toothed smile, overly pleased with himself at his nasty little joke. He had shown this android bitch that Dragons did not lack a sense of humor.

He turned to Ota. "I'll sign that manifest now." He strode over to the bioform and grabbed the clipboard from its paws. He rudely ground his right thumbprint into the scanning plate, then thrust it back. "You!" He pointed to the robot, Shariba-Jen. "You may begin trans-ferring these containers to the landing-shuttle security bay. Kask, Keeda—you will supervise." He turned sharply and left.

In their cages the puppies wailed abysmally, their tails drooping.

Robin turned to Ota; but Ota shook its head sadly. "I ache worse than you do, but . . . I can do nothing." The bioform put a restraining hand on Robin's arm. "Let it go. The universe will find its own punishment for that one."

MESAPORT

The planet turned, baking in the oppressive gloom of the giant red star. The inhabitants called it Devil's Heart and other things even less complimentary. Pilgrims find no grace or welcome here, only hellish days and bizarre nights.

The fading old sun gave off very little light, only a dull, gloomy presence; but it still had the heat to scorch the air and shatter the rocks. Dayside, the huge dark furnace scoured the planet's face and burned the deserts. The atmosphere crackled with coronal effects; Thoska-Roole writhed under a steady onslaught of particle bombardment that left the weather churning, the mountains burning, and the atmosphere faintly glowing.

But somehow, as it always does, life endured. It even thrived.

The few real cities on Thoska-Roole remained untouched by the fiery days; they hid well inside the walls of the planet's deepest fissures. These scars ran deep—once sliced with the cuts of ancient mines, now they shone with the lights of civilization. Here, down beneath, safe from the winds, safe from the solar flares, the interior precipices churned with life, the constant continual thrusting, pushing, clamoring for uncommon living space.

Follow the walls of the rift downward and behold the teeming slums of the vertical city: bright hanging markets, plunging complexes of hivelike apartments, the terrifying overhang of greedy business districts, and precarious perpendicular gardens, dripping with yellow and black fripperies; everything tightly clustered, jammed one against another in a desperate grasp for purchase. And all these exterior structures represented only the open face of the crowded city; most of the real dwellings burrowed deeper into the bedrock, tunneling sideways into dark cramped warrens. Many of the denizens here had never seen real daylight. Below, the bottom of the chasm disappeared in darkness. Above, far above, the sheltering roofs distilled the dayside heat into faint red gloom. Between the dark and the day, the rift-cities fattened and prospered.

Twenty klicks to the southwest, a twisted spire of rock reached upward, as if grabbing for the sky—MesaPort; three kilometers tall, high enough so that its broken peak stood easily above the worst of the scouring winds and the restless dust and lightning storms. Here, in the gaudy palace that crowned the peak; and here, deep in the caverns that honeycombed the mountain; the Nobility lived, deliberately isolating themselves from those they fed upon. And here, at the very topmost peak of MesaPort, on the mountain's flattened crown, the skyboats came to nest at the safest place to land in a radius of five hundred kilometers.

The lights of MesaPort blazed upward through the gloom, shining beacons in the gray-and-orange dust. Pseudo-white lasers roamed back and forth, restlessly carving the day into quadrants. And then abruptly they paused. Everything hesitated, waiting. . . .

A glow appeared in the distance, a faint rumble of

noise accompanied it. Those few attendants standing on the outer surfaces of the palace turned to look. Others, waiting at the edge of the landing field, powered up their service vehicles and lowered their goggles over their eyes.

At last Lady Zillabar's lander came floating out of the distance, a luminous apparition of light and color. The sky-boat came down gracefully, all beams flashing and strobing in a brazen display of pride and victory. The craft glided past the minarets and spires of the palace, slowing, lowering, and finally coming easily to rest in the huge Imperial docking bay.[19]

Her secrecy destroyed, Lady Zillabar had no choice but to make the expected gaudy entrance. Had anyone downside noticed that the Lady had arrived at Thoska-Roole aboard the disreputable *Lady Macbeth*? They *all* had noticed. The failure of Lady Zillabar's attempt at discretion had spread a rippling confusion of rumors throughout the palace. Some expressed glee at the Lady's discomfiture; others despaired, already fearing the wrath to follow her arrival. Would anyone mention the subject to the Lady—? Of course not. Fear more than courtesy ruled the court. Had the Lady lost face? Absolutely. To reestablish her authority, she would have to ... take bold steps. Everyone knew it.

The Regency Heralds began enthusiastically trumpeting the "Ceremonial Flourishes" the moment the Imperial lander touched down. The brassy fanfares rattled across the High Pavilion, echoing like a hellish brigade. The waiting dignitaries rustled impatiently.

Opposite the stairs the Great Balcony looked down upon the distant surface of the Iron Sea, a bleak and empty wasteland of rust and broken rock. The ghastly

[19]The Regency maintained the only *authorized* landing port on Thoska-Roole. All licensed commerce had to go through MesaPort. Illegal commerce, of course, found its own channels of delivery.

desolation confronted arriving travelers like a warning, staggering them with their first clear sight of the true nature of Thoska-Roole. Some thought it beautiful. Others recoiled, awestruck, shocked or horrified. The ancient red desert lay in rumpled bloody sheets, a nightmare vision under a flaming red sky. The view did not inspire sanguine thoughts—except occasionally to Vampires. The colors of Thoska-Roole often reminded them of sweet fresh blood.

The crowd at the bottom of the stairs looked haggard. Few of them cared about the vista anymore. Some complained loudly to one another; others, more experienced at survival, kept their thoughts carefully to themselves.

The Prefect of Thoska-Roole, an aged Phaestor named Zarr Khallanin, had summoned this gathering of Nobles to the palace fifteen hours ago, immediately upon receiving word of Zillabar's imminent arrival. He had allowed them frequent rest and refreshment, but he would not allow anyone to leave until after the welcoming ceremonies to celebrate the Lady's arrival had fully concluded. Protocol demanded a five-star welcome for a Lady of her rank, and because Zillabar ruled the Zashti clan, she required the presence of every Noble Citizen at Mesaport, nothing less. So Zarr Khallanin calmly held his ground. He insisted that the gathered Nobles await the Lady's landing—and they must continue waiting until dismissed by the Lady herself; but the Prefect also implied with subtle suggestions that the imposition of this demand came from the Lady's House, and not his own.

Beside Khallanin stood his protégé, a young starlord named Kernel Sleestak d'Vashti, a thin, bloodless-looking Vampire. d'Vashti had brought his squadrons of Marauders to Thoska-Roole two years previously, looking for an industrial world where he could refit and rebuild. He had immediately offered his services to the administration of Zarr Khallanin. Thenceforth, he

had secured for himself an appointment as one of
Khallanin's most trusted advisers by the skillful application of scurrilous information about Khallanin's other
most trusted advisers. The resulting perceptions created
not only an increased sense of paranoia in the Noble Prefect, but a perfect opportunity for an ambitious underling
as well.

d'Vashti waited patiently beside his political mentor. He recognized that the crowd had long since grown
restless and frustrated, almost to the point of anger. He
didn't care. It suited his purposes—his mentor's
purposes—to have them feeling angry and resentful.
They would blame the Lady, not the Prefect. Later he
could make quiet unofficial personal amends to each and
every one of them—not on the Lady's behalf, not even on
the Prefect's, but on his own. He'd make sure they got
the message. Slowly, he would build support.

He glanced across the room and noticed the
Dragon Lord, the supreme father of the entire race of
Dragons. The Lord of All Moktar and Lesser Breeds had
long since grown much too large for any but the most
ceremonial of occasions; only the largest of rooms could
hold him comfortably. He stood more than five meters
tall. His tail alone had more length than a Vampire. Even
those Nobles who considered it an honor to stand near
the Dragon Lord still gave him ample space to move.
The Lord stood in the center of his own wide clearing in
the crowd, his great head split in a ghastly grin, revealing
yellow teeth as long as a young man. His armor glistened
with an ebony sheen. He loomed huge over his end of
the room. The thick towers of his scaly hind legs and the
great curving claws at the base of them attracted nervous
glances from those closest by. The Lord himself gave no
notice of the attention he drew. He seemed lost in some
ancient reptilian dream. His great eyes had closed against
the glittering boredom; the monster looked as if he'd
gone to sleep.

d'Vashti knew better. He had no illusions about the Dragon Lord and the power he controlled. The Dragons remained the dominant military authority in the Regency, partly because their inability to surrender—you could kill a Dragon, you couldn't defeat him—made them essentially unbeatable, and partly because the commanding physical presence of even a single Dragon inspired feelings of stark terror in most species, especially the mammalian ones. A troop of Dragons simply marching through a village made for an excellent textbook study in naked panic.

Even the highest of the Phaestor gave their Moktar allies an apprehensive respect. d'Vashti had seen the Lord of All Moktar and Lesser Breeds in action more than a few times, and the memory still gave him uneasy nights. Even an *ordinary* Dragon controlled an appalling strength and viciousness. The master of all of them commanded the incredible physical authority necessary to control his entire species. He had once killed a Captain and his entire family of sons for committing the terrible insubordination of *massing* more than he did. The act had represented a naked challenge, and the Dragon Lord had quickly demonstrated his wrath. Since that time no Captain, ambitious or otherwise, had even dared to fertilize that many eggs at one time.

Most observers assumed that if the Dragon Lord could continue to manage the actions of his Captains this ruthlessly, the inevitable day of political challenge would not occur for at least another century or three—but when it did happen, Dragon blood would flow like wine. The last time the Dragon Lord had faced a serious challenge, fully one third of the major Dragon families—those who had supported the loser—had forfeited their lives. The loyal survivors had thereafter enjoyed many years of free breeding.

The thought of all that coiled and brooding Dragon energy troubled d'Vashti. Someday the Dragons might grow even more ambitious. The Moktar Dragons could easily crush the much weaker Vampires; both species knew it, and their alliance remained uneasy. The threat remained unspoken, but the thought of all that naked power coming to bear against the Vampire aristocracy continued to worry the highest councils of the Phaestoric Authority. No Vampire had yet conceived of a way to protect against that eventuality—except, perhaps, the continued maintenance of the present state of mutual advantage. The two species would simply have to continue sharing the great overripe plum of the Regency.

Beside the Dragon Lord stood Lord Drydel, the Prince-Consort. Drydel looked up suddenly and noticed d'Vashti's speculative interest. He allowed himself an amused expression that could mean almost anything. d'Vashti returned the Prince's glance with a delicate nod and an opaque smile; he held eye contact with the other man for a long violet moment, then deliberately, languidly, let his gaze slide sideways toward the ranks of pretty page boys. He wondered how many of them Lord Drydel had seduced. Probably at least as many as d'Vashti himself had.

Rumor had it that the Prince still maintained a remarkable private harem—a dangerous mistake, if true. If d'Vashti could only find a witness—or even just a soiled bed sheet; the most minuscule fragment of proof would suit his damaging purpose—and if he could, *without revealing his participation in the matter,* somehow maneuver the damning evidence of Drydel's transgression into the Lady's hands, it would certainly mean the end of this Prince's reign. No Lady ever objected to private harems of lustrous boys; powerful leaders often needed outlets in which to sublimate their overwhelming mating urges, and the tradition of the personal harem had a history as old as the Phaestor—but the tradition did not extend to include the lusts of Noble Consorts, and any Lady would surely take offense at her selected partner bedding down these pubescent trifles instead of servicing her own desires. A Lady's devouring passions must always take precedence.

d'Vashti considered alternate possibilities. He still fancied his presumed opponent. He had once admired that whole swarm of rosy Phaestor boys—fat, naked, chubby, tasty hatchlings all—eventually fastening his attentions on the sharpest of the survivors, the youthful Drydel himself. This had happened long before the Lady's intolerable selection, and although the male/male mating dance had never had the chance to come to passionate fruition, d'Vashti still keenly felt the hunger. He knew that Drydel felt it too; he had not mistaken Drydel's frequent frank examinations, both before and since his coronation. But he knew that Drydel could just as easily assassinate him as take him to bed, depending on the politics of the moment. The dilemma that d'Vashti pondered troubled him deliciously: how to ascertain which of Drydel's lusts held sway at any given moment.

The idea of a dalliance with Drydel troubled him. What advantage might he gain from it? Even more disturbing, what advantage might Drydel gain? Certainly, he could not allow his own mentor, the Noble Prefect Zarr Khallanin, to discover his lusts. Khallanin stood tall and pink and shining beside him, an example of elegance in power for all to see and admire. What a peculiar dilemma for the both of them, d'Vashti thought. What a remarkable moment in the game! Both he and Drydel stood pinned to the board by the power of their own desires as well as the power of their respective mentors, yet each wanted to trade one for the other—at least d'Vashti perceived it that way. He wondered if he had made a mistaken assumption about the Prince-Consort and his intentions. He didn't know. And he didn't know how to safely find out. The risk remained too great.

d'Vashti shook his head as if to clear it and pushed all thoughts of consummation aside. He didn't dare. Across the room Lord Drydel flashed a dazzling smile purposely in his direction—much more than just a simple greeting—an invitation or a challenge? d'Vashti groaned inside. The danger and allure would surely drive him mad.[20]

---

[20]Before he fell out of favor, the late poet Aristol once called the Vampires, "a nightmare wrapped in a scream." The Phaestor interpreted it as a compliment.

Historically, the Phaestoric redesign represents humanity recreated on the model of the wasp—the insect's concept of life superimposed upon a mammalian frame. Ungodly, selfish, mechanistic, and hungry; the Phaestor exist without compassion or mercy. They feed, they breed, they kill, and they die. Given human intelligence, they still lack even the simplest of human motives; instead, they use their cunning to scheme and plot intrigues against each other. They manipulate, they plan, they cheat, they lie, they calculate and bedevil their allies and their enemies alike. Possessed by their own terrifying appetites for blood and power, the Vampires must control everything. Whenever a Vampire reaches out to grasp a fact, it also immediately tries to apply that circumstance to its own profit. A Vampire has no more choice in its lust than a moth possessed by a pheromone; the same process obtains in both cases.

Consider:

Because a female Vampire can lay thousands of fertile eggs after a single mating, the Phaestor consider individual lives to have very little value—even those of their own children. The lives of individuals of other species have even less value to them; slaves and cattle simply don't count. A Vampire lives only for the continuation of the family line; because only from its family can a Vampire derive authority, fortune, and power. A Vampire will do anything it must to advance the goals of its family.

Furthermore, because most of the eggs hatch into males, and only a few produce females, the Phaestoric culture has deliberately structured itself around this severely skewed ratio. Warrior classes abound. Angry duels, ritual killings, blood sacrifices, reasonless murders, impassioned homosexuality, unbridled cannibalism, thrillseeking gangs, mass hysteria, violent swarming, feeding frenzies, mating frenzies, violent frenzies of all kinds—every appalling form of savagery occurs routinely among Vampire youth. Only a small per-

Even for a Vampire, Lord Drydel had a stunning presence. Exceptionally tall and slim, and oh, so pale-bright golden, he shimmered with angelic poise. He moved with the grace of a sparkle-dancer and spoke in tones so soft and gentle that beholders often likened him to a lovely wraith, some kind of pretty holiday ghost. Drydel's exquisite manners only enhanced the illusion. Indeed, he seemed delicate almost to the point of effeminacy.

The Lord had the high, pronounced cheekbones and the small, slightly protruding mouth common to all of the Phaestor, which usually afforded them a sharp, sinister, al-

---

centage of Phaestor males survive their adolescence; even so, the unforgiving ratio still remains badly out of balance.

As a result, only a small percentage of males ever achieve the opportunity to mate. The horrendous competition, even for an unlicensed Vampire female, exhausts the skills of most males. Among the aristocracy, the grueling rivalry for mating rights produces unspeakable savagery.

Naturally, Phaestoric society rules itself along matriarchal lines, with the most power held by the oldest and most fecund female. When disputes between age and fertility occasionally occur, the power almost always goes to the female who has given birth to the most offspring—because she has the largest army.

Phaestor young do not bond emotionally with either parent; instead, they bond chemically to the carriers of specific genetically linked pheromones. This produces in every individual a remarkable loyalty to the members of its own bloodline—a loyalty that *cannot* break by any means short of massive chemical confusion. Additionally, this chemical bonding automatically extends to every other individual that carries a related genetic mix; the closer the mix, the stronger the connection. A Phaestor child defines his identity through the linkage to his siblings and to his maternal parent. Ultimately, the Phaestor young become the foot soldiers in the undeclared wars of their mothers, grandmothers, and greater ancestors.

A Vampire may have allies, it will never have friends. The family scent controls every Vampire motive, outweighing every other possibility before it has a chance. As a species, the Vampires have no gods but themselves—they *cannot*. They have no higher vision, no purpose other than their own all-consuming hunger.

most ratlike appearance, but which in Drydel's case produced instead a brooding, thoughtful expression, which served somewhat to offset the startling clarity of his appearance. His lips seemed almost too red for his lustrous skin, his eyes too wide and bright, his hair too silverglowy. The deceptive elegance of his features belied the sharp mind behind them. His extraordinary appearance served as a useful distraction; he used it skillfully to his advantage; it confused the unwary.

But Drydel possessed a mysterious attraction that went far beyond mere beauty; he unnerved even his own kind. An enigma lived behind his liquid blue eyes, something every bit as wicked and as devious as the Lady Zillabar herself. Somewhere deep inside this brilliant puzzle lay the source of his enchantment. Some suspected that the purest essence of Vampire hunger lived behind those eyes, a hunger so intense that it would even feed on Vampire flesh. If true, then it explained everything. Other Vampires, unused to the frank appraisal of a higher kind of predator could only submit to his raw power.

The Lady Zillabar herself had fallen prey to Drydel's notorious charm at their first meeting. Drawn initially only to his beauty, she had quickly found herself entranced by his delicious wit and ultimately his wicked sense of how to handle power gracefully. Eventually, and not without considerable careful planning, she selected him as her Prince-Consort.

As Zillabar's favorite plaything, Lord Drydel enjoyed the Lady's unlimited favor while it lasted. He had studied Zillabar's history; he knew she could grow bored too easily. Drydel planned to have his own intrigues in place before that happened; he had the wit to keep both his ambitions and his vanity hidden.[21]

---

[21]The position of Prince-Consort not only carries great status and power, it also comes with its own set of unique dangers. Breeding fe-

Drydel knew about the stories circulating. He knew how they had started and had long since taken care of any evidence that might incriminate; the voluptuous little boys had long since fed their brothers. Lord Drydel took no foolish chances. He served the Lady's purposes with loyalty and zeal—and with considerable caution. She'd find no fault with him; not by any action of his own.

As for d'Vashti—well, even though Lord Drydel still enjoyed the immediate advantage of the Lady's favor, he knew better than to depend on it. While at the moment the Lady still found d'Vashti ill-mannered and presumptuous, a mere surrogate for Khallanin's senile fumblings, Drydel knew better than to expect that her opinion would remain unchanged for long. In Zillabar's case, desire often reflected the particular vicissitudes of politics and power—and, under Khallanin's tutelage, d'Vashti had a growing sovereignty here on Thoska-Roole. Even Zillabar didn't dare abuse his courtesy too badly.

For his part, Drydel didn't share the Lady's particular disdain; he found d'Vashti's cruel ruthlessness attractive. That d'Vashti stank of dangerous ambition only made him more interesting, not less. If d'Vashti kept on consolidating his authority, who knew what might happen—especially if Khallanin suddenly disappeared from the political equation. Would d'Vashti pick up all the pieces? Or would they scatter like spores on the

---

males often change their tastes abruptly.

Should a Lady become tired of her consort, he could die in sudden and mysterious circumstances. Should another suitor seek the Lady's favor, almost a certainty to happen, again the Prince-Consort could have an unfortunate and unexplainable accident.

Nevertheless, the competition to win a Lady's favor goes on and on and on. The explanation for this lies beyond the simple power of the pheromones: Every male Vampire believes that he has the personal authority to escape the law of averages.

wind? How many would land in his garden? Or the Lady's? The situation held no small potential—and Drydel
had his plans too.

—Finally, at long last, the Imperial Heralds raised
their horns and blew their most expectant notes. Everyone present looked up in anticipation. And then, as if in
answer to a prayer, the towering dark gates at the crest of
the stairs parted in majestic glory, opening to reveal a
lambent white blaze of light beyond.

Now the Heralds trumpeted with new excitement,
and a procession of glistening warrior-lizards entered in
proud, precise formation; they wore the black-and-scarlet
uniforms of the Zashti clan and carried the colors of their
individual Houses on high standards. They all had gaudy
ornaments and war paint appropriate to their high stations. As they descended, each pair of Dragons peeled off
from the front of the march and took up ceremonial positions on either side of the staircase. Thus, they lined the
course of the Lady's downward procession.

Following them came the Lady Zillabar's personal
retinue, Captain Naye-Ninneya and the squad of six personal Dragons. Much larger than the warrior-lizards,
more brutal looking and more dangerous, they came
down the stairs as if they owned them. They fanned out
at the bottom and waited.

The Heralds paused—the silence smelled of heady
expectation—then proudly, the musicians played the
"Zashti Entrance March." The blaring notes of triumph
filled the hall, and as they echoed grandly, the Lady
Zillabar appeared. . . . She looked almost tiny in the towering light of the doorway. She waited for the applause to
start and then began a stately, measured descent to the
floor of the gallery.

Having found discretion impossible, the Lady had
gone for impact instead. She wore a luminous blaze of
twinkling diamond mist and sparkling crystal
shards—no color at all and all colors at once, it reflected

and dazzled and blinded. The Lady Zillabar had become a fantastic apparition of woven light. One could not look directly at her; neither could one look away politely.

d'Vashti squinted and frowned and shielded his eyes. His vision burned painfully. He could see only blurs. The Lady had outsmarted them again, himself and Lord Khallanin. She had upstaged the Prefect in his own palace. The applause came thundering in waves around him. It rose and rose, roaring in his ears like the Lady's own rebuke; the tumultuous clapping went on and on and on. He glanced sideways at his mentor, not surprised to see Lord Khallanin applauding as enthusiastically as all the rest. Whatever feelings he might have written on his inner face, he showed only delight on his outer one. The Prefect had not survived this long by luck.

d'Vashti had to admire the Lady's style. He recognized the elegance of her maneuver. She'd never say a word about this; she wouldn't have to. Instead, she'd treat him with exquisite courtesy while he squirmed in shame and resentment.

She approached. Lord Zarr Khallanin and Kernel Sleestak d'Vashti both went down on one knee before her, bowing their heads low and spreading out their arms in total deference. The Lady let them stay that way for a long, painful moment, much longer than usual, while she regarded them both dispassionately. She made them hold the position to the point of embarrassment; her way of reminding Lord Khallanin—and in particular, d'Vashti, the architect of this moment—exactly where the real power still rested. d'Vashti thought he heard a stifled laugh behind him; he flushed with anger; later he'd run the tapes and find out exactly who found his public mortification so amusing. He'd show that one the meaning of true humor. At last the Lady acknowledged their devotion with a nod and bade them rise.

To Lord Khallanin she displayed her most gracious smile. She did not hold him responsible for the attempt at her public embarrassment. The Lady knew better. She allowed him to kiss her outstretched hand, and she responded with a throaty purr. "Your service always brings me satisfaction." Then she turned to d'Vashti. She did not extend her hand, she merely met his shadowed eyes with cruel study. "Never forget," she said so quietly that only he could hear, "that service must flow upward before it can flow down again."

Kernel d'Vashti stifled the first thought that came into his mind. Instead, he carefully inclined his head in a curt, socially correct, nod of gratitude. "I thank you for your wisdom, Lady Zillabar. As always, you bring— *enlightenment*." He spread his hands wide to include the painfully bright, shimmering veils that enveloped her. Soon his eyes would begin watering. If he used his handkerchief to dab at the tears, people would notice. If he did not, they would still notice. *The cunning witch.*

"Thank you for noticing." Zillabar beamed disarmingly. She looked to Khallanin and said, "Come now, let's conclude this tedious ceremony and all go someplace where we can sit and chat together." She reached for Lord Khallanin, pulling him forward in her wake, and then she paused as if remembering, turned back, and laid one delicate hand across d'Vashti's arm—a touch that felt disturbingly like the cold flicker of a snake—and she smiled sweetly. "Do please join us. I have so much to say to both of you."

d'Vashti bowed again, a gracious and courtly movement. "I welcome your words, my Lady."

"How kind of you to say so."

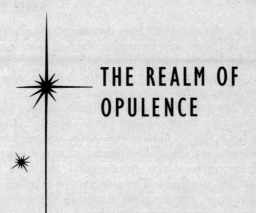

THE REALM OF
OPULENCE

The Pavilion of Night appeared to float high above the distant red-baked sands.

Towering panels of diamond-flecked obsidian outlined the hall. Tall windows opened out onto the distant desert floor so very far below. The lights of the rift-city glimmered softly on the horizon. The foreglow of the Eye of God had already begun to light up the edge of the world, and the entire vista had taken on a peaceful, desolate quality that only a Vampire's eyes could truly appreciate.[22]

Lady Zillabar took her time admiring the view and collecting her thoughts. She wanted to let the others stew for a long terrifying moment in their own anxiety, but at

---

[22]Vampires have the ability to see well into the infrared and ultraviolet. They perceive colors beyond the range of normal human or animal vision and find the radiation-blasted surface of Thoska-Roole a dazzling panorama of light and shade. Several Vampire poets have even composed thousand-stanza cycles about the indescribable beauty of the Thoska-Roole aurora. Unfortunately, most of the more dramatic colors of the planet's aurora remain invisible to lesser creatures.

the moment she didn't have the patience. She still carried too much anger and frustration; she had to let it out *now*. Despite her temporary return to dreamtime, she knew that she still remained much too irritable. She would have to keep this meeting short.

Abruptly, she turned to Khallanin, to d'Vashti, to Drydel, and to the Dragon Lord. "The TimeBinder on Burihatin appears to have died—or so my sources believe. Unfortunately, this death apparently did not occur in circumstances conducive to our goals. We have not yet found the headband. The officers who accepted the assignment of procuring the headband did not complete their mission satisfactorily—they have also died." She looked to each of them in turn; her piercing gaze stabbed from one to the next. "I hope that you will have much better news for me . . . ?"

The Dragon Lord did not react. He yawned deliberately. He knew the Lady would never threaten him. She didn't have the power to hurt him. He examined one steel claw abstractedly. Beside him Drydel waited silently. Nor did Lord Khallanin speak.

Kernel d'Vashti kept both of his faces impassive, the inner as well as the outer. He would not demonstrate any weakness of any kind. He would not volunteer anything. He would wait passively and allow the Lady herself to control the course of the discussion; in that way he would control her—by letting her have her way.

Lady Zillabar moved to a glowing couch and settled herself gracefully onto its evanescence. Again she became hard to look at, hard to see clearly. Lord Drydel moved behind the Lady, to stand as protector and Consort. She glanced up at him with only casual affection, then she looked across the room to d'Vashti and said, by way of small talk, "I trust that you have taken the appropriate care of my vessel. As I recall . . . ?" She let her sentence trail off into ominous silence.

d'Vashti returned her cold smile with an expression

equally polite. He ignored the Lady's sly implication. He had not *deliberately* subverted the maintenance of her powerful war-cruiser; he had simply allowed the occurrence of a few small logistical delays, enough so as to ensure that the completion of several necessary modifications would not transpire in time for the Lady's mission to Burihatin. A number of important replacement modules had mysteriously become unavailable. And the personnel who could have installed them in time had prior commitments elsewhere. d'Vashti had thought to neutralize some of the Lady's grander ambitions, at least temporarily, by delaying her departure from Thoska-Roole and allowing him time to complete his own schemes. His plan had almost worked.

Had d'Vashti's subtle efforts not subverted the Lady's intentions, the resources of her flagship would have given her efforts at Burihatin a significant advantage; instead the lack of those resources had seriously crippled her efforts. Under her original plan, she would have had the authority of her personal Guard to enforce her wishes on the moons of the great ringed world, but her inability to provide transportation for them on her personal warship had brought her instead to a dependency on the sympathies of Burihatin's local authority. d'Vashti had believed this made the possibility of her success in the matter problematic.

d'Vashti had expected her to recognize that. He'd expected her to cancel or postpone her trip. Instead, the Lady had secretly shifted her plans and secured other transportation—*lesser* transportation—and slipped away into the dark between the stars. She had opted for secrecy, and ... exactly as d'Vashti had predicted, she had failed.

Now she had returned with vengeance in her mouth.

The Lady knew of his efforts on her behalf—and

she hated him for those efforts. But, he wondered, *did she hate him enough?*

d'Vashti put on his sincerest outer manner, the one he always used for dissembling. "You may rest easy, Lady Zillabar. The previous state of affairs no longer maintains. We have punished the parties responsible. Those who failed to live up to the standards you require will no longer have the honor of working in your Stardock. As long as I have the privilege of this responsibility, you will never again have to suffer the indignity of seeking an alternate conveyance for your desires." Behind the Lady, Drydel frowned at this double-edged reference. d'Vashti noted the other's displeasure only in passing. "Your vessel now stands ready to carry you to the far reaches of the Cluster—and beyond—if you so choose."

"And ... what punishment did you apply to those who failed?" The Lady asked with only the faintest show of interest.

"They fed the Dragons," d'Vashti replied. "A task they executed with no small enthusiasm."

"Yes. I can imagine."

The Dragon Lord belched loudly. Neither the Lady Zillabar, nor Lord Drydel, nor Kernel d'Vashti acknowledged his comment. Lord Khallanin looked as if he had fallen asleep; d'Vashti would have bet otherwise.

The Lady's gaze remained fixed on the rival of her Consort. She understood the subtext of these events even better than the participants. Idly, almost casually, she let the nails of her right hand trace a delicate course up and down the line of her exposed cleavage. Precisely as she intended, the action drew d'Vashti's instant attention. She smiled inwardly. She could control this man. That made him worthy only of her contempt. She stroked herself meaningfully; she would arouse him to the point of lustful irresponsibility ... and then she would rebuke him; a rebuke of deliberate sexual fury and rejection that would inflict the most painful sting.

d'Vashti's eyes followed the movements of her fingertips. But he did not react as the Lady intended. He had prepared for this meeting by dosing himself with an especially powerful restricting agent. Let the Lady wonder at her inability to arouse him and it just might increase his mystery to her, and eventually his attraction as well.

Abruptly tiring of this ebb and flow of subtext, Lord Khallanin looked up and waved a slender finger at someone unseen. A servant-wasp appeared instantly from behind a screen, wheeling a silver cart before it. On the cart stood slender wineglasses and a decanter of frothy pink liquid. "Would you care for some refreshment, m'Lady?"

Zillabar ignored the invitation, her gaze still focused on d'Vashti. Her eyes narrowed suspiciously—she understood immediately. d'Vashti had made himself immune to her sexual pheromones. By so doing, he displayed not only his intention of independence, but he implied a greater insult as well—that he might not choose to mate with her, even if given the opportunity. The Lady considered these subtle taunts a very dangerous game. And yet—d'Vashti clearly understood that she found *danger* stimulating.

Drydel had recognized it too. He placed one hand gently on the Lady's shoulder. She acknowledged the gesture by glancing backward at him; then she allowed her diamond-tipped claws to slice delicately across the back of his hand. The gesture had a twofold meaning; she demonstrated ownership of his affections at the same time as she rebuked his impulsiveness. To Drydel's credit he left his hand on the Lady's shoulder, even though delicate beads of blood appeared where her nails had drawn their edges.

Watching, d'Vashti wondered if this time, perhaps, her nails contained a poisonous essence. One day soon, he knew, she would tire of Drydel—but Drydel wouldn't know it until *after* the stricture had closed his throat for the last time.

They waited in silence, each studying the others, while the servant-wasp poured the wine into the goblets. The creature wheeled the cart around for each to select a glass. The Dragon Lord waved her away, but the four Vampires each helped themselves.

"A toast, perhaps?" d'Vashti invited the Lady.

"Give me something to toast," she demanded icily.

Here d'Vashti made a mistake. He should have let the matter drop. Instead, he allowed the merest fragment of his ambition to show; he said, "The service of Lord Khallanin's people, perhaps? Surely their performance has brought you satisfaction and pleasure?"

"The performance of your Lord's servants ...?" The Lady pretended to consider the thought. "The servants' performance always reflects that of the master, Kernel d'Vashti. Don't you agree?" The faintest edge of metal appeared in her voice.

d'Vashti nodded. "As always, your words ring true."

"Yes, thank you," she said. "I would apply the word *adequate* here, as an appropriate descriptor of the performance of your master and his servants."

d'Vashti realized his error too late. He had given the Lady an opportunity to rebuke himself and his Lord—and in front of a wasp! Why not just announce it to the entire world? He bridled at her delicately phrased assault, but he held his silence and waited stiffly for her to continue.

The Lady Zillabar placed her wineglass on a table, the wine still untouched. "Have you located the TimeBinder of Thoska-Roole yet?" she demanded of Lord Khallanin.

The Prefect sipped from his goblet, appearing unconcerned. He had ignored the Lady's insult. What else could he do? He met her angry glare with equanimity.

"The work proceeds. The task carries many complications."

"Your answer lacks certainty," the Lady replied.

d'Vashti put aside his own wine, untasted. He spoke up aggressively. "We have several historians in custody. Before many more days pass, we shall have the TimeBinder as well."

"Oh?" The Lady raised her eyebrow skeptically. "And from where does all this confidence arise?" She exchanged a laughing glance with Lord Drydel. Drydel's eyes flashed with merriment, as well as with a suggestion of unashamed lust. But targeted at whom? Did Zillabar see it too? d'Vashti wondered again at Drydel's occupations.

Annoyed, he pushed the thought aside and turned his attention back to the Lady's question. "We have implemented an absolute security net. I believe you encountered it on your final approach. The forces of our most powerful ally—" Here d'Vashti nodded gracefully to the Dragon Lord. The Lord of All Things Black and Beautiful merely grunted in response. d'Vashti continued, "—have done an excellent job of establishing and maintaining a global containment. Nothing goes up or down that they do not control it. In addition, we have authorized a generous bounty. I doubt that you shall have to wait much longer, my Lady."

"I should not have to wait at all," she said, furiously standing. d'Vashti expected her to confront him, but instead she advanced directly on the highest law of the land, the Prefect of Thoska-Roole. "I expected that *you* would have captured the eye-damned TimeBinder by now, Lord Khallanin. You've had more than long enough. How do you waste my resources?"

Suddenly, d'Vashti understood the elegance of the Lady's mind. She knew that d'Vashti's maneuvers had brought them all to this point, but instead of attacking d'Vashti directly, she would destroy his protector and leave the real architect naked, humiliated, and powerless to do more. d'Vashti realized with horror that if she dared to assault the Prefect directly, then she must have progressed much further in her own ambitions than he'd thought possible. d'Vashti had privately regarded the Lady's goals as unrealistic and unreachable. Now he wondered just what else she had accomplished on Burihatin.

Lord Khallanin refused to accept the Lady's anger as his own. He spoke calmly and with quiet resolve. "The wilderness of Thoska-Roole covers most of the planet. We could have scoured every square meter, but I felt a more intelligent use of our resources would please you more."

"You may *still* have to scour every square meter. We cannot proceed without the TimeBinder's headband. You have wasted valuable days."

Inwardly, d'Vashti stiffened. Her impoliteness had a distinct taste of menace; but Lord Khallanin continued to ignore her bad manners. "The days have not ended yet," he said with cold strength. The Lady sniffed distastefully.

d'Vashti knew he couldn't let this argument cascade. He had to do something to deflect the Lady's wrath. He stepped forward briskly and offered an additional thought. "If we began the kind of search-and-seizure operations that you suggest, my Lady, we might trigger a renewed rebellion on this world. May I remind you that we have pacified this population only too recently."

"We—?" The Lady Zillabar regarded this last remark with deliberate contempt. "I don't remember seeing your Marauder squadrons engaged in the battle to secure the peace on Thoska-Roole. Indeed, if I remember correctly, during the days of the hardest fighting, you had not yet even announced your intention to base your squadrons here. If I remember correctly, *we* pacified this world, not you. Please tell me, Kernel d'Vashti; do I misremember?"

d'Vashti smiled generously. "My Lady, I thought

you had a larger vision than just a single world. When I spoke the word *we,* I intended it to include all of the members of the Palethetic aristocracy, regardless of origin—or species." He said this last with a nod toward the Dragon Lord. "*We* have greater goals in mind than the simple ownership of real estate. But my real point remains. The population of this world still carries strong resentment against us. If we push them too hard, they will not bother with the distinctions of class; they will make us *all* targets.

"We would win again, of course, but none of us eagerly seek that task, do we? It would require a great expenditure of resources, and none of us would gain anything worthwhile in return. Indeed, even after our victory, we would still have less than before—and a repair bill large enough to stifle economic growth for a decade. This planet hasn't yet recovered from the last war. Your people still carry the scars. Or do you forget how many of your own died before you and your Moktar allies finally achieved a tenuous measure of control here? With all due respect, you *need* the authority that I and my squadrons have brought with us."

"I remember the events of the rebellion well. Better than you, d'Vashti. You don't need to remind me." The Lady focused her chilly gaze on him. "Every war carries a price. We ourselves—the Phaestor—represent the price paid in the great war against the predators."

"I appreciate the history lesson, my Lady," d'Vashti replied, adding a florid, expansive gesture that expressed courtesy, respect, and sarcasm, all at the same time. He met her eyes directly. "But if I and my commanders must go to war on your behalf—or *anyone's*—we want to fight in a war of advancement, not retreat."

The arrogance of d'Vashti's presumption startled Zillabar. How dare he rebuke her! Inwardly, she seethed. She had not expected her opponent to have such a stiff backbone. Perhaps, in her absence, he had gained more influence among the Phaestor Lords than she had previously considered possible. She would have to find out whom d'Vashti had invited to his bed recently. Outwardly, she remained unmoved. "Do you have anything else to say?" she asked dispassionately.

d'Vashti looked to his mentor for support. Khallanin looked back at him, studying him oddly—as if he had never seen him before. d'Vashti realized that Khallanin had no intention of lending him support in this discussion. He would let d'Vashti stand alone to bear the hellfire of the Lady's wrath. d'Vashti put aside his surprise and bowed respectfully to the Lady Zillabar. He knew how to dance with the Dragon. He would dance again now.

"I do not speak for my Lord, only for myself," d'Vashti began, "but I know that all of us entrusted with the responsibilities of your service have pursued our tasks as aggressively as you have come to expect. We have done all that you have asked of us and more. We continue to scour this planet, even as you and I speak. We ask for no gratitude from you, nor do we expect it. Our service alone carries its own rewards."

"Yes," the Lady agreed. "That much you have correct. I will give you no thanks. And I will wait to see the quality of your service." She stressed the word *your*. "And now, you may go." She dismissed him with a curt wave. "I will speak alone with your master."

d'Vashti bowed. Zillabar ignored his bow of compliance. She had already turned her attention back to Lord Drydel. They bent their heads together and laughed softly over some private joke while Lord Khallanin waited stiff and silent.

d'Vashti straightened quickly and exited, betraying no sign of anger. He'd miscalculated, but so had the Lady. She had clearly recognized the threat that he presented to her ambitions. She'd seen through his maneuvers—and neutralized them. He'd failed here, how badly he didn't know. Perhaps Lord Khallanin might even have to invite him to sacrifice his life before the Lady. He doubted that matters would go that far, but he also knew now that Khallanin would offer him little protection.

But on the other hand ... he'd also learned something equally important. The Lady's failure on Burihatin told him that she too had weaknesses. He intended to find them and exploit them. He would consult his spies as soon as he considered it safe to make contact.

d'Vashti hurried away, his mind racing furiously. His footsteps echoed up and down the corridor, ringing like metallic taunts.

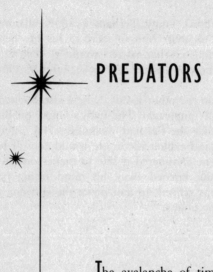

PREDATORS

The avalanche of time sweeps everything before it. Every individual instant hurtles into oblivion, drowning out the obliteration of the instant immediately preceding it, and then it too disappears under the onslaught of the next and the next and the next. When the avalanche has shuddered past for a long enough time, the perception of the past evolves. Distant events grow beyond mere history and take on the weight of legend.

For instance:

Many thousands of years ago, humans had spread across the great Milky Way galaxy. The bold diaspora, this tidal wave of sentience, rippled outward from the spiral arm, discovering, exploring, colonizing, and settling wherever life could make a stand. Human plows broke the ground under scores of new suns. Human children tumbled and laughed in alien skies.

The expanding sphere of humanity enveloped hundreds, then thousands, and finally countless numbers of new worlds. Necessity gave birth to grand technologies. A golden age of freedom had begun. Humanity grew and rejoiced in its growth.

And then, according to legend, the first *predator* arrived, floating silent and undetected out of the deadly night.

The first world died in puzzlement, without its inhabitants ever understanding what mysterious force had enveloped them. Comprehension did not come easily. The hungry predators represented an order of *life* that lay beyond the limited understanding of common men and women.

Many years later a second world died while still puzzling over the death of the first. The colonists on the third world had more time and much more warning, but little more understanding. As the decades slid away, a fourth and a fifth world also died. By now a line of death stretched like a dagger aimed at the heart of human worlds. A seventh world also died, but in the process of extinguishment, gave up the identity of its killer.

The mysterious predator showed up on no displays; it didn't have enough mass to register. Instead, it drifted as a vast amorphous veil of spider silk, stretching across an area larger than the average star system. Those who finally discovered and studied the thing found it difficult to conceive of it as alive; not life as ever previously imagined. Nevertheless, it functioned like something alive. It searched, it fed, it reproduced—and perhaps, maybe, it could also die.

No one knew.

Mindless and hungry, the predator seeks out the brightest sources of electromagnetic radiation in the sky, the kind emitted by technologies common to inhabited worlds. The predator moves through space like a cloud. It floats upon the cosmic winds, the ebb and flow of light and radiation in space. The pressure of photons across its vast, and nearly massless, surface gives it the motility it needs to soar from world to world. It steers itself by furling and unfurling itself like a sail, tilting its plane to catch the maximum possible push in the direction it wants to go. When a predator finds a world with a bright radio spectrum, it begins to wind itself around and around the planet in an ever-tightening shroud.

The extinguishment of a world lasts for many days, weeks, even months—as the sky becomes darker, the air grows thicker, and the filmy mass of the predator grows in monstrous accretions across deserts, lakes, mountains, forests, seas, snowcaps, volcanoes, and cities. When the predator pulls its entire mass into a single planet-sized shroud, it becomes a crushing burden—an envelope of desolation, gray and all-consuming. The predator devours energy. It feeds on heat.[23]

When the predator has fed enough, when it has satiated itself, consuming all the warmth it can from the victim world, it begins to expand, unwinding slowly, allowing its billions of separate layers to rise ever higher, pushing the topmost threads of the shroud high into space where they begin to slowly unravel. The predator pushes itself up as far as it can go, all the time fraying and unwinding and unfurling at its edges, and finally after it has extended itself in a vast silky corona out beyond the gravity well, it begins to pull the rest of its mass up and off the now dead world, strand by strand by strand. It leaves behind a bleak and blackened sphere. No life remains anywhere on the planet. And now, as the predator unwinds to its fullest dimension, stretching itself out again for the its next long leap into darkness, it has grown substantially larger, spreading itself across an area of space many times greater than before.

It may not have life, but it feeds.

---

[23]Predators appear *instinctively* to avoid intense gravity wells. A predator will not feed directly on a star, but will take as much nourishment as it can from a close approach.

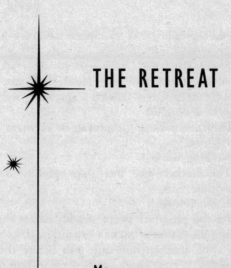

THE RETREAT

Many theories exist about the origins of the predators.

Some think that the creatures began as a doomsday machine, a weapon of war that continues to destroy long after its creators have passed into dust. Genuinely immortal, the predators may not even have begun in this galaxy; some scholars believe that they wandered here hungrily after exhausting the resources of their own birthplace.

Whatever the truth, all defenses failed against this predaceous onslaught of spiderwebbed hunger.

The first predator stretched itself and split into two parts after its seventh feeding, and the offspring split and reproduced again after their seventh meals. And again and again. Slowly, the things spread, so slowly that no one realized the danger, no one took them seriously for much too long a time.

But over the course of a thousand years, more than three thousand inhabited worlds and moons died. Try as they might, humans could not stop all of the delicious emissions of their various technologies; and the radio emissions of all the previous generations betrayed their existence in an ever-spreading call to dinner for every hungering predator to see.

Eventually, that first single predator spawned a hundred and thirty prowling clouds of doom. The star charts of their progress showed a spreading web of horror, death, and panic.

Humans tracked the predators. Humans attacked the predators.

Nothing worked.

The attackers died, their ships enfolded, and so did their worlds.

Humanity fled.

As the predators swept steadily across the galaxy, following the course of human expansion, destroying one world after another, humanity ran before them. The predators cut a great swath across the worlds of the dying exodus. As long as ripe worlds remained, the silent horrors spread their webs, fed, grew, and split. Humanity would not survive the next millennium.

Humanity had no choice but to take "the long voyage." The great ships began a new diaspora—out of the galaxy. Many fled to the Palethetic Cluster, a tightly packed ball of stars drifting high in the galaxy's wake. Even the largest and fastest starships found it a long and arduous journey. Most of the voyagers made the trip in hibernation; many did not survive.

Those who did searched, discovered, settled, and built—and made a vow: "Give us a place to stand and we will reclaim the stars."

It took three millennia for the survivors to settle throughout the Cluster and begin rebuilding what they had abandoned and lost in the home galaxy. For a long while ships continued to arrive across the great empty gulf, each vessel bringing fresh reports of the continued scourging of the growing swarm of predators, each report spreading new despair and discouragement.

Then the ships stopped coming.

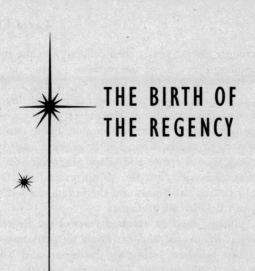

THE BIRTH OF
THE REGENCY

And then the first predator appeared in the Cluster.

Panic reigned supreme.

The TimeBinders of twenty-seven worlds met at a Gathering and mind-linked. They authorized the creation of the Palethetic Regency to oversee a vast military organization. Each of the Cluster worlds would share a proportional part of the financial burden. The Regency's sole purpose: to protect the Cluster from predators.

The Gathering proposed a daring and courageous plan. The most brilliant engineers in the Cluster would design and build a giant radio-emitting target that would attract a predator like the ripe technology of an inhabited world. Perhaps the predator would perceive it as an inhabited moonlet. When the predator had fully surrounded and enshrouded the target, the defenders would evoke a pinpoint black hole at the heart of the structure.[24]

---

[24]At that time the evocation of artificial singularities, although theoretically possible, remained only a tantalizing, but unachieved, goal.

The entire device would then collapse into the singularity, pulling every bit of the predator in after it.

To carry out this plan, the Gathering authorized the creation of a military aristocracy—the Phaestor—and also creation of the Moktar Dragons as an elite corps of troops to serve the Phaestor. These two species would form the backbone of Regency authority. The Regency would create and adapt other variants of humanity as needed, but the Vampires and the Dragons would rule as the brains and the brawn needed to seek out and destroy all predators.

During the first hundred years of the Regency, the Phaestor discovered and destroyed six predators. In the next two hundred years they discovered and destroyed only one small predator. During the next five hundred years, they discovered no further predators in the Cluster.

Without the galvanizing external threat, the Vampire aristocracy grew bored. Worse, the worlds that supported the Regency began to resent the high cost of maintenance for the Regency fleets. Internal tensions began to accumulate. The collapse of the Regency became a very real possibility. The Phaestor grew alarmed; they decided to act to prevent the collapse of authority.

Nearly a thousand years after the first Gathering, the Phaestoric aristocracy declared itself the rightful ruling class of the million worlds of the Cluster. Individual families expanded their authority to replace the institutions of their resident worlds. Where rebellion occurred, the imposition of order quickly followed. The Moktar Dragons compelled the loyalty of the aristocracy's subjects.

The justification for this assumption of power? The Vampires lived at the top of the food chain. Food did not

---

Subsequent to this, and due to a massive research effort, the technology became not only practical but widespread in application.

have rights. The Phaestor began to systematically revoke the citizenship of any species that did not feed at the top of the pyramid. Soon they declared themselves the master race, the species destined to rule over all others.

Those who had lived as loyal citizens of the Regency suddenly found themselves servants. Those who had served found themselves slaves. And those who had existed as slaves became property.

Civil wars broke out in many parts of the Palethetic Cluster, and the Regency fleet suffered great losses in putting down these insurrections. The Vampires suffered many costly victories.

But ultimately they won.

And they intended to savor their triumphs for a very long time.

THE POETRY OF DRAGONS

The puppies fretted restlessly. They yelped and whined and pulled on their leashes. They looked tired and wan and they whimpered pitifully.

Kask had the reins of three of the dog-children; Keeda held the leads of the other three; but Kask held his too closely, and the puppies pulled away from him as far as they could, complaining strenuously and wailing. The close proximity of the huge Dragons frightened all the pups; several of them had already urinated all over themselves in fear, and the stink rose offensively.

The smallest of the pups kept twisting away, yanking at his leash and chewing frenziedly at it. The smell of Kask's hot breath terrified the little pooch; its eyes had gone all white and crazy.

Kask noticed the dog-child working at the ornate ceremonial restraint, and he yanked it hard, sending the small animal sprawling. He growled warningly at the little creature, but instead of quieting it down, his deep bass rumble only drove it into a greater frenzy. It leapt about in wild panic, upsetting its littermates; they began crying and pulling too.

Captain Naye-Ninneya, larger and darker, came by then, lumbering heavily across the marbled floor. "Can't you keep those brats quiet?" he demanded.

Kask wanted desperately to explain. He wanted to talk about the inherent intractability of these foul little creatures and make the Captain see the sheer impossibility of the task, but he knew better than to try. Too often explanations carried the foul stink of excuses. He hung his head in shame and conceded his failure. "My Captain, I admit that I cannot."

"Hmpf," rumbled the other. "Let me show you." He took a deep breath—his heavy tail straightened out behind him—and gave out with his loudest and most deadly roar. He aimed it at the frightened little dog-children, a furnace blast of orange rage.

And as suddenly as he stopped, everything fell silent. The children froze where they stood, too frightened to move, too paralyzed even to whimper. The smallest pup grabbed the loop of his leash and bit it nervously, shoving it deep into his mouth, a terrified reaction. He resumed his frantic chewing at the leather. Kask deliberately ignored it; better that the damn thing should chew than cry.

Captain Naye-Ninneya grinned wickedly. "You see? Always put the fear into them first. When in doubt, terrorize them. It *always* works."

"Yes, my Captain."

"Hmpf." Naye-Ninneya glanced over the puppies, as if he'd never seen them before. He snorted loudly through his nose. "Disgusting. Tiny little morsels. The six of them together wouldn't satisfy me. Not enough here to fill the roar of a healthy Dragon, let alone his belly. Barely enough for a taste. Just when you get one in your mouth and start crunching away—what then? One swallow and your hunger still gnaws. The Lady calls them fancy gourmet delicacies—*hmpf*. And hmpf again. A frivolous waste of time. I want a meal, not a snack. I say, feed me something I can *eat*. Something I can sink my teeth into deeply, so I can feel the blood spurting and pouring, filling my mouth and flowing over my teeth. I like it when it runs down my chest. I like the smell of it, I love the hot wet feel of it. Give me a good fat bullock any day. Remember this always. If you want the Regency to flourish, you have to feed your Dragons well—not this frippery, not these insults. Hmpf." He concluded his discourse with a contemptuous snarl, and he lashed his tail with a vigorous flourish, by way of punctuation.

Then, having nothing else to say, Naye-Ninneya took a moment to study the uniforms of the two warrior-lizards. He narrowed his gaze like that of a warden and frowned, and he tapped at the metal studs ornamenting Keeda's chest armor. He did not feel satisfied that either of the two warriors would pass inspection before the Dragon Lord, but the time had passed for correction. He grunted. "We will present the Lady's gifts soon. Do not discredit me. Listen for the chime." Not expecting any answer from his subordinates, he turned and stamped heavily back to his waiting room.

Kask exchanged a knowing glance with Keeda. The Captain's anger derived more from the ignoble disgrace of guarding a litter of *food* than from the alleged superficial quality of the meal.

Keeda said, "He makes me hungry. All this talk of killing and eating. When it comes to food, the Captain has the soul of a poet."

Kask nodded in agreement. "He does it on purpose—he comes down here to torment us. I'll bet you he's already stuffed his fat face tonight. We still haven't gotten the taste of space rations out of our mouths, and he gorges himself on fresh pig and brags about it to us."

"When you become a Captain, my brother, you'll do the same."

"When I became a Captain, my brother, neither of us will have to stand and wait for oatmeal. We'll eat sausage every night." He grabbed his big fleshy belly and rubbed it vigorously. "Right now I'd rather have a meal that moos than a gold sunburst on my uniform."

"Me too." Keeda shrugged and looked at the dogs. "I could even eat a couple of these wee things. No problem at all. I don't share Naye-Ninneya's distaste."

Kask made a low-pitched chuckling sound. "Help yourself. They'll make for a tasty last meal—but not a very filling one."

Keeda returned the grin. "The Lady and her guests can have my share. I seem to have lost my appetite for dog." He laughed roughly; the rumble came from deep in his throat. Two or three of the puppies looked up nervously. The little one began chewing even more vigorously.

GIFTS

Lord Drydel whispered into the Lady's ear. "I admire your strength. You handled him magnificently."

Lady Zillabar allowed herself a smile of acknowledgment. The expression on her outer face, however, had no relation to the feelings of the self known as the inner face. Privately, Drydel's comment annoyed her, because it carried the stench of his judgment, and that implied that he believed he had the right to make a judgment on her activities. She also recognized the sycophantic quality of his approval, and that annoyed her further. She knew that in truth, she had handled the moment badly.

Her exhaustion and irritability had overwhelmed her wisdom. She had left d'Vashti simmering in his own anger. She had probably created more problems than she had resolved. She knew all too well how much store d'Vashti put in personal justice. She wondered if she should ask for his death. As much satisfaction as that might give her, it would unfortunately leave Lord Drydel holding too much power. She couldn't do it.

She had no misconceptions about Drydel's

loyalty—or *any* male's loyalty, for that matter. She knew her species well enough. Males existed to serve females, to bring them pleasure as well as service. Concepts beyond that had little value to a member of the Phaestoric aristocracy. Nevertheless ... relationships still required lubrication. Loyalty, like service, must flow downward before it can flow upward again. The Lady Zillabar turned her cold gaze to her Consort and said, "I have brought you gifts that I know you will enjoy." She motioned to the Dragon Lord. "You may present the gifts now."

The Dragon Lord made no apparent movement of any kind, but a moment later the service door dilated, and Captain Naye-Ninneya stepped proudly into the room, followed by two massive warrior-lizards incongruously herding six little balls of dirty fluff. The dog-children. Stained and soiled, with their tails tucked between their legs, they cowered and trembled.

Drydel's eyes flashed with interest—but his blood-lust faded quickly as the stink of the animals reached his delicate nostrils. The Lady Zillabar sniffed and reacted even more strongly. She felt a terrible roaring in her head. Her expression paled, then hardened into frozen anger. She advanced on Captain Naye-Ninneya. Behind her the Dragon Lord came rising to his full height, towering over everyone in the room.

The Lady looked at her gifts in astonishment. She moved from one to the other, letting the full range of her horror show on her features. The displeasure on her face sent icicles slicing up Naye-Ninneya's spine. At last she turned her eyes to the Dragons holding the leashes, and finally to their Captain.

"What in the name of darkness have you done to these creatures?" she demanded. "I intended them as gifts. A matched set of six. Look at them. Smell them!"

Naye-Ninneya cringed. He'd made a terrible mistake. He should have listened to the whinings of the android when he'd had a chance. He'd spoiled the Lady's gift. She could kill him for this. No apology could erase his crime. The Captain wondered if she would at least allow him an Honorable Suicide.

The Lady still screeched. "Why didn't you have them cleaned?" she demanded. Behind her the Dragon Lord growled low in his throat. He didn't like seeing his troops upbraided by a Vampire—but neither could he allow their failure to go unpunished.

Somehow Naye-Ninneya managed to get his words out. "I ordered the servants on the ship to do so. Obviously, they did not do their job."

"And you let them get away with that? You accepted this disgrace? This *insult*?" The Lady pulled a perfumed silk from the sleeve of her gown and held it to her nose to block out the distasteful stench. "This disgusts me. They stink of their own urine. They've soiled their clothes. They wear more dirt than fur. You have betrayed my trust. I cannot present these gifts. It would shame me to give such inferior-looking creatures even to d'Vashti, let alone to my Consort—" And then she stopped herself before she said anything further.

She realized that she had lost control. She had allowed a spark of her anger to show. She reasserted control, stiffening rigidly. She allowed herself several long, slow breaths, as close as she could come to evoking the dream state in real time.

The Lady Zillabar turned around slowly, studying the reactions to her display of temper. The warrior-lizards hid their eyes; Drydel looked grim, possibly dismayed. The Dragon Lord's expression remained hungry and unreadable.

To Captain Naye-Ninneya she said, "Have these creatures cleaned and fed. I will inspect them again tomorrow." To the Dragon Lord she added, "I trust that you will take appropriate disciplinary actions here."

The Dragon Lord hissed—not quite an acceptance of the Lady's order, but enough of an acknowledgment to avoid the appearance of disrespect.

Lady Zillabar gathered her flowing cloak around herself and swept out of the room.

ESCAPE

Safely back in the service corridor, Kask and Keeda growled unhappily at their charges. They had not enjoyed the ground-zero experience of the Lady's wrath, and they, in their own turn, passed their unhappiness on to the unfortunate dog-children in their care, terrifying them greatly. They allowed themselves some small pleasure in the panic of the little animals. The pups shrank away, cowering and urinating helplessly. Nearly frothing at the mouth, the littlest one continued to chew madly at its leash.

"Hey—" Keeda pointed. "If that one makes a mess of that leash, you and I will have to pay for the damage."

Kask grunted resentfully, but he jerked the leash sharply, spinning the puppy around and sending it sprawling. The little dog-child yelped in terror. It panicked and tried to run. Its naked paws scratched helplessly across the shining floor, scrabbling and clawing for purchase.

Remembering the Captain's words, Kask took a deep breath and gave a mighty roar of anger. It didn't work; higher-pitched than the Captain's noise, it only frightened the little brown-and-white creatures more. The smallest one redoubled its efforts to get away, leaping and jerking into the air, yelping horrendously. He cast anxious glances backward at the giant Dragon, then scrabbled frantically against the leash again.

Now all the other puppies started crying too. They panicked and began pulling madly in several different directions. Just hanging on to their leashes suddenly demanded the full attention of both Kask and Keeda.

"Big help that," Keeda growled. "Next time just smack him."

"No next times—" Kask said. He lunged for the pup. It squirted out of his grasp. "Come here, you!" He yanked the leash—it snapped. The puppy had nearly chewed it through, and under the sudden sharp strain it simply came apart at the weak spot. The dog-child leapt—and this time nothing held it back. It kept on going, sliding and scrambling down the long marble hall.

"Goddammit!" Keeda roared. Kask's growl had no words. He handed the other two leashes to his brother Dragon and launched himself after the fleeing morsel.

The dog-child ran for its life—Kask pursued. Hell's fury chased the puppy, but Zillabar's fury pursued the Dragon. If the dog escaped—Kask couldn't imagine what the lady might do. He charged down the endless corridor.

On and on the child raced; once it fell, sliding and skidding across the slick-surfaced floor, its claws scraping helplessly. It yelped, collided with a wall; it rolled and came up running again, half by luck, half by the sheer madness of its terror; it kept on. Only once did it glance back—it saw a furious Dragon pounding hard in its direction—the puppy cried and scooted sideways, dashing into a side passage, a service corridor, a hallway, through a door, another door, looking for the outside, anywhere, a place where Dragons couldn't follow—he couldn't stop, he wouldn't risk it, he just kept running madly, scrambling through the legs of servants who yelled and tried to catch him, leaping after him and grabbing, but they didn't have the speed or strength of Dragons; they didn't have the power either. The child caught its garment on the corner of a towering table—it yanked; the garment shredded, the narrow table toppled. Something large and made of glass came sliding, crashing to the floor. The little shaggy wide-eyed thing leapt away in sudden fright. This room stretched endlessly; the ceiling echoed in the distance, the walls all flashed with mirrors. And servant-wasps everywhere—spindly and black, with multifaceted eyes—came closing in toward him. And somewhere still behind him, he heard the Dragon's roar again.

He had to keep on going, had to find the way—maybe he could find the kind lady on the spaceship. Maybe she would help him—and his littermates—and take them home to Mommy. Dear sweet Mommy and her big warm belly and her soft red nipples. No time to think, a servant grabbed, the dog-child bared its teeth and snapped; he missed, the servant missed as well; the child scampered quickly, wildly toward a distant opening, another hall, another door, another endless passage—*oh, no!* At the end of this one stood the Dragon Keeda with five puppies cowering against a corner. He'd gone around a giant circle! And Kask still came thundering huge behind him. "Run!" he shouted to his two brothers and three sisters. "Run with me!"

They wanted to, but they couldn't—Keeda held their reins too tightly. The warrior-lizard turned toward him then, crouching low, advancing. He dragged the other puppies with him; they fought the leashes frantically, but also futilely. They yapped and snarled and hollered to their brother. "Get away! Get away!"

The puppy skidded. He had to help his siblings—but how? And coming up behind him, Kask bellowed furiously, "Don't let him get away."

"I've got him!" Keeda said.

The puppy hesitated, torn between his desire to rescue his littermates and his own need to escape. He made the only decision he could. He turned, caught purchase on the floor, and charged back the way he came—straight toward Kask. The Dragon tried to head him off. He reached out with giant scooping hands, but the puppy moved too fast; he curled frantically around the outstretched grasp—the Dragon caught him by the leg, yanked him upward suddenly. The child kicked, *connected*, writhed frantically against the Dragon's hand; he bit and clawed. He screamed, a high-pitched rasp, startling himself and Kask as well. The Dragon hadn't caught him firmly, the puppy wriggled and came abruptly free; he twisted as he fell—the Dragon clawed for him, but the child hit the floor already running.

Out of breath and out of hope, he fled.

He found a hole, jumped into it, and fell forever, down and out into empty space—

THE SEARCH

"Ibaka[25] got away!" the other puppies yelled. "He got away!" They bounced up and down excitedly in unconcealed glee. "He got *away*! H'rray! Ibaka got away!"

Keeda had already punched the communicator on his belt, sending out a call for immediate assistance. The other Dragon Guards came running at once. Captain Naye-Ninneya came pounding down the hall as well, shoving aside anyone who got in his way, sending two of the warrior-lizards sprawling clumsily across the floor. His eyes flamed angrily. "What the hell—?"

Keeda reported shamefully, "One of the morsels escaped, my Captain. The leash broke."

"You stupid son of a—" Naye-Ninneya punched his own communicator. "Red Scramble! Red Scramble! Intruder Alert! Go to Security One! Repeat: Security One! Emergency Lockdown! Do it now!" He looked at Keeda, glaring; but he didn't say aloud what he thought. Instead,

[25]Pronounced Eee-bah-ka.

he merely jerked the leashes out of the witless lizard's hands and thrust them at another Dragon—no, two Dragons. "No more mistakes! Both of you do this!" He pointed at the five remaining puppies. "Freeze them— put them in a cage. Put them where they can't escape. But whatever else you do, don't screw this up!"

"Yes, sir!" Together the two huge warriors began dragging the puppies away down the hall. The dog-children wailed in distress as the Dragons herded them along.

Naye-Ninneya forgot them immediately. He spoke to his communicator again. "Dispatch: I want three search teams on the roof, working down; three on the service level, working up. Full menu. Scanners *and* sniffers. Do it now! Red Scramble! Red Scramble!"

He paused to listen to the reply in his headset for a moment—then clicked to the all-talk channel and started snapping instructions back: "All right, everybody listen up. One of Lady Zillabar's gifts has escaped, a morsel, a dog-child. Less than a meter tall. Brown and white—" Naye-Ninneya looked to Keeda. "Which one?"

Keeda shrugged. "The littlest one, uh—Kask went after him." He remembered what the other puppies had cried, and added quickly, "Ibaka. He answers to Ibaka."

"Ee-ba-ka," Naye-Ninneya repeated to the communicator. "The child answers to Ee-ba-ka. Handle him with care. I do *not* want it injured in any way. You may *not* kill this creature. He must remain unharmed. He belongs to the Lady Zillabar! The animal has no weapons—" The Captain stopped himself again and turned to Keeda. "No weapons, right?"

Keeda tried to remember. "I don't think so. He didn't have any that I saw."

Naye-Ninneya grunted something unintelligible. He resumed his patter of instructions and information: "I repeat: The animal has no weapons. Consider it fragile and vulnerable. I want it caught without damage. If any harm comes to it, I'll personally inflict ten times the damage to the idiot who did it and every member of his family! Dispatch: report!" He listened for half a moment, then nodded to himself. "All right, do it. And scramble a vermin team too. Traps, gas, stunners—I'll have the whole palace scanned if I have to. Right. And I want a report every five minutes until you catch the creature." He clicked off.

Captain Naye-Ninneya took a long, slow breath. He took another. And then a third. He turned to Keeda. His voice went as low and deadly as Keeda had ever heard it. "I have to let you live for now. And you had better pray that we do catch the animal. I do not have a reputation for easing my victims pleasantly into death. You and Kask—my half-witted children—I thought I did you a favor here. How foolish of me to trust the two of you. I should have my chromosomes checked. Obviously, I carry the genes for stupidity and incompetence! Look how you turned out. I give you the simplest responsibility, the one thing that you two absolutely cannot possibly screw up—and what do you do? You betray me. You disgrace my judgment. You let the animal escape! And I'll have to wear this stain forever—and if I do, I promise you that your punishment will last ten times as long as mine—unless, of course, we catch the cursed thing before the Lady hears about it. Then at least you may commit dishonorable suicide."

He stopped only to take a breath, then thought of something and spoke to his communicator again. "What about the service tubes? Can he escape that way? He can't? Why not? I don't believe you. Check it anyway." He switched off again, glared at Keeda sullenly, then turned to look at all the other lizards standing behind him, waiting. "Well, what do you reptiles want? Quarter this level, now!" He pointed off down the hall, waving halfheartedly in the direction of the palace core. It didn't matter. Wherever the creature had gone to, these incompetent lizards couldn't find it if they had a road map and a guide—but at least they could look busy.

Naye-Ninneya didn't want to consider what would happen if they didn't find the creature. Lady Zillabar would simply have them killed—all of them—and probably quite painfully. Or maybe ... no, she wouldn't dare do that, although—Naye-Ninneya frowned at the thought. Once upon a time, they said, the Vampires used to like the taste of Dragons. Rumor had it that some of them still did.

Sudden fear burned in his stomach. To use Dragons as *food*—no, even the Vampires wouldn't shame their warriors like that. They wouldn't dare. But the idea still tormented Naye-Ninneya. He couldn't think of anything else so degrading. The Lady would think so too.

He comforted himself with one thought. The creature couldn't escape the palace. He might find a place to hide for a while, but he wouldn't find a way out—and he couldn't stay hidden for long.

As if on cue, his communicator beeped. "One of the sniffer teams has a trace on the main service level," the dispatcher reported.

"On my way—" He turned back to Keeda. "You! Follow me. If he went down a sewage pipe, you and Kask will go after him."

"Yes, my Captain."

They dropped down a service shaft to the bottom level of the palace. The mutable gravity field managed their descent. They stepped out of the well and trotted rapidly up the passage toward the distant sniffer team.

Designed for speed more than strength, the pursuit troops had a much leaner and hungrier look than their bigger, better-armored brothers. They had longer necks and narrower flat heads. More birdlike, and brighter-colored than the Dragons, these slender lizards bobbed and weaved with a slightly uncertain, nervous, uneasy quality. Lithe and sleek, they looked like re-creations of the ancient Deinonychus.

Holding their tails high and lashing them wickedly back and forth, the tracking team moved up and down the wide corridor, waving their gas-testing devices slowly through the air and listening to the resultant signals on their headsets.

"He came down here," Lieutenant Jheeter, the team leader, reported. He spoke in quick, clipped phrases. He had a whistling, high-pitched voice. Naye-Ninneya hated the effeminate sound of it. "He came down the same shaft you did. He went through the storage bays to the corridor on the other side, he came out in the master kitchen—almost right into the butcher's arms—then he panicked and dashed back into the service corridor. He found another drop-shaft and went down two more levels. We've tracked him as far as the recycling section. I've sealed the floor. He can't get out."

Naye-Ninneya gave as much of a compliment as he ever did, a noncommittal grunt. "Let's go." He strode off down the passage, Keeda and the trackers following hastily behind.

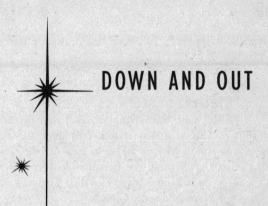

DOWN AND OUT

The recycling section smelled of garbage and methane. Waste material of all kinds lay piled in great unsorted heaps of filth. Someone had just dumped it here, day after day, week after week, without regard for sanitation.

Naye-Ninneya suppressed a shudder of distaste. He tried to close his nostrils against the stink. It didn't work. He still could easily identify the different flavors that filled the air: spoiled meat and rotting fish, wilted vegetables, rancid cheese, stale vomit, blood and offal from the butchery, the stink of urine from some unidentified mammal, and a more unpleasant odor that made his stomach churn—the distinctly foul smell of human shit. *Someone should do something about this disgrace,* he thought. *This dishonors the palace.* He said nothing aloud, however. Instead, he turned to the twitching team leader. "You tracked him through this stench?"

"Only this far," Jheeter piped in reply. "We've had to send for the heavy-duty sniffers. We didn't expect this—this unfortunate decay." The smaller Dragon chose his words carefully, not wanting to say anything that even *implied* disapproval. A palace lizard already had enough enemies.

"Who runs this section?" Naye-Ninneya asked blandly.

"Dhrynnka Moloch."

"Ahh," said Naye-Ninneya, as if that explained everything. And in a way it did. Not quite a Vampire—merely a ghoul, Moloch liked to feed off the dead flesh that others left behind; but first she liked to wallow in it. Of course she'd keep a place like this. The reek and filth disgusted Naye-Ninneya. Ghouls![26]

Naye-Ninneya had confronted Moloch on more than one occasion. She affected the pretense of mild and pleasant demeanor; she wore a bland, wide-eyed expression and spoke in quiet, gentle tones; but she fooled no one. Her face still gave her away. Dhrynnka Moloch had a mouth like a torn pocket, a tiny, twisted pucker of permanent acidity—and despite the presumed gentleness of

---

[26]A bastard subspecies of Vampire, the ghouls have the single worst reputation in the Regency. Not even their clients speak well of them. Most observers consider ghouls a significant genetic mistake, and most Phaestor Nobles publicly agree with this perception. Nevertheless, the ghouls have demonstrated a remarkable aptitude for a variety of unsavory tasks that the Phaestor prefer not to handle themselves and remain unwilling to trust to license-holders and clients. For instance, ghouls make wonderful attorneys.

The gene-designers who had originally created the Phaestor Vampires had also attempted to create an even nastier species by crossing the Phaestor with several members of the order of Rodentia. Only one of the hybrid species proved immediately viable, the mix of Vampire with Rat. Not wanting to see either their genetic purity or their reputations damaged, the young but growing population of Vampires quickly moved to suppress all further research in this direction, except for that which they directly controlled themselves. Later, for reasons of their own, the Phaestor redeveloped the rat-vampire species, now called *ghouls*.

At the specific request of the publisher, the author will *not* include a description of the mating habits of ghouls.

her voice, the content of her words too often carried deadly import. Moloch served as the Lady Zillabar's personal adviser on legal matters, and in the Lady's absence acted as her representative. Naye-Ninneya would have liked to kill her. Not eat her—only kill her. Some things even a Dragon won't touch.

He had killed other lawyers in the past. He particularly enjoyed it. He planned on dispatching many more in the future. More than a hobby, he considered it a personal responsibility to reduce the numbers of these vermin whenever he could. Fortunately, the Lady Zillabar used up attorneys at a fearsome rate. He doubted that Moloch would last too much longer—although, to give the darkness its due, Dhrynnka Moloch had lasted much longer than any other the Captain could remember.

Anyway, that not only explained the mess down here—it also explained why the mess would continue. Dhrynnka Moloch wanted it to feast on, probably with the rest of her grisly ghoul friends. Naye-Ninneya tried not to think of it.

A sound distracted him. He cocked his head sideways, trying to locate the source. He closed his nostrils against the stink and began moving around the nearest heaps of refuse. He had to go much farther into the room than he wanted to before he found what made the noise—Jheeter followed him; so did Keeda. They came around a pile of blackened bones, charred and broken, and found Kask stomping desperately across the trash. Kask barely glanced up. "He came this way. I saw him." His tail lashed rapidly back and forth in frantic agitation.

Captain Naye-Ninneya stopped and stared. He held himself back. He had too much anger boiling in him. If he tried to speak, his language would fail him and he'd just end up killing Kask and Keeda both. And probably any other creature who came close before his fury ebbed again. He forced himself to turn away. Keeda started to follow—

"Keeda, help him," Naye-Ninneya managed to say. He headed quickly back out. If nothing else, the futile pawing through refuse would keep the both of them from causing any more harm. He only wished Lieutenant Jheeter hadn't seen the disgraceful performance of these two idiots.

"I can spare some troops to help them," Jheeter said, following him diplomatically.

"No. They earned the right to pursue the animal without help."

"Ahh," said the wise Lieutenant. "Yes."

Naye-Ninneya looked at the smaller Dragon, frowning. Jheeter stared innocently back. They both knew that everything depended on the heavy-duty sniffer now. If Jheeter found the fugitive morsel, the Captain would carry a heavy obligation.

"The dog-child?" Naye-Ninneya asked. "Could it hide in all this mess?"

Jheeter waved its head from side to side like a snake. "I doubt it very much. Intimidating as this refuse may seem, the industrial sniffers do have the sophistication to isolate the creature's scent out of all this, uh—decay. I apologize for the delay, my Captain. We were all upstairs, unobtrusively sniffing Kernel d'Vashti's guests before the arrival of the Lady."

Naye-Ninneya's tail lashed impatiently. He forced himself into an attitude of patience. "No problem," he said stiffly. "You sealed the level. The creature can't escape." He didn't dare risk antagonizing Jheeter—not now. And especially not if he succeeded. He hated this—having to let a subordinate plant an obligation on him.

"Ahh." Jheeter whistled brightly. "Here we go. The unit has arrived. Now we'll find your creature for you. This will take only a few moments."

Jheeter took one of those moments himself to give instructions to his troops, specifically to direct the efforts of the three who carried the heavy-duty sniffer; then he turned back to Naye-Ninneya again. "If I may offer some advice, you should let this creature rest before you eat it. All this exertion, all the strain, will make the flesh taste gamy. I'd give it at least a week myself. A gentle killing preserves the flavor best—"

"The creature belongs to the Lady Zillabar," Naye-Ninneya interrupted curtly. "A gift for Lord Drydel."

"Ah. Oh, yes. Of course. My mistake. Nevertheless, if you could suggest to the Lady ... well, you know. I mean, if she wants to please her guests—"

"The Lady Zillabar has significantly more culinary skill than either you or I—or both of us together, for that matter—will ever possess. Vampires have much more delicate palates and pay significantly more attention to their diets than do Dragons. I have no doubt that the Lady will know how to prepare the creature appropriately."

Jheeter looked crestfallen. His tail drooped at the Captain's rebuke.

Naye-Ninneya remembered too late how emotional the lesser breeds had become. A sign of decadence—or latent insanity—no doubt. But he added quickly, "However, your suggestion does have merit. I'll pass it along to the Lady. She should know that this creature has suffered a good deal of strain today, and it could affect the flavor of its blood."

"Thank you, Captain. You do me great honor."

"No. You do the honor to yourself when you serve your masters well. Remember that." A thought crossed Naye-Ninneya's mind. Maybe he could just kill Jheeter when this situation ended. It would certainly simplify the whole affair.

Jheeter had lowered his head in polite deference. Abruptly, his headset chattered in his ear. "Ahh," he said. "We've picked up the trace." He pointed. "This way—"

Naye-Ninneya pounded after the lighter Dragon as they threaded their way quickly through the repulsive heaps. The muck squelched under his boots with a queasy, sticky sound. He'd probably have to discard them when this affair finally ended.

"Here!" pointed one of the troops. "It went down here—" The bright-colored Dragon pointed through a hole in the wall. The gas-tester kept chiming happily to itself.

"Where does that go?" Naye-Ninneya frowned as he peered into the dark hole.

"I think this space contains nothing but insulation," said Lieutenant Jheeter. "Who has the map?" One of his troops produced a map-board immediately.

"It looks deep," said Naye-Ninneya.

"Hmm." Jheeter scratched his chin worriedly. "On the other side of this insulation, I believe, you'll find the ruins of the old catapult." He pored over the map. "Not to worry. It doesn't seem to go very far."

Naye-Ninneya grunted. History held little interest for him. The early settlers of this world had carved mountains of ore out of its surface and smelted it into massive ingots. They had carved a catapult right up through the center of the towering MesaPort peak and boosted the ingots into low orbit by magnetic acceleration. When the mines ran out, the catapult fell into disuse and disrepair. Although no reason remained for anyone to stay on Thoska-Roole, life has a peculiar habit—once established, it stays. Sometimes it even thrives. On Thoska-Roole it just held on and maintained.[27]

"The launching catapult needed very heavy insulation and shielding," Jheeter continued explaining. "The

[27]the Vampires had their own reasons for staying on Thoska-Roole—possibly because their control of its interstellar commerce had also given them a unique control of the planet's economy. This gave them both a lever, and a place to stand. From here they could apply pressure to the economies of many other worlds. And just as possibly, they may have enjoyed the bleak and desolate spaces of the planet which served admirably to hide a multitude of darker deeds.

mountain provided most of it, so the builders installed only a few access tubes into this space—"

A terrifying thought suddenly occurred to Captain Naye-Ninneya. He turned immediately to Jheeter. "The catapult. The catapult itself. How far *down* does it go?" He let a hint of menace color his voice.

Lieutenant Jheeter blinked. And then he realized what the Captain had asked. He gasped. "Oh, darkness, no. It goes all the way down. *All the way down to the surface.*"

Naye-Ninneya groaned.

He knew what would happen next. He could see the whole future laid out like a map. He would send Kask and Keeda down the hole after the vermin—and Lieutenant Jheeter's troops too. He would mobilize every Dragon in the palace. He would send troops down to the surface to comb the rabbit warren of tunnels at the base of the catapult, hoping to catch the fugitive coming out of one of the outlets. They would set traps and tracers. They would sniff the air and scan kilometers of desert. They would send probes up the tunnels. It might work. It probably wouldn't. Incompetency fed on itself. His troops had never trained for this. They could win a war—but they couldn't catch a mouse.

Soon he would have to tell the Lady Zillabar that he had failed in his responsibility. His elite Dragon Guards had allowed one of her gifts to escape. The size of the search would not mitigate the failure. The Lady accepted only results, never excuses.

The Dragons had soiled the Lady's grace. Even if they caught the creature now, it wouldn't erase the stain.

His life had ended.

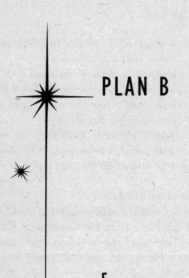

PLAN B

Finn Markham hung spread-eagled in energy chains, halfway up a bleak stone wall in a cavernous chamber. A drab gray light gave the cave a dank, oppressive look. Beside him, his brother also dangled against the wall, pinned in a spiderweb of soft-glowing beams. The bare rock floor remained tantalizingly out of reach.

"Can you move?" Sawyer gasped his question.

Finn grunted in reply.

"Does that mean yes or no?"

Finn shrugged. He *tried* to shrug. He couldn't move. Even the simple act of breathing took a tremendous effort that left him teetering exquisitely between exhaustion and anoxia. "It means no," he managed to say. He had to whisper to get the words out.

"If you move slowly—"

"—I'll pass out. Do you have any other ideas?"

"As a matter of fact ..." Sawyer had to stop to catch his own breath, then he continued, "I do have a plan—"

Slowly—oh, so slowly—Finn Markham turned his

head to look skeptically at his brother: his famous raised-eyebrow look.

Sawyer grinned feebly back at him. "Ah, you *can* move," he said. "Awright. You overpower her, and I'll run for help—"

Finn let out his breath painfully.

Below them a gargantuan shape moved through the gloom. Murdock lumbered among her equipment like a great shambling beast absentmindedly looking for a pair of misplaced ballet slippers. She moved through a maze of bulky racks and chambers, cylindrical vats, and several luminous workstations, all scattered helter-skelter across the floor of the cave without apparent plan or design.

Abruptly, she found the object of her search, one of the workstations. She studied its screens for a long thoughtful moment, then made a minor adjustment. Abruptly, Sawyer and Finn felt themselves moving higher up the wall, all the way up to the ceiling until they banged their heads against the rough stone roof. It gave them a better view of the layout of Murdock's installation but also effectively made the possibility of escape even more remote. Satisfied, Murdock began stripping off her cloak, her helmet, and her body armor.

Sawyer shivered where he hung. "I've seen some ugly women in my time, but—oh, God, no. I wish she wouldn't do that."

Below them the titanic figure peeled off the last piece of armor. She wore a dingy singlet that concealed nothing of her true shape. Sawyer blanched and tried to turn his head away. "Oh, my dear God in heaven, whatever I've done to offend Thee, I heartily apologize and beg Thy forgiveness. Please take this abomination away from my eyes."

"I had no idea you had so much religion."

"I didn't—until she started taking off her clothes." He looked helplessly to Finn. "I don't think I'll ever have the courage to touch a woman again. I—I don't think I could perform with the memory of her in my head. Some things a man just shouldn't see, just shouldn't even imagine—"

Finn understood. "If you decide to go in for homosexual rechanneling ... I'll understand. In fact, I might consider it myself. Murdock gives new meaning to the words *big* and *ugly*."

"She can't have come from human stock, Finn. She *can't* possibly—"

"She must have some human ancestry. Remember, I found her with a boy."

"The poor thing—I hope I never get that hungry or that desperate." Sawyer had turned quite pale at the thought.

"I think most normal men would share your reaction. Comfort yourself with this thought. Whatever she's devolved from, her subspecies can't possibly last beyond this present generation—because of the total lack of anyone perverse enough to father the next."

"Do you think she can hear us?"

Finn shrugged. "Do you think she cares?"

Sawyer thought about it. He watched Murdock's lumbering form in horror. She scratched herself abstractedly, paused to sniff under one armpit, scratched again, tugged her underwear out of her crotch, and then waddled heavily over to another workstation.

"Y'know," Finn said thoughtfully, "I wonder if we haven't stumbled into a trap...."

"Uh ... what gave you that idea?"

"No, I mean—even the commission to collect Murdock might not have a legitimate author. The more I think about it, the more trouble I have with the idea that somebody actually wants this—this *woman* badly enough to pay anyone to track her down."

"I agree, but maybe the local Dragon Lord has different tastes. The contract had his seal on it."

"I remember. This commission had one of the largest escrow accounts attached to it we've ever seen—the single richest, fattest prize, you should pardon the expression, in the Regency. You have to ask yourself, with that kind of a price on her head, why does Murdock still have her freedom? Every tracker in the Cluster must know about Murdock. Can you imagine anyone resisting the temptation of this bounty? I can't."

"Actually," said Sawyer, looking doubtfully downward, "I think I can."

Finn ignored the comment. "Soy, either no one else has the courage to come after her, or—"

"—or none of them have survived long after capturing her." Sawyer lowered his voice. "You know what'll happen next, don't you?"

"I can imagine. This woman specializes in organ-legging and slave trading. She sells bodies, body parts, special-purpose bioforms, and modified androids. We'll probably leave here in pieces."

Sawyer took a long, slow breath. He called down to the mammoth woman below, "If you surrender to us now, it'll go a lot easier for you in the long run."

Murdock ignored him.

"All right," said Sawyer, dejectedly. "Let's go to Plan B."

"Plan B?" Finn raised his eyebrow again. "I thought we already had."

Murdock stepped to another console to look at the result of her scanning programs. She frowned unhappily; an avalanche of wattled flesh collapsed into a mean and squinty-eyed expression. "Not prime," she said with audible disappointment. Her voice had a rasp like a bulldozer in pain. She rumbled deep in her chest, a volcano clearing its throat. "Not even choice. Hardly worth the trouble."

She glanced upward, considering another idea. She assessed the two brothers dispassionately. "Cute—" She nodded appreciatively, a leviathan gesture. "No real market value. But still ..."

Sawyer looked worriedly to Finn. *Cute?*

"I think she likes you—"

"No, no. She likes you much more than she likes me." Sawyer said it hastily. "Trust me. I know these things. She likes you. She doesn't like me at all. Really."

Murdock studied them thoughtfully for a moment longer, ignoring their frantic gestures and denials. Eventually, whatever small spark passed for intelligence behind her piglike features came to a reluctant decision. She discarded the thought. "No—not strong enough." She shook her giant head in slow, ponderous dissatisfaction and turned her attention back to the screen on her console. She punched a code and a moment later began talking to someone.

"You wanted a tracker? I have two." She listened, then answered with a laugh like a rusty gate; she wheezed. "Yeah. The same. I catch more trackers that way. They never learn. No, I'll only sell them as a set. You have to take both or not at all. Same price. No, not two for one. Each—" She haggled a bit longer, but finally came to terms with the unseen buyer and accepted the deal.

"To tell the truth," she added, "I don't want 'em nohow. They don't suit my purposes, but they might suit yours a lot better. Yeah. Yeah. They'll probably find much more happiness in your arms than in mine—" She laughed again, this time even louder and nastier than before.

THE VAMPIRE'S TABLE

By the time the Eye of God had crossed the sky and commenced settling its glory into the desolate west, Lady Zillabar's temper had eased enough for her to consider not only refreshment, but the next step of her plans. She returned to her own towers and, after several precious hours of dreamtime, began summoning various of her followers, citizens, and servants. She issued orders with crisp detachment, sweeping through the ranks of her clients without regard to their individual problems or concerns. By now the stories of her day-long tantrum—and the subsequent unfortunate death of the Captain of her personal Dragon Guard—would have gotten worldwide circulation; she might as well make good use of the resulting temerity of her subjects.

She retired to her private chambers for an informal dinner with several of her underlings, all Phaestor. All male, of course. No Dragons. Not after the events of earlier in the day. Too dangerous.

The servants had set the tables with a delicate repast, and as the evening deepened, her guests fed themselves liberally. The Vampires chatted and laughed among themselves, but all took care to keep their conversations light and noncommittal. Lady Zillabar allowed herself to enjoy the graceful beauty of Lord Drydel without, for once, wondering about either his loyalties or his ambitions. Whatever plans her evanescent Consort might have laid, they would lie fallow for a long while after today; certainly long enough for her to take steps to neutralize either the plans or the planner.

She pushed the thought aside and shared a goblet of green wine with Lord Drydel. His eyes flashed with desire, and she considered the possibility of a shared dream, later in the evening after the last of the guests had left. Perhaps ...

A servant-wasp approached to a polite distance, waited for the Lady's gesture, then presented her with a folded note. Zillabar barely lifted the card off the tray, unfolded it gracefully with one jeweled nail, glanced nonchalantly at the message inscribed inside, nodded to the servant, and dropped the note back on the plate. The servant withdrew.

Drydel looked inquisitively to his mate. She answered his look with a touch to his lips. "We have another guest." She clapped her hands twice, and the table servants began withdrawing the evening's buffet. Other servants quickly slid a set of ornate panels into place to hide that end of the room. Lady Zillabar moved to a dais and settled herself on its throne. Lord Drydel moved to stand behind her. Her guests had already taken notice; they took their places at the sides of the room to wait politely while the Lady conducted her business.

All conversation dimmed when the High Justice of Thoska-Roole entered behind the servant with the tray. Every dark eye in the room turned to study the corpulent man—a *human*, fat and filled with hot red blood.

The man wore a white toga and a black cape with a red border. The toga barely concealed his fleshy gut.

Whatever his age, he wore it well, though he looked like a man in his midfifties. He did not seem overawed by his surroundings or by his host. He glanced around at the furnishings and the other guests with unashamed curiosity.

The servant-wasp stepped to one side and announced in a chitinous voice, "The Arbiter of the Regency on Thoska-Roole, Justice Harry Mertz."

Mertz did not wait for the Lady to speak. He stepped forward and asked, "Do you require my services in an official capacity, Lady Zillabar? Or have you invited me to your quarters to share the quality of your table?"

What an impudent little man! The Lady allowed herself an edge of annoyance. How dare he! But instead of demonstrating what she felt, she merely smiled. "I apologize for this late summons. I know you have many concerns elsewhere, but the business I wish to discuss with you has no place in the official arena. You honor my house by your acceptance."

Mertz allowed himself an expansive bow. "You flatter me, Lady Zillabar. You and I both know that my credential has only a ceremonial function. I have honor without weight, glory without responsibility. The need for Arbiters[28] has long since passed into history. The job has disappeared with the need. Only the title remains."

The Lady smiled graciously. She descended from her dais and approached the Justice with easy familiarity, even though she knew that the man felt a profound repugnance at the nearness of her approach—his repug-

---

[28]The office of Arbiter carries only honorary importance, the legal equivalent of a Poet Laureate. The Arbiter speaks for justice, impartially and as a detached observer. He may act as a friend to any court in the land. In past times the Arbiters served as the consciences of their worlds.

nance probably equaled hers. He concealed it well, but she could still smell the stink of fear in his sweat. She held out her hands to him. He took a precautionary step back and opened his palms in a gesture of caution. "My Lady. I know you dislike touching. I would not have you uncomfortable."

Zillabar lowered her outstretched fingers. "People speak of your wisdom, Justice Mertz. You impress me now with your insight as well."

"Please, Lady—may we skip the flatteries. You wish something of me? Counsel perhaps?"

"Walk with me," the Lady invited. She gestured silently, and Lord Drydel moved up to flank the Justice on his other side.

Harry Mertz glanced from one to the other. "I cannot easily refuse this invitation, my Lady, can I?" he remarked wryly. If either of the two Vampires caught his inner meaning, neither of them showed it in their reaction.

They proceeded for a while through a shadowy arcade. After a bit the Lady spoke. "I think you will appreciate *this* invitation, Harry—may I call you Harry? Lord Drydel and I want to invite you to participate in a grand adventure with us. You see, now that we have restored the authority of the aristocracy here on Thoska-Roole, we intend to expand our vision to include the dynamic of the entire Cluster. The aristocracy wants to reinvigorate the Regency with a strong new purpose. All of us will benefit from an expansion of our influence in the Regency. We foresee a new age of enlightenment."

"In all honesty, Lady Zillabar, Prince Drydel, I have paid so little attention to matters that do not concern me that a street urchin would probably have more wisdom on these matters; I wouldn't presume to give you advice—"

Zillabar exchanged the quickest of glances with

Drydel. *This stupid human believed that they wanted his counsel!* She returned her focus to the Justice. "We need a man of your wisdom and reputation to address another area of our concern." She stopped and faced Harry directly. "As you must know, most humans have a deep irrational fear of the highest level of the aristocracy, the Phaestor—"

"Yes. Some humans call you Vampires."

"We take pride in the title. We drained the life out of the predators."

"To humans, however," Harry said, "the name carries another, much darker, meaning. In some quarters the word stinks like an epithet. No offense intended, of course." Smiling, Harry bowed politely to both of his hosts.

"None taken." Lady Zillabar smiled graciously and refocused on the task at hand. It took her a moment; this bastard had no intention of letting her proceed easily! He insisted on using that all-too-human thing they called *humor*. She didn't understand humor. It always looked like naked hostility to her. "However," she continued, "the existence of that fear, irrational or not, gives us great pause. We wish to work as partners with *all* of the species here on Thoska-Roole."

"I see," said Harry.

"We need someone to speak for us, someone who has respect and authority."

"I have neither, my Lady. Surely, you know that—" Harry grinned at her and her Prince-Consort.

Lady Zillabar found the sight of all those flattened teeth disconcerting and actually glanced away before she let her distaste show on her outer face. Turning back again, she said, "We need someone who can reassure the human constituency that the Vampire aristocracy means them no harm. He would enjoy the privileges of the aristocracy, and as your people began to see the value of Chris's partnership, then they would also begin to understand that they too can work with us without the enmity and rancor that has colored so many of our relationships in the past."

"A noble sentiment. I hope you will find someone of suitable authority and wisdom. Of course, I will do whatever I can to aid you in your search."

"We believe that the Arbiter of Justice should perform this service," said Lord Drydel, deliberately placing his hand firmly on Harry's shoulder.

Harry glanced at the hand, glanced up into Drydel's eyes, then looked to Lady Zillabar. Her eyes carried the same deadly message.

"The office no longer carries any weight, my Lord—" Harry offered, but Drydel interrupted him.

"We know that the office has devolved into a shell of its former glory, a mere honorary position; but that state of affairs needn't continue. We wish to restore the authority of the Arbiter to a much more meaningful level. You would *enjoy* a great deal of power, Justice." As he spoke, he continually looked to Lady Zillabar for signals—a nod, a frown, a subtle gesture.

Harry looked again from one to the other. Despite the fact that the words had come from Drydel's throat, he knew who had really spoken them. To Zillabar he said, "With all due respect, my Lady—I have never *enjoyed* power. I have always found it a most troublesome burden. Fortunately, any power I have had has also attracted a great many people who happily want to relieve me of that burden. So I have cheerfully given it up to others whenever and wherever I could. My shoulders have become too fragile and stooped to carry much weight of any kind anymore, so I would do the same in this case too."

"I think you misunderstand," said Lord Drydel. "As the Arbiter of Thoska-Roole, people look to you as the soul of justice. You cannot pass away this credential that you carry—you carry the trust of the people."

Zillabar caught Drydel's eye; the two of them steered Mertz gently to a nearby alcove, paneled with ornately engraved screens. On the table therein lay a document and a golden stylus.

"We have a Regency Order for you to sign," said Drydel. "With your signature it will validate the Regency's custody over all entities that do not presently hold full Regency citizenship: all robots, bioforms, androids, and uplifted-intelligence animals. As you know, the local Charter leaves nonsignatory species in a legal limbo. This will help to resolve that gray area of the law. After you sign, you may keep the stylus."

Harry did not reach for the document. Instead, he fumbled in his toga for a moment—until he found what he searched for. He pulled out a pair of ancient eyeglasses and fitted them carefully on his nose while both of the Vampires watched in obvious distaste.[29] At last Harry picked up the document and read it through carefully. As he read, he made small clucking noises in his mouth.

At last, satisfied that he understood the nature of the document, he laid it down again. He folded up his spectacles and returned them to whatever place they rested inside his garment.

In a tone of deceptive calm and courtesy, Harry said, "I can't sign this. The Regency doesn't have the right to assume this custody. And even if I did sign this order, it wouldn't make it right. And Lord Khallanin would never accept it anyway. He knows better. This will trigger riots."

Lady Zillabar's expression remained unchanged, as did Lord Drydel's—and yet, even without apparent outward sign of either Vampire's displeasure, the tension in the small alcove increased appreciably.

---

[29]Vampires have an intense dislike of any kind of disability. They perceive it as weakness.

Zillabar touched the parchment with a jeweled fingernail, sliding it carefully away from Harry's easy reach. Lord Drydel spoke first. "Perhaps you haven't heard yet. This afternoon Lord Khallanin retired from his position as the Prefect of Thoska-Roole."

"Lord Khallanin *retired*?"

"Permanently," added the Lady.

Harry selected his reaction carefully. "I see."

"He'll have a beautiful funeral," said Drydel, "as only befits one of his exalted station."

"The Regency Military Authority has already stepped in to ensure that order maintains here. We'll have no chaotic rebellions breaking out again. But, obviously, you do recognize the problem confronting us. Under the provisions of the restored Authority, the recommendations of the Advisory Council no longer carry the authority of law, so they cannot select a replacement, thus leaving us in something of a constitutional crisis; under the terms of the security agreement, we must have a representative of the Regency to coordinate all the various constituencies of Thoska-Roole's diverse population. Because of my rank in the Phaestor aristocracy, the Dragon Lord has asked me to step in—temporarily, of course—to ensure continuity, stability, and order. As soon as we can find an individual qualified to assume the reins of permanent conservatorship, I will gladly pass the baton of authority." She said this last without once looking toward Prince Drydel. "I have responsibilities elsewhere that I must attend to as well."

"Ah, I see. Of course." Harry smiled weakly. "Shall I assume then that without Lord Khallanin's further opposition, the Zashti clan will proceed with its plans to convert the Starport into a staging base for Marauder squadrons so that you can expand your influence even deeper into this region?"

Zillabar's expression remained unreadable. After an uncomfortable silence, Drydel answered for her. He

destepped the Arbiter's embarrassing question, staying
ocused instead on the more immediate purpose of the
onversation. "Justice, please. We must ensure that the ci-
ilian population remains calm. You can help us. Your
isible support will steer the conscience of the people."

"May I speak candidly?"

The Lady kept her voice calm. "I would consider it
n insult if you did not."

"I have heard stories—many of us have heard these
umors. Whether they have basis in fact or not, the sto-
ies still circulate. Perhaps you know the stories I
nean—? If so, you can spare me the necessity of refer-
ing to them further—?"

"On the contrary," prompted Drydel. "We have no
vay of knowing unless people like you tell us."

Harry looked uncomfortable. "We have heard sto-
ies about how the Vampires have dealt with *other* civil-
n populations, rumors of atrocities and ..." He trailed
ff unhappily.

Neither of the Vampires demonstrated a reaction.
hey simply exchanged a dark glance. After a moment
rince Drydel replied. His expression remained cold.
Malcontents and traitors have created these falsehoods. I
ssure you that when we find these troublemakers, we
vill deal with them harshly."

Unseen by Harry Mertz, Zillabar frowned quickly
nd shook her head at Drydel. Drydel decided abruptly
o study the ornate engraving of the ceiling ornaments.
Zillabar faced Harry directly. "You need not concern
ourself with that. I'll ask you only one more time. I will
ive you a choice. You will sign this document—or your
uccessor will."

"Yes," said Harry. "I see." He nodded his under-
tanding. "You allow me no choice at all. You know,
ady, I must share this with you. In the days of my
outh, in my studies of the Zyne,[30] I found an old saying

that has guided me all of my life. It goes like this: You will find it easiest to ride the avalanche in the direction it already travels."

Lady Zillabar allowed the slightest of smiles to appear on her face. Again she glanced at Drydel—a look of satisfaction. *We've won.*

Harry shortened her burst of triumph with his next words. "Yes. My successor will have to sign the document."

His calm defiance caught Zillabar off balance. Her face flushed with terrible anger. Even Drydel blanched as he saw the rising of her rage.

"You fool!" she spat. "Don't you realize that you stand before one who could kill you without blinking an eye?"

Harry met her gaze without flinching. He straightened himself and replied with equal strength, "More the fool you! *Don't you realize that you stand before one who can die without blinking an eye?*"

Zillabar stood speechless. Stunned. She had no suitable response for this. The blood-rage continued to suffuse her skin, until even Drydel worried what she might do.

But she did nothing. Instead, she stiffened, caught her breath, and swept angrily out of the alcove, leaving both the Vampire and the human wondering what would happen next—

---

[30] An ancient philosophical discipline, alleged to have its roots on Earth, the legendary birthworld of humanity.

AN OFFER OF EMPLOYMENT

Among Thoska-Roole's various fames, the imagination of the architects who designed its jails, prisons, dungeons, and other places of confinement, remains unacknowledged; yet the skills demonstrated in these constructions certainly rank among the best in the Palethetic Cluster.

Consider, for example, the accommodations in which Sawyer and Finn Markham presently found themselves. Murdock having relinquished all custody over them, their new patron—still unidentified—had generously arranged accommodations for the trackers in Thoska-Roole's most prestigious Incarceratorium.

Imagine a cylinder twelve times the height of a man. Imagine its cross section, a disk only two man-lengths in diameter. Imagine this cylinder set on end in a totally dark chamber. Imagine Sawyer and Finn sitting alone on top of this cylinder—waiting in a cell without walls.

"What do you think?" Sawyer asked his brother. "Do you like this place any better?"

Finn shrugged. "At least the view has improved."

"Immensely," Sawyer agreed.

They sat in silence for a while. Several centuries passed.

After a longer while they heard a faint scraping noise.

"Did you hear that?"

"Shh."

They listened harder.

The noise came again. It sounded like metal-heeled boots on a stone floor.

Abruptly, the lights came on. A bright beam of blue-white radiance struck down from somewhere high above. It pinned them where they sat. Finn and Sawyer both had to shield their eyes against the glare. They could not see very far into the darkness beyond the edge of the disk.

"Stand up," a soft voice commanded. It sounded very close. Bones creaking, muscles aching, they both pulled themselves to their feet. They could not determine from which direction the voice had come, so they simply faced outward.

Another light came on then, this one at a distance. It highlighted the bleak form of their new custodian. The Vampire stood alone on a matching platform opposite their own, illuminated in stark relief. It wore an attitude of bemused superiority and a black traveling cloak. The blue glow gave the figure an aura of lingering death.

"Uh-oh . . . ," said Sawyer.

"Ah, yep," agreed Finn. Vampires did not have a reputation for kindness.

"Do you recognize me?" the Vampire asked.

Sawyer scratched his neck, considering his response. His usual flippant reply would probably not gain him any advantage here. Fortunately, Finn spoke first. "No, Your Excellency. We don't recognize you."

"Good. For the moment that works to your advantage. I have a job for you."

"Ahh," Sawyer ventured carefully, "we already have employment."

"I see that," replied the Vampire. "Your present office speaks volumes about the quality of your success."

Sawyer started to answer, but Finn nudged his brother to silence. He whispered, "Shh. I think we need to hear what this fellow has to say."

The Vampire inclined its head in a polite nod. "Your brother gives you very good advice, Sawyer Markham. Follow it." The dark figure added, "I wish to have a man located. A human. A very important human. So you shouldn't have too much trouble ascertaining his whereabouts. But I want him immediately, and for that I need two good trackers."

Sawyer and Finn exchanged a glance, each trying to gauge the other's feelings. Neither looked happy. Finally Sawyer spoke up. "We don't work for governments."

The Vampire hesitated. "Why do you say that?"

"This installation."

"What do you mean?"

"The Miller-Hayes corporation built this detainment four hundred years ago for the Regency's most dangerous prisoners. Despite the government's strategic campaign to convince the public that the facility no longer exists or operates, despite the fact that the location remains unknown, our presence here demonstrates that the government still finds the facility useful. Only those at the highest level of the Regency would have access to this secret restraint. Therefore, the job you offer must benefit someone high in the Regency, perhaps even yourself—especially if the job requires some secrecy. Whoever you represent, clearly you stand here in some official capacity."

"The Prefect of Thoska-Roole has died," said the Vampire. "I have the responsibility of managing certain affairs pertaining to that death. You don't need to know anything more."

"We still don't work for governments."

"Then you choose the alternative ...?" The Vampire's tone had a dangerous sheen.

"Uh—"

"Wait a minute, Soy." Finn touched his brother's arm. Speaking carefully across the wide intervening space between themselves and the Vampire, he asked, "If we might impose upon your good nature, would you, um— explain the alternate option?"

"Death."

"Ah, I see. I thought so. Well, yes—that simplifies everything, doesn't it?"

"Yes, it does. I can promise you a very interesting job—or a very interesting death. Would you like to reconsider?"

Finn and Sawyer looked at each other.

"You tell him."

"Nope, I told him last time. You tell him."

Finn sighed. He turned back to the Vampire. "We have nothing to reconsider. We won't work for *any* government."

"As you wish." The Vampire turned quickly and strode away out of the light. It winked out with terrible finality.

A moment later the light above Sawyer and Finn also went out, plunging them again into utter blackness.

"Well," said Finn, his voice sounding very loud in the gloom, "you've done it again."

"Me—?"

"Look around. What do you see? Nothing! Another fine mess you've gotten me into."

The silence echoed with the accusation. After a long, long time Sawyer answered meekly, "I apologize, Finn."

AN ALLIANCE OF LIFE

Not every prison on Thoska-Roole had the elegance of the Miller-Hayes construction. The Old City detainment, for example, had little charm; its designers obviously did not have the same aptitude for this work as Miller and Hayes. In addition, they labored under the greater handicap of having to adapt an already-existing structure. Nevertheless, despite its artistic failings, the Old City detainment still served its purpose every bit as efficiently—perhaps even more so, because its miserable aesthetics served as part of the punishment.

Imagine a crater far out on the plain beyond the towering mesa. Imagine a gray-metal dome over the crater, and carved out of the ground beneath it, a huge dark chamber. Imagine a dank underground lake spotted with junk, debris, and sewage. Imagine never-ending humidity and heat.

Now let your imagination get baroque. Imagine a fetid stench, so strong it can peel the paint off walls. Install a scattering of flat circular islands in the lake, each one rising only a hand's width above the surface of the water—all made of stone, each one a different size. Imagine a bizarre rabble, spread across these islands—dirty, sullen, vicious, violent, and insane. Look up and see the catwalks of the guards hanging high over the prisoners.

The guards patrol ceaselessly. Here day and night both look the same, a dull gray sheen. Imagine swarms of terrible hungry things swimming in the lake: sharklins, piranhoids, lawyer-fish, and other dark things that trouble the sleep of fishermen. Among the deadliest things found in this water lurk the deadly mayzel-fish.[31]

The prison had only one real escape. Whenever a guest tired of the accommodations, he could go for a swim. Those who died of old age—or other causes—also left the prison the same way. The water would froth for a moment, and then become still again.

From above, a ramp lowered down to the largest island. And down this ramp came the Arbiter of Thoska-Roole, Justice Harry Mertz. Despite his circumstances, he wore an unusually calm expression. With every step he took, he demonstrated his willingness to ride this avalanche in the direction it already wanted to go.

He reached the bottom of the ramp. As he stepped off, it swung up quickly behind him. As he looked around at his new surroundings, his companions on the island also stood up to look at him. A more bizarre collection of life-forms had not gathered in one place since the last Cluster-Con of biological engineers.

"Good afternoon, gentlemen," Harry said, addressing them all. "Justice Harry Mertz, at your service—" He bowed elegantly. "But do not expect justice from me, for my words no longer carry weight. Nor should you expect justice to arrive from above. It no longer lives on Thoska-Roole. When justice gets sent to prison, there you will also find the free men of society. You may quote me on

---

[31]Dragons in particular like the flavor of mayzel-fish, but then Dragons have no sense of taste. Ask any Vampire about Dragon aesthetics.

that. It gives me great pleasure to make the acquaintance of each and every one of you. I had wondered where all the free men had disappeared to."

A sudden realization swept across Harry's features—recognition followed by horror. "I know this place. I knew it in my youth—a thousand years ago."

Several of the prisoners laughed at this bold claim. "You come here often, then?"

"Not if I can help it." Harry joined in the laughter. "But—this place did not always serve as a prison. In my youth people came to these chambers seeking arbitration and peace. The goddamned Vampires have desecrated a temple of true justice."

Harry shook his head in despair and looked around for a place to sit. The floor presented itself as the only available furniture. Harry shrugged sadly. "You can tell a lot about a civilization by the quality of the people found in its jails." His gaze fell upon two sad-looking warrior-lizards. Their name badges identified them as Kask and Keeda. "For example," he asked, "what crime did you commit?"

Keeda grumbled deep in his throat. "We committed the unpardonable sin of allowing the Lady Zillabar's gift to Lord Drydel to escape from our custody. They would not even allow us to commit dishonorable suicide."

Harry nodded gravely. "There. You prove my point."

The Dragons didn't understand, and Harry had little eagerness to explain himself to them. He turned around and surveyed the rest of his companions—the scum of ninety worlds, if Lady Zillabar had spoken truthfully in her vivid description of his future accommodations. Among the inmates Harry counted many humanoids, some androids, some bioforms, a few uplifts—but no particular emphasis on any one mix. The Vampires had no prejudices; they hated all other forms equally.

Harry noticed two men off to one side of the disk. They looked like natural humans to him; they wore the clothes of professional trackers. He stepped past them cautiously. They didn't even look up. The tall blond one seemed very concerned about his companion, a darker, bulkier man who slept fitfully on a rumpled mat. He wiped at his partner's forehead with a damp handkerchief, until the other awoke and pushed his hand away in annoyance. "Stop that. You don't have to worry about me."

Nearby, sitting glumly on its haunches, a LIX-class bioform, wearing the kind of jumpsuit most frequently seen aboard a starship, listened curiously to the angry rantings of a short red man; his skin had the color of blood and leather. Harry recognized him as a member of a clone family, possibly one of the Lees, a mix of Chinese, Navajo, and Martian genes—and probably a political prisoner. The Lees had caused the Vampires no small amount of trouble.

Harry smiled as he listened. This little radical spoke like one who knew his history. He understood his situation much too well: "You laugh, but I know the truth. I stand next in the succession. If anything happens to the TimeBinder of this world, I'll put on the headband. The Vampires can't afford to let me go free. The fact of my arrest proves that the Vampires plan to eliminate the office of the TimeBinder. If they do that on enough worlds—and they will—then we can never again call for a Gathering of all the Cluster worlds. If they can, they'll kill all thirteen remaining TimeBinders and prevent anyone from succeeding to the office."

"But what does this have to do with me—?" asked the LIX bioform.

"Listen, Ota—I subscribe to a very radical philosophy, in fact, a very *dangerous* idea. I believe that all of the races of the Cluster can unite together to throw off the heavy yoke of the Vampire aristocracy. The Regency has become oppressive under the rule of the Vampires; but the Vampires rule only because *we* let them."

Nearby, listening to this rant, both Kask and Keeda reacted with annoyance. One snorted, the other *hmph*ed. "You know nothing about the Vampires," Keeda rumbled.

"And you do? If you have such expertise, how did you and your brother end up here?"

"You spout dangerous ideas," said Kask.

The red-skinned man answered with a grin. "What can they do to me? Throw me in jail?" This triggered a round of derisive hoots from all the other prisoners. Seeing two of the noble Dragon Guards disgraced gave them a great deal of satisfaction.

Then the speaker noticed Sawyer Markham's interest in this discussion and pointed good-naturedly at him. "What do you think, tracker?"

Sawyer shook his head. "I don't believe in getting involved with governments—or resistance movements. My brother feels the same way."

"I would have thought that you would sympathize with a rebellion."

"All the rebels I've known," said Sawyer, grinning, "have too much anger, too much intensity for their own good—and rarely liven up a party."

The angry man, the intense man, poked Ota. "Listen to him. There, my friend, speaks the voice of a political illiterate." That phrase caught Harry's interest, and he settled himself nearby to listen to the rest of this ad hoc seminar in revolution.

"This world had beauty once. And the Regency meant justice. Now we see an empire in the final stages of collapse and decay. We have seen nothing but civil war for hundreds of years, a plague of oppression and death that sweeps from world to world in the Vampires' wake. Do you really need proof? Look around at Thoska-Roole's wasteland condition. That alone demonstrates the

Regency's inability to maintain its own authority before the Vampires' hunger and greed.

"Once the Dragons lived as the most respected moral authority in the Cluster. Now the Dragons grovel like everyone else—" He aimed this taunt deliberately at Kask and Keeda. "The Dragons serve the Vampires' wishes, not the Regency. Even their own Lord has fallen under the control of the Zashti family." Kask and Keeda both let loose with warning rumbles at this. The prisoners around them began to edge away, but the leathery little man continued unafraid. "You wouldn't rumble at me unless you recognized the truth of it. If I spoke falsely, you'd have no need to warn me off." Kask and Keeda looked at each other, uncertain. They fell back and continued listening.

The man with a cause said, "Once the Vampires held the trust of every race and form within the Regency. Once the Vampires lived among us all as equals. Now they live as terrorists and Lords—a deadly combination."

"But what do *you* want?" asked Harry. "What would serve the man who speaks?"

"Justice," he replied simply.

Harry snorted. "Justice?" Amusement spread across his face. "Most people say they want justice, but they don't really want justice. They want revenge. They want to see the pain spread around equally. May I ask, what do you want? *Really?*"

The revolutionary looked up, startled. He seemed to notice Harry for the first time. "You seem to know a lot, old man. But have you ever fought in a revolution?"

Harry sidestepped the question with a shrug. "I've seen my share of wars, thank you. Only people who haven't lived through a war advocate it so eagerly."

"I don't advocate starting a war at all," said the rebellious man. "I simply wish to win the one that already swirls around us—the war that the Vampires have inflicted on every other species in the Cluster.

"The Regency collapses around us, even as we blather," he continued. "Civil war simmers on a thousand worlds throughout the Cluster. The Vampires commit atrocities in the open, unashamedly, no longer even bothering to keep their crimes a secret. Their fleets have plundered helpless worlds. Populations have vanished. Our civilization burns around us!

"The Call must go out, my friend, for a new Gathering of TimeBinders. The last Gathering gave us the Regency. This Gathering will dissolve the Regency and create a new republic, in which all species hold true and equal representation. Thirteen TimeBinders must issue the Call for a new Gathering. Twelve have already declared. Soon the TimeBinder of Thoska-Roole will add his voice, and then not even the Vampires will stop the sword of social justice."

His eyes shone with the fire of true belief now. His voice took on a deeper resonance. The man with the fury spoke to all of them. "I give you this vision—an Alliance of Life, an Alliance in which all sentient entities shall hold equal shares of responsibility and privilege, an Alliance with a place for each and every one of us. Imagine—a world that works for everyone, with no one and nothing left out."

Some in his audience heard his passion and allowed themselves to share the tiniest bit of it. Others, however, had not yet climbed that high on the evolutionary ladder. His words brought hoots and catcalls of derision from some of the bitterest and most skeptical of the prisoners.

"Treat robots equal to humans? Machines? Pfah! I can still do one thing a machine can't," hollered one squat, gray-looking man.

"And faster, too——" jibed his partner, an equally squat and gray-looking male.

"And what about androids and bioforms?" called another. "Shall we break our bread with them as well?"

"Not to mention clones and other synthetics. Would you want your brother to marry one?"

The man with the vision ignored the jokes. He held up a hand for silence. He stood up so everyone on the disk could see him. "*Every* life exists as a sacred spark. Every life, everywhere. We who believe in the values of the Resistance hold this truth as a self-evident proposition."

Harry looked around. Sawyer and Finn remained interested observers, but from a careful distance. Kask and Keeda looked angry. Clearly, they heard this radical speech as treason, and their Dragon Guard training demanded that they act. Kask mumbled something about seeing the man thrown in jail for his lies about the Regency; he did not realize the irony of this thought.

"Listen," said the man with the vision. "Consider this—*imagine it*. Imagine that all the forms of the Cluster could put aside their differences and cooperate, even if only for a very short time. Imagine what we could accomplish! Dragons, for example—" Kask and Keeda perked up what they used for ears at this remark.

"Without the Dragons, what power would the Vampires have? What could they impose upon the rest of us? As long as the servant races—all of the races, but especially the Dragons, continue to cooperate with the Vampire masters, they help—*we* help—them to perpetuate their power."

He turned back to Ota now, a question on his face. The LIX-class bioform shook its head. "I prefer not to have an opinion on this. The practice of war still lies beyond the horizon for my species, and I hope it stays that way forever. The business repels me."

"May I remind you, gentle-beast," the red man said, "that you now reside in the same jail as the rest of us, and that makes it your business too."

"I refuse to accept this responsibility," Ota said. "Humans created bioforms as servants, not warriors."

He snorted in contempt, but Sawyer grinned and called, "The beast makes better sense than you. Take the money and run."

"Hah! The tracker speaks—the voice of greed. The paid huntsman. Another kind of servant." The scorn dripped from his voice. He added with contempt, "Another fool!"

Sawyer took no offense. He merely grinned and scratched himself. "Here we sit, my friend—both in the same prison. We must both look like fools to our masters, but given the choice, I'd rather look like my kind of fool than yours."

Another inmate spoke up then. "I'll believe in an Alliance of Life when a fleet of ships arrives and wipes out the Vampires and their Marauder squadrons."

The red man finally allowed his frustration to show. "Don't you get it? The Alliance of Life starts with your declaration—not somebody else's. Ota? Surely you understand?"

"Sorry," said Ota, shaking its head. "I see enough violence just serving under Star-Captain Campbell."

Meanwhile, Keeda had finally decided that he had heard enough, and at last, laboriously, he levered himself erect. Beside him Kask also began to lift himself. The sight of a Dragon rising to its feet brought silence to the prisoners on the stone island. The sight of both Dragons erect terrified them. The prisoners rose to their feet nervously and readied themselves to jump out of either monster's way.

Keeda roared low in his throat. He towered over all these little men, but in particular he focused his hungry gaze on the small one with the skin like red leather. "By what right do you speak such treason? Who dares to stand before this Dragon and speak such shit?" All of the other prisoners began backing out of the way, leaving a clear space between the Dragon and its prey.

The revolutionary stared back unafraid. "My name? Don't you know? Can't you tell who stands before you? Don't you recognize a brother?"

Keeda pointed back to Kask. "There stands *my* brother. My *only* brother." Keeda lumbered forward. "I repeat, what name do you go by?"

The angry little man stepped boldly forward. "You see before you a member of the Martian Lee clone-family. Number 1169."

Keeda rasped something unintelligible. His eyes reddened. "Say your prayers. Prepare to die," he commanded. "I have sworn a blood-oath. No one named Lee will ever escape my wrath alive."[32] The Dragon lunged—

Kask tried to stop Keeda. He grabbed for his brother's arm, bellowing, "That debt has died. It no longer holds!"

---

[32]The source of this enmity lies some seventeen standard years prior to this narrative, at which time an "unfortunate incident" took place in the small agricultural community of Kilpatrick's Folly on the rocky planet Morpaline. A troop of Regency Dragons sought revenge for an inadvertent insult to one of their number.

The insult itself did not develop out of any action of any member of the local community, but instead occurred when a visiting traveler, known only as Mr. Costello, who identified his profession as "hero," accidentally espoused a philosophical position somewhat at odds with the Dragons' perception of personal integrity. Unfortunately, the Dragons' response grew severely out of hand. They slipped into a killing rage and ran amok through the settlement, killing one hundred and seventeen of the one hundred and eighty-three inhabitants.

The Regency Prefect of Morpaline, a member of the Lee clone-family, summarily ordered the entire troop of Dragons dishonorably executed. This judgment triggered a violent three-year campaign of assassination and terror by the Moktar Dragons directed against any and all members of the Lee family throughout the worlds of the Regency. At no time would either the Lees or the Dragons accept arbitration or reconcilement. As a result, the blood-war never officially ended—the Dragons simply ran out of Lee clones to kill.

"No matter!" roared Keeda. "This death wants no price. This Lee *needs* killing."

Keeda picked up Lee and held him over his head in one great hand, ready to fling him out into the water. He paraded around the perimeter of the disk, shouting and hooting his defiance, taunting Lee to stop him. "I'll give you the only appropriate reward for traitors—"

Sawyer and Finn both leapt to their feet shouting, "No!" Sawyer ran to the Dragon, pulling at its arms, hanging from them, kicking and punching and trying to stop Keeda from concluding his deadly game. Keeda ignored him. He lifted Lee high and—

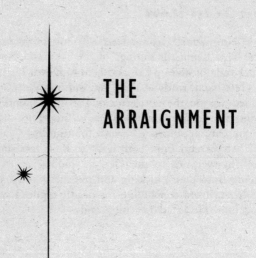

THE ARRAIGNMENT

The first shot sizzled just past Keeda's left ear. The scream of air imploding and the sudden burst of steam from the fetid water beyond slapped him like a hammer blow. Silence rippled outward like an aftershock. Sawyer let go of Keeda's arm and dropped back down to the stone floor of the disk-island.

Keeda whirled around and bellowed his defiance at the guards on the catwalks above. "Don't stop me!"

The second shot scorched the stones between his feet. They glowed red and gave off an oily smoke. The sound of the blast stung everybody's ears. It echoed across the lake for long angry seconds.

Keeda hesitated. The rifleman remained unseen. Finally the heat from the burning stones forced the huge Dragon to take two steps backward away from the painful surface.

"I've taken a blood-oath," Keeda called, but his whooping cries lacked their previous angry defiance. "He *needs* killing."

A spotlight pinpointed the huge Dragon, and a

penetrating voice rolled across the vast underground chamber, rippling the surface of the lake and bouncing off the distant walls. "Put. The. Man. Down."

Still, Keeda hesitated. What could they do to him? Kill him? At least he would die with honor, and in the fulfillment of a blood-oath. He hissed in angry confusion. He looked up at the man squirming in his great claw. He really wanted to throw this son of a primate into the hungry water of the chamber.

Sawyer looked up at Keeda and whispered, "I don't think you should do it."

Finn moved a few steps closer and added his encouragement to his brother's; he spoke in the Dragon's own tongue. *"It would dishonor your family to kill him this way—this manner of killing has neither style nor virtue."*

"I have never dishonored my family." Keeda glowered down at the two men. He looked past them to Kask. "Ask my brother."

"Then don't start now," Sawyer said. *"You* ask your brother."

Keeda looked uncertainly to Sawyer and Finn, then beyond them to Kask.

Kask nodded to Keeda. While he couldn't directly admit the accuracy of Finn's words, still he couldn't deny them either. "If nothing else, we must keep our honor," he grumbled.

Still Keeda hesitated. He didn't want to give any human a reason to think he had triumphed over a Dragon. At last he lowered his hand so he could stare directly into Lee's eyes. He roared at the man, "You deserve killing, and I will kill you someday. Not today, but someday I will give you a death that I can brag about. Count on it. I will not betray a blood-oath."

"I ask of you one thing only," said Lee. "Hold true to the largest loyalty you can. Someday, perhaps, you might give that loyalty to the Alliance of Life."

Keeda snorted. Even in death the man still

preached treason. Incredible! He lowered Lee-1169 the rest of the way to the stone surface. He lashed his tail angrily and stamped away. Kask followed him.

Sawyer and Finn exchanged a look that revealed both fear and relief. Lee-1169 looked at them oddly. "Why did you save me?" he asked. Sawyer shrugged. Finn shook his head. Both turned away quickly to avoid showing how the moment had affected them.

Now the lights above came up. On the high ledges and the gun emplacements surrounding the lake, the Dragon Guards stamped and shuffled impatiently; they swiveled their weapons and targeted one prisoner after another, picking them out with red targeting beams.

The watchers on the slender catwalks above became visible as stark black gnomes hanging directly over the islands. They appeared as gaunt and mysterious figures behind their narrow blue-white spotlights. The lines of light pierced the gloomy murk, probing and searching like radiant fingers, until each one had isolated a specific prisoner on one of the stone islands. All over the chamber the inmates began standing up, shielding their eyes, and peering fearfully up into the brooding and ominous glare.

A spectral catwalk led out to a central platform that hung high over the whole chamber. The prisoners could see a tall, thin Vampire sweeping angrily to that vantage point, followed by two aides. The Vampire took up his position, leaning out over the railing to look down on his unfortunate charges. He flung back the hood that cloaked his features, and a whisper of recognition swept across the islands below. The Vampire smiled, revealing his gleaming teeth. His incisors glistened long and needle-sharp.

"d'Vashti," said Harry to no one in particular.

Kernel Sleestak d'Vashti had a needle-beam in his left hand. He glared down at Keeda with anger-reddened eyes; he pointed down at Keeda and pinned him in the targeting beam of his weapon. He shouted across the entire chamber, his voice amplified like thunder; he aimed his words at the Dragon Guards hulking in the high gun emplacements. "Pay attention! Disobedience never goes unrewarded! Failure never goes unpunished!"

d'Vashti's beam changed color then, became a ray of throbbing amber power—a tractor beam. Keeda struggled against the pressure, but no Dragon had the strength to resist the repulsive power of a focused singularity field. He began slipping and sliding backward across the stone surface of the island toward the dark water beyond. He glanced once over his shoulder, grunted in dismay, and struggled harder. His huge tail lashed furiously back and forth, but the deadly beam kept pressing him ever closer to the water. At last he could resist no longer. Waving his arms helplessly, he toppled backward into the murky, wet stink.

The water boiled around him. It turned red. It frothed. The Dragon struggled, screaming, surfaced once and scrabbled at the edge of the stone island—for a moment he looked futilely into his brother's eyes, then he slid back and disappeared forever. After a moment the surface of the lake became still again.

Kask stood rigid, horrified. He trembled like a thing possessed. The words came unbidden to his lips. "Keeda did not deserve such a dishonorable death." Fortunately, he spoke this thought too softly for d'Vashti to hear—or the Vampire would have sent him quickly to join his brother.

Now d'Vashti glowered around the chamber like an avenging demon. His beam regained its harmless color and began searching through the prisoners, focusing first here, then here, and finally here. The inmates cowered under his terrible gaze. "We will now proceed with the process of selection."

A groan rose up among the poor creatures on the stone islands. From a hundred throats it came—a multi-

tude of voices, united in a sad chorus of despair. Sawyer
and Finn exchanged a worried glance.

"Selection?"

"I don't want to know."

A series of ramps came rising up out of the water,
bringing rank sewage and dead things with them. Like
the spokes of a wheel, they connected all of the islands to
an ominous platform at the edge of the lake framed by
an ornate curved proscenium. A dark door dilated open
in the depths of the arch, revealing a deep crimson glow
beyond.

From his vantage above, d'Vashti began picking out
prisoners, directing them across the spokes and through
the glowing door. His selections included all of the
bioform and chimera species, none of the humans. Picking their way carefully to avoid stepping on the most distasteful of the objects left on the still-wet ramps, the
varied creatures crossed over to the narrow shelf of stone.
They looked uncomfortable and afraid. d'Vashti selected
Ota with an offhand gesture, and the LIX-bioform followed the others with resignation. It disappeared after
them into the red gloom.

Of all the nonhuman prisoners, only Kask remained unselected. He stood alone, wondering if he
should call d'Vashti's attention to his existence, or if wisdom dictated silence. Remembering Keeda, he opted for
silence.

The dark door closed, and the ramps sank quietly
back into the dank and brackish water. As they did, a
new set of stone walkways rose up; these ramps stretched
between the various islands. They locked into place, and
d'Vashti began pointing again, directing various prisoners
from one disk to another, sorting them into groups by
some criterion known only to himself.

He pointed and pointed and pointed again. "You—
cross to that platform. You—stay there. You—cross over."

On the central platform one prisoner dropped to his

knees, weeping. He lifted his arms up to d'Vashti, wailing for mercy and forgiveness, but d'Vashti had already moved on. He strode out onto the catwalks to call down to specific prisoners—again and again, his beam stabbed and selected. The other prisoners moved nervously away from the one who still wept alone and forgotten.

d'Vashti stopped as if he had suddenly remembered something. He looked back at the pitiful man and appeared to consider his plight. "I've reconsidered," he said calmly. "You may stay there." Using the slender catwalks like a spiderweb, he circled around the chamber, once again rearranging his choices, ignoring the grateful slobbering thanks of the man he had seemingly spared.

Shortly, Sawyer, Finn, Lee-1169, Kask, and Justice Harry Mertz all found themselves assigned to the same stone island. They crossed to it and stood around uncomfortably, looking at each other. What happens now? None of them had either speculation or comment on their situation.

Sawyer whispered to Finn, "How bad do you think it will get?"

Finn whispered back, "*Very* bad."

"Oh, good."

"Good?" Finn raised his eyebrow at his brother.

"I guessed right."

Above, the selection process appeared to have stopped. d'Vashti made one last circuit of the webwork, prowling and peering until he felt satisfied. He moved two more prisoners, telling them to swap their places on different islands. He smiled as he watched them cross, first one, then the other.

At last he straightened. As the prisoners watched in fear, d'Vashti gave a signal to someone unseen, then turned his attention downward again.

Several of the stone islands began to sink away under the prisoners—including the central platform, still bearing the man who had begged so pitiably for his life.

The waters began sweeping up and over the edges. The prisoners on them danced and hopped from one foot to the other. Some of them dived into the water and tried to swim—the water frothed around them—others died where they stood. The pitiful man rose to his feet and screamed enraged curses at d'Vashti. "You betrayer of souls! May you fall into the night forever! I hope that your dying lasts for the rest of your life." He continued cursing even as the things in the water pulled him down and away, even as he flailed against them, until his final words dissolved into a desperate gurgling rattle.

The dank waters continued to froth and bubble and rage; it seemed as if the horror would never end. d'Vashti watched without comment. When the water at last began to quiet again, he straightened up and gave an order to the Captain of the Dragon Guard. "Send the rest of them to trial."

And then he exited. The darkness wrapped itself around him and then floated down like a blanket to smother the remaining prisoners as well.

In the gloom Kask began to wail in despair—a series of long, low whoops of grief and dismay over the death of his brother. The sound had a horrendous quality. It rolled out through the stench-ridden air, bounced off the walls, and left the nerves of all who heard it raw and quivering.

THE COURT OF BLOOD

A crowd of several hundred had gathered for the day's proceedings, filling the Imperial chambers and spilling out into the corridors beyond. Rumors had circulated all over the city about the petitions before the court, and the many Lords and their fewer Ladies had arrived in their best finery to make a day of it. Because of the great number of Vampires in attendance, the representation of the lesser races had visibly diminished. Nevertheless, the chatter of excited curiosity seekers filled the ornate-paneled room. Delicately carved screens separated the various court areas. Crimson trim illuminated the pale velvet panels on the walls. Tiny ornate figures peered down from the cornices above—the little gargoyles concealed a battery of recording devices, not to mention an additional battery of assorted weaponry. Just in case.

Sitting in the dock, Sawyer nudged his brother. "You can almost smell the blood-lust."

"I wish you wouldn't talk like that."

"How do you feel?"

"Like a Dragon booger. Green and slimy. Leave me alone."

Abruptly, the murmur of excitement rose. A magnificently clad Herald had entered the room. He wore a stiff red square tunic with the Imperial shield emblazoned on the front of it in evanescent gold. A flutter of gasps came from the audience; both the men and the women reacted visibly to the beauty of this young Phaestor. He stepped up onto his perch and the crowd began quieting. The buzz of speculation, hovering above the room like a swarm of lies, diminished quickly as all the various liars and lawyers came to attention.

"By the special appointment of Lady Zillabar," the Herald announced in a voice like a violin, "Lord Drydel will now hear all outstanding matters before the Regency." The last few whispers faded away.

Lord Drydel entered then and took his place behind the high desk at the front of the court. Lady Zillabar entered quietly at the side of the room and settled herself in a curtained reviewing box. Drydel could see her; almost no one else could. He settled himself and began organizing his papers. He had extensive notes on the podium in front of him. Plus, he had a screen that relayed Lady Zillabar's thoughts as well.

In the dock, among others, sat an Imperial warrior-lizard named Kask, a traitor named Lee-1169, former High Justice Harry Mertz, a scraggly tracker named Sawyer Markham, and his equally disreputable-looking brother, Finn Markham. Drydel noted with interest that Finn Markham did not look well.

Lord Drydel spent a few moments poring over the various petitions in front of him, before deciding to get the nastiest one out of the way first. He handed it to the Bailiff, who logged it and handed it to the Herald. The Herald stepped up onto his podium and called, "Lord Drydel will now hear the matter of Star-Captain Neena

Linn-Campbell and her special petition seeking redress in the matter of an appropriated LIX-class bioform."

Captain Campbell stepped boldly forward. She wore a black uniform and a black traveling cape. Behind her came a husky-looking female android and a sullen-faced high-gravity dwarf. All three took their places at the bar and waited respectfully.

Drydel laid the petition aside and studied the Star-Captain with curiosity. He didn't see many human women on Thoska-Roole.[33] He assumed that other humans might admire her presumption in dressing like a Phaestor aristocrat; himself, he found it arrogant and offensive. No matter. He would decide this case on its merits alone—as he always did.

He waved a hand languidly toward the human woman. "Do you wish to address this issue?"

"My Lord—" She acknowledged his rank with a curt nod. "Agents of the Customs and Immigration Authority boarded my landing shuttle and performed an illegal search. They seized the person of my First Officer, a LIX-class bioform. The Authority maintains that the bioform had no license for this world; but the bioform never left the confines of the shuttlecraft, and therefore never left the legal territory of my vessel, the *Lady Macbeth*. Therefore, the officers had no right to seize the creature. I demand its immediate return. You have copies of my guardianship papers attached to the petition."

Lord Drydel exchanged a smile with Lady Zillabar, then looked back to the arrogant Star-Captain. "This court has read and studied your petition. We acknowledge that the officers of the Immigration Authority acted with impropriety, and we have issued a stern warning to

---

[33]The Regency did not freely license female embryos, and of those who survived to breeding age, few remained on the planet. Thoska-Roole maintained its reputation as a good place to leave quickly.

them that such flagrant disobedience of the law has no place in a civilized society. However, as we have studied this matter in some detail, we must also find that the guardianship papers of this bioform have no validity in a Regency court—"

Captain Campbell's expression hardened with sudden fury. She looked like she wanted to say a good deal more, but she prudently held her silence. Lord Drydel looked down from the bench at her with a deliberate smile, then continued.

"—due to the direct and immediate failure of Captain Campbell to secure appropriate licensing and registration from the offices of the Confluence of Bioform Management. Therefore, the Regency denies your claim of proprietorship." It pleased Drydel to see the Star-Captain's suppressed rage. He would enjoy the next part immensely. "The Regency has accepted custody of the LIX bioform, designate Ota. We have already transported the beast to a detainment center for reassignment. Next case—"

"I challenge this appropriation," Neena Linn-Campbell interrupted. "By what authority does the Regency assume custody of my personal servant?"

Drydel maintained his cold smile. "Perhaps you remain unaware of the reconstruction of authority that has occurred here. Because of the very real possibility of civil unrest, the Regency has had to assume custody of all unlicensed, unsecured bioform entities on Thoska-Roole. The order became effective last night."

"Excuse me, m'Lord—?" The interruption startled Drydel. For a brief instant he had no idea who had spoken. Then he recognized the voice and refocused his attention. Justice Harry Mertz had stood up in the dock to speak. Now he added, "I advised you last night that such an order would have no merit under the law. You leave me no choice but to speak now and declare that order illegal."

A murmur of consternation swept through the

court. Drydel tapped at the bell on his desk again and
again until silence returned to the bright paneled chamber.

Drydel knew better than to declare Mertz out of
order. In fact, he had planned on having Mertz in the
courtroom for precisely this declaration. The fat fool's interruption had come at the perfect moment. Almost everyone in the room recognized High Justice Harry
Mertz, but for the record Drydel asked, "Sir, would you
please make yourself known to this court."

"I go by the name of Harry Mertz. I hold the office
of Arbiter of Thoska-Roole. I admit that my placement
here in the dock instead of in the advisory box appears
unusual—but considering the current state of affairs, I
cannot think of anyplace more appropriate for me to sit.
Nevertheless, my dear Lord Drydel, I speak to you as a
friend of the court, as mandated by my office. And I repeat, I hereby declare this order illegal under the charter
of the Regency under the rule of which all sentient species share equal privileges and equal responsibilities *under
the law*."

Drydel glanced quickly to Lady Zillabar for direction.
She shook her head curtly. Drydel nodded his agreement to
her.

"An interesting position, Citizen Mertz," Drydel replied slowly. He hesitated while he selected his next
words with care. "But you have presumed an authority
which you do not have. You yourself, in fact, have acknowledged that the office of Arbiter exists only as an
honorary position."

Harry opened his mouth to speak again, but Drydel
held up one exquisitely manicured hand to stop him.
"Additionally, Citizen Mertz, I must point out that even
if this court could recognize your office, your arguments
would still carry no legal merit." Drydel looked through
the papers on his desk. He found the one he wanted and
touched it with an extended index finger. He slid it away
from the others, licked his lips as he read it. "In order to

secure domestic tranquillity here on Thoska-Roole, and to
ease the process of determining the fair and equitable al-
location of personal and property rights in the courts of
the world, the Regency Authorities have had to recon-
struct the definition of *sentience*. We recognize that certain
other classes of artificial entities have substantial cognitive
and language skills and that these skills represent a significant simulation of consciousness. Nevertheless"—Drydel
glanced   smugly   across   the   ornate   courtroom—
"Nevertheless, the true quality of sentience lies not only in
an entity's ability to communicate rationally, but in the
much larger domain of personal responsibility; and in that
regard, we do not mean the small responsibilities of personal survival, but the much larger obligations and commitments that one has toward one's family, one's society,
and even for the survival and success of the communities
of all sentients as expressed in the Regency Charter. By
that definition we have no choice but to find that certain
classes of creature do not qualify as sentient—"

Harry snorted. Loudly.

"I beg your pardon?" Lord Drydel interrupted
himself. He glanced across the courtroom to Harry
Mertz, one exquisite eyebrow arched skeptically. The
spectators looked back and forth between the High
Bench and the prisoner's dock. Captain Campbell took
advantage of the confusion to whisper something to
Robin. The android did not allow her concern to show,
but she began measuring the distance to the exits.

Harry spread his hands in apology and spoke with
deference. "Please excuse my impolite and emotional outburst. Such explosive displays of emotion have no place in
a civilized courtroom—but, with all due respect, your
declaration has a fececious[34] quality that I have not seen
in a legal argument since the worm Ouroboros ate its

---

[34]Fececious: full of feces.

own tail." Unwilling to wait for Drydel's comprehension of the analogy, Arbiter Harry Mertz continued quickly. "Regency laws prohibit robots, bioforms, androids, uplifted-intelligence animals, and certain other augmented entities from holding positions of social status, responsibility, or economic impact. Now, by virtue of the fact that such entities do not hold such positions, this decree denies the possibility of sentience and the claims to legal protections contained therein. Frankly, sir," Mertz concluded, "I expected much better from you than this. I can only confess my great dismay and disappointment in such shoddy legal reasoning."

And, having said all that, Harry Mertz sat down again. Lee patted him once on the shoulder. "Well said," he whispered. Sawyer and Finn glanced over and shook their heads in regret; they admired Harry's courage but retained serious doubts about his wisdom in challenging the court so bluntly.

For his part, Drydel remained calm. He pushed the paper aside, folded his hands together, and leaned forward in his seat. "Nevertheless, Citizen Mertz, the court remains bound to follow the law, however sound or unsound the reasoning behind it." To Captain Campbell he said, "The ruling stands. The Regency has taken custody of the bioform Ota. May I suggest to you that you accept this all in good grace, lest the Regency also decide to examine the status of the robot and android members of your crew."

He turned his attention back to the other prisoners in the dock. "As you have brought yourself so directly to the attention of the court, I will now read the court's ruling on the dispositions of the responsibilities relevant to your case." He looked directly at Harry Mertz. "You will live out the rest of your days in the labor camps. The same sentence will apply to your fellow conspirators in the dock." Drydel read through their names, quickly and without real interest. "Lee-1169, the Dragon Kask, Sawyer Markham, Finn Markham, et al."

"Hey!" said Sawyer, leaping to his feet. "Don't we get a trial?"

Drydel didn't even glance up. "You just had it," he replied. "Take them away."

As they filed out, Lord Drydel turned his attention back to Star-Captain Neena Linn-Campbell. "I see that you still wait. You have another matter? Another request, perhaps?"

Neena Linn-Campbell met Drydel's glance without fear. "Brinewood," she said. "This planet needs a dose of brinewood."

"I beg your pardon?"

"Never mind."

Captain Campbell crossed to the side of the room and abruptly yanked back the curtain shielding Lady Zillabar from the gaze of the lesser people. "I thought so," she said. The Lady flung herself back in horror, so off balance by this effrontery that the shock actually registered on her face. "You've staged this whole charade for my benefit, haven't you?" Captain Campbell accused.

Lady Zillabar stood up, seething. "You forget yourself!" she hissed and spat.

Robin grabbed at Captain Campbell's arm. "Captain, please—we have no legal recourse here. Let's go." *Let's go before you get us jailed for treason—or worse.*

Campbell suddenly realized the danger that her outburst had put them in. She let go of the curtain and turned quickly back to Drydel. "May we take leave of this court?" she asked, politely curtsying.

Drydel missed the sarcasm. He glanced to Zillabar. No help there. The Lady had already swept out of her box. Drydel dismissed Star-Captain Campbell with a gesture; he had reached the limit of his authority. Captain Campbell turned and exited swiftly, followed by her dwarf and her android, both hurrying to keep up.

Lord Drydel watched them go with little pleasure. Despite his rulings, he did not feel triumphant.

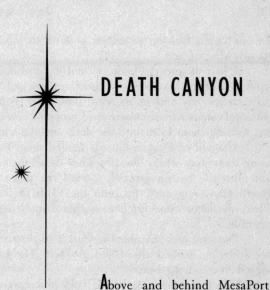

DEATH CANYON

Above and behind MesaPort lies a range of stiff jagged mountains, all tumbled and broken with ghastly canyons. Here the unwary explorer will find places where the surface of the world looks shattered, as if by the repeated blows of a gigantic ax. At the bottom of Death Canyon, for instance, the ground opens up in a terrible deep crack that smokes with hellish fumes and gases.

Here lies the garbage pit of a civilization that doesn't care. At the bottom of the canyon, a dismaying sprawl of garbage, junk, and sewage stretches away into the distance, the detritus of a thousand years. The reek of decay hangs over everything like a burdensome cloud. Things live in the garbage, prowl and hunt through the discarded slag—disturbing things, *hungry* things.

Here, lost among the ruins, wander the forgotten and condemned of Thoska-Roole, a dreadful population of renegades, runaways, and rebels—the remnants and wreckage of a higher, now unreachable, plane of life; every form save one has its representatives here. The bottom of Death Canyon resembles nothing so much as a narrow slice of hell.

A pair of spidery elevators climb up and down the sheer side of the Mesaport cliff, providing the only access between the city and its dreadful underside. Today the clunking cabins released a wretched group of new prisoners, spitting them forth into the dark and the stink.

A squad of Dragon Guards herded them forward, using their sting-whips liberally. They drove the convicts out onto the barren ground, toward the place where Death Canyon opened up onto the Plain of Sorrows. There the labor camp lay like another discarded tumble of trash.

The prisoners shambled toward it in despair. Sawyer and Finn looked ahead and groaned. The barracks sagged like a dying beast.

"Oh, hell—cheer up. We've had worse accommodations."

"I can't remember where."

"Give me time—I'll think of something. We have to have had a worse experience somewhere."

"Not necessarily." Finn grunted painfully. Then he added, "But think of it this way, Soy. We can only go up from here."

Behind them Kask shook his heavy head. "Nobody escapes from Death Canyon. No one ever has."

"Well, then," said Sawyer, "Finn and I will claim the honors of the first. You may come with us, if you wish. Harry? Lee? Will you join us?"

Lee looked skeptically at the tall blond man. "Tracker, your jests have everything but laughter."

"You have my apology, sir. But I don't share your dismay. I've finally found the place where the sun never shines. Now I can stop wondering."

Lee just sighed and shook his head. He wandered away from Sawyer and Finn. The two would not last long here. Of that, he had a strong premonition. They didn't take the situation seriously enough. Lee shielded his eyes with a leathery red hand and stared up into the canyon, wondering how far it extended, wondering how far the guards would chase a man before they gave up and turned back.

The piles of pipes and casings, broken engines, wall panels, half-filled trash containers, shattered girders, twisted frameworks of all kinds, gave the landscape a weird, metallic, evil, and surreal quality. Here and there orange fires smoldered. The smoke rose upward, twisting slowly in the wind, disappearing into the gray haze that hung over everything.

Lee squinted and wondered who lived up there, up beyond the towering garbage. Who prowled through its tunnels, haunted its narrow canyons, lurked inside the metal caverns? Who came crawling down out of the night to prey upon the prisoners of the labor camps? If the inmates of the labor camps lived on the bottom rung of Thoska-Roole's ladder, then what kind of horrors lived beneath them, where no rules existed at all?

"You, there!" growled the Dragon Guard. He lashed his stinger-beam across Lee's back. "Don't go too far! We have to put a collar on you first!" Lee fell to the ground, writhing in pain, twisting and turning and trying to get his arm around to touch the band of fire the Dragon had laid across his spine.

"How do you like your Alliance of Life now?" rumbled Kask as he yanked Lee to his feet and flung him back in the direction of the others.

Lee shook his head in disbelief. A prisoner like all the others, and Kask still identified with his oppressors. Lee staggered to his feet and followed the rest of the prisoners on toward the hut at the center of the camp—where they would have their slave-bands installed.

Following behind, Sawyer and Finn looked as broken as the rest. Finn mumbled as he walked, a steady stream of quiet, inventive curses. Sawyer had long since stopped asking him for explanations of some of the more esoteric terms. He grabbed Finn quickly to keep him from stumbling and asked him softly, "Can you make it?"

Finn grunted. He looked bad. A lot of the color had drained from his face; his body seemed racked with chills and fever. But he merely nodded and said, "I can handle it. The spells remain bearable."

"Finn—they keep getting stronger. And closer together. You don't have enough time to recover from the first one before the next one begins."

"I have six hours between them now. I'll manage." He shrugged off his brother's grasp. "I'll make it. Or I'll die trying."

"Yes," agreed Sawyer. "That's what I fear. If we intend to get out of here, we'd better do it quickly, while you still have the strength."

"Don't worry about me."

"I have to. I promised your mother."

And then the Dragon Guards nudged them forward with their whips. Sawyer and Finn exchanged their last two looks as free men—and then the Dragon pushed the slave-bands down onto their heads.

TOP SOIL

Thoska-Roole had no indigenous life of its own. Whatever lived here, whatever survived here, had arrived as a stranger. The starships had delivered their cargos of passengers and stowaways. Along with the miners had come the rats and parasites and the diseases.

Some of the more foolhardy—those who couldn't find a reason to leave—believed that Thoska-Roole might someday bloom. They knew that all life depends on six inches of dirt. If they could manufacture that six inches, they could turn the deserts into forests. They believed that they could make a paradise here.

So they created hell. They turned it on and let it run—and conveniently forgot that hell cannot exist without the damned. Here huge infernal machines clatter and bang, clunk and churn. They grind the rocks into powder, then mix them with garbage, sewage, and tailored bacteria to make a viscous "rock soup." Then the resulting mess sits for a while in great stinking heaps. It ferments, it simmers and stews and generally gives nature a very bad name—but eventually it turns into topsoil. The natives say that you can tell the ripeness of the soil by how bad it smells. Indeed, the smell alone constitutes cruel and unusual punishment.

Here at the bottom of Death Canyon, where it opens up onto the Plain of Sorrows, lay the topsoil factories for the sprawling farms of New South MesaPort. The labor camps provided the arms and the legs and the backs. MesaPort provided the garbage, the waste, and the prisoners to replace the ones who died.

The condemned men lived and breathed rock soup. It clung to their skins, it filled up their lungs, it grayed their hair, and it dulled their senses until everything smelled and tasted and looked the same. They worked until they died, and then their bodies became part of the soup as well.

The prisoners shoveled and wheeled and carried all the sewage and manure without complaint. They *couldn't* complain. On the day they arrived, they had their slave-bands installed, unremovable prisons wrapped around their foreheads, binding them and steering them. Whether they wanted to or not, the slave-bands would *make* them work. They retained just enough consciousness to know how much they hurt.

All the races—all except the Vampires, of course— had fair representation among the damned; but humans, of course, had the majority share. The Vampires hated them the most—perhaps because the humans represented the *true* species from which all others descended, if not in fact, then certainly in spirit.

Only a single Dragon labored here among the lesser races, a deliberate insult to him and the family whose crest he wore, but an insult deemed appropriate to the crime he had committed. Sullenly, Kask bore his burden, terribly shamed by his dishonor; but he resented even more the dishonor of those who had sent him here.

High up on the slopes of trash and refuse, a tiny creature gasped in recognition. He knew this Dragon.

This monster had brought him and his siblings across the light-years to this terrible place. He growled deep in his throat—an embarrassingly high-pitched sound—but then, as he saw the stinging whips come slashing down, he began to realize that this Dragon, and all the other poor creatures accompanying it, had come here as unwilling slaves, and his growl became a whimper of dismay. His tail drooped pitifully.

Little Ibaka couldn't stand to see even a Dragon in pain.

THE CHILDREN

The pack of orphans—all ages, all sizes, ragged and dirty, some human, most not, all scrawny—prowled hungrily through the garbage of Death Canyon. Today they had ventured dangerously close to the edges of the labor camp.

A new child had begun running with the pack of pitiful children—Ibaka, the dog boy. Smaller than the rest, he had learned fast how to survive in this metallic wilderness. One of the older children, a gender-female human boy[35] named Slash, had taken a fancy to him. She

[35]Genetically male, but bioformed to function as a female.

Several centuries previous to this narrative, the Regency had begun a deliberate policy of adjusting the availability of breeding licenses to restrict the ratio of female births in various sentient species. While this admittedly heavy-handed method of social engineering did have the desired effect of limiting the growth potential of any race that might grow in sufficient numbers to challenge the Phaestor aristocracy, it also produced widespread "mating psychoses" and "bonding frustration" among the many young unpartnered males of the affected races—particularly humans. The Regency responded by li-

took him under her protection, not entirely for unselfish reasons. She had already figured out that she would rather cuddle up around a warm furry pup on a cold night than shiver alone under a thin blanket. Slash had no illusions that Ibaka could provide her any protection against the occasional rapist, but Slash had already worked out her own defenses for that possibility.

"Listen to me," she explained, pointing down the steep slope of trash and slag. They studied the labor camp with impugnity. "I know it looks dangerous to get too close to the labor camp, but if you take care, you should try to stay as close to the camp as you can—at least at first, until you learn how to survive higher up the canyon. The prisoners can't hurt you, not while they wear those silver bands on their heads. See, look—if they haven't finished eating when their break ends, they have to leave their food rations behind. We can sneak down and get them."

They watched for a while. Slash knew that even if someone below spotted them, they could hide in the endless tunnels undermining the trash before anyone could even aim a scatterbeam. She pointed out landmarks in the camp and explained the actions of the guards and the prisoners.

Abruptly, she ordered him to hide. "Get down!" Slash whispered, pulling him down out of sight. Duckwaddling, she crept along the gully of trash. Ibaka started to follow, but his curiosity made him hesitate. He held back just long enough to take a quick peek over the edge.

censing the development of "synthetic females" for mating and bonding, but not for breeding. By the time of these events, the implementation of these policies had become so widespread that many human males on the most rigidly controlled Phaestor worlds had never even seen a real female of their own species; gender-females remained the only experience of human femininity available to them.

Down below, a new group of prisoners came marching briskly out of the camp; they headed diagonally across the bottom of the slope toward the place the other children called the stink-farm. All the prisoners wore silvery bands around their heads. Ibaka wondered what the pretty headbands meant. The people who wore them all seemed so busy. For a while he wished he could wear a headband too. His brothers and sisters would all envy him so much—

And then he remembered. And realized. He would probably never see any of them again. And not his mother either.

He began to whimper. He sat there whimpering for a long time, until Slash came back and pulled him down into the dark corridors of slime and sewage where they both could find a pretense of safety and security. Slash had a hidden lair. They could go there. They could hold each other close and pretend they did it only for warmth.

She didn't ask him why he cried. She didn't need to. She simply held him in her lap and petted him gently. After a while, as a way of distracting himself, he asked her about the headbands on the prisoners.

She answered carefully, explaining to the best of her knowledge what she believed the headbands did. "See," said Slash. "The headband has little needles that drill into your head and take over the working of your body. Then anybody who has the controller unit can run you like a robot. Your poor body will have to do whatever the controller tells it to do, no matter what you want; no matter what you think or feel or choose."

At first Ibaka didn't believe her; then, when he did, he began to cry again—this time in even greater distress. He had never heard of anything so frightening. He hadn't dreamed such horrors existed.

"But can't they take the headbands off?" he asked when his whimpers finally began to subside.

"If they try, they die."

"But—" Ibaka pawed at his muzzle in confusion. He understood less and less every day. He had to find a way to rescue his brothers and sisters. He had to find a way for them all to go home. But nobody wanted to help him. Everybody only explained to him why nothing would work. "—don't they ever get to go *home*?"

Slash smiled sadly. How could she explain to this poor naive little waif? He had no concepts for this. She shook her head and patted Ibaka gently, smoothing his fur and pulling him to her. "Listen to me, sweet one," she said. "You must never let yourself get caught by the guards, or they'll put a headband on you too. They don't care. All criminals look the same in the stink-farm. And they get paid by the amount of topsoil they produce. So they'll work you and kill you and throw you in the rock soup with everything else. You must take great care. Promise me?"

"I promise." Ibaka looked to Slash as a surrogate mother. She gave him warmth and reassurance and helped him find food. In Ibaka's eyes Slash glowed like a radiant creature; her long stringy hair took on a heavenly glow. Her pinched features and squinting eyes became beacons of kindness. Her thin arms and legs had the strength of a warrior. Her voice, when she sang to him, soared like an angel's.

Ibaka had surprisingly little pretense about his situation. He could not imagine himself safe here or anywhere, not ever again; but when he cuddled himself comfortably into Slash's protecting arms, at least he didn't hurt quite so much as he did before.

THE SPACERS' GUILD

Star-Captain Neena Linn-Campbell did not find satisfaction at the Thoska-Roole offices of the IOG.[36] Instead, what she found left her so

---

[36]Because of the distances and the speeds involved, no interstellar authority has ever succeeded in imposing a uniform code of conduct where the participants have not already embraced it willingly.

Other than the technocratic feudalism of the Regency, which does not function as a uniform authority in any case, but only according to the goals, desires, and whims of its individual Lords and their Ladies, the only significant effort to define a uniform standard of conduct and authority in the Palethetic Cluster comes from the Spacers' Guild.

Ideally, the government of every planet or moon that hosts interstellar travel—every authority that operates a legitimately recognized Starport—has also signed the Minimum Basic Agreement of the Interstellar Operations Guild, committing itself to a standard of behavior that all space-faring vessels can depend on. Without the IOG seal of approval, a Starport cannot operate. No Guild member would allow his ship to land or receive goods at an outlaw facility.

The Guild handles the collection of all taxes for the representative worlds; disciplinary matters of its own members as well as ground-based employees; and arbitrates all disputes over contracts

appalled that she made an irrevocable decision, one on a level with the famous brinewood betrayal that had eventually toppled a government.

The meeting had not begun well. From there it went downhill. The local Vice Applicator-Adjutant refused to hear Captain Campbell's claim against the Thoska-Roole Regents' misappropriation of her First Officer, a LIX-class bioform named Ota.

"You have my sympathies," the Vice Applicator-Adjutant said, putting on his sincerest expression. "But unfortunately, the Guild lacks authority in this kind of matter."

Neena Linn-Campbell wasn't fooled. This pompous preening popinjay had a perfumed pompadour piled high upon his head. He stood on his podium, wearing pink ruffled silks and a dark-blue velvet jacket. He seemed about as sympathetic as a candied vulture.

Captain Campbell glanced quickly to Robin and Gito; she made a surreptitious *keep still* gesture. *I'll handle this.* She turned back to the Vice Applicator-Adjutant.

"You refuse to provide assistance to a member of the Guild?"

and breaches thereof. The Regency could not function without the approval and cooperation of the Guild.

On most worlds IOG officials also run most of the ancillary operations of the Starport, taking an additional percentage off the top to cover the operating expenses of the local Guild offices. In reflection of this fact, IOG installations usually tower over all the other installations at most Starports. Nevertheless, on some worlds IOG authority remains tenuous.

On Thoska-Roole, for example, the IOG held on to its venue only by strategically applying bribes and kickbacks to the ruling Vampire authorities. The Phaestor had long had their eyes on the power of the Guild and had begun looking for ways to appropriate first the Guild's operations, and ultimately its access to the spreading wealth of the interstellar community.

"It appears to me that you have exhausted all of your legal options."

"Not me, you fool! Ota! The bioform carries a second-class license!"

"You don't have to insult me. I understood you the first time. I tell you again, the Guild cannot act on your behalf in this matter. The local authorities take precedence in matters of criminality—"

"What criminality?"

The Vice Applicator-Adjutant shrugged and shook his head. "You would know that better than I. The arrest of your First Officer did not simply happen accidentally, did it?"

"Lady Zillabar seized the bioform because I would not give it to her as a gift. She used the law to steal what she couldn't obtain legally."

The Vice-Applicator Adjutant coughed with embarrassment. "May I remind you, Captain Campbell, that we routinely record the operations of this office for later review. The Regency also maintains access to the recordings. It would not do for you to make statements that might appear ... ah, seditious."

Gito rumbled warningly. Robin put a hand on his rock-hard shoulder to hold him back. Captain Campbell ignored them both.

The Vice Applicator-Adjutant looked around nervously. He appeared to make up his mind about something, then switched on a device hidden under his rostrum. Annoying sounds, vaguely resembling music, began to fill the room. Campbell, Gito, and Robin exchanged curious glances.

The man now stepped down from his podium and approached them gingerly. He wore patent-leather slippers and knee-high leggings of shimmering white that showed off the delicate curves of his calves to best advantage. He chose his steps—and his words—as carefully as if he danced on knives. "If I could speak candidly," he whispered, "I would advise you to forget this entire matter, return to your ship as fast as you can, and break orbit immediately."

Captain Campbell raised one eyebrow skeptically. "I assume that you have a reason for offering this advice?"

The man shook his head. He appeared to regret having made his initial statement. He started to turn back to his podium, but Captain Campbell grabbed his velvet sleeve and insisted, "Tell me!"

He sighed. He lowered his voice almost to inaudibility. "The Lady Zillabar has filed additional complaints against your ship and your crew for failing to provide the standard of service she contracted for. She has withheld payment of her fee. She has filed suit. And her arbitrators will probably rule in her favor tomorrow. Unless you've departed before then, she'll seize your vessel to guarantee the claim."

Neena Linn-Campbell released the man's sleeve in shock. He quickly retreated back to the safety of his podium, before she could grab him again.

"And the Guild allowed this?" she demanded, not caring if the recording devices picked up her words or not.

The man waved his hands impatiently at her, trying to hush her, trying to get her to keep still, or at least lower her voice. It didn't work. "The Guild has no authority in this matter," he insisted. His voice had taken on a tone of exasperation. "Besides, the matter involves only a bioform. Forget it. Buy another!"

Star-Captain Neena Linn-Campbell did not believe what she had heard. *Buy another?* "The bioform paid its Guild dues. And you continue to insist that you will not act on behalf of a dues-paying member?"

The Vice Applicator-Adjutant grew more annoyed and uncertain. "I can offer you the appropriate insurance forms. You can file a claim on the animal's loss. I can't offer you anything better than that."

"I see," said Captain Campbell. She turned away for a moment, muttering something to herself—either a curse or a spell or an incantation; certainly not a prayer, not in that tone of voice. Gito and Robin both backed away. Robin studied the plaster ornamentation of the ceiling, Gito examined the marbled tiles of the floor.

At last Captain Campbell stopped. She had reached a decision. She took a breath. She quickly unpinned her Guild insignia from her black uniform and held it out to the Vice Applicator-Adjutant. "Here," she said. "I have no further need of this."

"I beg your pardon?"

"What value does this trinket have? Certainly, it displays no artistic merit."

"Madam, you cannot possibly mean this!" The man's words tumbled out in a fluster of confusion.

"I can—and I do!"

"But—but you can't turn in your Guild credential."

"Why not? As a credential it certainly has no worth. The organization behind it lacks all willingness to enforce its authority—so it has none. If not here, then not anywhere. I refuse to pay dues to support a Guild that has no teeth. I'll turn my vessel into a freebooter before I'll wear a Guild insignia again."

"I must warn you"—the Vice Applicator-Adjutant drew himself up to his full bureaucratic height—"that whatever freedom you may claim as a freebooter, you will pay heavily for it. Wherever you go, the planetary authorities will suspect you of piracy and other renegade actions. You will not have the Guild to stand behind you and protect you."

"I don't have the Guild standing behind me and protecting me now. Thank you, but I can no longer afford the dues of this organization. Come, Robin, Gito—let's get out of here and go someplace where we can breathe without having our nostrils filled with the stench of sanctimony and fraud."

"You would do well to watch your tongue, Madam—" But Captain Campbell and her crew had already vanished out the door.

The Vice Applicator-Adjutant debated with himself for a moment. Eventually, greed won the debate and he opened a communication channel. "Get me the Regency Liaison Officer."

A DRAGON'S WILL

Under the slave-bands Sawyer and Finn retained just enough awareness of their situation to appreciate its hellishness. The Eye of God glared down on the camp and turned everything gloriously bright. The trash sparkled like diamond filigree. The heaps of stinking refuse took on a gorgeous pink aura. The towering cliffs of Death Canyon glistened and shone in shades of brooding magenta and crimson wine. The sky gleamed.

The prisoners could not appreciate it. Their bodies moved mechanically, rhythmically, dreadfully. The pain crept up their arms and legs, rooted itself in their spines, and clawed its way up toward their eyes. First the sweat, then the tears, and finally the blood poured down their arms and legs. They wailed and cried for mercy, but still their bodies hammered on.

Despite his continued dizziness, Finn still worked—he staggered, but he had no choice. As long as his body remained physically capable of working, it would work, regardless of his feelings or intentions. The world took on a hallucinatory atmosphere. Lights and

colors sparkled and faded. Sounds jangled at him in a
symphony of confusion. He existed in a wondrous daze.
Things and people lost all relevance—everything floated
in and out of his consciousness without meaning, while
his hands and legs continued to move, continued to act
and work, totally out of his control.

Even before the end of their first shift Sawyer had
become despondent. He wondered how long they could
survive. Finn would certainly die first. He, Sawyer,
would get to experience the full range of Death Canyon's
repertoire of despair: first rage, then futility, then madness, and finally death—

Occasionally, the Vampires who controlled them
gave them breaks—more often when the controllers grew
tired than when the prisoners did. The Phaestor aristocracy did not consider the control of prisoners a prestigious assignment, regarding it at most as a convenient
out-of-the way hole in which to tuck those best kept
away from polite company. They had placed too many of
their youthful troublemakers and fools here.

The high-spirited young controllers considered the
whole operation a game. They would laugh among themselves and make bets on how long this one or that one
would last. Sometimes, when they grew truly bored, they
would make the prisoners perform ghastly puppet shows,
dancing and capering and gibbering like baboons. Other
times they forced the prisoners to perform obscene antics,
either alone or with each other. The poor victims
couldn't look at each other after sharing such a shame.

On their breaks the prisoners never spoke of the
controllers' actions, but the urge for revenge lived in the
hearts of each of them, stared out through their eyes.
Each of the creatures enslaved by the bands wished for
only one thing: just a single opportunity to have his
hands around the throat of one of those who treated
them with such unholy contempt.

During the first break Justice Harry Mertz had

spoken up clearly, "If this represents all the hospitality that Lady Zillabar offers her prisoners, then she doesn't deserve to have any." But since then he hadn't said anything at all. He seemed almost a broken man. Sawyer wondered if Justice Mertz would last even as long as Finn. Finn, at least, had the advantage of youth and physical endurance.

Elsewhere the other prisoners also suffered. One old man had already collapsed and died. Another probably wouldn't last the night. Most pitiful, the lumbering Dragon, Kask, still struggled with the painful confusion of his slave-band. During the infrequent rest periods, he staggered around the compound, trying to pry the headband off, trying to resist the painful shocks that kept slamming him down to his knees, grunting in agony.

Even when the controllers had them working, Kask still resisted—his incredible physical strength refused to submit to the will of another mind. Several times the controllers had tried to recalibrate his slaveband, but each time the results proved unsatisfactory. No Dragon had ever worn a slave-band before; no one knew how to calibrate the system for a superaugmented battlefield-grade nervous system.

Once Kask thought he had seen Ibaka up on the cliffs, watching them. The little dog-child had ducked quickly down behind a rock, but Kask had seen enough to have certainty. He dropped what he carried and struggled again with his headband. The controllers shocked him into unconsciousness that time. His body flung itself back and forth upon the ground, writhing in the sewage until at last sheer exhaustion brought his frenzies to a labored halt.

Since that moment Kask had worked to retain his awareness; no matter what orders his body had to obey, his eyes remained ceaselessly searching the surrounding hills of trash. If Ibaka appeared again, Kask would know it. He tried to husband his strength, but the effort of resisting the slave-band tired him even more than cooperating with it. And yet—Kask remained unbowed. Somehow he managed to retain enough of his own will to resist.

Kask had a plan.

He had begun to leave his rations only half-consumed. Although the hunger racked his belly, he did it deliberately, day after day, meal after meal. He had studied the hills very carefully. He knew that packs of hungry children lived up there, waiting, sneaking down while the prisoners labored, to search around the fire pit for unfinished rations. Kask had seen the children out of the corners of his eyes. He never saw them when he stood up straight and looked for them, but he had seen the quick flickers of motion as they ducked and hid. He knew.

He knew that the orphans who lived up in the hills of trash paid closer attention to his movements than the controllers did who took turns operating his slave-band. He knew that they would come down for the food he left behind. Sooner or later Ibaka would come. And then he would catch him. He hadn't worked out the details of that part yet, but he would.

Kask hadn't seen any of the ragged children watching him today. Nevertheless, he remained certain that his actions did not go unobserved. The scroungers had picked up every ration pack he'd put out for them. Now he held his unfinished ration pack high over his head, deliberately taunting the unseen watchers in the hills. He turned around and around with it, then he made sure to place it carefully on the large flat rock he used as a place to sit. There it would not escape the notice of the hungry dog-child.

Somehow he would catch Ibaka. He would return the pup to the Lady. The Lady would forgive him. Perhaps she would even honor him for his unswerving loyalty. In this way he would erase the stain of dishonor from his name and from his family. Yes, he would catch

Ibaka, and that would make everything right again. Kask had a very simple vision; he could not imagine that the Lady's attention might have already moved on to larger and more pressing matters.

Kask had patience. If not today, then tomorrow. If not tomorrow, then the day after. He would wait. Eventually, he would catch Ibaka. Eventually, he would get out of here. He *would* reclaim his honor.

The slave-band began to tingle in warning. The meal break had ended. Kask's mind remained aware, but his body began to move of its own volition. It turned away and trudged heavily back to work. His tail dragged in the mud behind him.

It didn't take long for the bait of Kask's unfinished meal to catch the attention of his intended prey. Almost immediately, Slash and Ibaka came darting down the slope. They had gotten too hungry and too careless. Lured by Kask's fat ration, they hurried quickly toward the circle where the prisoners ate. They kept well into the shadows for as long as they could. Finally, at last, they dashed across the open ground.

Slash circled quickly around the fire pit, inspecting the other discarded ration packs. Ibaka ran immediately to the one that Kask had laid on the rock. He knew that Kask had left it for him; he didn't care. He would grab it and run away and fool the Dragon again. He'd done it before—

Abruptly, across the compound, Kask smelled them.

Despite the slave-band, he straightened up to look around—half a klick away, his controller fell out of his chair from the feedback shock. The Dragon didn't even notice. He sniffed the air again, looking around. His nostrils flared. His powerful arms and legs began to flex, temporarily under his own control again. And then he focused—

Across the compound Ibaka, the dog boy, caught in

the act of reaching for the half-consumed meal, stared back at him in a strange mix of curiosity, fear, and even pity.

Kask grunted, and his eyes widened as he recognized the little pup. His blood began to surge.

And then everything happened at once.

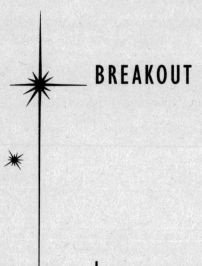

BREAKOUT

It began with a terrible roar that issued from Kask's throat like a volcano preparing to erupt. And then he moved. He started lumbering toward the dog-boy, like an avalanche, building speed as he ran, accelerating like a battle-tank. His heavy tail lashed furiously behind him.

In the control tower at the center of the camp, the operators struggled vainly to bring the roaring Dragon down. But Kask had shifted into battle-frenzy; he had become immune to pain, and all the staggering electric shocks they sent pouring into his body simply went unfelt—or at least, unheeded. Kask went roaring across the camp.

Ibaka broke and ran; so did Slash. Confused, the dog-child scrambled first one way, then the other. The furious Dragon came pounding after him. Kask couldn't match the little pup's maneuverability—he skidded and slid—but he picked himself up and kept on coming.

The sirens went off everywhere. They blasted their warnings up and down the canyon. The ear-splitting shrieks had the force of hammer blows.

Slash had headed for the hills, then stopped uncertainly when she saw that Ibaka hadn't followed. Ibaka couldn't get to her. The Dragon blocked his way. He started running headlong into the center of the camp, hoping to circle around. Reluctantly, Slash followed, trying to avoid the other prisoners, but also needing to stay close to her friend.

The Dragon bellowed and charged. He came crunching through the piles of slag, and even the occasional hut. Whichever direction the puppy ran, that way Kask came following. Anything in the way got crushed.

As Kask's operator worked in vain, the other Phaestor joined him, trying to override the raw power of Kask's furious intention. Nothing could stop the monster. The young Phaestor began to panic. Their own charges went forgotten while they frantically tried one control circuit after another. All over the camp the prisoners began to straighten in wonderment and confusion. Nothing like this had ever happened before.

Ibaka ran for the big tower in the center of the camp. Maybe he could hide under that. But when he got closer, he saw that it stood on high stilts. It would provide no shelter at all. He ran through its legs and kept on going. Kask followed—he came crashing through the same space, unmindful of the discrepancy of sizes.

Kask knocked out one of the tower's spindly legs. The tower teetered—the prisoners cheered as they turned and realized. The tower began to topple. Slowly, slowly, it came tumbling down. A great roar of triumph went up. The prisoners came running, carrying their pitchforks and shovels. Those without tools picked up pieces of jagged metal from the ground, or even rocks.

The Vampire controllers tried to leap free of the tower, but the growing mob of prisoners chased them across the broken ground, herding them, sweeping them up against a fallen wall. The grinning slaves caught their masters and brought them savagely down. The pitchforks rose and fell, stabbed and stabbed again. The shovels thudded into the bloody bodies. They clubbed the Vampires viciously, over and over again, flinging their limp forms back and forth. The Vampires had long since died, but the prisoners didn't care.

Sawyer and Finn did not join in the riot. When Sawyer saw the tower start to tumble, he ran toward it. When the controllers ran, he jumped into the debris, looking for a weapon of any kind. Lee-1169 came in right behind him. Sawyer grabbed the first rifle, tossed the second to Lee, and a third for his brother. Lee grabbed the last weapon, and the two of them leapt free. All around them the control consoles sparked and sputtered as their self-destruct fuses began activating. Exultant prisoners began pulling off their hated headbands and throwing them to the sky as hard as they could. They knew they had only seconds to spare before the Dragons sent out an all-band paralyzing signal—or worse, the death impulse.

Sawyer, Finn, and Lee discarded their own headbands, then ran as hard as they could—the blast of the exploding tower flattened them to the ground, deafened them—but they jumped up again immediately and kept on running. Sawyer grabbed Finn; the stocky man stumbled, but he kept up with the others. "Come on!" Lee yelled. "Rations! We'll need food!" And the three of them ran for the hut that served as the camp's kitchen.

There they found Harry, also unbanded and stuffing a sack with packets of food and other supplies. He grinned and tossed them sacks of their own, and the four of them began pulling down piles of stores from the shelves—weapons, battery packs, blankets, everything.

Outside again, they hesitated—out onto the plains? Or up the canyon?

From here they could see prisoners running in all directions. Many had already scattered up into the junk piles where the orphans ran. Scrawny children who had come out to watch the riot now came scrambling down the hill to look for food and clothing. The prisoners scattered and fled.

And now, coming through the rubble like a crushing machine, bearing his struggling prize high over his head, Kask strode like a conquering giant. Ibaka screamed and yelped. Slash came shouting after, bating at the giant with a stick. Mostly, he ignored her. Once he stopped and turned and started after her, but she ducked away. Kask had no interest in the boy-child, so he continued back on course. And again Slash came hammering after.

"The main access elevators up the cliff?" suggested Lee. "I know the city. We can disappear—"

Sawyer shook his head. "Too many guards at the top. They'll shut off the power. Then they'll come down in force." He pointed up. "And besides, they have gun emplacements everywhere. No. We'll have to go up the canyon and hide out until we can find another way up."

"Why not the desert?"

"No chance. Where can you go? They'll scan us from the air and pick us off like vermin."

"All right," Lee agreed with a nod. "Let's go."

"Finn?"

"I can travel."

Harry shouldered his pack and followed. "If you fellows don't mind, I'd like to come with you."

"If you can keep up—"

"I can keep up."

The four of them hurried away from the labor camp. In the distance they could already hear the sirens of the Dragon Guards. Soon the high-pitched shrieks of their beams would follow.

THE CAPTAIN OF
THE GUARD

The battle-robots and the
Dragon Guards came pouring out of the elevators; first
one elevator emptied, then the other then they immediately sped back to the top of the cliff.

The Dragons took up immediate defensive positions around the base of the elevator tower; the robots
moved out beyond them, picking their way like spiders,
their periscopes scanning in all directions. They shot at
anything that moved.

Again the elevators dropped to the surface and disgorged another cargo of Dragons and robots. Again and
again the elevators repeated their trips, until a whole
company of warriors had taken up their positions around
the base of the tower.

Now the battle-robots began spreading out across
the broken ground toward the labor camp. First one line
of robots would advance and take scanning positions,
then the next. The Dragon Guards moved stolidly behind
them. In this way they advanced steadily toward the canyon.

Occasionally, the robots would slash out with their

beams, cutting down anything larger than a rat that moved. Pretty soon nothing moved. Only a few bodies lay smoldering in the acrid air.

A roar came bellowing out of the distance—a Dragon's voice. "Don't shoot," it called. "Don't shoot."

The robots swiveled their guns to focus on the probable target. Something waited behind a heap of metal pipe casings.

Captain Lax-Varney, the Lady's new Captain of the Guard came forward and peered across the intervening space. He thought he recognized the voice. "Hold fire," he ordered the robots. He roared out his answer. "Who goes there? Identify yourself."

"I have the Lady's gift. I caught it. I want to bring it in and reclaim my honor," the voice called back. "I hatched from the egg of Yetzl. I trained on Gzorny. I served under the glory of Naye-Ninneya. I wear the name of Kask and bear the insignia of the Jeweled Dragon, Left Hind Claw, Fourth Cusp."

Lax-Varney rumbled unpleasantly. He did not like this task, but he had no choice. He had just gained this promotion. He wanted to keep it. If he failed here, in this task, he would die in the same disgrace as his predecessor. He suspected a trap.

He considered his options. The escaped prisoners would certainly seek to regain access to the city. He didn't dare let that happen; but without access to the master-devices for the headbands, he had no means of regaining control over any individual prisoner. Fortunately for Lax-Varney, this situation already had a clear resolution—the Dragon Lord had given him definite orders.

He called out, "No such name as Kask exists. No such person exists. The Claw no longer records that name. The family no longer acknowledges it. No such person as Kask ever existed. You lie."

"I stand here now. I'll come out and you can look at me."

Captain Lax-Varney gestured to his troops; they moved up to flank him. "Come on out, then," he called.

From behind the heap of rubble, something moved—in the brightness they could clearly see the shape of it—a Dragon. He held something small and furry above his head. The thing squeaked and squirmed unhappily.

Lax-Varney recognized the Dragon. He wished he didn't. He wished he didn't have to give his next order, but he did. He turned around slowly, ponderously. He turned his back on the unfortunate Dragon. "He lies," the Captain said to his troops. "Therefore he dies. Kill him."

Across the intervening space Kask realized immediately what the turning of the Captain meant. "No!" he shouted. "I have served honorably! I deserve loyalty!"

"Kill him!" Lax-Varney bellowed at his troops.

They hesitated. They had never had to shoot a brother Dragon before. Some of them knew this warrior-lizard. Most of them believed that killing a brother would disgrace the corps. They couldn't do it. They couldn't believe that Lax-Varney had even ordered it.

"Let me approach!" called Kask. "Let me have a fair hearing! I carry the Lady's gift. She wants it back!"

Lax-Varney lashed his tail angrily. He growled something at his troops. They lowered their weapons, but now they turned their backs to Kask as well. "Robots!" ordered Lax-Varney. "Fire at will. Destroy the target. Now."

But even before Lax-Varney had completed the order to shoot, Kask had already leapt sideways, back behind the cover of the moldering refuse. The beams of the robots slashed into it, igniting it.

Kask took off headlong for the hills—

DEATH CANYON

The beams sizzled through the air. Suddenly, the robots spread out through the camp, moving faster than a man could run. They fired their weapons in rapid bursts, burning and blasting a path for the Dragons to follow.

Kask ran for cover. He held Ibaka close to his chest and charged toward the broken opening in the cliffs. He didn't think he could outrun the robots in the open. Maybe he could dodge them in the rubble. "No! No! That way!" squealed Ibaka, squirming in Kask's heavy grip, and pointing toward a gap. Without thinking, Kask followed Ibaka's course—around the mounds of fermenting soil, the path widened and gave Kask room to run at full tilt.

Suddenly, it forked—Ibaka pointed again. "To the left! To the left!" Kask went charging to the left. He realized where Ibaka wanted him to go—*up Death Canyon*. He lowered his head and bellowed like a bull. "If I must go into Death Canyon," he recited,[37] "then I will do so *at a run!*"

---

[37]*Owed to a Dragon*, by the poet Aristol.

It thrilled him oddly to pound across the ground like this, up the slope and into the heart of legend, the place where unnamed horrors lurked. He loved the blood-surge of action, the excitement of the chase. Up through the rubble and wreckage, up the slopes, up the hills, up the hidden pathways of the children—again and again he followed Ibaka's direction.

Ahead now, the path became narrower and more jagged. Some of the prisoners had come up this way. Some of the scrawny children too. Kask overtook them and pounded on. They leapt out of his way in panic, then stared at him in amazement as he hurtled past.

Sawyer, Finn, Lee, and Harry heard him thundering and roaring long before he reached them. "Dragon coming—" said Finn.

"Dragons scream when they come?"

Finn pulled his brother out of the way just in time. Kask charged past them without even noticing their presence. Down below, the sound of the battle-robots came screeching up the canyon. Kask had more pursuers than they realized. Sawyer and Finn exchanged terrified glances. "Uh-oh—"

Lee and Harry heard it too. "Come on!" they shouted.

A gender-female human boy, skinny and dirty, came running after them. "No, not that way—that leads to a dead end!" But too late. They didn't hear her. She followed after, screaming incoherently.

Kask reached the end of the path first—some kind of abandoned installation. Pipes and tubes lay tumbled everywhere, broken and scattered. Sawyer and Finn came skidding in after the Dragon; then Lee and Harry. They stopped in dismay. Three other prisoners came running after, almost bumping into them; Sawyer recognized them from the slave camp. Still more came hurrying up the path.

"Which way?" demanded Kask.

Ibaka pointed at a hole in the wall, the outlet of a pipe. The faintest trickle of dirty black water dripped unsteadily from it.

Kask and the humans all looked at each other. They looked to Ibaka.

"Well, I can get into it," said Ibaka. And then he understood. "Oh," he said.

"I'll kill him," Sawyer muttered. Ibaka flinched.

Slash came hurtling into the clearing then. She ran directly up to Kask. "Give me the puppy," she demanded. From down the canyon came the noise of guns.

Kask ignored her. He looked to Sawyer and Finn. "We must fight!"

"We can't win!"

"Then we'll die like heroes—with honor!"

"You can have my share of honor! I have other plans," Sawyer said. He started looking around.

Kask expressed his opinion of that course of action. He spat at Sawyer's feet. Sawyer stepped back distastefully. The puddle of Dragon spit smoldered and smoked. "Nice," he admitted, with wry admiration. "Very nice."

A beam shattered the rocks overhead, triggering a small avalanche. They ducked out of the way as part of the cliff came sliding downward, missing them by only a few meters.

Finn Markham nudged his brother in the ribs. "I like this better. This looks like much more fun than shoveling shit for the rest of my life."

Sawyer grinned back. "But at least this we have experience with."

Finn grunted. "Well, I sure hope you have a Plan B—"

"*Me?* Why don't you come up with a good idea once in a while?"

"I did, remember? And we ended up here."

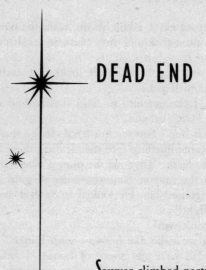

DEAD END

Sawyer climbed partway up the cliff so he could look down the canyon. As bad as the carnage sounded, the view of it looked even worse.

The battle-robots had no compunction about killing. They shot prisoners and children with equal accuracy. They didn't care. They swept back and forth across the canyon, crashing through the rubble. They smashed and destroyed everything that lay before them. Their beams stabbed out with sudden fire, slashing and burning.

Sawyer jumped and skidded down from his perch. He'd already seen too much. But the terrible sounds continued—the screams of the injured and the dying, suddenly cut short by the higher, nastier screams of the beams of the battle-machines. They could hear them crunching steadily, nightmarishly after them.

"Come on!" shouted Slash. "Let's get out of here!"

For the first time they all looked at her—a gender-female human boy? Giving orders?

"Well, do you want to get out or not? This way!" She pointed.

Sawyer and Finn exchanged a what-have-we-got-to-lose look, shrugged, and followed after. The others came behind them, even Kask; he still carried the struggling Ibaka.

"What did they do here?" Sawyer asked her.

"—drainage, for some kind of installation farther up the canyon. Nobody uses it for anything anymore." She led them quickly up to where the water fell from a series of broken pipes into a brackish catch basin. The water flowed over the top, down a scumble of white rocks, and disappeared into the dark opening of a huge sluice tube. "Down that way!"

The growing crowd of prisoners pushed close, eager to get away; they looked fearfully back down the canyon. Lee held them back. "Where does it lead?" he demanded.

Slash shook her head. "To another catch-basin, and then another, and another, all the way down."

"Down to where?" Impatience edged his words.

Harry stepped forward. "I know where—you won't like it. This goes all the way down to the tank at the bottom of the Old City detainment. You remember that, don't you? This water feeds the pool."

"Ugh," said Finn, wrinkling his face in disgust.

"Wait a minute—" said Sawyer. "We can get out before it empties into the pool."

"I wish I had your faith in Ghu—" said Harry, "—so I could wish as eagerly to meet my maker."

"I don't need faith," said Sawyer. "I majored in urban plumbing." He sat down on a rock and began pulling off his boots. "This thing has to have an access before it pours into the prison tank." He tossed his boots into the sack of rations he carried and tied it to his belt. He slung his rifle over his shoulder.

"And what if you've made a mistake?" asked Finn.

"Then, my dear brother, I won't have to worry about it, will I?"

"You, Soy, have taken all leave of your senses."

"I know that. Do you have a better idea?"

"Yes! Let the Dragon go first."

"Huh?"

"So he can catch the handle and open the access from the inside. What if you don't have the strength? He will. Then he can pull the rest of us out."

Kask shook his head and rumbled unpleasantly. "No. I will not let go of the dog-boy."

"Give him to me. I promise you we'll bring him if you'll pull us out on the other end," said Sawyer.

Kask frowned. "I have never trusted a human before. Why should I trust you now?"

In answer to his question, a sizzling beam came screaming through the air, slicing a great chunk of rock off the cliff above them.

"How about that for an argument?"

Kask grunted and nodded his head. He thrust Ibaka into Sawyer's arms. "If you don't bring the dog-boy with you, I'll kill you."

"Yeah, yeah. I got it. Let's go."

Kask grunted again and began lowering himself into the tube. Just before he vanished, Finn called to him, "The rest of us will follow at one-minute intervals. You've got to catch us."

"I will."

"Okay, then—"

But Kask had already let go. The pipe swallowed him up, and he slid away into the darkness.

DOWN THE TUBES

The air stank of smoke and burned flesh. The scorching beams came more frequently now. Rocks tumbled from the cliffs on all sides. The abrupt screams of the dying sounded frighteningly close.

"They won't stop until they've cleaned out the entire canyon—" Lee said. More prisoners kept arriving every moment. They crowded into the narrow space surrounding the catch-basin, shouting in panic.

"Wait!" said Sawyer. "We have to time this. One-minute intervals!"

"But you have to go first," Lee told him. "You have the dog-boy."

"All right, all right. Make sure Finn gets sent down after me."

"It'll happen. Get going!"

Sawyer handed Ibaka to Finn and climbed over the edge of the channel, a much harder step for him than for the big Dragon. The water churned coldly around him— and it stank. He gritted his teeth as he sat down in it. The wet chill seeped up into his pants and straight up his back. With his left hand he held tightly to the edge of the channel—a task made all the more difficult because the cold rushing water pushed at him so strongly. Finn pushed Ibaka into his arms—"Good luck!" Sawyer managed a weak grin and released his grip on the rocks. The surging water swept him and the dog-child on his lap instantly away and down toward the blackness of the tube. He didn't even have time to wave.

Darkness swallowed them up. Ibaka screamed in terror. Sawyer screamed too—half in jest, half in sympathetic resonance. The dirty water pushed them headlong into total blackness. The light behind them vanished. Down the tube they hurtled. They had no idea what the channel held, what traps or twists or sudden drops.

At one time this great channel had described a graceful course of loops and curves as it wound its way down the canyon. At one time it had fed a whole series of efficient drainage basins and beautiful green filtration farms. Now it lay buried beneath rubble and debris, the detritus of the fabled city on the towering cliffs above. Now it lay forgotten, its channels covered, its basins clogged, its fields filled with waste and wreckage. The city didn't even remember the river it had built here. But the water still rushed down and down, beneath the piled trash, beneath the dirt, beneath the heavily armored legs of the Dragon Guards and the cold spider-feet of the robots—all unnoticed—around the jagged hills and raw escarpments, the great channel sweeping down the gullies, looping, turning, curving, dropping suddenly, then rushing madly forward again for a sudden almost-level dash. The water rushed in liquid panic, headlong and always down.

Inside the sluice tube, Sawyer and Ibaka did not share the same joy of construction as the long-dead architect of the channel. In the darkness all the terrifying loops and curves gave their ride down the conduit anything but a sense of grace and smoothness. Unexpected twists and turns punctuated their journey, always catch-

ing them by surprise. Sudden drops into nothingness left
their stomachs clenching and their hearts pounding. And
always they hurtled on in utter blackness.

On and on the water carried them. The ride went
on forever. Sawyer began to fear that he had made a big
mistake. His mind went into overdrive, summoning up
one possibility after another. Suppose the channel had ob-
structions in it or sudden breaks? What if razor-sharp
pieces of jagged metal lay ahead, waiting to rip great
slices out of them as they slid by? But, no—the Dragon
would have cleared away anything in the channel,
wouldn't he? His great bulk alone would push everything before him—

—unless he had become jammed somewhere up
ahead, unable to break free, drowned and clogging up the
tunnel with his body, like an armored cork, and the water damming up behind him in the pipe. Sawyer's heart
began to thud in panic at the thought. Everyone who
came after Kask would come slamming up against him,
adding their own weight to the dam, each one caught
and drowning in his turn, with no way up or out, and
the others piling up behind, no way to warn them. Sawyer could already feel the chilly water filling up his lungs.
He gasped for breath and hung on tight, trying not to
panic. But in the darkness, time stretched out forever.

The rushing water chilled and stank. Sawyer's
mind raced almost as fast. He couldn't escape his own
worst fears—all the things that might have gone wrong.
What if Kask had missed the access? Or what if someone
had permanently sealed it? Or what if the Dragon
couldn't grab him fast enough? Or what if the battle-
robots and the Dragon Guards stood waiting?

As they continued to bounce and tumble, the certainty grew in Sawyer that he had made a terrible mis-
judgment about the nature of this channel. Maybe it had
no access to grab at all. Maybe it just led inevitably to the
lake at the bottom of the Old City detainment. Maybe,

one by one, all the terrified prisoners would jump into the tube, and one by one, each and every one of them would end up sliding right back down into the waters of the dungeon where they'd started, only this time the deadly mayzel-fish would fatten on their flesh.

Finally even fear began to ebb, gave way to boredom, and then cold wet impatience. How far did this thing go, anyway?

And then, just when he had given up all hope— light!—and a hand the size of a wall reached down and plucked them both from the stream. Sawyer gasped in surprise and almost let go of Ibaka, but the dog-boy clutched at him, and Kask pulled them both, dripping wet and starting to shiver, up from the access pipe with ease. The giant Dragon laughed with delight at his prize. His gleaming teeth and the booming roar from his chest terrified Sawyer and Ibaka both.

TUBAL
LITIGATION

Kask grabbed Ibaka from Sawyer and started to rise. "I go now—"

"Wait a minute! You promised to pull us out!"

"I pulled you out."

"All of us."

"I made no such promise."

"Then you have no honor!" Sawyer shouted at the Dragon's back.

Kask stopped. He whirled around, his tail lashing against the stanchions and rocks that surrounded the pipe. "I have honor!"

"No, you don't! If you don't pull every single one of us out of that pipe right now, I'll tell the world that Kask the Dragon lies like a—a lawyer."

Kask hesitated, indecision struggling across his features.

"Now!" demanded Sawyer. "Get to the pipe!"

Holding Ibaka awkwardly in one hand, Kask squatted again by the access. He reached and scooped— and missed. The prisoner went screaming past. "Missed him," Kask grunted. "Sorry."

Sawyer stared at him, astonished at his indifference. "You did that on purpose!"

"No, I didn't. I'll get the next one," Kask said, without much enthusiasm. He shifted his position, anchoring Ibaka under his armpit, and reached down into the pipe even farther than before. He yanked—and pulled out Harry Mertz. He tossed him aside like a flopping fish.

"Finn? Did Finn go ahead of you?" Sawyer demanded.

Harry finished coughing and shook his head. "No, he didn't. They started to panic up there. They don't want to listen to Finn and Lee. Finn had to use his gun. He promised to stand guard until Lee and the girl-boy got down, but some of the others jumped in anyway—" Harry glanced around in confusion.

"Kask missed 'em. Once he had the pup again, he wanted to leave. It took a minute to convince him to keep his promise." To Harry's curious look, he added softly, "I had to rub his nose in it."

"Big job," Harry acknowledged. "I'll never underestimate you again."

Kask flipped another rider out of the sluice tube, this one skinny and shaking—Slash. She leapt away from the Dragon, glaring at him suspiciously. Ibaka yelped at her excitedly. She started for him, but Sawyer grabbed her and held her back. "Let him work—"

Kask grunted in annoyance. "Missed another one. They didn't space themselves out like you said." The screams still echoed in the tube.

Harry and Sawyer exchanged a glance and shuddered. Harry whispered. "Kind of like watching election returns come in—" Then, seeing Sawyer's face, he added, "Sorry. I thought you liked jokes."

"Ask me again after we get Finn out of there."

Kask yanked another prisoner out of the tube, one that neither of them recognized. He fell wetly to the ground, then began to crawl painfully away. He looked injured. Another prisoner came flopping down almost on top of him. And then a third. The Dragon had found a rhythm to his task. He missed another prisoner—muttered something nasty in a language no one understood—then reached back in the pipe and pulled out Lee-1169. "Aha!" he laughed. "I caught a traitor!" But he tossed Lee aside like all the rest and bent back down to the access pipe.

"Stop missing them!" Sawyer shouted, terrified that Kask would let his brother slip by. "Let go of the dog-boy."

"He'll get away!"

"Give him to me. I'll hold him." Sawyer ran to Kask and grabbed; the Dragon pushed him back. Another prisoner slipped past. Kask grunted, "Now, see what you made me do!"

"You made a promise!"

"Damn your human eyes!" the Dragon roared. He shoved Ibaka back into Sawyer's arms. "If you lose him, I'll kill you."

Sawyer made a show of holding on to Ibaka firmly. Ibaka started to squirm, but Sawyer rapped him sharply on the snout. "Keep still!" Then, stepping back out of the way, and feeling guilty, he whispered, "I won't let him hurt you. Trust me, little one."

Ibaka looked up at him with big round eyes. Trust? A human?

Slash approached and held her hand up to the puppy's face. He sniffed at her, then licked her fingers tentatively. Sawyer looked down at Slash with curiosity, but he maintained his rigid grip on the little dog-boy's squirming body. "Shh," he said. He rubbed the puppy's head affectionately and hugged him close. After a minute Ibaka stopped protesting. Sawyer turned around again to watch the Dragon.

More prisoners came tumbling down the sluice tube

now, one after the other; Kask pulled them out as fast as he could, reaching first with one hand, then the other. They came out gasping, swearing, coughing, staggering, and exhausted. Many had injuries—burned and ragged flesh. All had horror stories: the battle-robots, the panic, the fighting to get into the tube—

Sawyer pushed through the crowd of ragged and dirty men. "My brother, Finn! What happened to him?"

"The guy with the gun—? I don't know. I didn't see—"

Sawyer yelled to Kask. "Keep watching! Watch for Finn!"

But Kask just shook his head. "Only dead ones now." He pulled another body out—only half a body. Sawyer flinched in horror. The battle-robots had melted the poor man's face. Kask let the body fall back into the sluice tube. "No more." He looked down at Sawyer. "I guess he didn't make it."

In his revulsion and dismay, Sawyer's grip on Ibaka loosened, and the puppy took immediate advantage. He leapt from Sawyer's arms with an excited yelp. Kask forgot about his promise and charged after Ibaka, shoving Sawyer and twelve other men out of the way. Ibaka scrambled between their legs, ducking back and forth, until he finally saw an opening. He dashed for a gap under the access pipe and slid under it. Kask followed with a roar; he scattered the men like tenpins and reached quickly into the gap after Ibaka—the puppy snarled and bit, but the Dragon grabbed him by the leg and pulled him out.

Meanwhile, Sawyer had leapt up onto the top of the pipe and struggled desperately to reach into it, grabbing frantically and shouting, "Finn! Finn—" The bodies swept past him, each one in worse condition than the last. Sawyer couldn't look—but he couldn't look away. He had to stay there for Finn. He hung down into the water, waving his arms and grabbing at everything that came surging past.

"Crazy man," grunted Kask, nodding toward Sawyer.

"Of course, you wouldn't understand," said Lee-1169. "He only wants to save his brother."

Kask reacted sharply to that. "I had a brother. I understand."

"Then help him!"

"Why? My brother died? Why should I save his? His brother probably died too. Why waste the effort pulling a dead body out of the pipe?"

Lee made a noise of frustration. "Dragons!" He started to turn away—

"I've got him!" shouted Sawyer suddenly. "I've got him! Somebody help me! Help me, you goddamn son of a lying lizard! You promised!"

"You let the dog-boy escape!"

"Help me save my brother!" Sawyer gasped out breathlessly. "I can't hold on!"

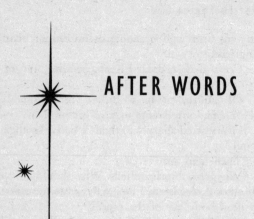

AFTER WORDS

Sawyer hung on frantically to Finn's limp body. He didn't know if Finn still breathed or not, but he didn't dare let go. Whatever had happened, he had to know for certain. He strained to hang on as hard as he could, but he didn't have the strength or the leverage. He could feel his grip on Finn's shirt weakening. And he felt himself sliding as Finn's weight pulled him forward into the tube.

"Help me!" he shouted again—and then suddenly, he felt hands grabbing at him, pulling him. "Get Finn! Get Finn!" he cried. Somehow Sawyer hooked his fingers into the sleeve of Finn's jacket and pulled. Someone else reached past him, also grabbing—

—and then, amazingly, Finn reached up and grabbed his arm! They hung on to each other, staring into each other's eyes, both wet and grateful, while all the other hands pulled and tugged at them. Slowly, Finn came rising up out of the surging water; he flopped over the edge of the pipe and hung there gasping. Harry and Lee pulled him the rest of the way over and laid him down on the wet ground. Sawyer sagged down next to him, one arm still wrapped around his brother. "I thought I'd lost you."

"You almost did," Finn coughed. "It got pretty hairy up there."

"What happened—?"

"Later. I'll tell you later."

Harry and Lee and a couple of other men that neither recognized stood around them, concern showing on their faces—and relief that Finn felt well enough to sit up to cough and spit the dirty water out of his lungs.

And then Sawyer remembered. He jumped to his feet and advanced on Kask. The Dragon had pulled Ibaka out from the hole under the pipe; now he lifted him high in the air like a prize, where he squirmed and squealed and tried to bite the hand that held him.

"You tailless son of a lizard!" Sawyer started shouting. "You couldn't keep a promise if the Lady Zillabar herself nailed you to it!"

"You let the dog-boy go! I caught him," Kask roared back. "I can reclaim my honor now."

Ibaka screamed down at him, a high-pitched yapping sound. "I saved you! You can't turn me in! I showed you the way!"

Slash began beating at Kask's legs, shrieking her rage too. "You owe me! I helped you escape! Give the puppy back to me! You have the honor of a pig!"

Kask remained resolute. "I have found the Lady's gift. I have erased my shame. I can return to my rightful place." He lowered his hand in front of his face and gave the squirming dog-child a furious shake. Ibaka calmed down immediately. "You must not run away."

Ibaka spat at him. "I saved your life. You owe me!"

Lee-1169 also added his voice to the argument. "Join the Alliance of Life, Kask. We *all* saved each other here. Don't betray that."

Slash continued to pound on the Dragon's thigh. "You have to listen to them! Give me my puppy!"

Harry Mertz, former High Justice and Arbiter of Thoska-Roole, pushed forward. "Listen to the dog-child, great Dragon. He saved you—to give him back to Lady Zillabar would bring an even greater dishonor to your family. Everybody would know what you had done."

Kask started to look confused. "You people know nothing about honor," he said, turning around in annoyance. "You don't even deserve to have an opinion about honor."

The humans traded dumbfounded looks. Dragons!

"So much for your 'Alliance of Life'," Sawyer said to Lee.

"They breed them for strength," Harry explained sadly. "Not brains."

With Sawyer's help Finn had pulled himself to his feet. "Well," he said, "now we know how far we can trust him."

"What do you know about trust?" Kask rumbled.

Finn shook his head. "You'll never know."

Kask started to answer, then—in annoyance he reached down and swatted the insistent Slash away from his side, knocking the boy tumbling. "Go away," he said. "Or I'll kill you."

"If you do, you'll die here!" Slash shouted, picking herself up. "The Guards will find you and kill you. Or you'll starve to death in the desert. I know how to get out of here. You don't."

For the first time the men began looking around. Even Kask stopped to consider Slash's words. They stood in a rocky gulley scattered with boulders the size of houses. Beside them the pipe led down to a covered reservoir—and from there to the dirty gray dome of the Old City detainment. It blocked their access to the desert. It lay across their path like a wall.

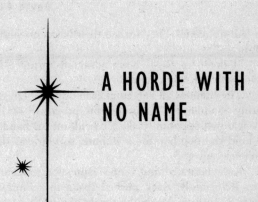

A HORDE WITH NO NAME

"Maybe we can go back up?"
Lee suggested.

Slash shook her head. "It won't work. I know this place. You don't. You'll all die here if I leave you."

A couple of the prisoners shook their heads in contempt. "Only a fool would listen to her. We'll go up." They turned and began climbing roughly over the huge rocks that lined the broken channel.

Three other prisoners started working their way downward. "If we keep to the cover of the rocks, we can find our way around the dome."

Sawyer and Finn looked at each other. Finn said, "The kid brought us to the sluice tube. I think we should trust her." Sawyer agreed with a nod. The brothers looked to Harry and Lee. "Don't you agree?"

Kask had followed all this with interest. "This doesn't affect me," he grunted. "I have the Lady's gift. I can go back."

"They shot at us, you stupid worm!" Ibaka screamed. "Have you forgotten that already? They said you had no name! They turned their backs on you! They shot at us!"

"I don't know—" Kask admitted abruptly. He sat down with a heavy thump.

The humans all looked at each other. A Dragon admitting ignorance? "Consider this progress," said Finn. He sat down opposite Kask. He held out his hands. "Let me hold the dog-boy for a minute, so you can think. I won't let him go."

Kask hesitated, but Finn's expression remained resolute. Reluctantly, Kask pushed Ibaka into Finn's arms. "Here. Take him. Maybe he speaks the truth—I have to think about this."

Slash came over and sat down next to Finn. She reached over and stroked Ibaka and made reassuring noises. "We'll figure something out."

Now Lee came over and sat down too. He had an expression of great concern on his face. Finn looked at him curiously, but Lee held up a hand as if to say, "I have a thought here. Let me try something."

"Kask," Lee said. "May I help you remember one thing?"

The Dragon didn't respond. He glared at Lee—the traitor, the man for whom his brother, Keeda, had died—but he didn't turn away either.

"You, Dragons, you have a—a wonderful discipline. The whole family of warrior-lizards has a proud heritage. Everybody envies the strength of the Dragons. I don't have to tell you that. You already know it. But I can tell you something that you don't know. And that may help you make the right decision here."

Lee hesitated, waiting to see how or if the Dragon would respond. Kask merely continued staring at him.

Lee-1169 took that as assent and continued. "You have a tradition that one Dragon defends all, and all defend one. You belong to the family of Dragons. Well, the rest of us want to have that same kind of tradition in our lives—some people call it family, others call it community. I call it an alliance of life."

"You humans can't know," Kask protested, but without real enthusiasm.

"Yes, I know. But if we could know," Lee said, "we would want to have the same spirit among ourselves that you have among your brothers." Lee stretched out his hand and laid it on the Dragon's broad claw. "You can help teach us."

Kask looked up at that. "Teach? Me? What do I know?"

"You know right from wrong. You know honor."

Finn touched Lee's arm. "Let me say something. Kask—" The Dragon's gaze shifted warily. "Your brother died for the honor of your family. You will too, if you have to. Let me ask you this—can you imagine an even greater honor? One worth *living humbly* for?"

Kask didn't answer, but both humans knew that he had heard their words. The great Dragon had actually begun considering the import of what they had said. After a moment he grunted. "This confuses me. You start talking and I understand even less. If I had the honor of my family, I would have killed you both, long before this."

"Yet you trust me—as you trusted my brother—to hold the dog-child."

"I had no choice—"

"Yes, you did," said Finn. "You chose the honor of life instead of the honor of death."

"What you did," explained Lee, "perfectly demonstrates this idea of an alliance of life. We helped each other, all of us."

"Dragons don't help," said Kask. "Helping fosters weakness. I have brought dishonor to the Dragon's Claw."

"And gained a *larger* honor," Finn put in quickly.

"Can you imagine an honor held by *all* life? An honor so big that no individual race can hold it all?"

"No," admitted Kask. "I can't." And yet, even as he admitted that he couldn't, the two humans saw his armored forehead furrowing in concern. Even as he shook his head in denial, still his patient mind had already begun trying to encompass such a strange and terrifying concept.

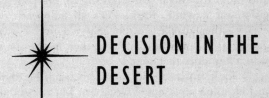

DECISION IN THE DESERT

By now a small crowd had gathered around the group. One or two of the remaining prisoners grumbled, "Why waste time with the Dragon? Let's go." But others insisted on waiting. Finn glanced around, counting. He saw his brother, Slash, Harry, and three other men waiting nearby. He didn't like it; they would make too large a group—too easy to spot, too slow to move.

But ... he and Sawyer had no choice. If nothing else, they owed a debt to Slash for showing them the sluice tube, and they could repay it only by achieving the freedom of the little dog-boy. Finn sighed. He hated situations like this.

"I have a suggestion," said Sawyer. He had put on his shoes again and had slung his weapon over his shoulder.

Kask looked up. A suggestion? Nobody ever *suggested* anything to a Dragon. They always ordered. He found the human's courtesy an intriguing and disturbing new behavior.

"Let's get out of here before the Dragon Guards

and the battle-robots start tracking us. Postpone your decision for a while, Kask. Let's all help each other to escape—then maybe we can help you find a way to regain your honor. If not *this* way, then maybe some better way. How does that sound?"

Kask frowned and shook his head. He didn't like it. Indecision represented weakness. But . . . so did everything else here. He said so to Finn, whom he trusted more than Lee.

"Humans call it a no-win situation, Kask. And yes, we find it just as troubling as you do."

Kask grunted, a sound without meaning.

Finn stood up, hoping that Kask would take the hint and stand up too. "Sawyer's suggestion makes sense. Come on. We have to get going."

"All right," conceded Kask. He began levering himself back to his feet. "But I haven't given up my claim to the dog-boy. I will carry him." He bent down and plucked Ibaka from Finn's grasp. Carefully, he put the dog-boy on his shoulder. "You will ride there, little one. You will show me your honor by not trying to escape? Do you understand?"

Ibaka looked around the group. Finn and Lee both nodded to him. So did Sawyer and Harry Mertz. But only when Slash nodded her approval did Ibaka accept the situation. "All right," he said softly. "But no growling, okay?"

Kask considered. "No growling at you, unless you deserve it."

"Done," said Finn. "Now, let's get the hell out of here."

Sawyer turned to Slash. "Lead the way, fair maiden—"

Slash gave him a dirty look. "Sorry. Neither."

"My apologies—" Sawyer bowed politely. "But do please get us out of here?"

"This way." Slash pointed up the arroyo. She led

them up and over the rocks and boulders until they reached a point where they could crawl onto the top of the enclosed sluice tube. From here they had a much better view both up and down the gully. The pipe wound back and forth, up and down over the rocks, all the way down to the distant dome of the Old City detainment.

"There—" Slash pointed. "See that?"

"What?" Sawyer shielded his eyes against the glare of the Eye of God.

"See where the canyon goes deep? See that cut in the side of the hill? We go up that cut, then down the other side to the old canal bed."

"We follow the canal bed?"

"Not quite. The Guards patrol the canal, in case someone tries to attack the prison. We cross to the other side. See how the hills stretch all the way out into the desert; they block the view from the dome and from the canal. The ghouls live there, so we have to take care, but once you get past the dome, you can drop down into the canal bed and follow it all the way to—I don't know, but you can follow it a long way."

Sawyer looked back at Finn. "What do you think, Finn?" He had a double purpose to his question. The concern showed in his eyes.

Finn nodded reluctantly. His voice had a ragged edge to it. "I can handle it. I think I have a few more hours before I'll need to rest again."

"Good. Harry? Lee?"

The two men nodded. "But let's get off this pipe. I feel awfully visible up here."

"Right."

FREEBOOTERS

Star-Captain Neena Linn-Campbell stormed into the hangar where the shuttleboat of the *Lady Macbeth* rested. Her footsteps sounded like gunshots shattering the silence of the night. As she walked, she reeled off orders to Robin and Gito, who hurried to keep up with her.

Abruptly she stopped and stared at the shuttle suspiciously. "Shariba-Jen?" she called.

The door to the shuttle's airlock popped open, and the robot came gliding quickly across the intervening space. A work of industrial poetry, Shariba-Jen moved like a dancer. Its flexible copper skin glistened in the reflected glow of the night; the red-and-gold trim gave it a crisp military appearance.

"Has anybody or anything entered this hangar since we've left?"

The robot replied, "Nothing, Captain. Not even insects."

"I don't believe it," she snapped. To Shariba-Jen she explained, "I believe you, Jen. But I don't trust *them*."

She spat out the last word like a curse. "Inside—" She pointed. "We have work to do."

Her crew followed her up into the airlock. As soon as the door popped shut behind them, she started issuing orders. "Sweep us for bugs—including nanos."

"In progress even as we speak," Shariba-Jen reported. "We have ninety percent confidence. What else?"

"Can you work in the dark? Of course you can. We'll need the boat repainted to make it look like a Regency patroller. Darken the hangar. Make it look deserted. As soon as the goddamn Eye of God sets, I want to get out of here."

The air lock finished cycling—a precautionary measure against airborne dust-probes—and the Captain pushed into the cramped quarters of the shuttle. She flung herself down at a workstation and thumbed the screens to life. "EDNA," she demanded. "Update these maps and show me Ota's location."

The starship's computer replied immediately, its voice relayed directly from the *Lady Macbeth*. "Captain Campbell, I have a duty to warn you that an attempt to retrieve the LIX-bioform by force will constitute a serious violation of local Regency statutes."

"Thank you, EDNA. As always, you offer valuable advice. However, the world of Thoska-Roole has already forsaken the law far beyond anything we intend to do. Log it that here the law serves the purposes of tyranny, not justice. Cooperation with the authorities of this world would only validate their crimes. Our commitment to a higher standard requires that we break the agreement to abide by their rules when those rules do not serve justice."

"May I also point out, Captain, that a rescue attempt will violate the Articles of Noninterference by the Interstellar Operations Guild."

"Thank you, EDNA. For your information, I've turned in my Guild insignia. We cannot support a Guild that does not protect its members. In the future this ship will function as an unlicensed trader. If we have to, we'll establish our own code of standards and live on our reputation. Please begin the necessary steps to register the *Lady Macbeth* as a freebooter."

"Yes, Captain. In progress."

"Now show me the maps. Where have they taken Ota?"

"At your orders, Captain, each member of this crew carries an internal locator chip. To prevent against scanning, we have implanted organic-based transponders. To my best knowledge the Regency did not detect the chip implanted in the bioform. Six hours ago I began transmitting flash-burst signals to activate the device. On my first orbit I detected no response; this falls within acceptable parameters. On the second orbit I repeated my flash-burst transmissions in case the Regency had detained the bioform in a shielded location.

"Twenty minutes ago," EDNA continued, "I received a response from a location in the desert south of MesaPort."

Captain Campbell studied the screen. EDNA had superimposed the location on an expanded map, showing not only surface features, but also scanning and defense patterns as well as potentials for counterattack and pursuit.

Robin looked over her Captain's shoulder, a hard look on her face. She pointed at the map. "Come in here, just north of the camp, touch down, send in an assassin?"

"Uh-huh," agreed Captain Campbell. "And if I had an assassin to spare, I'd consider that."

"You want to go in blasting like hell?"

"Look at that installation—" Campbell pointed. "Who do you think built it? And why?"

"It looks like a farm to me," said Robin. "Or a ranch."

"Precisely. Livestock."

"Livestock? What kind of—" And then she realized. "Oh, my God. You don't think—"

Campbell swiveled in her chair and looked at Robin, at Gito, at Shariba-Jen. "I don't think anything. I just want to kill the Vampires who kidnapped Ota. How does that sound?"

"I know what Ota would say," Gito growled. "It doesn't sound very *enlightened*."

"Well, Ota will just have to wait to vote—until after we rescue it."

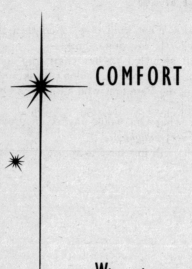

COMFORT

When dawn crept over the edge of the world, Thoska-Roole grew dim. The Eye of God slid down in the west, and the orange gloom of the day flooded in from the east. The desert turned red, as if blood had poured across it. The sky became a ceiling of ruddy terror as the swollen orb of the primary rose above the horizon in bloated splendor.

This far south the canal bed flattened out as it approached its final destination, the great salt reservoir. From there Lee-1169 suggested they should strike out overland to a remote transit station that the Resistance occasionally used as a temporary safe house. The ragtag group of escapees still hadn't agreed, but no one had come up with a better alternative—not even Kask, who remained curiously subdued. He even let Ibaka down to walk on his own, knowing that the puppy could not run away here—not without Kask quickly overtaking him.

As the last of the starlight faded away, everything became a rosy blur. Finally they decided to stop and rest for a few hours. They climbed up the sloping wall of the canal and found a place of tumbled rocks and ruins. Sawyer insisted that they *had* to stop. Finn had begun shaking again, suffering the onset of another one of his spells. Sawyer laid out a ragged blanket he had found with the stores, and Finn lay down on it gratefully. Against his better judgment, Lee switched on a thermal-pack, and they all crowded close to its yellow warmth.

They passed around ration-packs and speculated on the territory ahead. They had reached the limits of Slash's knowledge, and she had begun talking about heading back the way they had come, back up to her familiar canyon. Lee advised against it. The Regency would leave the battle-robots patrolling Death Canyon for a long time to come. She'd find no safety there.

"By now the Vampires will have cataloged the escapees, listing those killed, recaptured . . . or still missing. I intend to stay in the latter category, and I doubt that we can do that by heading back the way we came."

Slash grumbled and moved away from him. "Have it your own way. I can't help you anymore."

Lacking hard information, most of the other prisoners stayed silent. Finn's apparent agonies unnerved them. They hadn't seen his spells before, and they worried among themselves about contagion.

Harry came over and sat down next to Sawyer. "This will pass, right?"

Sawyer nodded. "He gets these spells. You don't need to worry. He'll shake for a while, but he'll come back strong."

From across the glow of the thermal-pack, Lee asked, "What does he have?"

Sawyer fumbled with his answer. Finally he said, "You can ask him when he gets better."

Lee spat to one side. "Tell the truth, tracker. Don't hide behind your brother."

"I don't speak for my brother. You can ask him tomorrow."

"He has the blood-burn, doesn't he?" suggested Harry sympathetically. "I've seen it before."

Sawyer didn't want to answer; it showed in his eyes. Harry and Lee exchanged a meaningful glance. Harry shrugged. Lee shook his head. Slash, sitting next to Lee, asked softly, "Blood-burn?"

Lee whispered back, "Very bad. Very painful. It just gets worse and worse. And you take a long time to die."

"Does the blood-burn *always* kill?"

"I've never met any survivors."

Slash shuddered. She got up and moved away from the glow, looking again toward Kask. The Dragon growled at her. He clearly didn't trust her. He sat alone, with Ibaka jammed uncomfortably under one arm, while he peeled open ration-packs and stuffed them into his mouth. "We should have let the Dragon go off by himself," she said. "He eats too much."

"If we do," said Lee, "he'll take the pup."

"I know—"

Slash called to Kask. "Hey—don't get greedy, you big lizard! Give some of that to Ibaka."

Kask looked over at her and grunted. "Why?"

Harry stood up then and approached. He put an arm on Slash's shoulder to keep her from speaking out of turn. "Because the pup probably wants to eat, just the same as you. The last I heard, those little things get very hungry."

Kask reached into the sack beside him and pulled out another ration-pack. He peeled it open and began feeding Ibaka like a doll. "You eat. You stay healthy. But you don't try to escape again. You belong to the Lady, and until I can take you to her, you belong to me. You act with honor, all right?"

"You and your honor—" one of the other escapees snorted, a tall, spindly man named Arl-N.

Kask growled deep in his throat. "You know nothing about honor," he said. "All of you. What do you know? You talk of honor as if anyone can know it. Dragon honor comes from the"—Kask fumbled with the words—"from the egg. Dragons honor their brothers from the nest. Can you understand that? No matter what anybody says, I have a personal honor to my brothers. No matter what the Lady says or anybody else—" His voice became uncertain as he remembered Captain Lax-Varney's rebuttal of his claim. He shook it away angrily. "—No. It doesn't matter. I have my own integrity. I will keep true to my brothers as they would to me."

At this, the small hairball under Kask's arm began to whimper. Kask looked down at Ibaka curiously. "What troubles you?"

"I miss my brothers—and my sisters." The little dog-child started crying in piteous, unconsolable yelps.

Confused and startled, Kask held Ibaka before him and watched the little animal's torrent of emotion. Finally he ordered, "Stop crying. Crying demonstrates weakness." Ibaka ignored him and continued to weep.

Slash said to Kask, "Don't you get it, you big wart? Whoever sold this pup to Lady Zillabar took him and his siblings right from their mother. You at least had a chance to grow in your own nest. Somebody taught you honor. These dog-children never even had that much chance."

Kask looked troubled. He hadn't considered that thought. He looked at the sobbing puppy in his hands, then back to Slash again. "How do you make him stop?"

"Give him to me. He needs comforting."

"I will comfort him. How do you do this thing?"

"I don't think you could—" Slash shook her head. Kask insisted. "I will try. What do I do?"

"Pet him."

"Pet him—?"

"And tell him you won't let anyone hurt him. Tell

him you won't led Lady Zillabitch get her filthy claws on him again."

"I can't tell him that."

"Then you can't comfort him."

"But he needs comforting. You said so."

"I'll do it." Slash moved to take Ibaka from Kask's big hands.

Kask hesitated. "You won't try to escape with him? If you do, I'll kill you."

Slash just sighed. "Give him to me, you stupid reptile." She took Ibaka in her arms and held him close. "I love you, Ibaka," she said. "Come sit with me and we'll get warm together."

Kask growled in disgust, a terrible low sound of repugnance. "This comforting business—it looks like weakness. They act like egg-carriers. I don't think I want to learn how to do it."

"You don't have to worry," Harry reassured him. "I very much doubt that anyone will ever ask you."

HISTORY

On the other side of the glow of the thermal-pack, Lee huddled inside himself and watched the transaction taking place between Slash and the Dragon. He smiled ruefully and pointed with a nod. "The Alliance of Life looks like that," he said. "But they'd only deny it if I tried to convince them." He sighed sadly and added, "I wish my brothers could have seen it, though. Many of them didn't believe it either."

Harry lowered himself painfully back to the ground next to Lee. Under the punishing red gloom of the day, he looked like an ancient gargoyle. "My bones ache," he complained. "I haven't had to run like this since the Amazon freebooter caught me with her daughter—" He shut up as Slash came and sat down on the other side of Lee with Ibaka in her arms. She sat close to the warmth and cooed softly at the pup.

Harry looked at Lee suddenly and perceptively. "Your brothers?" he asked.

Lee hung his head low and stared down at the ground between his feet. "You don't know much about clone-families, do you?"

Harry shook his head. "No, I don't."

"At our peak the Lee family numbered more than two thousand identical members. All ages. We had estates on twenty worlds. We had houses and gardens and schools. We had political power too—enough to seriously threaten the authority of the Vampires in some places." He glanced across at the Dragon. "Kask thinks he knows honor. He knows nothing. He and his brothers all hatched from different eggs. My family—every single one of us, we shared the same genetic heritage. Imagine it— each and every one of us, the same! If we dishonored our family, we dishonored ourselves. We couldn't do that. He thinks Dragons have integrity—we learned integrity as a family identity." Lee looked frustrated. "I can't explain it in this language. We don't have all the words I need."

"You miss them, don't you?" Harry said perceptively. He noticed that both Slash and Ibaka listened with curiosity.

"Of course I do. I miss them like I miss myself. I have nothing without my family. I have no identity. Regency Dragons have killed most of the Lees throughout the Cluster." He grinned ruefully. "They don't like us. We don't like them. They won't stop until they have hunted the last of us down and eaten his liver. I don't know where any of my brothers have gone to ground anymore. We did that on purpose. That way they can't torture it out of us. I don't know if any of my brothers still live. Who knows? You might have the honor here of spending time with the last living Lee." He looked across the glow of the thermal-pack at Sawyer's unhappy expression. "You don't like hearing this, do you?"

"No, I don't," Sawyer replied. "It makes me uncomfortable." And then he turned to Finn again and resumed mopping his brother's feverish forehead with a damp cloth.

"You all have brothers," Harry said, a tangential thought. "Sawyer and Finn. Lee—you may still have many brothers out there, even if you don't know it. Kask still has brothers, even though he can't go to them. Ibaka has brothers and sisters. He only wants to rejoin them." He sighed. "I never had a brother—"

"I had no brothers," Slash said. "I had sisters." At their looks, she explained. "They bred us for nurturing. Our parent-group had a contract, so they produced gender-females to order. We had a happy time for a while—" She fell silent again, hugging Ibaka closer to her.

Lee looked at Slash, and at Harry Mertz, with compassion in his eyes. "In the Alliance of Life, you would share brotherhood with all of us."

Harry didn't respond to that. He'd seen too much in his long life to have much enthusiasm for the concept. Instead he stood up, adjusting his robe and muttering that he had to see a man about a dog. He grinned at Slash and Ibaka as he stepped past them, but as he crossed in front of Sawyer, he looked regretfully down at Finn. "They'll come after us, you know. Can he travel? Otherwise—"

"He'll travel," said Sawyer, as if his determination alone would make all the necessary difference. "He has to make it. *He has to.*"

A PLACE IN THE SUN

When the spell finally passed, Finn fell into a deep red sleep. And finally Sawyer allowed himself to breathe easier too. He lay down next to his brother and moved up next to him, more for comfort than for warmth. Back to back, they lay there, while the ruddy sky above burned and burned. Eventually, Sawyer slept too.

He came awake with a start—Finn sat up beside him shaking, not with illness, but with fear. "Did you hear it?"

"Hear what?"

"A flyer. Not close, but—I heard it clearly."

"I didn't hear anything." Sawyer looked across to the others. "Did you?"

Harry and Lee had awakened. The rest still slept. Lee shook his head. Harry rubbed his eyes and yawned and made morning noises.

Finn stood up impatiently. "Let's take a look around." He looked and acted more refreshed than any of them. He bustled with nervous energy. That made Sawyer worry even more. "Come on, Soy," he urged. "We need to scout ahead. Something smells wrong."

Sawyer looked at his brother sideways. "I don't smell anything."

"Think about it, Soy. Where does this channel lead? Who built it? And why? What kind of installation does it serve?"

"Ghosts."

"Or maybe tunnel worms—?"

"Okay, so I made a mistake. So sue me."

"They'll have sent out flyers looking for us. Maybe they've set a trap farther down the canal. I think we need to scout ahead." Finn remained insistent. "Come on."

"All right," Sawyer agreed. He looked to Lee and Harry. They nodded their reluctant agreement. *Let him look.*

Taking only their weapons, two ration-packs, and a water bag, they headed south along the dry canal bed toward a distant rise. They didn't talk for a long while. Finn didn't have anything to say and Sawyer didn't want to ask.

As they approached the low hill, they began to feel a deep thrumming vibration, like the kind made by a flyer idling on the ground. They looked at each other in wordless agreement. Sawyer pointed, and the two of them headed toward the top of the hill. Just below the crest they dropped down to the ground and sidled the rest of the distance on their bellies. They looked over the top of the hill suspiciously.

The installation beneath them looked like a small village; it glowed with lights of all colors. Several large buildings lay in a large circle around a central plaza. Nearby, a flyer idled on a landing pad. Beyond stood several dome-shaped barns.

"Do you think we can capture the flyer?" Sawyer asked.

Finn grunted. "Let's wait and see who it belongs to."

"Finn," Sawyer said slowly. "Don't play stupid. You

know who built this place. You know what purpose it serves."

Finn didn't reply.

"We have to tell the others."

"We have a problem," Finn agreed.

"We have a lot of problems," Sawyer corrected.

They studied the buildings a while longer. At last three figures came out of one of the structures and crossed to the flyer. A moment later the flyer lifted off and headed first to the west and then north toward MesaPort. Sawyer and Finn slid quickly back down the hill to keep out of sight.

They trudged most of the way back in silence. Finally Sawer asked glumly, "Do you think we can turn any of this to our advantage?"

"I don't think anything," said Finn. "Not even about survival anymore."

"Don't talk like that. You can't give up. I won't let you—"

Finn looked at him. "The decision belongs to me, brother."

"No, it doesn't. Because whatever you decide affects me too."

"Think about it, Soy. If I choose to die, can you stop me?"

"You think about this, Finn. If you choose to die, I'll follow you into hell and drag you back by your hair."

"If you go to hell, you'll go alone. I intend to go to the good place, get drunk, and tumble as many redheaded angels as I can find. Of either sex. I won't play favorites."

"Don't joke about it, Finn. We have a *commitment*."

"I know about our commitment. And if I didn't joke about it, then I'd have to cry. So just leave me alone. As long as I remain upright, I'll do ... whatever I have to."

Sawyer accepted that as a victory and fell silent. The two of them continued on back to the camp, each one lost in troubled thoughts.

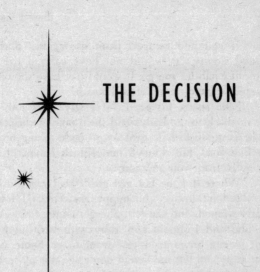

THE DECISION

Kask snored like an earth-quake. Each intake of breath rumbled and shook the Dragon's entire body. Each exhalation whistled like the blast from a steam engine. The decibel level would have shattered glass. Eventually, his nasal symphony reached such a peak of enthusiasm, he even woke himself in startlement. He came instantly awake, leaping to his feet and looking around for the source of the attack, growling and hissing his defiance. "What?" he shouted. "Who?"

And then he realized and fell abruptly silent. Sleep did that to him sometimes—scared him into a fighting stance. He sank back down on his mighty haunches, his armored muscles folding and compressing under him.

Ibaka sat across from him, staring with large round eyes.

Kask frowned in puzzlement.

Ibaka hopped a little closer, as if waiting for Kask to pick him up again.

Kask made no move to grab the dog-child. "Why didn't you run away?" he asked. "You could have."

"We talked about it," Ibaka admitted.

"If you had escaped from me again," Kask explained slowly, "it would not have carried the same shame if I had let you go. It would just have shown your cleverness against a big slow Dragon."

Ibaka shook his head. "If I stay with you, you'll take me back to the Lady. And she'll take me back to my brothers and sisters. I want to go back to my brothers. Just like you." He climbed into Kask's hands. "I won't run away from you anymore."

"Where did the boy-girl go?" the Dragon asked.

"I don't know," the puppy answered. "I told her what I wanted, and she left. She got angry. She yelled at me. She said I should run away with her, but I don't want to run anymore. I just want to go home. So she went away and left me here. I don't like this place. Please take me back."

"Hrpf," said Kask. Sometimes he thought he understood, but most of the time he didn't. Obviously, all these other animals had different ways of thinking than he did. That realization left him confused and troubled. He wanted to live in a simple and orderly world, but the way people acted kept making that impossible. He shook his head in dismay and rose back to his feet just as Sawyer and Finn Markham came trudging sullenly back into camp.

"What did you find?" asked Lee. He could see it on their faces.

"Trouble," said Sawyer.

"Two klicks away. A Vampire village of some kind. I think we can go around it. We can avoid detection if we strike out east."

Kask rumbled gravely, "Then we will part here. I can turn in the dog-child at that settlement. They won't shoot at me there."

"Um, Kask—" Finn tried to approach the Dragon with reason. "I don't think you should do that. I don't think it'll make either you or Ibaka very happy." But the

Dragon had already begun lumbering toward the canal. Sawyer and Finn both rushed to follow him. "Kask! Listen to me. You don't know what they do there—"

The Dragon ignored them. He stumped across the broken ground like a rock-crushing tank. The humans had to run just to keep up with him. "Kask! Wait! Wait a minute—listen to me!"

"The dog-child wants to go back. I want to go back. We have nothing to discuss."

Sawyer and Finn both came around to the front of the Dragon and tried to restrain him physically; they could have easier held back an avalanche. He brushed them aside and kept on heading toward the distant hill.

"Kask, wait! Before you go down there, stop and look! Look and see what happens in that place!"

"I don't have to listen to you anymore," the Dragon rumbled. But in his arms the dog-child began to whimper. "Kask, what did they see? What did they see, Kask?"

Abruptly, the Dragon stopped. He whirled around, lashing his tail so furiously that he almost knocked over Sawyer and Finn. The others came running after, out of breath. "What do you all want from me? Leave me alone! Go away."

"We want you—" Lee managed to get the words out only with great difficulty. "We want you to do the right thing."

"I know the right thing!"

"We want you to have certainty!"

"I have certainty!"

"No, you don't. You only *think* you do." Finn explained, "Before you take the dog-child down into that camp, look and see what they do there. Then you'll have certainty."

"You talk in circles. How can I understand?"

"The same way anybody understands anything! Look and see!"

THE DISCOVERY

At the top of the ridge Kask stopped. He stood solidly at the crest and studied the camp below. To the others following him, he appeared silhouetted by the wall of light coming over the eastern horizon. The Eye of God had begun to open. The radiance poured over the horizon and lit up the entire landscape with a fairy-tale glow.

The others caught up with him and pulled him backward to keep any observers below from seeing him. "What should I look for?" Kask asked.

"Just watch," said Finn.

"For how long?"

"Until you see what the Vampires do here."

Kask grumbled, but he settled down to watch and wait. The humans lay flat on the crest of the hill. Kask squatted down beside a boulder, flattening himself as best as he could. As the Eye of God drifted higher and higher into the sky, the valley below began to shimmer like a translucent bowl.

"There—" said Finn. He pointed.

"Oh, my God," said Harry.

"I knew it," said Lee.

Kask rumbled uncomfortably in his belly.

Sawyer didn't say anything at all.

"The Vampires eat their prey live," said Finn.

"Son of a witch," said Arl-N, the tall, spindly man. "That violates the Charter—"[38]

"Where?" demanded Ibaka. "What?"

Sawyer grabbed the dog-boy and tried to pull him back, desperately trying to cover the squirming child's eyes. Ibaka snapped and bit. "Let me see!" Ibaka broke free and leapt to the crest of the hill. He looked down at the golden bowl below.

"My brother!" screamed Ibaka. "I see my brother, Ubaja!" He started shrieking. "See? See? The little running dog? But why does he run? Why do they chase him? Oh, no! No! I have to help him—" He started running down the hill.

Sawyer started after him, but Kask overtook him. Kask pounded after Ibaka and snatched the dog-boy up into his arms before he could get very far. Quickly, he brought him back over the ridge; Ibaka screamed and pounded at the Dragon's chest.

"You knew about this! Didn't you?" Ibaka accused.

Kask didn't answer. He looked troubled and uncertain and even terrified. Holding Ibaka close to his chest, he began to growl. The growl rose in loudness and pitch, becoming a hideous rasping sound. Now Kask threw his head back and let loose a terrible roar of anguish, one that rattled the bones of all those who stood near him. He raged up at the Eye of God with a vile dreadful curse in the guttural Dragon language. The sound echoed out to

---

[38]Article Two of the Regency Charter strictly forbids the use of sentient creatures as prey animals. This prohibition serves as one of the most fundamental tenets of the Regency Authority.

the horizon, prolonged and painful, and then came rolling back again.

When Kask fell silent again, he looked around at the stunned humans. "I didn't know—" he said to them. He repeated it to Ibaka. "Not like this." He held the sobbing dog-child close to him and began patting it gently on the head. "The Vampires have no honor. How could they lie like that? How could they violate the Charter? I can't reclaim my honor this way," he admitted. He sounded close to tears himself. "I can't restore my honor by giving them this child. That would make me a party to the violation." He held Ibaka and patted him again and again as gently as he could. "Forgive me, little dog-child. I will have to find another way to reclaim my honor. I promise you, I will not let the Vampires get you. I will not let the Lady Zillabar hurt you. You have my word on that."

The humans stared at Kask, astonished. None of them had ever seen a Dragon make such a declaration before.

"Well, damn my eyes," whispered Lee in amazement. "The Alliance of Life *does* work."

"You doubted it?" asked Harry.

"Never for a moment," said Lee. "I just didn't think it would happen in my lifetime."

Ibaka continued to sob in the Dragon's arms.

HONOR

Sawyer started to say, "We'll have to go around—" but Kask hadn't finished speaking. He'd made a decision.

"We have to kill the Vampires."

Sawyer looked to Finn. "Kernel d'Vashti won't like that very much." They both grinned at the thought.

Harry said, "I have a responsibility to point out that such an action would violate the laws of Thoska-Roole."

"You don't have to come," said Lee. He unslung his weapon and began checking its battery load.

"I didn't say I wouldn't come. I just wanted to say that it violates the law."

"Count me out," said one of the prisoners, a man whose name Sawyer had never learned.

"Me too," said his partner. They both began sliding back down the hill.

"I'll fight," said Arl-N. "I want to kill Vampires."

"We'll need to reconnoiter, make a plan—" began Finn.

Suddenly, Sawyer looked up. "Kask!" he shouted. The others looked. The big Dragon had made his deci-

sion and hadn't waited to see if the others would follow.
He had already traveled halfway down the hill toward
the camp.

"Oh, shit!" said Finn.

"Come on! Let's back him up."

"Right! To hell with Plan B!"

They began charging down the hill after Kask.
Skidding and slipping on the rocky slope, they couldn't
catch up, but they had a great view of what happened
next.

Kask strode straight into the center of the camp.

As he walked, the Vampires—all male—began
gathering around him. They followed him in, a crowd of
thirty or forty of them, lustrous and beautiful and intrigued that a Dragon would come out of the desert and
into this very private place of Phaestor recreation.

Kask stopped in the center of the plaza. He looked
around at all the golden Phaestor faces. Some of them
still had blood trickling down their cheeks.

"Take me to the Lord of this place," he demanded.
"I have information that he must hear."

The Vampires crowded around Kask, laughing in
high musical voices. Almost childlike in their amusement,
they seemed both delighted and dangerous at the same
time. Kask ignored their merriment. Resolutely, he
headed for the main hall of the villa. It sprawled like a
palace. It wore a crown of red-and-black filigree, ornate
decorations, and lanterns of green and pink and pale
blue.

The huge door dilated to its full diameter to allow
Kask to enter. He strode directly into the spacious central
chamber where Lord Drydel laughed and feasted drunk-
enly with his friends. He wore a frivolous-looking, pink-
silk daygown with red trim and a purple sash. He stood
upon the head table, holding a bloody leg of something in
his hand, waving it about while he caroled obscene verses
about eating and killing—in that order. He paused in his

recitations only to pull raw wet chunks off the leg and gulp them down salaciously. The other Vampires, almost all young and pretty boys, had goblets of blood in their hands, and they toasted their host's every utterance with broad, high gestures, loud cheers, and raucous jokes.

Drydel held up a hand for silence. "I demand respect!" he insisted. "For soon, very soon, I shall stand before you as the most powerful Vampire in the Regency."

"Don't let Zillabar hear you say that," cautioned one of his consorts, a ruddy boy with a scornful lip.

The drunken Drydel strode down the length of the table to the boy who'd spoken. "Falex, you always bring me such dreary warnings," the Lord confronted him with a deceptive laugh. "I shall have to call you Cassandra to honor your skills at precognition." He bent down low and took Cassandra's chin in his bloody hand, tilting the boy's face up to his, almost close enough to kiss. "The Lady has named me her Consort. We have posted the bans, and soon we will exchange our formal vows. *I* will father the next generation of Vampires in the Zashti line. And do you know the first thing I intend to do?"

Cassandra managed to shake his pretty head. His ringlets of curls bounced around his face.

"The first thing I will do ... I will eat d'Vashti's sky-damned heart." He said it with such fury in his eyes that no one dared to speak. "And for dessert," Drydel taunted, "perhaps I will eat one of you. Or maybe just a part of one of you."

"I will cheerfully volunteer for such a *death* my Lord," Cassandra offered. He lowered his long lashes seductively, but before he could amplify his remarks, the room fell curiously silent. Drydel released his grip on Cassandra and straightened. He turned to see who dared intrude on his private pleasures. His eyes widened at the sight of Kask. His anger began to rise. "How dare you—"

The huge Dragon bowed low. Despite his dirty appearance, he still made an impressive sight. Behind him, the rest of the Vampires came crowding in, giggling and tittering like children.

"Forgive me, my Lord, for interrupting your feast. I acknowledge my bad manners and humbly beg your pardon for this breach of courtesy. But I have information that you must hear at once, and the need for immediacy outweighs the lesser concerns of courtesy." Kask bowed again.

Drydel's eyes narrowed. He had no intention of granting any forgiveness easily—not to a Dragon, not to anyone, and certainly not today. Truly important information came only from Vampires. Nevertheless, he wanted to hear what the Dragon had to say. He strode across the table and sat down languorously on the edge of it, adjusting his gown and preparing himself for whatever curious information this crude Dragon might have to impart. "Go ahead." He waved casually.

"Thank you, my Lord," Kask said. "I have the solemn duty to inform you that this place and this gathering and the Phaestor who celebrate with you have all violated the most sacred oath of the Charter of the Regency. I regret to inform you that my duty to the honor of the Dragon's Claw requires that I kill each and every one of you immediately. I will try to make it painless. Please do not resist, as that will only make the job more difficult. Thank you."

Drydel's jaw had fallen open as Kask had spoken. Now he started to laugh. He laughed loudly—but he did not laugh long.

He died with the laughter still choking in his throat.

NIGHT OF THE DAMNED

Despite his size Kask could still move quickly. He seized Drydel's neck in his claw and squeezed until he heard it crack. Perhaps he overdid it— Drydel's head came off in his hand and bounced away across the floor.

Panic and pandemonium.

The Regency had designed the Dragons as warriors. The Vampires never had a chance.

Half the boys in the room went scattering and screaming, crowding toward the exits; some went scrambling for their weapons—and some died fighting. They hammered futilely at the Dragon. He waded into them, plucking them out of the crowd, first with one hand, then the other, and squeezing them easily to death in his claws. The blood spattered on the walls. The screams became horrendous.

Kask grimaced as he worked. A rictus of anger and ferocity spread across his face. He could not enjoy this killing as he would enjoy a battle; he could only perform the distasteful task with dispatch and duty. One after the other, he broke their backs and their necks and flung them aside. The Vampires screamed and begged, they shrieked and wailed. The shining Phaestor children scrambled and slid across the floor, slipping in the blood of their comrades. But they couldn't get out the door fast enough to escape the Dragon's wrath—Kask just lunged and grabbed. The bones went *cra-ack*, and he threw the boys away without emotion. The golden bodies slammed against the walls and collapsed in ghastly postures.

Behind Kask's back one of the Vampires had found a hunting rifle. He scrambled to aim it at the Dragon's broad back; Kask moved like a fury; the ruby-red targeting dot of the laser slid across the wall as the Vampire tried to follow him, tried to focus—

The Vampire with the gun exploded in a blast of light! Two beams simultaneously pierced him. Lee and Sawyer came tumbling into the room from the back, shooting wildly in all directions, puncturing the screaming Vampires like hot needles stabbing into a pack of frenzied cockroaches. The noise became intolerable.

Finn and Arl-N pushed into the room from the front. They had to climb over the bodies. They caught their bearings and aimed—

The silence fell suddenly. One last scream of a Vampire in Kask's grasp—and then it too ended in a choke and gurgle. The body thumped limply to the floor. Kask turned around slowly, looking to see if he had missed any of the Vampires. His cruel gaze swept the room like a smoldering searchlight.

Finn turned quickly to the door to stop Harry and Ibaka. "Don't come in here. Keep him out—"

Arl-N asked, "Huh? Why—?"

Sawyer pointed grimly to the remains of the meal spread across the table—a gender-female human boy. "They must have caught her last night."

Outside they could hear Ibaka screaming, "Let me in! I have to see!" He burst into the room and skidded, slipped to a terrified halt.

Harry rushed in after the dog-child. "Sorry," he said. "He bit me."

Finn tried to grab Ibaka, but the little pup squirmed away. Very casually, Sawyer tossed a fallen drapery across the center of the table, so that Ibaka wouldn't see what lay there.

The dog-child stood alone in the center of the room, staring in horror at the carnage around them. After a moment he bent down and picked up one of the Vampire's weapons. He held it stiffly in front of him and turned around slowly, in case any of the dead Vampires dared to move.

Harry said to Sawyer, "Only a few came out the front. We got them all."

"We got the ones who tried to come out the back."

Finn said, "We'll still have to scour the camp. We don't dare let any escape to tell." He pointed. "That way—"

Kask grunted. "I'll lead." None of them argued. Only Ibaka saw Falex-called-Cassandra rising from under the table with a needle-beam in his hand, aiming at Kask. Ibaka fired without thinking. The upper half of Cassandra's body disappeared in a flash, along with half the table. The remaining half collapsed with a heavy crash. The bloody goblets shattered, the silver utensils clattered on the floor. The bloody sheet-covered lump rolled aside, but remained thankfully covered.

Kask looked at Ibaka, astonished. "You defended me—why did you do that?"

Ibaka stared back at Kask in anger and annoyance that the big Dragon would even have to ask.

THE TRANSPORT

The alarm still shrilled. Now, in the sudden silence in the hall, its noise became intolerable. Lee went prowling through the service bays behind the decorative screens, looking for the main data-console. After a moment the alarm choked off, but when he came back into the room, he wore a grim expression.

"What?" Sawyer asked.

"I think the attack triggered a remote alarm. We don't have the all-clear code. That means that we can expect a squadron of Dragon Guards and Vampires any time now. We've got to get out of here."

"No," said Finn. "Let's find a way to defend ourselves. This place has armor and guns."

"And if we don't find them, they'll pick us off like stinkbugs."

"They'll do that anyway. You saw the countryside around here. Where can we hide?"

Harry spoke up then, "I saw transports and flyers out back. We could use one of those to escape."

"I like that idea best," said Lee.

"We can't take a flyer. They'll shoot us down."

"One of the trucks then," said Lee. He headed for the door with Harry and the others following. "We'll head out into the badlands. We can use the summer-tunnels."[39]

"Come on, pup." Sawyer came around the edge of the table, and carefully guided Ibaka toward the door and away from the cloth-covered lump.

Finn gave Kask a heavy shove. "You too, lizard. I don't think you'll have many friends among the Phaestor after today."

"I don't want friends among the Phaestor," Kask rumbled. "They have no honor." He let Finn push him toward the door.

The largest of the transports rested in a shallow pit, like a giant nesting tortoise. It looked like a fat red pumpkin seed. Harry came around the back of it and stopped abruptly. Lee and Kask came up beside him quickly. The others followed—

Several bioforms sat disconsolately in the back of the sealed truck. They looked sad and desperate. They sat with their heads in their hands or curled up in fetal positions.

Lee said an oath in some unfamiliar language and

---

[39]Because of Thoska-Roole's elliptical orbit, it suffers extremes of both heat and cold. During winter, for instance, much of the atmosphere freezes, and those inhabitants who remain during the six-month freeze must stay in the pressurized and heated habitats of the winter-caves. During the peak months of summer, when the planet passes through the outermost fringes of the red star's corona, the oppressive heat also drives the population deep underground. As a result, most of the long-term residents have grown to regard the surface of the world with a mixture of distrust and fascination. Horror and mystery prowl the surface, watched by the Eye of God. Security lives deep under the covering rock. So profoundly do the planet's inhabitants feel this revulsion of the empty sky that many of them refuse to venture to the surface even during the long safe months of passage between the extremes.

began unlocking the rear hatch. He climbed into the truck and went to the largest of the bioforms, a familiar-looking LIX. He put his hands on its muzzle and tilted its face upward to look at him. "Now, do you understand, Ota? Now, do you see? This struggle has your name on it too. No one may claim neutrality when the Vampire wants to feed."

Ota didn't answer. The creature barely even recognized Lee. It stared at him, almost unseeing, almost as if its eyes had lost their ability to focus and its brain had lost the power to resolve.

"Drugged?" asked Harry.

"No. Vampires don't like the flavor. Probably just traumatized. I don't know if it can recover."

Ibaka pushed forward, hopefully. "My brothers?" He scrambled into the back of the truck, looking around. "Ujama?"

"Sorry, kid," said Lee. "No dog-children here. We've got to go."

"What about these poor creatures?" asked Harry. "We can't leave them here—"

"We'll take them with us. Everybody get in."

"No!" shouted Ibaka. "My brothers. We can't go without my brothers. I have to find my brothers!" He ran out toward the dome-shaped barns on the other side of the villa.

"Uh-oh," said Finn.

"We have to have certainty—" Sawyer said with resignation, and headed out after Ibaka. The others followed.

Ibaka called out names as he ran, "Ujama! Ikaba! Ribaba! Can you hear me?" He ran pell-mell from one building to the next. He dashed into the gaping doors of the largest barn and—

The others heard a yelp. And then silence.

Finn looked knowingly to Sawyer. "Your turn to take the point."

Sawyer entered the barn cautiously. He took slow, careful steps and scanned the lofts above, as well as the stalls on either side of the entrance. Heavy chains and metal cages and various pieces of restraining gear filled several of the stalls; Sawyer didn't recognize some of the other devices, but none of them looked as if they served any noble purpose. Above, the lofts groaned with the weight of many sacks of dry meal—another indictment. The grain served as evidence that the Vampires brought their prey here to fatten it before they fed upon it.

The place smelled bad. Sour and dank—like something decaying. He knew this smell, but he couldn't remember where he had first encountered it. The memory had unpleasant associations, and he could feel a shudder starting to creep up his spine.

For just one swift moment, he had the eeriest feeling of déjà vu—

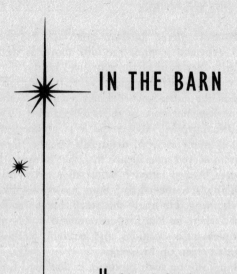

IN THE BARN

He felt it before he saw it. The ground shook underfoot. He turned, bringing his weapon up before him. Murdock came charging out of the darkness, wielding a club twice her own height.

Sawyer groaned, "Oh, no!" and leapt sideways. He felt the impact of the air as the tip of the club missed him by a whisker. He leapt backward again, stumbling to keep from falling. Murdock swung the club around over her head and prepared to bring it down again.

Sawyer fired. The beam splattered off her armor, throwing molten specks in all direction. He kept firing— and the beam caught the base of the club near her meaty paw. He flung himself to one side, falling and rolling. The club thumped on the ground next to him. He knew she had missed on purpose. The bitch liked to play with her food! Finn had guessed right. She *did* like him.

Sawyer aimed at her eyes, but her visor protected her from the blast. "I've. Had. Enough. Of. You!" she grunted. She towered over him. "Time to die."

"I agree!" said Sawyer. He fired again—not at Murdock this time, but at the beams above her, the ones holding up the loft. The first one splattered. The second one exploded. The third one crunched and broke. The loft began to sag. Murdock hesitated. She looked up, alarmed. She lifted her club up over her head as if to stop the imminent collapse of the upper story of the barn. Sawyer scrambled back in panic, rolling and kicking.

And then the whole thing came down in a great rush. The beams cracked and shattered. The sacks of meal split and poured. All the weight came roaring down on top of Murdock. She struggled for an impossible moment against this avalanche, longer than Sawyer would have believed possible ... and then, at last, she began to weaken. The bags of meal slid down on top of her, one after the other, pummeling her about the head and shoulders, finally knocking her down with their repeated poundings. She sagged and toppled. She took forever to fall. She screamed in anger, a pitiful sound, like some enormous prehistoric beast wailing out its doom as it sank inexorably beneath the tar. Murdock struggled vainly against her collapse, but still the sacks of grain came tumbling down, smacking her heavily in the chest or in the face. They pinned her great white body to the ground. She looked like a beached leviathan. The debris of the loft continued to pile up around her, pouring down in a dusty stream, covering her, until at last she disappeared for the last time beneath the rubble and the beams and the growing heaps of grain. The dust rose up in yellow clouds.

"Do you need any help?" came Finn's voice from the other side.

"No. I don't think so," Sawyer called back, "I've got everything under control now."

The others entered the barn slowly, picking their way carefully around the edges of the collapse. One of the beams cracked. Another gave way suddenly. A final sack of grain came toppling down from above, punctuating its impact with a grunt from something deep within the pile.

"You didn't kill her, did you?" Finn said. "Remember, we can still collect the bounty—"

"You would think of the money first," Sawyer rasped, trying to catch his breath. "She nearly killed me."

"But she didn't. I told you, she liked you."

"Please—do me a favor. Let the next one like you."

"We'll need chains—"

Sawyer pointed. "In the stalls." He studied the problem skeptically. "We'll need Kask's help. We'll have to start by getting her armor off her—" He shuddered. He didn't even like thinking about the logistics of this problem.

"You realize what we have here, don't you?"

"What?" Sawyer circled around the great mound warily.

"Proof," Finn said with disgust. "Proof that the Vampires have repeatedly violated the charter. Murdock supplied them with bioforms and slaves and runaways, all the creatures nobody would miss. They all ended up here. And the Vampires hunted them down for sport and ate them alive."

"You can't fight your genetic history," Sawyer muttered.[40] "From the looks of this place, they never even tried."

"Let's find the puppy." Finn headed deeper into the barn. Sawyer reluctantly followed after—not because he didn't want to find Ibaka. He feared what *else* he might find. Darkness filled this dome; what other nasty surprises lurked within?

Finn called out loudly, "Ibaka!"

---

[40]Sawyer referred, of course, to the rumors that the original genetic designers of the Phaestor had modeled their creations on wasps, spiders, and other carnivorous insects.

An answering whimper came back weakly. "Here—"

The brothers found Ibaka cowering in a cage. Murdock had trapped him and shoved him hastily into a restraining jacket. He lay in the dirt, unable to move his arms or legs. He couldn't even wriggle, he could barely breathe. Sawyer scooped him up and looked for the release, turning the little bundle over and over a couple of times before he found it. He unsnapped the catch and Ibaka tumbled out, gasping and panting. He yelped in dismay.

Remembering his age and all that had happened to him, Sawyer scooped him up in his arms and held the little child carefully. "Easy, fella. Easy. Murdock can't hurt you anymore. No one can." But Ibaka continued to scream and struggle, trying desperately to get away. Finally Sawyer had to ask, "What? What—?"

Ibaka pointed in fear—he could see something up above. Sawyer turned around to see what had caught the dog-child's attention. He almost dropped the pup in startlement.

Five little cocoons hung from a beam across the rafters of the barn.

THE FIRE THIS TIME

Wordlessly, Finn started lowering the cocoons to the ground. Before Sawyer could grab him and hold him back, Ibaka attacked them furiously, calling out the names of his brothers and futilely trying to peel them out of the spider-silk pods. He sobbed and wailed piteously, his voice rising in a hideous screech. He scratched at the webbing with his little sharp claws. "Ujama! Ujama! Ribaba! No! No! No! Don't die! Don't die! I've come back to save you! Please, please—" He looked around helplessly at the humans.

Sawyer went down on his knees beside Ibaka, not sure whether to help him or hold him back. Each of the tiny shrouds still felt soft and warm to the touch.

Lee and Harry approached silently, guns at the ready. They wore their horror on their faces. Kask lumbered up behind.

"Shit," said Lee.

The others looked at him.

He looked away unhappily, then brought his eyes back to the others. "After a Vampire catches his prey," he explained, "he cocoons it. He injects it with a poison to keep it paralyzed and alive for days, so he can feed on it at his leisure. You don't want to know the rest."

Kask made a decision. He grabbed the frantic dog-child in one great claw, scooped him up, and carried him screaming out of the barn. Ibaka snapped and bit and shrieked all the way.

Sawyer looked to Lee. He gathered the cocoons before him, straightening them gently as if the puppies within could feel and hear everything that happened around them. "Do they still live?"

Lee nodded grimly.

"Can we ... do anything?"

Lee hesitated. He shook his head slowly. "No. Not now. Maybe if we'd gotten here sooner—I don't know."

"Can they hear us ...?"

Lee shrugged. "Nobody has ever come back to report." He stared into Sawyer and Finn's eyes. "Do what you have to do." Then he turned and left.

Harry waited only a moment longer, his lips moving silently. "A prayer for their little souls," he acknowledged. Then he too exited.

Sawyer stood up unhappily. He could feel the tears welling up in his eyes, he didn't know why. He'd never let himself feel anything like this before. He backed away from the silken cocoons without looking at them. He reset the controls on his weapon and—still without looking—pointed it in the general direction of the five little objects.

He squeezed the trigger and the tiny pods burst into flame. He squeezed the trigger again and they turned white-hot. Once more, and they disintegrated in powdery flashes. In the distance they could still hear Ibaka shrieking in the Dragon's arms.

Sawyer turned and looked at Finn. "We've gotten into a very shitty business here."

Finn grunted. He looked uncomfortable and weak.

Sawyer started for him. Finn held up a hand to hold his brother off. "I can manage—for a while longer anyway."

"Listen, Finn."

"What?"

"If you ever find me wrapped up like ... like that, will you—you know?"

Finn nodded. "Yeah, I will. Me too." He met his brother's eyes. "Please?"

Sawyer realized abruptly what Finn had asked. In his brother's case the request had a terrifying immediacy.

"Finn—that won't happen!"

"You know as well as I what will happen! Just promise me." He grabbed Sawyer's arm.

"Please, don't make me—" Sawyer couldn't say it. He gave in to his brother's insistent stare. "All right. I promise."

"Thank you."

Suddenly, the sound of an airboat came from outside the barn. They both broke and ran for the door—

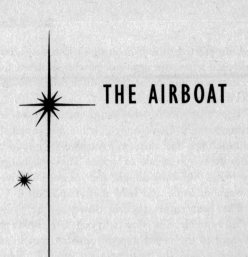

THE AIRBOAT

The airboat came bobbing up over the hills like an arrow, radiating a high-pitched electronic whine. The sound shivered up their spines and then back down again, leaving them shaking and nauseous.

"Slop field!" Finn cursed. "The goddamn Regency does that shit!"

"Regency colors—" Lee spat. He carried one of the heavy-duty cannons. He anchored it on the ground and started to take aim, but just as he locked onto his target, Ota came barreling into him. The bioform leapt and kicked, missing Lee, but hurling the weapon halfway across the yard. Lee started to turn to the creature, a curse forming on his lips, when abruptly a beam spat out from the approaching shuttlecraft and speared the weapon in midair, splattering it in a puddle of blazing light. The colors echoed in the air.

"They got us," said Finn. "I don't have the strength to run anymore." He held up his hands in surrender. "I give up."

"I don't believe you," said Lee, spitting his disgust.

Finn started to say, "You don't know—" And then he collapsed across the ground. Sawyer grabbed for him, barely catching him before he sprawled face down like a drunken sailor.

The boat circled the camp once, its lower guns swiveling to keep them in sight while it scanned the rest of the buildings. The slop field warbled even louder then, making them too weak to resist. They exchanged unhappy looks, but they all got the message. They tossed their weapons aside and held their hands up in the air.

The boat came drifting down to the ground as gently as a bubble. The slop field began to ebb as the rear access door to the vessel popped open. A female android and a high-gravity dwarf sprang out, weapons held at the ready. Both wore armor. They advanced carefully. Behind them the gun turrets of the shuttlecraft swung around to focus on the small band of escapees. A heavy-metal robot came down the ramp next. He had a heavy-equipment harness slung from his shoulders to help him support the high-powered cannon he carried. He wore a power-cell on his back and had enough firepower to level the whole villa just from where he stood.

Ota walked slowly forward. "I've seen better timing," it said with wry amusement. "These people have already secured the installation and killed all of the Phaestor. The battle ended some time ago."

"What?" screamed an angry female voice, amplified through the shuttleboat's speakers. A moment later a furious Captain Campbell came striding down the ramp. "What the hell do you mean winning the battle before we arrive?"

"My apologies," said Ota, remembering itself quickly. "I appreciate your rescue. I promise you, the next time I will wait for your full participation."

Behind the bioform the humans exchanged confused glances. "Excuse me?" Sawyer called. He straightened up slowly, leaving Finn sitting weakly on the ground. "This shuttleboat wears Regency colors—"

"Only until we get out of here," snapped Campbell. "Thank these people and get aboard, Ota. EDNA says a Dragon-boat has just launched from MesaPort."

"Wait a minute!" said Lee. He approached Captain Campbell quickly. "Will you accept a contract to deliver the TimeBinder of Thoska-Roole to the Gathering?"

Campbell scratched her sideburn thoughtfully. It took her less than a second to decide. "I need to break orbit and get out of here fast. I've got Dragons after me."

"So have we," said Lee. "Can you give me twelve hours?"

"If we can avoid the prowling Marauders, we can."

"You can hide your boat in any of the canyons in the badlands. The Marauders won't go there. Something keeps shooting them down."

"I'll need a guide—"

"I can do that," said Arl-N. "I grew up in the badlands."

"All right. Deal," said Campbell. "Robin, give this man a coded signaler." To Lee she said, "I had to leave thirty-three metric tons of industrial-grade three-month pfingle eggs on Burihatin. We pick them up first, deliver them, and then we'll take you to your Gathering. If we hurry, we can deliver them before they turn into six-week eggs."

"Pfingle eggs?" Lee looked astonished. "You want to carry pfingle eggs?"

Captain Campbell shrugged. "Why not? Somebody has to do it. At thirty-five hundred calories of pure protein per egg, this cargo has a Class-Double-A profitability rating."

Lee shook his head in disbelief. "And I wondered if you had the courage for this job. You do—"

"Enough talk. Load your people," said Campbell.

"We've got to move!" Captain Campbell began herding the group toward the shuttleboat.

Sawyer went back to Finn. "We have to help Lee—"

Finn nodded his agreement. "I know." He levered himself weakly to his feet. "Come on. We'll need a couple of antigrav sleds—"

THE THOUGHTS
OF DRAGONS

The Dragon Lord belched uncomfortably and picked at his teeth with a hardened claw. He peered down at the display table with dispassionate interest. A stereo map showed the terrain south of MesaPort. The image rolled slowly across the surface of the table, pouring off the edge and disappearing. Two ruby-red dots moved across the center of it.

Captain Lax-Varney pointed with a green finger of light. "They've made a very bad tactical mistake. They've entered a canyon called *the gullet*. They'll have to run the whole length of it. Fifty kilometers. We'll wait here and we'll catch them when they come out. They have no other exit."

The Dragon Lord grunted and studied his Captain skeptically. "Do you really believe that you'll catch them that easily?"

Lax-Varney bowed respectfully. "My Lord, the sleds have tracers. Wherever they go, we'll catch them."

"Yes, you do believe it," said the Dragon Lord. "You have all the wisdom of your predecessor. Let us hope that you have better luck." He swung his tail out of the way, turned, and studied the desolate red landscape scrolling away beneath the airboat. "This planet has too many places to hide," he cursed. "The wise Dragon believes nothing until after it has happened."

Lax-Varney felt troubled by his Lord's ruminations. He wondered if the old lizard had fallen senile. He knew he couldn't challenge him—not yet. He hoped the Dragon Lord had the strength to survive a while longer while he built up his strength. He thought for a moment. It might take as long as ten or twenty years. He would have to make sure that the warrior-lizard did not fall until he wanted him to fall. He pretended to study the display again, making a great show of it.

To all outward appearances, the Dragon Lord might have fallen asleep. His smoldering eyes had drifted shut. His huge mouth had parted slightly, and his breath came out in slow and heavy gusts. But only the great lizard's body rested; his mind raced through corridors of thought, examining possibilities, considering them, discarding them, and moving on.

Too much had happened here recently—and too much of it had involved Lady Zillabar and behaviors best left undiscussed. The question of honor loomed large in the Dragon Lord's mind. Honor meant loyalty—but loyalty to what? The Phaestor? The Zashti family? Zillabar? Or the intangible concept called the Charter of the Regency? It troubled him—a little. He knew too much. Not only that, he ate too much—too much of the wrong things. He shared the Vampires' shame.

The standards of honor demanded that he remain clear about his duty. But the question stood out in his head. Duty to whom? And to what?

Above all, he knew, stood duty to power. Without power, nothing followed.

And power brings perks. Why shouldn't it? Along with the responsibilities came privileges. He had his own little pleasures. A Dragon Lord could afford to have a habit or two, if he maintained discretion. But in that, he knew, his honor remained no better than that of the Vampires.

Nevertheless, he consoled himself, when you achieve the rank of ruler, you no longer follow the rules—you *make* them.

So he sighed to himself and allowed himself a pang of remorse for his deviations, knowing full well that the next time the opportunity presented itself, he would enjoy himself fully. He could justify it to himself, and his opinion had become the only one that mattered when he became the Dragon Lord.

Besides, if he really needed a justification ... he knew all too well that if he did not maintain the status quo, he would not maintain his authority either. He knew his history. Dragon Lords didn't simply retire. And he had no illusions how long he would last if Lady Zillabar chose to have him replaced. Not replaced. Assassinated. And if not from above, then certainly from below. Lax-Varney, for instance. The Captain of his personal guards had already demonstrated both his ambition and his stupidity.

The Dragon Lord hadn't decided yet how to kill the dim-witted lizard, but something would occur to him sooner or later. If nothing else, he could always send him out to patrol the badlands and let the rebels take care of this little problem. He liked that idea. It had honor. Always let your enemies weaken themselves fighting each other before you let them fight you.

He settled himself happily in his stall and waited for the airboat to land at the nether orifice of *the gullet*. The Dragon Lord snorted happily at the realization. He had a vulgar sense of humor.

CONTRACTUAL OBLIGATIONS

The desert smoked. Great rolling clouds of it obscured the horizon. The red sun poured through it like a glaze, until everything turned as gloomy as the inside of a Vampire's heart. The Dragon Lord allowed himself a smile of pleasure; he liked the gloom. He called it *hunting weather*. He liked to prowl through the darkness, following only his nose, seeking out criminals or prey—it didn't matter which; in the darkness he could eat without witnesses and without guilt.

The larger he grew, the hungrier he became. For years hunger had traveled constantly at his side. Perhaps if the great clouds of dust would roll this way, blanketing the remainder of the day, he could indulge himself again. What would happen if the criminals accidentally shook off their bonds? Why, then he would have to demonstrate just how he had earned his great rank, wouldn't he? He would have to go after them in person—and who knew what could happen in the darkness?

Already his stomach rumbled in anticipation. He waddled heavily around to where six gunners sat behind their cannons, waiting for the antigrav sleds to come slicing out of *the gullet*. "Listen to me," he said. "When they exit the canyon, the Regency override signal will cut in, and the power to their sleds will fail. We have blocked their access to the plain. They cannot get by. They will not even try. So don't fire unless I tell you to. I want to catch this human vermin alive. If you disobey—if you fire without my command, I will eat your livers. Do you understand?"

Both of the Dragons nodded quickly. "Yes, my Lord. Yes, sir."

"Sir?" Captain Lax-Varney called. "We have them in range. We should hear them any moment now—"

"Lax-Varney, you don't listen very well. For the past three minutes, the sound of their sleds has echoed in my ears."

"Sir—?"

The Dragon Lord held up a hand for silence. In the red gloom of the morning, the desert had an eerie stillness. He felt as if he could hear for light-years. He felt pleased with himself; Captain Lax-Varney might have his doubts about another Dragon's ability to hear the distant sleds, but he wouldn't doubt his Lord's word. The great Dragon had deliberately installed a seed of fear and doubt in the heart of his ambitious underling. Whatever plans Lax-Varney might have brewing, now he would also have to consider that his Lord could see and hear him in ways he had never considered. The danger remained, of course, that the Captain would only grow more cautious, not more respectful—but at this point the Dragon Lord did not expect his Captain to live long enough to develop into a real threat.

Now, very faintly in the distance, the heterodyning hum of two antigrav sleds began to rise. "They come," he said, satisfied, and turned to glare at the gunners. Quickly, they removed their hands from their fire controls.

The sounds of the sleds grew louder, warbling unevenly as the vehicles maneuvered their way through the narrow twisting canyon. The sound rose and fell; it splashed and broke in a torrent of confusing echoes that dopplered and reflected and ultimately rolled out of *the gullet* as a river of electronic noise. The whine of the sleds grew louder and louder. Suddenly, they appeared at the far end of the canyon—both of them, very close together.

The Dragon Lord frowned.

The sleds looked harnessed together. They moved in unison, bobbing and swerving like two stallions caught in a trap and racing to break free. They roared down the canyon toward the waiting cannons. Something big hung between them, it looked like an angry side of beef.

Abruptly, the Regency override signal cut in and the power to both sleds failed. The hum of their engines warbled downward, and they slowed and lowered to their skids. They came sliding the rest of the way out of the canyon, stopping only meters in front of the Dragon Lord.

Murdock lay stretched between the two sleds, tied by her own chains. Dirt and rage streaked her face. A heavy tag hung around her neck. The Dragon Lord approached cautiously. He lifted the tag with one talon and read it with growing rage.

The Markham brothers had attached their bill.

> *Posted Criminal Warrant #M21-S filled. Contract completed. Bonding agency notified. Please credit Markham trust account 131-534 at First Interstellar Bank. Reimbursement fees for lost and damaged equipment included in total; expense report filed. Also note additional charges for ancillary terminations of Murdock's employers, as per contract. Details on request, only to authorized parties.*

Employers—?

The Dragon Lord ripped the tag from Murdock's

neck and threw it to one side. Lax-Varney rushed to pick it up.

The Dragon Lord growled, a deep, disturbing rumble of frustration. The audacity of the Markham brothers' stunt only annoyed him. On one level he could even admire their style. But the tag around Murdock's neck—the bill for services—represented a much more serious matter. Not for what it said, but for what it implied. The potential for real disaster here troubled him much more than he dared show. And the Markhams had to know that too. He hated the humans for pushing him into this situation. If the knowledge of Murdock's crimes became public, that she had supplied bioforms and slaves for secret Vampire feasts, riots would break out in every city on Thoska-Roole. The Vampires wouldn't suffer. They had the means to escape. No, the Dragons would bear the brunt of the attacks.

He dared not oppose the Vampires, but he dared not release Murdock either. The damned Markham brothers had filed their damned claim through an interstellar bonding agency. Investigations would follow, no matter what. Investigations, revelations, riots—and massacres. The Dragons would lose much honor.

The Dragon Lord felt frustrated. No matter what he did, the action would prove disastrous for Dragons, unless—yes. That could work. The matter would end here if Murdock died while trying to escape. Indeed.

The Dragon Lord turned to study the criminal. She glared up at him, impatient for her release. Her flesh had a strong and muscular look to it. Juicy, even. Yes. Her great size decided the issue in the Dragon Lord's mind. For once he would sate his intolerable hunger. He began to salivate.

Lax-Varney approached his master cautiously. "Sir?" he asked. He held up the bill. "What about this? What should I do with it?"

The Dragon Lord grinned, revealing a cavernous mouth filled with glittering teeth. "Pay it, of course."

NO SUCH THING AS A FREE LAUNCH

The shuttleboat rested in a dark, shadowy canyon.

Ota tended to the minor wounds and scrapes of her rescuers, while Shariba-Jen passed out food and water. Kask ate hungrily, ignoring Gito's unhappy glare. Ibaka had fallen asleep in the Dragon's lap only after long hours of inconsolable tears. Every so often Kask would pat the tiny brown ball of fur gently with his great scaly claw.

Captain Campbell sat in the pilot's seat and glowered unhappily. EDNA had moved the *Lady Macbeth* into a deep elliptical orbit, where it would remain out of easy range for the Regency's Marauders. Unfortunately, the new orbit would also make an eventual rendezvous much trickier. The Regency didn't have to search for them on Thoska-Roole. They could wait until the *Lady Macbeth* made its closest approach and intercept them then. She would have to figure out an unlikely, but still cost-effective, way of returning the shuttleboat to the vessel.

Perhaps—she had an idea—if she put the shuttle

into a complementary orbit, she could elude the Marauders. Suppose they lifted into an elliptical orbit that extended away from the planet opposite the orbit of the *Lady Macbeth*. And suppose the only place where the shuttleboat orbit came parallel to that of the starship remained out of range?

It might work. She'd have to talk it over with EDNA. The mechanics of such an operation would prove tricky—

And then she had another idea. What if they launched the shuttleboat outward on a maximum-acceleration course? One that guaranteed that they would expend all of their fuel? The Marauders could eventually outrun them, but only at the risk of exhausting their own fuel and hurtling themselves irretrievably into deep space. An interesting idea that. The Marauders could not depend on the *Lady Macbeth* to intercept their course and rescue them. She could.

All right. Those plans worked. Now she needed only one more.

"Ahem, Captain?"

She looked up, then swiveled around. Gito and Robin stood politely waiting. "Captain?" Robin repeated. "We need to discuss something."

"I know that tone of voice," she said with resignation. "It always means bad news. Go ahead."

"You've resigned from the Guild, correct?" Robin asked.

Campbell nodded. "Yes."

"Well, that makes all of our contracts null and void. As the union representative aboard this ship, I have the responsibility of protecting the jobs and the rights of the crew—"

"I know the speech, Robin." The Captain sighed. "No one will lose their job. Conditions aboard the *Lady Macbeth* will remain exactly the same."

"No, ma'am, they can't. Freebooters operate without Regency guarantees. So even if you personally make a guarantee, no larger legal authority stands behind it. We have no way to compel behavior or compliance with a negotiated contract. In such a case the union requires additional bonding per voyage to guarantee the wages of the crew."

Campbell didn't reply immediately. She stared off into space, considering her options. It took her a moment to step past her feelings of anger and betrayal. After all, hadn't she just demonstrated her commitment to her crew—her family? Hadn't she just resigned in protest from the Guild so she could rescue Ota without sanctions? Didn't that count for something?

Apparently not.

But then, after she put her feelings aside, she recognized that Robin and Gito had a point. And in fact, as union members they had a specific responsibility to keep their shipmasters honest. She would have done the same.

Star-Captain Campbell nodded reluctantly. She studied her fingernails with a thoughtful expression. Finally she looked up at them both. "You know the financial situation of the Shakespeare Corporation. Robin, you and Ota handle most of the bookkeeping. We can't afford the extra bonding."

"You should have thought of that before you resigned from the Guild," grumbled Gito.

"And leave Ota to the Vampires?"

"You didn't have to resign!"

"We couldn't have afforded the Guild penalties if I didn't!"

"We worked hard for that insignia!"

"Yes, we did. I didn't say I liked what I did; but I did what I had to do. And you would have too. So let it lie, Gito."

Gito opened his mouth to reply, but Robin placed a hand gently on his arm. He shut up with a scowl.

"All right," Captain Campbell said. "What do you want?"

Robin looked apologetic. "We know about the financial situation of the corporation. And we stand prepared to shoulder our share of the burden."

"Would you translate that into my language, please?"

"If we have to share the dangers of freebooting," interrupted Gito rudely, "we want to share in the profits too."

"What profits?" Campbell asked blandly.

"Whatever profits we earn in the future," Robin said.

"I see. . . . I go freebooter to rescue the crew, and the crew votes itself shares in the corporation. What a lovely plan."

"You can't run the ship without us!" Gito insisted.

"You have a contract," Campbell replied quietly. "Regardless of Guild membership, the corporation will honor all of its current contracts. I expect the crew to honor its commitments too."

"Without a Guild insignia, you have no way to compel enforcement."

"True, but you gave me your personal guarantee. Doesn't that count for something?"

"But you can't give us a corresponding guarantee, Captain. Don't take this personally, but we now have absolutely no protection against possible abuses by the corporation."

"How can I *not* take that personally? I own all the shares."

"If you make us shareholders, then we have protection. We become your partners."

"I don't want any partners. I like it this way."

"Captain, we don't feel comfortable working without an enforceable contract. This would give us fair representation. We'd have more real input."

"Shares of stock reflect ownership, bought and paid for with real value. What have you invested in the Shakespeare Corporation?"

"Our labor, for one thing."

Captain Campbell didn't answer that directly. "I can't deny the value of your labor," she admitted. "But your idea, Gito, doesn't have a lot of appeal for me. The way you tell it, I get to carry the financial burden—you share the profits."

"What profits? We've all seen the books."

"My point exactly." Captain Campbell grinned. "I can't afford your plan."

Gito looked flustered. He sputtered for a moment in helpless anger. He looked to Robin. The android spoke quietly. "This plan protects you as well. It guarantees against labor stoppages—"

"I don't pay protection. You know that."

"If you agree to this, we all stay in business."

"At a loss, yes!" Campbell laughed. "What'll we do? Make it up in volume?"

"Captain. We all need each other. We ask only an acknowledgment of that."

"Acknowledgment I can give you. All you want. But shares in the corporation—? Well ... I'll gladly sell a proportional share to any of you, but I can't give shares away. We've all worked too hard for that."

"We need a lawyer—" Gito said in frustration.

"It seems to me that you've already had too much exposure to lawyers for one voyage."

"We have an Arbiter aboard—" Gito pulled Harry to the front of the vessel. "Ask him."

Harry held up his hands in protest. "I don't barge into arguments uninvited. And besides, I charge for my services."

"Oh great," said Campbell. "Something else to pay for."

"We'll trade you safe passage in return for your legal advice," Gito said.

"I make the deals here—" Campbell interrupted.

"Without a deal nobody goes anywhere," Gito snapped right back.

Campbell studied Harry with little regard. "I've shoved lawyers out the airlock before. I won't hesitate to do it again."

"Hm," said Harry. He stroked his chin thoughtfully. "This case has some interesting complications. It may take me some time to make a ruling. I'll have to study the situation at length. I would advise in the meantime"—he glanced around the cabin, meeting the eyes of each of his listeners—"that all complainants maintain their duties until such time as I can determine an equitable resolution."

Gito stared up at him. "What does that mean?" He looked to Robin. "Can he do that? Does that have legality?"

"Ahh, you need a little application of Latin, do you?" Harry said wisely. "Try this. *Illegitimi non carborundum.*"

"Eh?" Gito frowned in confusion. Captain Campbell concealed her smile by biting her lip and turning to the plotting screen.

"I'll translate," Harry said. "Let's get out of here as fast as we can. We'll figure out the details later."

THE CORRIDORS
OF NIGHT

MesaPort only pretended solid-
ity. Within the towering rock lay a hidden network of
caves and tunnels. Generations of dwellers had spent
their summers and winters expanding their warrens like
worms tunneling through soft cheese.

Here, inside the mountain, a whole other civilization thrived—a civilization unknown to the Vampires
and the Dragons and all the various pretenders and idle
worshipers who served them in their glittering halls. Secret passages led down to the roots of the broken canyons,
wove their way even deeper than that, tunneling down to
huge underground reservoirs and the rivers that fed
them. Here, hidden from the Eye of God, and hidden
from the Regency as well, churned the machineries of human survival.

Using only a single red lamp for illumination,
Lee-1169 brought Sawyer and Finn up through a series
of narrow passages. The journey took several hours. They
had to stop several times, once while Finn suffered another of his crippling spells, another time for rest and a
meal break; a third time they rested at the edge of a vast

black reservoir and filled their canteens. The inky water echoed with distant voices. The stillness of the chamber enveloped them with dark echoes.

They pushed on. Lee explained the necessity of this roundabout route. It would protect all of them if they did not know their destination or how they had reached it. They climbed up a seemingly endless ladder that paralleled a huge vertical tube. The tube throbbed with energy; it thrummed with mechanical life. Both Finn and Sawyer stared with awe and wondered about the energies it focused. They also wondered what would happen to MesaPort if a saboteur could wrap a section of the tube with explosives. They made a mental note to ask Lee about this later. Purely as a hypothetical exercise, of course.

At last they arrived at a long room carved out of the naked rock, with a ceiling so low, they could not fully stretch their hands up over their heads. It gave them a claustrophobic feeling. At one end of the room narrow windows opened out onto a view of Death Canyon. They could see the lights of the labor camp glimmering far below. Already a new crew of prisoners toiled under the slave bands. Sawyer shuddered at the memory. Had they really escaped from that terrible place only two days previously?

He turned around to see a group of four men entering the chamber after Lee. One of them stood so tall and spindly that he couldn't completely straighten up in this room. The man wore a red cloth wrapped around his head and carried a rod that looked like a walking stick. He entered the room at a crouch and moved directly to a stone bench, where he settled himself comfortably. The others arranged themselves around him. Even in repose he loomed taller than anyone else in the room. The man grinned down at the much shorter Lee, his expression an acknowledgment of the difference in their sizes. "Your apartment hasn't gotten any taller, my friend."

"I don't need the extra height," Lee retorted. "It would just take that much longer for the blood to reach my brain."

The tall man laughed, a large good-natured sound. "Tell me about your escape."

Lee pointed to Sawyer and Finn. "These two trackers, Justice Mertz, a Dragon, a dog-child, and others—we discovered the Alliance of Life lives everywhere, all the time. You spoke the truth, sir."

"No," corrected the tall man. "I spoke words. *You* discovered the truth of them."

Lee allowed himself a sheepish look at the correction. "I still have much to learn," he acknowledged.

"You will continue to do well," said the tall man.

Sawyer and Finn approached and joined the circle. Sawyer couldn't decide if the other men in the group acted as guards or worshiped as acolytes. He decided that they served both functions and kept himself wary. Despite his obviously weakened condition, Finn nodded courteously and said, "You have the advantage of us, sir."

The tall man opened his hands in the universal gesture of peace. "I wear the name of William Three-Dollar." He unwrapped the red cloth from his head to reveal a shimmering band of blue-white light. It sat like a halo on the crown of his skull; it gleamed across his forehead and around his temples, disappearing finally under his long jet-black hair. The brightness of the band made a stark contrast with his dark red skin. His piercing eyes shone almost as bright. Sawyer had the eeriest feeling as he looked into the man's face—as if somehow he stared directly into one of the many faces of God.

William Three-Dollar spoke in a voice like the wind. "I serve as the TimeBinder of Thoska-Roole," he said.

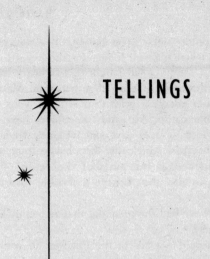

TELLINGS

Sawyer and Finn exchanged a glance. For a moment neither of them knew how to react. Finally Finn—holding on to his brother for support—went down on one knee in a bow. "Father, I beg your forgiveness for all of our crimes—those in our past as well as in our future."

The TimeBinder blinked in surprise. He stretched out one long arm and laid a huge hand on Finn's head. As he did so, a grave look of concern came over his face. "Unease rides within you, my son. And something else—" His eyes narrowed. "I cannot cure what troubles you. But the medicine does exist."

"I have searched for years, Father—I have never found it."

"You have to look in the right place, my son. Keep looking."

"I beg your forgiveness, Father."

"If you can forgive yourself, Finn, you won't need mine."

Finn nodded his acceptance. "I have heard it said

that a TimeBinder never gives you anything, except what you haven't asked for."

William Three-Dollar laughed. "I've heard that one myself." He gestured. "Please sit down, Finn Markham. Rest. Save your energy. I want to hear about your escape from the labor camp. All kinds of rumors have swept through the city for two days, but we've heard nothing from the Phaestor. And now they have all gone into hiding—panicked at the news of the death of Lord Drydel. Apparently, they believe a terrible insurrection has begun."

"If only we had the men and matériel to make that so—" Lee said.

"You would not accept the Phaestor in your Alliance of Life?" the TimeBinder asked speculatively.

"I cannot imagine a Vampire accepting the Alliance. Would a Vampire forsake its family, its honor, its greed, its *hunger*, for the privilege of associating with prey? I doubt it very much."

"And suppose such a one did exist? Could you accept him?"

"When I meet such a one," Lee-1169 said bitterly, "then I will consider that question. But not until then."

Three-Dollar nodded his acceptance, knowing that even this little bit represented a major concession for Lee. "Tell me about your escape," he said to them.

Quickly Lee, Sawyer, and Finn recited the details of their escape from the labor camp, their trek south through the dry canal, and the surprise attack on the Vampire villa. The TimeBinder expressed little surprise at Kask's acceptance of a new brotherhood. "Dragons have simple and direct souls," he said. "That remains their strength as well as their weakness."

The men concluded their narrative with an explanation of the trick they had played on the Dragon Guard. "—so we took Murdock's transport. The Vampires had given Murdock a safe-passage transponder, so it wouldn't even show up on the Dragons' screens. And even if they did spot the transport, they still wouldn't imagine that anyone could have overpowered Murdock. That creature abandoned all pretense of humanity a long time ago."

"We destroyed the transport," Lee said. "It has joined the rubble at the bottom of Death Canyon. If and when the Dragons ever find it, we will have long escaped from this place."

William Three-Dollar sat silent for a long moment, considering the import of their words. His long fingers drummed silently on his bony knee. His expression faded away, as if he focused on something a million light-years distant. "No TimeBinder has ever left Thoska-Roole," he said finally. "Not since the first Gathering."

"This Gathering cannot happen without you," Lee argued.

"I know that, son." He fingered the rod that lay across his lap, and an uncomfortable expression came across his features. "I have no experience with star travel," he admitted. "The thought disturbs me. Does that startle you? That a TimeBinder can experience fear? It shouldn't. The TimeBinder must remain open to all experience. Here I remain safe. The Regency can't find me in the warrens of MesaPort. Out there—we all become vulnerable. I wonder if this Gathering might not represent a much greater threat to us than to the Regency."

"We have to take the risk."

"Not you—I. And I do not share your enthusiasm for this task. First, I must believe that no better alternative exists." He held up a hand to forestall Lee's next words. "I know what you want to say—and what your respect stops you from saying. No, my son. Trust me when I say that you do not fully understand. I would make the journey if I could see the absolute necessity of it. At this moment I have doubts that I must resolve. I cannot decide immediately. I must *transcend* this moment to a larger perspective. I will need dreamtime."

"We don't have time," Lee said impatiently. "Captain Campbell won't wait."

"She will have to, or I won't go. I will not embark on a voyage of this importance without certainty."

THE BINDING OF TIME

Those who convened the first Gathering made two important decisions.

In the first of those decisions, they assigned the protection of the Regency to the fast-thinking Phaestor and the undefeatable Dragon Guards. In the second decision, they created a means by which the Regency could reinvent itself should such a need ever arise.

In the history of sentient affairs, one fact remains apparent—that those who do not learn from their history will attempt to rewrite it.

So the TimeBinders created themselves as a direct connection with their own heritage. Each of the TimeBinders wore a crown of wisdom. The identities, knowledge, experiences, and intelligence of every previous wearer rested in the band. When a TimeBinder died, he passed the band to a chosen heir; as each new 'Binder put on the band, the wisdom of the past would begin to infuse his soul, and likewise, his spirit would begin a life-long migration into the substance of the crown, so that every TimeBinder who wore the crown after him would have the same access to his knowledge and experience.

The contribution of any individual remained insignificant. Across the centuries criminals and saints alike wore the bands. The crowns had little tangible value in the immediate world, and those who sought the crowns for personal gain first discovered disappointment, and later enlightenment.

The wisdom of the band lay in the cumulative experience of all the wearers, and no TimeBinder ever escaped the heavy weight of the centuries. Whatever he or she or it brought to the process, the headband brought even more. As the generations of wearers passed steadily into history, the quality of the individual who accepted the band became much less significant to the process. Even the experiences he carried had little importance when measured against the great mass of personal history the headband carried. Ultimately, the headband transformed the wearer into a true TimeBinder, whether he desired it or not.

Although the TimeBinders had little real authority in the day-to-day operations of the Regency, as the generations passed and the wisdom of the headbands began to accrue, the observations of the TimeBinders began to gain wider and wider respect. The TimeBinders became the living voices of each world's heritage. Ultimately, those who ignored the combined wisdom of the generations often lived long enough to regret their errors. The TimeBinders came to represent an extraordinary moral and ethical force across the Regency.

While much of the raw information of the band remained always accessible to the wearer, the real wisdom lay in the dreamtime experience. In the dream state the TimeBinder's present identity merged with the stored identities of all of his/her/its predecessors. The perceptions, decisions, observations, realizations, words, and actions that resulted came not from a single soul, but from the merged souls of all who had ever worn the headband.

In the dreamtime, the TimeBinder became immortal, living simultaneously in both his past and his future. He could embark on no path without this centering of self.[41]

---

[41]The TimeBinder's dream state bears little relation to the Phaestor dream state. Where the TimeBinder communes with the shared identities of every individual who has previously worn the same headband, the Vampire communes only with his or her own hallucinogenic center. Wisdom drives the TimeBinder, but only hunger drives the Vampire.

THE TIMEBINDER
SPEAKS

When he returned to that state that others called consciousness, William Three-Dollar rested for a long moment before arising from the mat.

The ancestors of this body had come from the legendary Earth. They had lived high in a mountain range called the Andes, the backbone of a continent called South America.

He sat up slowly, giving himself a moment to reorient to his surroundings. He wore his ancestors' features; he had high, wide cheekbones and narrow black eyes. The crown of his head bulged slightly wider than his distant progenitors' had; the effect conferred wisdom, not grotesquerie.

He rubbed his eyes as he brought himself back to the immediate moment. He realized anew much of what he had always known but had never consciously *experienced*. The dreamtime gave him access to the insight of history. Sometimes it troubled him; mostly it didn't. It never got any easier; if anything, each subsequent submergence into the dream state felt more difficult than the last—but each time he always emerged stronger.

He stood up in an uncomfortable crouch and returned to the main room of Lee-1169's apartment. He settled himself again on the stone bench and waited until the others had gathered around him again.

He began to speak quietly and patiently of the situation in the Cluster Worlds. He looked to Lee. "You believe that the authority of the Regency will soon collapse."

Lee nodded.

"In that belief, my son, you have projected the hopes and wishes and fears of yourself and those who follow you."

"So you say the collapse will not occur?"

"On the contrary, Lee. The collapse has already occurred."

For a moment Lee and the others struggled with their confusion. Everybody spoke at once, questioning, demanding, interrupting each other with their hurried words. "How do you know this? Where did you get this information? Why didn't you tell us?"

William Three-Dollar held up his hand and waited patiently. The room fell instantly silent.

"I have swum in the oceans of time. All knowledge dwells in that sea, if you have the strength to dive for it. What I have seen—in this life and all the others—tells me the truth about the Regency Marauders that have taken over this world. Why *this* world? Have you ever considered what strategic value this broken rock possesses? It has none. It lies away from the center of the Cluster. It has little industry and only enough agriculture to feed the barest of populations. We have no wealth here, no strength, nothing but our inaccessibility."

"Tell us something we don't know, old man," Lee grumbled.

Three-Dollar laughed at the child's disrespect. "You know it, Lee—and yet, you still don't know it. Think— why would the Regency send so *many* Marauders here? Do we need such protection—from whom? Or do we represent such a threat *to* the Regency that we require so many restrictive patrols? What kind of a threat could we mount? We don't even have the power among ourselves to demand the enforcement of the Regency Charter. So, the question remains: *Why* have the Marauders come here?"

Lee and the others frowned as they thought about the TimeBinder's questions. Clearly, he had seen something in the situation that they still missed.

Sawyer looked to Finn. Finn shrugged. "How should I know?"

"All right," conceded Lee. "Tell us."

"Most people don't know it yet. Kernel d'Vashti doesn't dare let the information out. But the Regency Marauders that have taken over Thoska-Roole represent all that remains of a much greater fleet. Think about it."

The TimeBinder explained. "The Vampire families have argued among themselves. The fleet has disintegrated, and each Vampire has supposedly taken his squadrons home. But think about Vampire males—they kill each other almost as fast as they kill the rest of us. Knowing that your potential enemy has turned his back to you, could you resist the temptation to sneak up on him in the darkness and thrust a knife into his back? Neither could d'Vashti. The Marauders here bear scars of battle. The Vampire commanders have squabbled among themselves. We'll never know how many ships died—but d'Vashti's presence here proves that no one won a decisive victory. And pay attention now—I feel certain that no single voice remains in authority. No one commands. We wait in silence while the Regency lies stunned, naked, and uncontrolled. A single strong hand can either seize its reins or rend it asunder."

"You saw this in your dreams?" asked Sawyer, skeptically. "What distinguishes this—this theory from the wishes of children or the hopeful speculation of old men?"

"You have little experience with TimeBinders," said William Three-Dollar. "I report what I see. Whether you accept my vision or not remains your choice."

"We have to take your word on faith, then?"

"You may use whatever you wish," the TimeBinder chided him gently.

Exasperated, Sawyer threw himself back in his seat. Finn shrugged helplessly at his brother, but the two turned their attention back to the tall Indian TimeBinder.

William Three-Dollar continued his careful discourse. "Kernel d'Vashti wants to wear the crown of Emperor. He wants to rule the Cluster. He has brought his squadrons to this world because our people lack the capability of mounting any serious resistance. Here he can replenish and rebuild the strength of his fleet without fearing a sudden assault from space. He did this under the protection and authority of the Prefect—until Lady Zillabar arrived and demoted him and killed the Prefect.

"But now, with Drydel's death, you have forced both his hand and Lady Zillabar's. The Lady will now have no choice but to make him her Consort. She had hoped to avoid this marriage, but now she needs him to enforce her family's power. Without d'Vashti, she risks civil war across the Cluster. They both know that neither can win such a conflict. It would last for centuries without a resolution. So she'll name him Consort, and he'll use the Zashti family's authority over all Vampires to advance his personal goals. He'll rebuild the fleet. And then he'll start moving against the other Cluster Worlds, one by one. But here he will practice his tyranny, perfecting it for tomorrow."

"And nothing can stop him?" asked Sawyer.

"If he can consolidate his power, he'll have the authority of the Regency."

"The Gathering can dismantle the Regency," said Lee. "We don't need it any longer. You have to go."

"I'll decide what I have to do," corrected William Three-Dollar.

"What happens at the Gathering?" asked Sawyer.

"The TimeBinders of thirteen worlds will link their souls," he explained. "The linkage will create an entity with the cumulative wisdom and spirit and vision of all thirteen TimeBinders—a living cross section of the history of the Cluster in a single man."

"And then what?"

Three-Dollar shrugged. "I don't know. If we knew what we would say, we wouldn't have to link ourselves to say it, would we?"

"You could reassert the authority of the Regency, couldn't you?"

"That could occur, yes. We would make that choice not because we want to or need to or even because we wish to—we would make it only because our vision of the future would dictate such a choice. We will speak for the wisest course we see in the possibilities before us."

"And that course," vowed Lee, "will see the destruction of the Regency."

"That possibility remains one of many," acknowledged the TimeBinder.

Sawyer snorted. Finn looked almost as skeptical. "Forgive us our disbelief, Father; but it sounds too much like mysticism to my brother and to myself for either of us to accept it easily."

"You don't need to apologize, son. I've seen skepticism before. It doesn't bother me." William Three-Dollar looked over at Lee-1169. "I will go to the Gathering."

JOB OFFER

This time of year the secondary tunnels saw little traffic. Nevertheless, the small band of rebels moved cautiously through the maze of passages, lest they encounter an unexpected security force. The TimeBinder appeared unconcerned as they negotiated the twists and turns of various dark corridors. Occasionally, he would offer a suggestion as to the suitability of one passage over another; he appeared to have absolute knowledge of the labyrinth. In contrast, Sawyer and Finn had become hopelessly confused. Neither had any idea at all of their location in relation to anything else.

"It took more than a thousand years to carve this network of tunnels," William Three-Dollar noted. "Most of them remain unknown to the Regency."

"The rebellion has lasted that long?" Finn asked.

"Oh, no. Before the Alliance of Life, smugglers used these caves. The smugglers carved the first tunnels."

"Ahh," said Sawyer. "That we understand. Profit. Greed. Money."

The TimeBinder studied the brothers with a practiced eye. "You don't approve of the Alliance, do you?"

Sawyer shrugged. "We don't have any opinion one way or the other. It doesn't really involve us, does it? We sell our services to whoever can afford our fees. Why do you support the Alliance?"

"I don't. I exist solely as a vessel to hold the heritage of this planet. The Alliance has the investment, not me. They choose to protect me from assassination by Kernel d'Vashti and Lady Zillabar. But if I die, another will wear the headband, and I will live on. The Vampires cannot co-opt the TimeBinder. They've tried elsewhere. It has never worked. It won't work here. In the meantime, the Alliance protects me because it serves their purposes. I cooperate because it serves my purpose of experiencing everything I can of the continuing history of this world."

Sawyer shook his head. "That sounds like a very roundabout justification to me. The rebels have the access to your wisdom. The Vampires don't. You represent an asset to whoever you cooperate with."

"Yes, I guess so," the TimeBinder said blandly. "So do you, of course. And your brother. You both have experience that the Alliance of Life could make good use of."

Sawyer shook his head again. This conversation had suddenly begun to make him uncomfortable. "No, thank you. It would feel too much like working for a government—a government in exile, a protogovernment, call it what you will. We don't work for governments or people who want to take over governments. It leads to bad habits and worse company."

Three-Dollar laughed genially at Sawyer's observation, but he did not allow the tracker's flippancy to distract him from his train of thought. "I think you have an inaccurate perception of the Alliance of Life," the TimeBinder said. "You keep equating it with organizational entities like governments and rebellions. The Alliance operates not as a government, but as an agreement

among many to create a different operating context for
all governments. The Alliance works to create a new
agreement, one of mutual respect for sentience, out of
which all the different species of the Regency can deal
with each other as partners instead of adversaries."
Three-Dollar interrupted himself to point down a final
corridor. "Here," he said. "This one leads to the transport." He led the small group toward the red daylight
seeping in at the end of the tunnel.

"You actually believe it will happen?" Sawyer
asked.

"What will happen, will happen," the TimeBinder
replied. "Lee and the other people that you see here—this
tiny group of rebels—they may succeed. More likely, they
probably will not. But the underlying philosophy will
transform the relationships of everyone who accepts it."

Sawyer shrugged. "Maybe. I don't know. I've seen
too much of Vampires and Dragons and humans to have
much faith in the inherent goodness of any of them."

"I promise you," the TimeBinder remarked, "I have
probably seen much more and much worse than you can
even imagine. And it hasn't dissuaded my convictions at
all. If anything, it has only strengthened them."

"Yeah, well—you have to see things differently.
You have immortality. We don't."

"Sawyer, Finn—" William Three-Dollar stopped at
the tunnel mouth and put one huge hand on each of their
shoulders. The oppressive red light of the swollen star enveloped them all. "You've both seen how the Alliance can
work. You've experienced how different species can work
together. You couldn't have escaped from the labor camp
without that cooperation."

The brothers looked at each other uncomfortably.
Finn said reluctantly, "We just did what we had to do,
not what we wanted to do."

"I see," said the TimeBinder. He looked disappointed. "So you don't feel any loyalty toward those who helped you . . . ?"

"What we feel has nothing to do with it. We work for money."

Three-Dollar didn't answer that directly. Instead, he focused on something in the immediate past and remarked, "It bothers me that Lee has placed so much trust in the two of you. I don't see a corresponding loyalty."

Neither Sawyer nor Finn responded immediately to that, so the TimeBinder tried another tack. "Forget the Alliance for the moment. What if I offered you a job? What if I asked you to come and work directly for me? Could I buy your loyalty?"

"Under ordinary circumstances, Father, you probably could," Sawyer said. "Unfortunately, we already have a job."

"What kind of job?"

"This kind," said Sawyer. He rolled up the sleeve of his jacket to reveal a beeper-bracelet on his arm. He activated the device.

"Father, forgive us," gasped Finn as he collapsed weakly to the ground.

—A sudden terrifying noise filled the air—it rose like a siren—Lee whirled around alarmed—

And then it hit them.

The slop field enveloped the men with a hideous whine. The sudden nausea toppled them like reeds before the wind—even the TimeBinder. William Three-Dollar grunted involuntarily and sank gracefully down to his knees, his hands clutching his stomach.

Sawyer gasped and dropped as the pain spiked through his abdomen all the way down to his testicles. He grabbed himself and screamed. He rolled back and forth in agonized seizures. Lee-1169 and the others also fell writhing to the ground, jerking and shrieking. Finn had already passed out from the shock; he sprawled limply, his body twitching in sympathetic spasms.

The hideous warble of the disablement field increased—until one by one each of the humans lost control. Every nerve cell in their bodies discharged. Their bodies twisted and stiffened in terrible seizures. Consciousness disintegrated. Frenzied hallucinatory flashes dissolved into madness and darkness beyond.

William Three-Dollar held on longest, and then he too went limp.

.
.
.

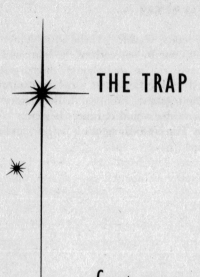

THE TRAP

Consciousness returned with a shock—the memory of the incredible pain still racked their bodies. They came awake gasping, screaming. They looked to each other in horror, their faces pale.

They had soiled themselves. Their bladders had let go and their sphincters had released. Some of them had coughed up blood or injured themselves in their seizures. Sawyer's arm felt stiff; he couldn't tell if he had broken it or not. Finn remained unconscious. William Three-Dollar looked shaken. Lee could barely move. The other men lay still in their misery and groaned.

For a long while nobody spoke. None of them had the strength or the coordination for it. They just lay there like broken dolls. Sawyer became aware of the vibration first. Somehow he managed to work his mouth enough to say, "Truck. They've put us on a truck." He opened his eyes. The dim red light hurt. Everything hurt. He could see a dark roof pressing close. He could feel the rumbling of the vehicle's heavy treads.

Eventually, he tried to sit up. He couldn't. He could barely manage to raise his head, but strong hands pulled at him and helped him into a sitting position. He found himself looking into William Three-Dollar's compassionate eyes.

"The headband gives me some protection," the TimeBinder said, tapping the bright halo he wore. "My body might hurt, but my mind has the power to disengage from the pain and move the muscles regardless."

"You could have escaped—?"

"Not quite. The band does have its limits. But I don't have to suffer as intensely as you." He smiled wryly. "I find it ironic."

"What?"

"Your job hurts you and your brother much more than it hurts me." And then he added softly, "Spiritually as well as physically."

Sawyer turned his head away. "Spare me."

William Three-Dollar placed a hand on Sawyer's feverish brow. "You don't have to hate me to justify what you did. You accepted your job willingly. You tracked me down. You turned me in. You don't need to justify it. You had a contract, you fulfilled it."

Sawyer stared in disbelief. "How can you say that?"

"Easy. I open my mouth, the words fall out. TimeBinders don't hate. TimeBinders experience. Out of experience comes understanding. You haven't hurt me, so I bear you no ill will. You don't need to hate me either."

"I don't hate you," Sawyer replied slowly. With Three-Dollar's help he eased himself up into a sitting position against the side of the truck. He looked around at the others. Lee glared weakly at him from the other side of the cabin. Finn lay unconscious between them. "I had to do it," he said. "We didn't have a choice. Kernel d'Vashti—"

He couldn't meet their eyes. He looked down at his hands in embarrassment.

"Go on," said Three-Dollar gently.

Sawyer got the words out painfully. "d'Vashti offered us something we couldn't refuse ... our lives."

Lee spat in disgust. "You cowardly traitors."

William Three-Dollar shook his head. "No, Lee. He speaks the truth. They had no choice."

"I did it for Finn," Sawyer said.

Lee remained unconvinced. "Everything they did, from the very beginning—I should have known we couldn't trust trackers. Now I know why you tried to stop the Dragon from throwing me in the water, and why you helped me escape from the labor camp, and why you stayed so close to me. You knew the sluice tube had to have an access—and maybe you even knew about the Vampire camp as well—because d'Vashti told you, didn't he? You did it all to win my trust, because you needed me to lead you back to the TimeBinder."

Sawyer acknowledged Lee's accusations with a reluctant nod. "We just want to get off this miserable planet. We should never have come here."

"I'll give you agreement on that, you lousy *traitor*!"

"No," said Sawyer, looking up for the first time and meeting Lee's eyes. "You don't understand. You never did. My brother and I could not have betrayed you—for the simple reason that neither of us ever swore allegiance to your cause. You assumed what you had no right to assume—our agreement. My brother and I have no allegiance to anyone except each other."

"And look what that loyalty bought you! Your brother lies dying at your feet."

"You idiot," Sawyer said. "The Regency poisoned Finn. What did you think causes these goddamn spells? The blood-burn doesn't work like that. Finn suffers from the Vampire's bite—look at him, damn you! The Phaestor poison flows in his veins. Did you ever wonder what happens inside those cocoons? Look at Finn and see! Every hour he gets weaker—and the antidote carries a very high price. Only the capture of the TimeBinder buys the cure!" Sawyer's anger rose to the surface; he let it. "You want me to feel guilty? Okay, I feel guilty. But I'd do it again to save my brother. Wouldn't you?"

"I've lost a thousand brothers," Lee said. "Every single one of them chose death rather than serve the Vampire's greed. So will I when the time comes. I won't do less than my brothers."

Sawyer opened his mouth to reply, but a hand on his knee stopped him—Finn's. The big man looked like a wraith, all ashen and gray. "Sawyer," he said weakly, "please don't argue with them."

Sawyer—almost as weak as Finn from the effects of the slop field—rolled over onto his side so he could face his brother directly. "We didn't know," he said. "We've always looked out for each other, no one else—"

"Shh," said Finn, reaching a hand out to Sawyer. "Don't talk. Don't argue. Don't waste your strength. They have honor. We have . . . life."

Sawyer didn't want his brother to see his dismay, so he just smiled and nodded and took his brother's hand in his own. "Right," he said. "But no more government jobs. Never again. Okay?"

"Okay," agreed Finn, and then he lapsed back into unconsciousness.

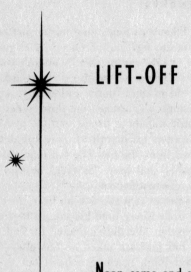

LIFT-OFF

Noon came and went. The locator signal did not go off.

Star-Captain Campbell swore in frustration. She paced the short length of the shuttleboat like a caged animal. Lee-1169 had not shown up, and she had lost valuable time. "I never should have trusted that red-faced little weasel. Rebels! Pfah! They always think their cause has more importance than any contract. They never keep their word."

"The Dragon Guard might have captured them."

"I doubt that. The Dragons couldn't hit the broad side of a hangar, firing from the inside."

"Shall we wait longer?" asked Ota.

"No. We've waited long enough."

"I do feel some obligation to them—"

"And I feel some obligation to thirty-three metric tons of pfingle eggs—a deep financial obligation." Campbell spoke to the computer. "EDNA? Download the latest launch and intercept course. We lift in fifteen minutes. Scan for local patrols and high-altitude interference. If necessary, I'll hedge-hop halfway around this damn rock, but I'd just as soon stand her on her tail and climb straight for the sky."

"Working," EDNA said politely, and then almost immediately after, "Done. I have also downloaded six alternate courses and evasion routines."

Captain Campbell muttered something unintelligible in acknowledgment and flung herself into the pilot's chair to examine the courses on her screen. "Gito! Robin! Jen! Cycle up the main batteries. Check your weaponry. Heat the thrusters. Eject all bystanders and nonpaying customers. Seal the hatches. Check for atmospheric integrity. Fasten your seat belts and stand by for liftoff."

In the aft of the shuttlecraft, Robin glanced over at Gito. "She loves doing that."

"She acts like a martinet," Gito grumbled as he sealed the hatch.

"But we chose to work for this martinet," Robin replied, glancing down a row of green lights on her workstation. "So we might as well enjoy her."

The Captain of the *Lady Macbeth* came stamping back to the passenger's cabin, with a glowering expression on her face. She looked at Harry, Kask, Ibaka, and Arl-N, all that remained of the original band of escapees. "Well?" she demanded. "Without Lee-1169, how do you plan to pay for your escape?"

Ibaka crawled into Kask's lap and huddled there. The big Dragon glanced over at Arl-N, the spindly man. "Should we get off and wait? Without Lee-1169, who will take us to the Alliance of Life?"

Arl-N grinned at the Dragon. "Wherever we go, we bring the Alliance with us, Kask. It works that way." He looked up at Captain Campbell. "We need to leave this planet before it kills us. The Justice has already paid his fare with an arbitration—"

"He did not!"

"Would you like to arbitrate that?" Arl-N smiled blandly. "In any case, I would like to suggest the same arrangement. Perhaps the Dragon and I have some skill or service that we can offer you in exchange for our passage."

"I have all the crew I need, thank you."

"Do you have contacts with the Freebooters' Circuit on Burihatin?"

Campbell hesitated. "Can you provide that service?"

Arl-N nodded. "My skill as a negotiator almost equals my fame as a poet."

"That news doesn't fill me with confidence. I've never heard of you before."

Arl-N spread his hands in a gesture of helplessness. "Then you will have to take my word for it—or throw us off. The Dragon, by the way, has agreed to work as my bodyguard. I don't think he'd allow it."

"I hate negotiations like this," Captain Campbell said. "We need to get out of here, not waste time arguing." But she allowed herself an appreciative nod. "On the other hand, I like your style of negotiation. I'd rather have you on my side of the table than opposite. I'll take you as far as Burihatin. After that, we'll see—"

"Thank you, my Lady. I will strive not to disappoint."

Campbell grunted and went back to the front of the boat. "All right," she called. "Lock and lift!" She waited until the last light on her board turned green, then eased the boat gently forward and up into the air. The tiny seed-shaped craft nosed up out of the canyon, slewed around to point eastward, and began accelerating across the broken hills to the desert beyond.

The shuttleboat raced hard across the desert floor, staying low and building up speed, until at last it swung its nose upward and sliced straight out into the hard red sky.

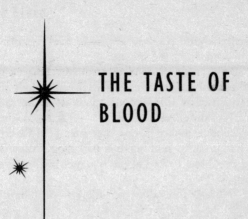

THE TASTE OF BLOOD

Despite her victory, the gloom of day filled the Lady Zillabar's chambers. Only a faint pink glow seeped up from around the edges of the floor. It did nothing to dispel the darkness. The ornate panels and screenwork remained hidden in shadow, and the pale silk draperies that framed the alcoves hung motionless and looked like empty shrouds. Above, the tiny animated gargoyles and imps that prowled the upper cornices had fallen silent and still; they curled up inconspicuously into their metal shells and waited patiently for the celebrations of night to return.

Four figures stood at the dark end of the hall—two Vampires, two humans.

Lady Zillabar towered taller than the others. She wore a black velvet cloak that enveloped her completely; its hood almost completely shielded her face. Her smoldering eyes seemed to glow in the air with only blackness around them.

Across from her stood Kernel d'Vashti, resplendent in his armor and medals and jeweled ornamentation. He wore his blood-red cape slung back over his shoulders so the sculpted and polished beauty of his breastplate could gleam brightly in the gloom.

Between them stood two humans. Sawyer, the thin blond; and Finn, the heavier dark one. Both the men held themselves stiff and emotionless before the Vampires. Tension edged the air.

Zillabar looked across the space at d'Vashti. "This day has brought nothing but bad news. What do you bring me?" She looked at the two men with ill-concealed distaste.

"I bring you what you ask for. As I have always done."

Lady Zillabar waited impassively.

d'Vashti explained. "You asked for the TimeBinder of Thoska-Roole? I have him in custody."

Zillabar inclined her head curiously at Sawyer and Finn. "And these two men?"

"These two men performed the difficult part of that service for us," d'Vashti explained. "You said you wanted to meet everyone responsible. Sawyer and Finn Markham tracked the enemies of the Regency—*your* enemies, my Lady—and brought them back to Phaestor justice. Let them taste your gratitude."

Zillabar's glance flickered briefly over the two humans, then returned to focus steadily on the ambitious d'Vashti. "My gratitude?" she asked in a voice like stone. "Do you know what your little escapade has cost me?" Zillabar's eyes pierced out of the darkness. "A band of armed escapees traveled south from the labor camp. They attacked and overpowered the guests at my private nest."

"Yes," acknowledged d'Vashti, unembarrassed. "I had heard of the difficulties." He added blandly, "If you had let me build that nest or provide the protection, it would not have happened." He allowed himself an outward smile. "I offer my sympathies—and I share your shock and outrage at the unfortunate discovery of the late Prince Drydel's unworthy behavior. On the other hand, perhaps you may take some condolence that you discovered his discourtesies now instead of later, when they would have caused even greater embarrassment."

Lady Zillabar stared across at d'Vashti, astonished at the boldness of his manner. Of course, she had known of Drydel's personal tastes; she'd never told him that she knew, but she'd made her nest available to him specifically so he could pursue his boyish pleasures in a safe and secluded location and avoid the possibility of bringing shame down on his name and a reflected taint on hers.

Obviously, by saying these hateful things in the presence of their human prisoners, d'Vashti intended his remarks as a ploy to embarrass her now. He referred to the matter as a deliberate show of strength, as well as a test to see what she had known and when she had known it. She didn't dare let him win this conversational battle. Only the most devastating of rebukes would do.

She let the anger flood up from her inner face, and she vented it on the pompous fool before her. "You engineered the escape, didn't you? You planned the entire operation. You pointed the criminals southward. You told them of the location of the nest. And you kept away the Dragon Guards who would have intercepted them. You sacrificed Lord Drydel to your ambition, didn't you?"

d'Vashti bowed in supplication, but not low enough. "My Lady," he said. "I wish I had the cunning that you believe. Did I have a plan for the prisoners' escape? Yes. Did they follow it? No, they did not. They found their own way of breaking the control of the slave-bands and overpowering the guards. The death of Lord Drydel has sorrowed us all. I myself must admit to some attraction to your Lord and remain deeply grieved at his loss."

At these impudent words Zillabar's face turned white with fury. Even d'Vashti saw it and reacted with concern. Perhaps he had miscalculated—

"I don't appreciate your insults, Kernel d'Vashti,"

Zillabar said with deadly intent. Her expression narrowed. "Do you believe me such a fool as to think that I would accept this fanciful tale of human ingenuity without question?" She snorted. "No human can outthink a Vampire."

D'Vashti's expression remained unchanged. "Nevertheless, my Lady, I would rather tell you an impossible truth than a polite lie."

Inwardly, Zillabar exulted. She had changed the subject, forcing d'Vashti to defend his own honor instead of challenging her authority.

Watching this, Sawyer and Finn exchanged a nervous glance. Sawyer began to doubt that they would leave this room alive. After letting them see such a naked display of her anger, would Zillabar really let them leave freely? On the other hand, maybe she intended to embarrass d'Vashti by deliberately upbraiding him in front of underlings. On the third hand ... who knew what ultimate goals motivated any Vampire's actions?

Zillabar turned away from the others, her black cloak sweeping around her like a tame tornado. "I know of your ambition, d'Vashti. You may forget your dreams. I promise you, they will not happen."

d'Vashti chose his words carefully. "I don't think I understand exactly what you mean ... ?"

"Don't play coy with me. You know exactly what I mean. You can't possibly think that I would now name you to take *his* place as my Imperial Consort."

d'Vashti replied calmly, "My lady, you will choose whoever pleases you. And I wish you every happiness and joy. But if I may venture one question, however rude it may seem—who else could you find who has the appropriate rank? Other than myself, of course?"

Zillabar whirled around to stare angrily back at him. "I'd sooner mate with a human—"

d'Vashti inclined his head in a polite nod. "You may have to. Here—you may practice on these two."

Zillabar barely glanced at Sawyer and Finn. She snarled, "Forget it, d'Vashti. You will never share my royal bed. I want a meal, not an hors d'oeuvre."

"Nevertheless," d'Vashti replied, keeping his voice incredibly calm and emotionless, "there may come a day when you will choose to feel otherwise. I shall remain enthusiastically at your service until then."

Zillabar realized abruptly that despite her anger, despite her deliberate attempt to belittle and embarrass him in front of these two miserable human wretches, d'Vashti had—by retaining his courtesy and calm demeanor—won the argument. He had embarrassed her with his oily display of loyalty. The realization only enraged her more.

Somehow—she steadied herself. She stiffened within her cape and reasserted her careful control over her feelings. She had enjoyed Drydel, and she had felt a deep sense of loss and betrayal at his death—she still felt it now, and would probably continue to feel the ache for some days to come—but to exercise her anger or seek undue revenge would only demonstrate that she had lost herself in the red wash of her emotions, forgetting the rigorous mastery of the Vampire dream state, the sweet delicious taste of the inner soul. The taste of blood.

Later, she told herself. *I will deal with him later. The time will come. . . .*

Carefully, she brushed the hood of her cloak back, revealing her exquisitely shaped features. "Your loyalty touches my heart," she said with a grim smile. "I will not forget what you have done on my behalf."

THE LADY BANISHES

Zillabar raised one delicate hand and spoke quietly to her Imperial Ring. The ornate seal gleamed bright in response as she commanded, "Prepare for departure. Set a course for Burihatin."

To d'Vashti's startled look she explained, "You make plans, you give orders, and you think you show cleverness; but your people behave as clumsily and nakedly as you do."

"You have what you came for—"

"*I do not!* I want to prevent the Gathering."

"If you wish, I'll form up the fleet to move on the rebel alliance—"

Zillabar gave him a sideways look of disbelief. "You'll do whatever you think will gain you power. What I wish will have little to do with it."

"Whatever you say, my lady."

"I have no intention of wasting any more time on this backwater rock. I return to Burihatin to finish my business there—then I'll deal with those who dare to challenge the Regency. I'll have some surprises of my own, you'll see."

"My people on Burihatin will place themselves at your service, my Lady—"

"Don't bother. Your people still haven't found the headband, and that makes it inevitable that a new TimeBinder will accept the crown. I'll find the damned headband—and anyone who still dares to wear it." She glowered at d'Vashti. "You may leave now—" An order, not a request. "The trackers will stay. I'll deal with them myself."

d'Vashti allowed himself a final polite bow, graceful and suave. He straightened, turned, and exited. His metal heels clicked loudly on the ceramic floor.

Zillabar waited until she heard the sound of the door dilating shut behind him. She turned to face the two silent humans.

Sawyer spoke up first. "We wish you no trouble, Lady Zillabar. We intend to leave Thoska-Roole. Kernel d'Vashti did have a contract with us, signed on your behalf, and we would appreciate payment for our services—the promised antidote—so we can make an immediate departure. The *King David* breaks orbit for Sherman's Planet tonight, and we'd like to catch the evening shuttle—if you don't mind, I mean." Sawyer fell silent under the Lady's withering glare.

The Lady continued to stare at him for the longest time. Sawyer had the feeling that his outburst had so astonished her, she remained unable to speak while she sorted through possible responses. At last she said, "I find your remarks amusing, to say the least. Your impudence demonstrates either naïveté, disingenuousness, or perhaps even simple stupidity. I, myself, would incline toward the latter interpretation had you not already demonstrated your talent for destructiveness. But perhaps d'Vashti's assessment contained some kernel of truth. Perhaps, indeed, you and your cohorts stumbled your way to success in your escape. In that regard, at least, we might spare Lord Drydel from having the stain of incompetency attached to his demise. After all, who could possibly defend himself against a wild and random occurrence?"

Sawyer held his breath. He glanced over at Finn. His brother looked paler than usual. He decided wisely that whatever funny remarks might occur to him now, he would save them for later. In fact, he might save all of his thoughts for a long long time before he spoke again. The Lady had a definite flair for intimidation. Yes, she did.

She studied him closely. "You didn't realize, did you, whose nest you destroyed?"

"From your remarks here, m'Lady—no offense intended—I would guess that you owned that nest—"

"And do you know who you killed in that attack?"

"As a matter of fact, um—actually, the Dragon did most of the killing. *All* of the killing, in fact. We didn't want to. We tried to stop him, actually. By the time we got down there after him, he had pretty much wiped out everything that moved, so uh—we didn't actually participate in the killing, and we really didn't want to, because killing tends to get messy and leaves a lot of bad feeling and—and ..." Sawyer trailed off ineffectually.

"You didn't answer the question. Do you know who you killed?"

"No, ma'am. We honestly don't know who the Dragon killed. We did see a lot of dead Phaestor boys. Apparently, the Dragon decided that his personal honor demanded all that unfortunate killing. I didn't understand why and I didn't have the opportunity to ask, but I think that it had something to do with—uh ... gee, I don't really know, do I?" Sawyer realized abruptly that he did not want to complete this sentence in front of the Lady Zillabar.

"You and your companions killed Lord Drydel and his personal retinue. They had borrowed my nest for a private retreat. Did you know that Lord Drydel and I would have taken our final vows today?"

"Uh, no, ma'am. We didn't. Um. You have our

deepest sympathies at your loss. Now, if we could just arrange some kind of equitable settlement here. My brother desperately needs an antidote—"

"I had plans. I had *delicious* plans. You and your ragged band of rabble and refugees have caused me great annoyance. It seems to me that I owe you an equal annoyance."

"Madame Zillabar, we have no wish for enmity on either side of this transaction. Obviously, that would benefit no one. Surely, you would agree. Perhaps before Finn and I leave Thoska-Roole, we could perform some additional service that would help to alleviate the, uh—the annoyance that you feel. Perhaps we could—" Sawyer shrugged. "I don't know, but certainly, if we could arrange for the antidote, we could proceed to negotiate some procedure for balancing the scales of justice so that we could part as—as—"

"Have you quite finished?" the Lady Zillabar said acidly.

"Uh, yes. Yes, I have."

"I have no intention of paying you for your services. I find your performance almost as incompetent and unacceptable as d'Vashti's. You, at least, have the excuse of your genetic deficiency. But in any case, the two of you have done quite enough damage for one lifetime."

"Well, yes, I guess so. Um, so then I guess we'll just take our leave and thank you for your kindness and— come on, Finn, let's stop wasting the Lady's time—"

"Kindness? Yes, I have always liked the sound of that word, whatever it means." Something about the way she spoke—Sawyer and Finn stopped in their tracks. The Lady Zillabar took a breath, a sound of quiet expectation. "I have decided to put you two away for now—to prevent you from wreaking any more havoc."

The Lady stepped back away from the brothers and waved one hand in the air; a graceful gesture, but also an imperious one. Immediately, a squad of armored Dragons came thundering into the room; the light blazed around them and they loomed like metal monsters. "Take these two worthless dregs and throw them into the holding tank with the rebels they betrayed. Let the one watch the other one die. And then the others can kill him."

Sawyer felt as if his heart had dropped out of his body. He felt betrayed. The anger rose in his throat like a bad taste. But even as the rage possessed him, he remembered his manners and phrased his words accordingly. "You leave me with no choice, Lady," he said as one of the Dragons seized him in both hands. "I hereby declare you in breach of contract and demand a full hearing under the auspices of an Arbiter of the Regency as required under the Holy Charter."

"An interesting demand," the Lady Zillabar replied as the Dragons started carrying the two brothers away. "But I believe you'll have some trouble enforcing it. You'll probably have to sue me," she said to their departing backs.

"I'll do more than that," Sawyer promised. He struggled desperately in the Dragon's grasp. "However long it takes, I'll have justice—human justice! *You'll live to regret this, you Vampire whore! I promise you!*"

Lady Zillabar laughed at the man's impudence, but the laughter had a hollow sound. The brothers Markham had already demonstrated their propensity for discoordinating the most carefully balanced machinery. She wondered if perhaps she should order them killed immediately. She shook the thought away; she had more important matters to attend to. She could plan a suitable punishment later.

When she had more time.

HOLDING PATTERNS

At least the tank smelled clean.

Sawyer sat on the floor with his feverish brother and kept a solemn death watch. He didn't think Finn had much time left. He cradled his brother's head in his lap and whispered softly to him. He doubted that Finn could understand or even hear much of what he had to say; but he said it anyway. He refused to believe in personal mortality. It seemed like such a—a slap in the face from God.

The other prisoners kept to the other side of the cell, well away from the two men they regarded as traitors. They whispered among themselves and avoided looking toward the Markham brothers. Sawyer wondered about their intentions, but he had more immediate concerns. Besides, if they intended to harm either himself or Finn, they would have acted already. Perhaps they didn't dare proceed without first conferring with their TimeBinder.

William Three-Dollar sat apart, composed and quiet. The tall man had folded himself into the lotus position, his long legs crossed in an impossible knot with his large feet placed precisely on top of his knees, and his hands resting gently on the thin bones of his ankles. His eyes remained closed, his features relaxed. He seemed totally at peace. Either he slept or meditated, Sawyer couldn't tell. Whatever his state, Sawyer sincerely doubted that the TimeBinder realized the profound danger of his situation.

Sawyer understood the peril. In this single instance, at least, he could see the single-mindedness of the Lady and the path she must follow as certainly as if she had given him her map. He wondered at the clarity of the vision. It had an almost hallucinogenic quality. Did the TimeBinders see the same way? If so, then William Three-Dollar had to know what the Vampire queen planned.

The Lady Zillabar had to destroy not only each of the present TimeBinders, but also the bands they wore. Or—perhaps she had found some way to assemble all the bands and claim their power for her own. Sawyer tried to imagine a Vampire queen with the wisdom of a thousand generations. He couldn't. He whispered his concerns to Finn, almost demanding that the darker man wake up and reassure him.

At last Finn opened his eyes and looked blearily up at his brother. He spoke weakly, but clearly. "You talk too much, you know. How do you expect me to sleep with you jabbering away like that? You sound like a fretful mother."

"You looked so pale, Finn. I thought that you might just slip away—" He couldn't bring himself to say the word.

"How can I die with you working so hard to distract me? Do you know what a noise you make every time you get worried that I might leave you alone? Grow up! I'll let you know when I finally get ready to die—all right? Until then, let me rest in peace."

"I don't want you to rest in peace!" Sawyer

snapped back. His brother's sour expression of contempt gave him much more relief than annoyance. "Do you want some water?" Finn nodded.

Sawyer held a canteen to Finn's parched lips, and the big man sucked at it thirstily, pausing only to gasp uncomfortably for breath. He shook so badly, he had to stop several times. When he had finally had enough, he pushed it away and raised his head to look around. "Where did they put us this time?" Finn asked. "I don't recognize this place."

"I have no idea," Sawyer replied. "But at least it doesn't smell as bad as the last three prisons we've seen——"

"Has it occurred to you, Soy, that most of our recent career moves have put us behind bars? Too many of the things we do keep landing us in jail. I don't want this to turn into a habit."

"But at least we've moved up to a higher class of prison. That should count for something."

"Frankly, I'd prefer a different sort of progress." Finn grunted as he levered himself painfully up into a sitting position. Just the effort of putting his back against the wall left him out of breath. "Unfortunately, the quality of our jailers hasn't improved." He noticed the men across the cell—Lee and the other three rebels—and smiled weakly at them; he lifted his hand halfway in a feeble gesture of recognition. Only Lee-1169 bothered to acknowledge it. He spat in Finn's direction.

The brothers ignored it. "He's had a bad day," Sawyer explained.

"We all have. Madame Zillabar's hospitality doesn't exactly inspire confidence."

"An understatement. I've decided not to like that woman. She has no integrity."

"No integrity?" Finn looked sideways at his brother, a skeptical smile showed faintly on his weakened features.

"None at all. She breached our contract. I don't know about you, bro, but I just hate it when somebody betrays a trust."

Across the room Lee-1169 exchanged incredulous looks with his companions. How dare these trackers complain about betrayal?

"Well—" said Finn, his voice almost a whisper, "now will you believe me? No more government jobs."

"I admit my mistake," Sawyer said. "I promise you, we'll never do that again."

"I think we can say that with some certainty," Finn agreed. "Shall we go to Plan B?"

"Yes, I think we should go to Plan B."

Both of the brothers looked up then, across the cell to the members of the Alliance of Life. As they did so, William Three-Dollar opened his eyes and came back to the present. He met their eyes with a curious yet dispassionate demeanor. "Yes?"

"Uh," Sawyer began cautiously. "About that job you offered us before—? Could we reconsider? We could discuss terms, if you wish—"

ABOUT THE AUTHOR

DAVID GERROLD made his television writing debut with the now classic "The Trouble With Tribbles" episode of the original *Star Trek® series*. Since 1967 he has story-edited three TV series, edited five anthologies, and written two non-fiction books about television production (both of which have been used as textbooks) and over a dozen novels, three of which have been nominated for the prestigious Hugo awards.

His television credits include multiple episodes of *Star Trek*, *Tales From the Darkside*, *Twilight Zone*, *The Real Ghostbusters*, *Logan's Run*, and *Land of the Lost*.

His novels include *When H.A.R.L.I.E. Was One Release 2.0*, *The Man Who Folded Himself*, *Voyage of the Star Wolf*, as well as his popular *War Against the Chtorr* books—*A Matter for Men*, *A Day for Damnation*, *A Rage for Revenge*, and *A Season for Slaughter*. His short stories have appeared in most of the major science fiction magazines, including *Galaxy*, *If*, *Amazing*, and *Twilight Zone*.

Gerrold also writes a regular column for *PC Techniques,* a computer magazine. He averages over two dozen lecture appearances a year and regularly teaches screenwriting at Pepperdine University.

David Gerrold is currently working on the new Chtorr novel, *A Method for Madness*.

COVENANT OF JUSTICE

the exciting sequel to *Under the Eye of God.* In the following excerpt, as the Phaestor progress in their conquests, brothers Sawyer and Finn Markham are invited to dine with Lady Zillabar for a meal they will never forget. *Covenant of Justice* will be available in bookstores this spring.

MY DINNER WITH ZILLABAR

A curious thought had occurred to Lady Zillabar. In space, no one can hear you break the law. After some consideration, she decided to wear the resulting smile on her public face but simply not explain it.

She hissed away her maids and checked her appearance in a full-length mirror. As always, she demanded an impeccable presentation. Tonight she wore a scarlet shroud wrapped tightly around her entire body, leaving only her head free. She could barely move. Her maids would have to wheel her in, serve her, feed her, hold her glass to her lips for her.

She enjoyed the feeling of helplessness—while at the same time remaining totally in control. She enjoyed taunting her privileged guests with this performance. Perhaps she relished her insect heritage. She fantasized about hives and queens. She thought about all the workers who lived only to service the queen, all the drones who lived only to mate with her. The queen lay in her chambers. She spent her entire life in glorious dreamtime. She ate and grew fat. She mated and grew fatter. She laid eggs, eventually at the rate of two or three a day.

Lady Zillabar didn't particularly enjoy the last part of that fantasy. She knew that she had the responsibility to further the Zashti line. Sometimes she wished that she could avoid it, but she knew that when at last she finally did mate with some unfortunate male, the hormonal surge would carry her into a state of psychotic desires. She would want nothing else but to eat and mate and lay eggs—and she would want nothing else until her reproductive storm began to ebb. With that in mind, she knew that she had to firmly consolidate her authority *before* the storm clouds began to gather over her bed. Otherwise ... events would sweep past her. She had to stop the Gathering; if she could do that, she could safely mate.

She thought about d'Vashti and laughed. She couldn't imagine him accepting her challenge. Without a challenger, she could go for years without having to risk mating. Hmm. Perhaps d'Vashti had done her a favor by arranging the death of Drydel.

Satisfied, she nodded to her maids. They maneuvered her gracefully onto a slanted board and wheeled her into the dining salon, where her guests waited—the senior officers of her starship, all Phaestor, several of her most trusted personal aides, and the Dragon Lord. They stood as she entered and applauded the glimmering audacity of her gown. Beyond the windows, the Eye of God stared balefully, a wall of blazing light that colored everything in the salon with an unholy aura. She loved it.

The Dragon Lord waited respectfully at the end of the table, his tail twitching patiently back and forth. Her attendants wheeled her the entire length of the room so she could greet him face to face.

"My Lady," he said, bowing his great head low enough to look her straight in the eye. "You look good enough to eat!" And then he laughed in that great booming rumble of his, loud enough to rattle the slender glasses on the table.

Behind her, Lady Zillabar could sense the shocked silence of her officers. Too straitlaced to visibly appreciate a joke as vulgar as this without approval, they waited for the Lady's reaction. Zillabar and the Dragon Lord exchanged a private smile; he enjoyed teasing her like this. They had shared this joke before. At last, mindful of her attendants and her officers, she allowed her amusement to break through to the surface. She replied with coy grace, "But, my Lord, you'll spoil your appetite for dinner."

"For such an hors d'oeuvre, I would gladly spoil a hundred dinners, a thousand!"

"But, my Lord, while I would willingly do anything in my power to offer you that pleasure, I fear that such an act of generosity might also spoil *my* dinner—and I would not have you bear such a stain upon your honor."

"As always, you think too much of me and not enough of yourself, madam. If it pleases you to climb onto my plate, I would not dream of stopping you. I will happily bear any shame, any disgrace, for such a treat."

"Ah, my Lord Dragon, you do me such honor, I shall surely swoon from delight. But, as you can see, my present attire makes such an act, no matter how much I desire it, impossible to implement. I lack the ability to make any move at all under my own volition."

"Gracious madam, if you will allow me the honor of touching your esteemed person, I would gladly place you myself upon my plate."

"Oh, Great Lizard, as much as the thought of your touch thrills me, I fear that such an action might appear presumptuous and greedy, for you would leave little for the rest of my guests."

At last the Dragon conceded the point and put on

his most sorrowful expression. "I shall remain forever disappointed."

"Not half as disappointed as I," Zillabar laughed in conclusion. "Eaten by a Dragon—who could wish for a more delicious death? You have me almost convinced to strip off this shroud and leap onto your plate right now. But, Great Lord, it occurs to me that you would not want to miss the entertainment I have planned for tonight's dinner, an entertainment in which I must play a particularly important role. You will appreciate its elegance, of that I have no doubt."

The Dragon Lord bowed. He lowered his huge head almost to the floor, then raised it again and towered over all the rest of the guests. Their banter concluded, the Lady hissed at her attendants and they wheeled her around to the head of the table.

ENTERTAINMENT

After the attendants had seated all the Lady's guests at their places, the two elegant chairs at Lady Zillabar's left hand still remained empty. The captain of the starship and several of the Lady's aides looked at the places with open curiosity. The Lady *never* allowed her guest list to unbalance her banquet table. The reputation of her hospitality, as well as the stories told about the sumptuousness of her sideboard, had spread throughout the Phaestor aristocracy; young Vampires all over the Regency aspired to an invitation to her table, so any gap in the seating arrangement could only provoke curiosity among the rest of the guests present.

Lady Zillabar waited until everybody had settled themselves, then nodded to one of her aides. The aide exited and a moment later returned with a very chastened-looking Sawyer and Finn Markham. The young Vampire led them silently to the empty places, directing Finn specifically to the chair closest to Lady Zillabar. The two brothers looked at the exquisitely dressed table and the array of lustrous guests, looked at each other with reluctant agreement, and sat down warily.

"How *sweet* of you to join us," the Lady said sweetly. "You don't look very well, Finn. I do hope you have the strength for this little celebration. I would hate to have your discomfort spoil anyone's evening. You will let me know if you begin to feel weak, won't you? Thank you." To the rest of her guests, she announced, "Gentlemen, may I introduce to you two of the very best trackers in the Regency, Sawyer and Finn Markham. They have provided many useful services, and this dinner in their honor allows me to reward them in an appropriate manner."

While her guests applauded, she nodded to a pair of medical aides who had discreetly entered from the side. Immediately, they stepped to Finn's side and while Sawyer watched in horror, one of them held Finn's arm and the other wrapped a medical band around it and connected an intravenous tap.

"You must promise me that you will eat well," the Lady said to him. "I would hate to have a stain on my hospitality. And besides, if you don't eat well, neither can I."

Already the servants had begun filling the wineglasses and placing delicately arranged trays of appetizers in front of each of the assembled guests. Neither Sawyer nor Finn recognized any of the meats, and neither felt immediately inclined to ask for annotation. While the other guests helped themselves, both of the men kept their hands politely in their laps.

The Lady Zillabar *tsk*ed in annoyance and nodded to the aides who waited discreetly behind the two brothers. Without further ado, the attendants spread cloth napkins on both of the brothers' laps and then, using a silver serving utensil, placed an assortment of savories on the golden plates in front of each of them. Still, neither Sawyer nor Finn moved.

The Lady's most personal attendants now began to tend to her needs. One held a delicate goblet to her lips, allowing her to take just the faintest sip of the bright pink wine it held. The other placed a tiny sliver of blackened meat in the Lady's mouth. The Lady chewed delicately and swallowed. She glanced to the servant and he placed another tiny sliver of meat on her tongue.

Sawyer and Finn exchanged a glance. Finn looked tired and haggard, but he held himself upright, refusing to let his weakness show in front of the Lady. Sawyer merely looked horrified. Whatever the Lady intended at this banquet, she could not possibly plan to let either of them survive. Not for long.

The Lady noticed Sawyer's expression then. She cocked her head curiously. "I fear that you have lost your appetite, Mr. Markham. Perhaps the chef has failed to prepare the food to your liking?"

"Uh—no, no. I don't doubt that your chefs have done their very best, madam." He pushed his plate away distastefully. "I just find it difficult to eat meat of such an uncertain ancestry. I can't help but wonder which of your former guests provided these particular savories."

The Lady's smile barely flickered. "You have such a remarkable way of looking at things. I confess that my palate has become so used to the elegance of my table that I often forget how others might perceive the fare served here. No matter," she said. "As long as your brother eats." She shifted her gaze to Finn and her eyes grew hard and cold. *"You will eat,"* she commanded him. She nodded to the servant behind Finn, who picked up a fork, speared a fragment of something dripping in red sauce, and held it up in front of Finn's mouth.

For a moment Finn thought to resist, but the attendant held something to the back of his neck, and he gasped in surprise. The fork popped into Finn's mouth and out again just as quickly. The attendant had obviously done this before. The next time the pale boy held the fork before Finn's mouth, he did not hesitate. He took the food quickly. Finally, reluctantly, Finn took the fork from the servant and began slowly feeding himself.

"Good," said the Lady. "Very good." The other guests at the table had watched this entire proceeding with elaborate interest. Now they too resumed their meal.

At the end of the table the Dragon Lord enthusiastically plucked maissel-fish[3] out of an especially reinforced bowl with his bare talons and plopped them happily into his gaping mouth. They looked like dead mice dipped in pond scum: soft, shapeless, and generally unpalatable. They also made terrible, disconcerting croaking noises. The Dragon Lord didn't seem to mind. He enjoyed eating them live. Sawyer almost felt sorry for the maissel-fish; then he reminded himself that these fish had very likely come directly from the Old City detainment[4] and he decided that they deserved what they got.

Sawyer turned back to the Lady. Her personal attendants had now begun feeding her some kind of squirming thing from a bowl of squirming things. He didn't want to look, but he couldn't look away.

"Yes, Mr. Markham?" she asked.

"I—uh, hope you won't think me bad-mannered—"

"I would never do that," the Lady interjected sweetly.

[3] Especially imported for his pleasure from the Old City detainment on Thoska-Roole.
[4] Actually a pretty good guess on Sawyer's part. One maissel-fish looks pretty much like another.

"But if I might presume to ask a favor of you? As you know, my brother suffers from a condition resembling tertiary blood-burn ..."

Lady Zillabar's laughter froze the words in Sawyer's throat.

"Oh, you poor dear. You have my profoundest apology. Of course, I should have explained this to you earlier. Kernel d'Vashti lied to you both. No antidote exists at all for your brother's condition." To the rest of her guests, the Lady explained, "Once again you see the problem we have with humans; they accept the wildest tales unfailingly. They always believe what they want to believe instead of seeing what actually lies before their eyes."

Before Sawyer could push his chair back and leap to his feet, Finn's hand came down on his arm, and even though Finn no longer had the strength to hold him in his chair, Sawyer got the message and restrained himself.

As if she hadn't seen this exchange between the Markham brothers, Lady Zillabar turned her attention back to Sawyer. "Besides, my dear, even if such an antidote existed, I wouldn't dream of offering it to your brother. It would *spoil* the taste." She added something in her own language, a command to her servants. Immediately, one of the attendants next to Finn bent to the intravenous tap on his arm and opened it. His dark red blood began sliding down the tube and into a silver goblet.

The brothers watched in fascinated horror as the servant closed off the tap and brought the goblet around to where the Lady Zillabar sat. The young Vampire held the cup to the Lady's lips and she drank from it eagerly. When she had finished, she licked her lips appreciatively, until finally another servant approached and delicately touched a silken cloth to each of the corners of her mouth.

The Lady Zillabar sighed. "Ahh. I enjoyed that." She looked at Sawyer and at Finn. "Finn, thank you so much. Truly a delicious experience. I intend to have you share all of your meals with me. Oh, do have some more wine. I would like to get wonderfully drunk tonight." She turned to the rest of her guests. "Would anyone else like a taste?"

DINNER THOUGHTS

The Lady's guests began to laugh then at the delicate irony of her words—indeed, the whole nasty situation had a certain baroque charm. Only a Vampire could appreciate all the nuances of pain in the situation; only a Vampire would want to.

The Lady knew that the young Vampire males would whisper among themselves for months, spreading the tales of this evening's merriment. They would talk of the bloodred shroud that left the Lady helpless and vulnerable, and they would stimulate themselves to frenzies of lust as each of them imagined what grotesqueries they might perform if they could have her in such a helpless circumstance.

They would repeat her every word among themselves. They would laugh at her jokes and allow themselves to experience delicious thrills of envy and desire. And yes, of course, all of them would hunger for an invitation to her table. All of them would want to taste the blood of her next victim.

The Lady smiled at the thought. She wanted exactly this kind of story whispered among her admirers. For one thing, it would drive d'Vashti insane with rage and lust. She wondered how long she could keep Finn Markham alive. The idea intrigued her—how long would it take to drive Sawyer Markham mad? She would have to drink sparingly of Finn to make it work, but the enjoyment would certainly justify the restraint. Yes, she would give the appropriate orders immediately after tonight's meal concluded.

At the opposite end of the table the Dragon Lord did not share the Lady's enthusiasm. He had enjoyed his earlier repartee with the Lady as an amusing conceit, a harmless flirtation wherein each of the partners gently tickled the other's sensibilities.

This shameless display of unrestrained blood-lust, however, he found extremely distasteful. Perhaps the Vampires found sport in the malicious taunting of the prey; it made him queasy. It reeked of dishonor. His progenitors had trained him to kill his meals quickly and cleanly. Additionally, he had always believed it the lowest form of dishonor to eat criminals. At least in public. Destroying the distinction between criminals and prey befouled the prey and diminished the meal. It insulted the service of the one and exalted the other. No, eating the wrongdoer did not constitute an appropriate form of punishment. And it implied that the eater's hunger had grown so far beyond control that he had abandoned all pretense of dining as an art.

That he himself had only quite recently devoured an appallingly large human criminal did not affect this judgment at all. He could justify that matter easily enough in his own mind. That particular human had tried to escape, and he'd had to personally track her down. Once a Dragon enters into the pursuit of a fleeing animal, all the ancient Dragon instincts come boiling straight to the surface of his soul. The hunt cannot properly conclude until the Dragon has eaten the heart of the hunted. In such a situation any arbitrary distinctions disappear.

Once having eaten the heart, the Dragon may also partake of the rest of the flesh, if he so desires. In this case the Lord of the Dragons had indeed desired. He had sated his hunger three times before abandoning the corpse to whatever predators waited in the dark red gloom beyond. . . .

Nevertheless, this situation wore a different face. To bring the criminal to the table and partake of his blood as a delicacy offended the Dragon Lord. Additionally, to taunt the prisoner for the entertainment of one's guests—well, maybe Vampires found amusement in that. Dragons did not.

After considering this matter for some time, the Dragon Lord at last came to a decision. He rose from his chair and excused himself from the table. The Lady barely noticed, so enraptured had she become with her jest. She did not see the Lord's grimace of distaste as he turned away and stamped heavily off to his own part of the vessel.

Along the way, he stopped to address the ambitious young Captain Lax-Varney. "I do not want any Dragons at all assigned to Lady Zillabar's section of this vessel. Do you understand?"

"Sir?"

"I want no tales circulating among my Dragons. What they don't see, they can't discuss. Keep them all away from the Vampires' part of the vessel. If you fail me in this, I will eat your heart."

"Yes, my Lord." Lax-Varney hurried quickly off to give the orders.